A Heart SUFFICIENT

the PENN-LEITHS of
THISTLE MUIR
BOOK FOUR

NICHOLE VAN

Fiorenza Publishing

A Heart Sufficient © 2024 by Nichole Van Valkenburgh
Cover design © Nichole Van Valkenburgh
Interior design © Nichole Van Valkenburgh

Published by Fiorenza Publishing
Print Edition v1.1

ISBN: 978-1-949863-20-8

To those who ache
for love and forgiveness.
May light find you.

And to Dave,
for always being
my guiding light.

He stepped down,
trying not to look long at her,
as if she were the sun,
yet he saw her like the sun,
even without looking.

—LEO TOLSTOY

PROLOGUE

APRIL 1841
LONDON, ENGLAND
A GARDEN PARTY

G uess who?"

Tristan Gilbert, Earl Hawthorn, tensed at the sound of a decidedly-female voice at his back.

He froze further when a pair of hands, clad in supple kid leather, abruptly covered his eyes from behind and turned the world dark.

"Come now," the melodious voice continued, fingertips pressing against his brow ridge, "surely ye ken who I be?"

The woman's lilting cadence held Scotland and a hint of laughter.

Tristan hadn't the faintest idea who she was.

Irritation constricted his chest, his jaw clenching.

Ten minutes. He had arranged to spend ten *bloody* minutes alone in the Duke of Montacute's garden—risking his father's wrath and Babcock's dismissal.

And now some managing miss had seized the opportunity to approach him in this unseemly manner.

"We are unacquainted, madam," Tristan replied, words vibrating with leashed anger. "Please remove your hands from my person."

She gave a startled *eep!*, her fingers instantly releasing him.

Glowering, Tristan pivoted around, a scathing tirade marshaled on his tongue.

But one glimpse of his assailant, and the syllables crumbled to dust.

He cataloged her in rapid bursts of imagery. Curls tousled and vibrant red. A trail of freckles across sharp cheekbones. A pert nose. Eyes the blue of summer cornflowers and dancing with mischief.

Lovely. She was lovely.

And then there was the lithe height of her, her forehead topping his shoulder. She would fit so neatly in his arms, he would scarcely need to bend his head to kiss her plump lips.

As for her lips . . .

An elegant gloved hand flew to her mouth, a scarlet blush rising up and over her cheeks before disappearing into the shadow of her cream bonnet.

Tristan tracked it with an almost unholy fascination, his pulse a punishing drumbeat in his ears.

She rendered him lightheaded, like a tumbler of brandy bolted too quickly.

"I do beg your pardon, my lord," she breathed, that refined trace of Scotland in her vowels. "I mistook your lordship for an old family friend."

My lord.

His mind snagged on the honorific.

"You know who I am?" He mentally winced at his brusque tone.

"Of course, Lord Hawthorn," she replied breezily, an impish smile peeking out. "I think any marriage-minded miss under the age of thirty would recognize the Duke of Kendall's heir."

No slow-top, this woman.

He added it to the rapidly-growing list of things he liked about her.

"And are you, then? A marriage-minded miss?" The question tumbled, unbidden, from his lips.

Tristan hadn't intended the words flirtatiously, but the young lady arched her eyebrows and flicked a gaze over his person invitingly.

"I could be, I suppose." She tilted her head, that same vivacity twinkling. "For the correct gentleman, that is."

Devil take it.

She was flirting with him.

Now what?

Tristan had never flirted. Not once. He had no need. As the heir to a powerful dukedom, ladies generally fell over themselves to capture his attention.

Granted, until this moment, he had never wished to flirt.

But for her, he would try.

"Ah." He gave a hint of a smile, his mind rapidly shuffling through possible responses. He landed on, "And what would one have to do to become that gentleman?"

Her eyes widened, and then a slow, delighted grin creased her cheeks.

Tristan's heart quite literally skipped in his chest, as if abruptly remembering that it needed to beat and sustain life.

Heaven help him.

He feared he would do a great many things to earn more of her smiles.

She tapped a gloved finger to her plump lips. "Mmm, a lady never shows her hand."

She was not a classical beauty in the Grecian sense, Tristan realized. Her eyes were too wide-set, her mouth too lush, her cheekbones too pronounced.

No, hers was the beauty of the unexpected. An oak tree in autumn coated in reds and golds standing amid still-green poplars. Or scudding clouds abruptly catching the last vivid rays of sunset.

She reminded Tristan of Allie, the twin sister torn from him a decade past—magnetic, clever, brimming with life.

Who *was* this young lady?

Had they been introduced, he would have remembered.

Tristan resisted the urge to look for Babcock. His protection officer would be returning soon. The man adored cheese, but it caused him severe intestinal distress, necessitating a rather lengthy trip to the water closet. Consequently, Tristan tempted Babcock with cheese at every opportunity.

Anything to garner a few precious minutes of freedom.

Only the Queen and prime minister had protection officers, but the Duke of Kendall insisted on one for his heir. How else was His Grace to ensure that every last thing his son said and did was inventoried and reported back?

Tristan did not want his tyrannical father to learn of this encounter. Not yet.

"A lady?" he asked, echoing the title she had given herself. "Is that how I should address you?"

"*My lady* would be appropriate."

Maddeningly, she provided no further explanation, but her arched eyebrow encouraged him to pick up the clue she had offered.

Only the highest-ranking, unwed women merited the honorific of "lady." But then, her rank was to be expected, Tristan supposed, given their location.

They stood on a small terrace in the Duke of Montacute's extensive gardens, partially hidden behind a pair of rhododendron bushes bursting with fuschia flowers. Below, guests strolled alongside a serpentine pond—gentlemen in tall hats, ladies twirling parasols.

The Duke and Duchess of Montacute only invited the highest echelons of Polite Society to the annual garden party on their sprawling estate outside London. It was the only reason Kendall had permitted Tristan to attend.

Therefore, this lady had to hail from some prominent family or another.

Hope, an imprisoned beast within his chest, rattled the bars of its cage.

Tristan never rebelled openly against Kendall. Lessons in obedience and compliance had been, quite literally, beaten into him at a young age. Thankfully, his father was too old to physically harm Tristan anymore.

But like a bloodhound, Kendall had an eerie ability to sniff out wants and desires—emotions he ruthlessly extorted to blackmail others, even his twenty-year-old heir.

It was why Tristan had relinquished all sentimental attachments—sister, mother, friends. If he appeared to want nothing, if Kendall had nothing to hold ransom, then he and his father would maintain their stalemate.

Tristan's sole goal was to obliterate his father's memory after the bastard's death. To accomplish this, Tristan aimed for nothing less than the Prime Minister's office and a seat at the right hand of the Queen. Such a rise to power would ensure the brilliant luminosity of his own star relegated his father to the shadows of history.

The correct bride—highborn, elegant, charming—was crucial to his plans. And now this glorious woman appeared.

He glanced around again for Babcock. *Please do not let Kendall learn of this encounter*, he silently pleaded. Tristan required time to conduct reconnaissance on the lady—to determine her parentage and the extent of her political connections—before Kendall inserted his caustic will.

Tristan merely needed to know her name.

"You have me at an advantage, my lady," he said with a smile. "I would love to know with whom I am speaking. Surely, we do not need to stand on ceremony."

The beautiful Scot raised an eyebrow in reply. "But where would be the amusement in making introductions?"

Her gaze was guileless, Tristan noted. Every emotion and feeling skipped across her expression—interest, delight, mischief.

"Amusement? Do you always base your decisions on their potential value as entertainment?"

"Do ye not, my lord?" She clasped her hands coyly behind her back, looking up at him through auburn-tinged lashes.

Tristan's pulse had migrated outward and now thrummed at the tips of his fingers, as if begging him to reach for her.

"Not generally."

"How tragic."

The faux innocence of her tone startled a laugh out of him. "Perhaps I am beginning to see the wisdom in it."

"A lady must guard her air of mystery, after all."

"Is that so?" Tristan mimicked her position, clasping his own arms behind his back. Was it his imagination, or did her eyes dart to his shoulders as if she found him attractive, as well? The thought filled his veins with champagne bubbles. "But what if mystery should turn to boredom?"

She chuckled, throaty and delighted. "Something tells me ye aren't bored, my lord."

"Not yet." He raised an eyebrow in challenge. "But mystery requires substance to thrive."

"That is your opinion."

"Hardly. It is a fact."

"I utterly disagree. Surely ye have studied the classics, my lord? 'Nothing exists except atoms and empty space; everything else is opinion.'"

"Democritus?" Tristan gaped in astonishment. "You blithely quote ancient Greek philosophers?"

She shrugged, that same teasing grin playing about her mouth. "We could move on to Shakespeare, if that is more tae your taste?"

Beautiful *and* well-read.

Tristan stared, utterly disarmed.

She vibrated with life. As if Newton's laws of gravity struggled to contain the buoyancy of her spirit.

Tristan's parched soul ached to hold that joy. To soak in the sunshine of this woman's light. To glut himself on it.

Yearning uncurled within him, ribboning between his ribs and swelling his lungs.

Heaven help him.

He wanted her.

Not just as a bride for his political goals but for her brilliant self.

He wanted . . . *them.*

Answering his silent plea, she leaned forward, as if to impart a secret. "Ye see, my lord, I have now added a level of intrigue tae my aura, as it were. 'Twould be a pity tae make introductions and dispel the allure of the unknown."

"Are you quite sure?" Unbidden, he matched her motion, bringing them nearer to one another. Scarcely a foot of space separated them. Close. Almost scandalously so.

Babcock could return at any moment.

Tristan risked much if his father learned of this encounter.

Yearning—wanting—was a dangerous emotion. Kendall would scent it and use it to twist Tristan to his merciless will. His stomach clenched at the thought of this beautiful creature falling into his father's snare.

"Oh, quite," she replied, those lovely blue eyes sparking. "I would hate tae ruin your enjoyment of the chase. Now, ye shall have to launch an inquiry into my identity. Every gentleman deserves an amusing pursuit. I have granted ye one."

"You assume I do not have other, more interesting, pursuits?"

He didn't. Everything in his life abruptly paled before her dazzling radiance.

She couldn't know that.

And yet, her smile turned enigmatic. "I shall take my leave of you, my lord."

She dipped a polished curtsy, the motion exquisitely graceful. The sort of curtsy an aspiring Prime Minister would desire in a wife.

Before he could think the better of it, Tristan snatched up her left hand, desperate for one final thread of connection.

The soft touch scalded him, her hand slender and delicate in his larger one.

She inhaled sharply—eyes wide—as if he had finally broken through the surface of her flirtation. As if, possibly, this encounter impacted her as deeply as it did himself.

Holding her gaze, he bent and placed a fervent kiss to the back of her gloved hand. She smelled of citrus—an Italian lemon grove in full bloom.

"Until we meet again, my lady," he breathed.

Expression as helplessly lost as his own, she squeezed his fingers.

It was all the encouragement Tristan needed. Instead of releasing her, he brazenly turned her hand over and pressed another kiss, lingering this time, to the sliver of pale skin exposed between her glove and the cuff of her sleeve.

She gasped at the contact.

"Aye," she replied, voice breathless. "Until then."

Gently, perhaps even reluctantly, she tugged her hand free of his grip.

Tristan watched her walk away, the bell of her muslin skirt swaying.

Abruptly, like a phenakistiscope he had played with as a child—images spinning round until they appeared to move—the future spooled out in his mind's eye.

This lady whirling to reach for his hand, her glorious red hair a blur, the wind snatching her bubbling laughter. Her, pursing her lips from a wingback chair beside the fire, Milton open in her lap as he argued a point. Her perfectly timed smile in reply to the Queen's witticism, earning Her Majesty's nod of approval.

Taking in a deep breath, Tristan turned back to the balustrade overlooking the garden, thoughts racing.

His unknown lady was correct, of course.

He would revel in finding ways to surreptitiously ask about her without alerting his father.

Because Tristan *would* uncover her identity.

He would find a way to court her. To convince her to love him. To somehow, someway, blackmail his father—like sire, like son—into accepting her.

And then, Tristan would make this beautiful, unknown lady his wife.

OVER THE FOLLOWING days, Tristan thought about the mysterious woman with obsessive intent—the trilling cadence of her laughter, the sharp crack of her wit, the sparkling merriment of her gaze.

He felt nearly fevered at times, such was the force of his infatuation.

Questions pummeled him.

Did she think upon him as often as he did of her? How was he to court her? To secure her affections? He had never successfully won a friend or lover, but for her, he would learn. He would try.

Uncovering her identity *should* be a straight-forward matter—go to White's, describe her to some acquaintances from Oxford, discover her name.

But that questioning would be reported back to Kendall. And too many years of brutality at his father's hand rendered Tristan cautious.

It was one of a hundred reasons why he kept his wants so small and few.

Moreover, Tristan rarely attended *ton* events as his father seldom came to London: The duke preferred to avoid the censure of his Peers.

His sire's sordid history remained a blight upon the family name. As a young man, Kendall had secretly married an unsuitable young woman, Catherine Ross. Then, several years later, he had publicly married the wealthy daughter of a Scottish earl, Lady Elspeth Gordon, despite Catherine Ross being very much alive. Lady Elspeth had given him three children, two boys and a girl.

Thirty years into their marriage, Kendall's bigamous behavior was uncovered by his second son, Lord Rafe. As the duke was still married to Catherine, his marriage to Lady Elspeth was dissolved and their children declared illegitimate. Kendall himself was censored and ostracized by his Peers, losing all political power.

True to his despotic nature, the duke retaliated swiftly.

He hounded Lord Rafe, wielding the economic and political might of the dukedom like a cudgel to pauper his now illegitimate son. Additionally, Kendall finally divorced his first wife, Catherine, and within a year remarried again, legally this time.

For his third bride, Kendall chose an Italian heiress, Lady Beatrice Barozzi. She quickly proved fruitful, giving birth to twins scarcely a year after their marriage—Tristan and his sister, Allegra.

But Kendall's actions continued to have weighty repercussions.

Angered over the duke's cruelty, the wealthy Earl of Hadley—Lord Rafe's closest friend—marshaled the might of his own financial empire to defend his friend. As much a man-of-business as a Peer, Hadley laid waste to the dukedom's coffers.

Eventually, funds grew so tight that Kendall did something wildly out of character—

He compromised.

Eager to save himself from financial ruin, Kendall granted Tristan's mother a divorce *a mensa et thoro*—a separation of bed and board. And in return, Beatrice surrendered her lucrative salt mines to her husband.

Desperate to escape her brutal marriage, Beatrice had signed the papers, taken Allegra, and absconded to Italy, leaving Tristan alone in his father's cruel clutches. After all, the duke had been willing to part with "the girl," but his heir had to remain.

In one fell swoop, Tristan had been separated from the only two people he loved—his mother and his twin. All precipitated by Kendall's vindictiveness and Hadley's relentless erosion of the dukedom's finances.

Having lost his reputation, fortune, wife, and daughter, Kendall tightened his grip on the one thing remaining—his ten-year-old son and heir.

Consequently, Tristan was granted no quarter and obedience was violently enforced. Kendall kept him on a very tight leash, watching his every move. The duke refused to let his heir attend any event where Babcock could not remain at Tristan's side, overhearing everything. Balls and routes were not permitted.

In short, the chances of Tristan now encountering the unknown beauty from Montacute's garden were not as statistically high as he would have liked. And a thorough perusal of *Debrett's Peerage*—late at night, in his bedchamber, under cover of darkness—did not narrow down the field of Scottish ladies. There were simply too many options.

Finally, in desperation, Tristan suggested attending the opera to his father. It was the best place to conduct reconnaissance, and Tristan required information before mustering a campaign.

"I have never attended an opera, and I find it a rather appalling lack in my education," he said to Kendall over dinner at Gilbert House, the family's London residence.

As usual, Tristan removed any sense of a request from his words. Apathy was paramount when dealing with Kendall.

"What an idiotic idea," Kendall harrumphed from his end of the long dining room table, pinning Tristan with his unsettling pale gray eyes. "Odious things, operas. Caterwauling women and plots that are as improbable as they are absurd. You are better off without them." He shook his head and stabbed at his roast beef with a trembling hand.

Tristan said nothing in reply. Manipulating his father was a chess match, and Tristan had years of experience. Words were weapons Kendall could twist to his own advantage. The less Tristan said, the more power he retained.

Mentally, the duke was as sharp and cruel as he had ever been.

But Kendall's physical decline became more apparent each year. Though it was said he had grayed young, his white hair had thinned dramatically and a tremor now racked his muscles. His skin, aged with liver spots, sagged over his bones like melting candle wax.

Most of the time, Tristan felt like he was merely waiting for the old bastard to die.

As Tristan hoped, apathy and silence won out in the end.

Three nights later, Kendall announced they were to attend the opera.

"I have decided it will be advantageous for others to see my heir," he proclaimed.

In other words, Tristan was to be trotted about like a show pony. A reminder to all and sundry that Kendall's scandalous behavior had not materially impacted his legacy.

And so, a week after the Duke of Montacute's garden party, Tristan trailed his father up the steps into the Theatre Royal Haymarket, Babcock following discreetly behind. They were fashionably late, of course, as Kendall wished everyone to take note of their arrival. The old duke held his shoulders high, giving the impression that the walking stick in his hand was more for fashion than stability.

Heads did indeed swivel their way as they entered the lobby. Though Kendall's expression remained haughty and aloof, Tristan could feel his father preening at the attention.

Covered in elegant carvings and gilt decoration, the interior of the theater was a feast for the eyes. However, Tristan's attention rested on the vibrant silks and glittering jewels of the assembled elite of London. Knowing Kendall would disapprove of gawking, Tristan feigned boredom, keeping his face carefully blank as he scanned the thinning crowd. Surely his lady's vibrant hair would stand out—a red cardinal flitting among drab sparrows.

She was not in the lobby.

He refused to be discouraged. The evening had scarcely begun.

Climbing the stairs to the first level, Tristan and Kendall wended their way along the corridor outside the aristocratic boxes, encountering few people as the notes of an opening aria had already sounded.

Abruptly, two tall, immaculately-dressed men stepped out from a box—one younger and the other gray-haired. The dim guttering gaslight rendered the doorway in shadow, masking the pair's identity.

Kendall's hiss of outrage and abrupt stop were Tristan's first clues.

Sir Rafe Gordon—Tristan's half-brother and Kendall's now-illegitimate son—stepping into the gaslight of the corridor was the second. A quick look confirmed the younger man to be Sir Rafe's eldest son, Mr. John Gordon.

Both men froze, obviously just as alarmed at encountering the duke and his heir.

"I knew coming tonight was a mistake." Kendall turned his pale eyes to Tristan. "Nowadays, you never know what bastards they will admit to formerly-respectable entertainment."

Sir Rafe laughed, a humorless crack of sound. "If I'm a bastard, 'tis only thanks tae the perfidy of my sire, would ye not agree, Father." He gave a mocking bow.

"You are no son of mine!" Kendall spat.

"Ah, I do believe a parish register at St. George's in Hanover Square would beg tae differ." Scotland threaded through Sir Rafe's voice, a nod to his Scottish mother.

Sir Rafe spared a glance for Tristan—and then for Babcock at Tristan's back—expression almost apologetic . . . but not quite.

Tristan kept his own mouth firmly shut. The less Kendall noticed him in this situation, the better. He preferred his father's vitriol to fall on Sir Rafe.

Tristan had not seen his half-brother in nearly a decade, though he had glimpsed Mr. John Gordon from afar once or twice at Oxford. Not long after being declared illegitimate, Rafe had been granted a baronetcy by then King George VI, becoming Sir Rafe.

The family resemblance between the four of them—duke, sons, and grandson—was astounding. All three of Kendall's progeny sported their sire's sharp features, broad shoulders, and striking height. Sir Rafe, Tristan noted, had a thin white scar that extended from his right temple to his cheekbone, the only mark on his otherwise handsome face. Tristan had to wonder if he himself would age as gracefully. His half-brother had avoided inheriting their father's preternaturally gray hair—Sir Rafe's good fortune, as ever, holding true.

For his part, Mr. John Gordon looked between his father and grandfather, eyes wide and guileless, before sparing a glance for Tristan. Though John and Tristan were the same age, Tristan doubted he himself had ever regarded the world with such unspoiled honesty.

Sir Rafe placed a comforting hand on his son's shoulder.

Anger and yearning Tristan had assumed long buried uncoiled and slithered out from the hole to which he had confined them.

Yes, Kendall might detest Sir Rafe for his part in uncovering his bigamy, but Tristan hated his half-brother for the promise of what might have been.

When Tristan had been most vulnerable, Sir Rafe had ruthlessly rejected and betrayed him, resulting in Kendall's virulent retribution. It had been one of his sire's earliest and most brutal lessons on the folly of *want*. On the futility of expecting love or affection from another human being.

Tristan turned, intent on dragging his father to their own box, when the door behind Sir Rafe opened again, admitting another tall, middle-aged man into the hallway.

Like Sir Rafe and his son, this man was impeccably dressed. And like them, he paused when his gaze landed on Kendall and Tristan.

"Kendall," he said, voice level and similarly laced with Scotland. "Hawthorn." He nodded to Tristan.

"Hadley," Kendall spat.

Ah.

So this was Andrew Langston, Earl of Hadley. At last, Tristan could put a face with the man who regularly took a scythe to Kendall's funds.

The Treachery of Lord Hadley was one of Kendall's favorite ballads, a refrain he never tired of bellowing. Of an evening, he would rage over how Hadley, a Scottish cit, had succeeded to an English earldom. How Hadley systemically paupered the dukedom. How Hadley continued to corrupt the aristocracy with his emphasis on trade and business, two activities in which a true gentleman did not engage.

Tristan had to agree with his father when it came to Hadley's love of commerce. The man might be as rich as Croesus, but he was hardly good *ton*.

Hadley had presence, Tristan begrudgingly admitted. Though the earl must be near fifty years of age, the breadth of his shoulders and depth of his chest pointed to a powerful physique. Tristan could see why the earl was admired by some members of the *ton*. However, those admirers remained a segment of Polite Society that cared more for money than maintaining proper decorum and tradition.

Tristan did not, and would never, share in that admiration.

And Kendall's vitriol aside, Hadley's actions toward the dukedom indicated he had no care for Tristan himself. Kendall was an old man and nearing the end of his life. Hadley's financial attacks hurt Tristan's future more than Kendall's, in reality. And given that, the earl's behavior was hardly sporting.

Hadley folded his arms and fixed the duke with an icy gaze. "I see they let ye out from underneath the rock ye call home, Kendall."

Kendall grunted. "Despicable," he hissed. "I cannot believe any of you are still received. Your crimes should be punished, not celebrated. It pains me to even breathe the same air." He turned to Tristan. "Yet another reason why attending the opera is abhorrent. We are leaving."

Panic sparked in Tristan's chest.

No! He had finagled and planned at length to reach this point of reconnaissance. His fiery-haired beauty might be just beyond the door of his father's private box. They couldn't leave now. Not without even five minutes to peruse the crowd in earnest.

Livid, Tristan shot Hadley and Sir Rafe a blistering look.

"If ye must, Duke," Hadley said congenially, as if Kendall's vicious words had been of no consequence. He smiled at Tristan. "Hawthorn is welcome tae stay, if he would like. We can see him home after the performance."

Tristan stilled.

Under no circumstances would he spend time with Hadley, even if Kendall permitted it. Being seen in the earl's company was anathema to Tristan's own goals for power and prestige. He could not sully his reputation so.

"Permit my heir to rub shoulders with vulgar riff-raff? I should think no—" Kendall broke off as the same door opened for a third time.

"Papa?" a feminine voice said. "Mamma asked me tae check if all is well."

A young lady stepped into the hallway. A lovely, red-headed lady.

No.

Please, no.

Tristan instantly recognized the beauty who had been haunting his dreams all week.

Dressed in a gown of palest blue satin that cinched her trim waist and shimmered in the candlelight, she looked at Hadley with a soft smile before noticing Kendall and Tristan. Her expression froze.

She was still achingly lovely—vibrant hair artfully piled atop her head and clusters of curls framing her fine-boned jaw as she gracefully sank into a polite curtsy.

But . . . she had called Hadley *Papa.*

Tristan's body jolted as if kicked in the chest by a temperamental stallion—stomach plummeting, heart thudding, ribs cracking in pain.

The evidence was as plain as day. His mysterious lady had been found.

But she was nearly the last woman he would ever take as a bride. The daughter of the only gentleman in Christendom that Tristan—not to mention Kendall—could not stomach: Lord Hadley.

The Scot lifted a hand to his daughter's elbow. "Ye can return tae the box," Hadley said gently. "I have this in hand."

Her gaze lingered on Tristan before sliding to Kendall and then back to her father. "Ye be sure, Papa?"

"Aye, Isolde."

Isolde.

Her name was Isolde.

Boldly, Tristan met her blue gaze.

Lady Isolde Langston, Hadley's eldest daughter, as Tristan's perusal of *Debrett's* had shown. He only remembered her name because of its close association with his own—Tristan and Isolde, the ill-fated lovers of Celtic legend.

Hadn't there been some scandal surrounding Lady Isolde Langston last year? Tristan recalled Kendall going on at gleeful length. Something about Hadley's daughter offending the Queen with her unbridled tongue.

Yet another nail in the coffin of his hopes regarding her.

Lady Isolde had known Tristan's identity—addressing him as Lord Hawthorn in the Duke of Montacute's garden. And of course, she would have been in attendance despite Hadley's standing within the *ton*; her mother was Montacute's half-sister. Another fact gleaned from *Debrett's*.

Swallowing, Lady Isolde spared a quick smile for Mr. John Gordon.

The sickening reality curled through Tristan. She had clearly mistaken him for John that day in the garden. From behind, they would likely have appeared identical.

Lady Isolde returned her gaze to his. As if she, too, felt the unnatural pull between them. As if she were just as aware of him.

The ache of her spirit—fascinating and so very alive—fractured something under his sternum, like rocks splitting inside the earth.

Her left eyebrow rose in challenge, daring him to do something now that he knew her identity.

That damnable yearning surged in his chest. She was simply so lovely, so fiery—

No.

No more.

Lady Isolde would never be for him, no matter how much his baser self admired her.

Even if Kendall were to die tomorrow, Tristan would not ally himself with a family of Hadley's ilk, with a lady of such tarnished reputation. To do so would be the kiss of death for his personal aspirations. And given the vitriol between their families, Hadley would never countenance an alliance regardless.

With a dismissive jerk of his chin, Tristan broke free of the lady's gaze.

He turned to Kendall. "Let us leave, Father. As you said, I have no wish to associate with vulgar riff-raff."

Lady Isolde's eyes flared wide at the hit.

"Indeed," Kendall harrumphed, pivoting away.

Tristan followed his father down the hallway toward the theater exit, the burn of the lady's gaze smarting between his shoulder blades.

He did not look back.

The sting of his folly scoured him.

How many times had life taught him that *wanting* only brought regret and suffering? And yet, like a damn fool, he had permitted himself to yearn for a pretty woman with a clever tongue. To build fantasies atop dreams of what their life might be together.

But in hindsight, a lady who impulsively accosted a supposed friend in Montacute's garden would not be entirely genteel.

Unfortunately, knowing himself to be an idiotic fool did not immediately stem the tide of Tristan's longing.

The spell of Lady Isolde lingered—the bright trill of her laugh, the crackling snap of her wit, the lemon scent of her skin beneath his lips . . .

For the briefest moment, he felt akin to Sir Tristan of legend.

As he recalled, the tale of Tristan and Isolde traveled a similar path to that of Lancelot, Guinevere, and King Arthur. Only in the former case, it was King Mark of Cornwall who tasked his loyal knight, Sir Tristan, with retrieving the king's chosen bride, Princess Isolde of Ireland. However, as Tristan and Isolde journeyed back to Cornwall, they were betrayed and fed a love potion. From that point, they both loved and hated one another in equal measure—helpless to fight their love-potion-fueled attraction while knowing their love to be a manufactured fiction.

Paradoxical emotions. Ones that Tristan now understood keenly.

No matter.

He had successfully overcome ill-advised bursts of longing in the past.

This too would be surmounted.

And perhaps, he would finally remember, once and for all, that *wanting* and *longing* were not emotions he was privileged to indulge. Unlike Sir Tristan of legend, this Tristan would cast his Isolde aside.

In order to erase his father's legacy after the man departed for the fires of Hell, Tristan needed to remain focused on his political and personal aims.

As he saw his father into the ducal carriage, he vowed to do precisely that.

SIX YEARS LATER

. . . Your betrayal is that of a viper—stinging, venomous, and fatal to my former loving affections. Return my letters forthwith and never speak with me again.

—PRIVATE LETTER FROM LADY ISOLDE LANGSTON
TO THE HONORABLE MR. STEPHEN JARVIS

Impulsivity would be her downfall.

Lady Isolde Langston pondered this reality almost daily.

She knew she acted without properly thinking through consequences.

Truthfully, she should enter drawing-rooms with a warning written large across her chest. Or, at the very least, engrave the fact upon her calling cards.

Lady Isolde Langston
Prone to reckless acts of incredible stupidity

Unfortunately, *knowing* she was impulsive and *doing* something to stem said impulsivity were two rather disparate things.

Ergo . . . her current situation.

With a steadying breath, Isolde quietly pushed the bedchamber door closed. Fortunately, the sturdy oak swung silently on well-oiled hinges—thanks in part, she was sure, to her mother's equally well-oiled staff.

Pressing her back to the now-closed door, Isolde surveyed the dim room.

To her left, a large fireplace stood—coals smoldering in the grate—with two tartan-clad wingback chairs angled toward it. The mantel clock ticked steadily, a nagging reminder of both the late hour and her need for haste.

Directly in front of her, a pair of windows stretched from floor to ceiling—shutters pulled shut and curtains drawn—a tall chest of drawers nestled between them. Beside the windows, gas-lit sconces sputtered, flames low.

To her right, a large fourposter bed, draped with lavish blue velvet fabric, dominated the room.

Most significantly . . . Tristan Gilbert, Duke of Kendall, lay asleep in the middle of the bed, the steady rise and fall of his chest lifting the counterpane. Gaslight from a nearby sconce rimmed the left side of his body.

Why had the duke chosen today, of *all* days, to arrive on her parent's doorstep?

Isolde took another steadying breath, fearful the frantic pounding of her heart would wake the man. Closing her eyes, she slowly counted to ten, willing her pulse to calm.

Truly, this entire situation was Kendall's fault.

If His bloody Grace hadn't arrived unexpectedly this afternoon, then Lady Hadley's best bedchamber—the one reserved for guests who outranked Lord Hadley—would have remained unoccupied.

And the private letters Isolde had hidden in the chest of drawers would have remained safe, both from her prying siblings and, potentially, the one person in all of Britain she did *not* want to read them—the Duke of Kendall.

But Kendall had sent word from Montrose Harbor of his arrival and rolled up the drive shortly after luncheon. His Grace purportedly wished to fetch his sister who had been staying at Muirford House. However, Isolde suspected the sudden visit to be another gambit in the endless chess match between the duke and her father.

Worse, His Grace then had the audacity to be wounded during an altercation with an Italian revolutionary. Isolde could scarcely blame the Italian for firing a pistol. Heaven knew, Kendall regularly inspired vitriol in strangers and acquaintances alike, even if they weren't brandishing a weapon.

When Old Kendall had finally passed four years ago, everyone had hoped the duke's heir would depart from his sire's autocratic ways. That perhaps Lord Hawthorn's tendency toward arrogance had been more for his father's benefit than truly innate.

But . . . no.

The current Duke of Kendall was every whit as high-handed and domineering as his sire. Even injured, he had sent Hadley's servants scrambling for a doctor, for French brandy, for hot water to bathe himself. Though superficial, his wound had bled to a shocking degree and required stitches. Who knew how long His Grace would remain at Muirford House convalescing?

Thankfully, the local physician had likely administered a heavy dose of laudanum after stitching the duke's shoulder, ensuring Kendall slept deeply and, therefore, granted them all a reprieve from his temper.

Isolde opened her eyes and spared another glance for Kendall.

The duke was in a rather surprising state of dishabille, even for a man asleep and recently wounded.

Before this moment, Isolde would have wagered that His Grace slept fully clothed—coat pressed, hair pomaded, cravat immaculately tied. Kendall always appeared so strait-laced and stern, it was difficult to imagine him as anything approaching human. He and Isolde might be similar in age, but His Grace gave the impression of a middle-aged man in a youth's body. Granted, his unnaturally gray hair contributed to the perception. Like his father, Kendall had grayed shockingly young.

But the gentleman currently beneath the counterpane was neither inhuman nor aged.

His hair flopped loose across his brow and stuck out around his ears like a haystack, the gray strands contrasting with his unlined face. The same could be said for the silver stubble rimming the sharp edge of his jaw.

His shirt was unbuttoned entirely—the ends of it disappearing under the quilt bunched around his waist. A white bandage wrapped his right shoulder and upper arm.

A light furring of hair—gray, of course—covered his chest that, even from across the room, Isolde could see was surprisingly muscled. What did His Grace do to acquire those muscles? Whip peasants? Berate underlings?

Most interestingly, like a wee boy fallen from an apple tree, he slept with childlike abandon, limbs loose and sprawled across the bed.

It was . . . unexpected.

Swallowing, Isolde tore her eyes from Kendall's sleeping body, running clammy palms down her dressing gown.

Enough ogling. Retrieve your letters and leave.

Stepping on tiptoe, she soundlessly crossed the room to the large chest of drawers between the windows. Thankfully, the thick pile of the expensive Savonerrie rug muffled the occasional creak of the floorboards.

Gently, a mere inch at a time, she eased the top drawer open. It appeared His Grace's valet had already stowed several neatly-folded neckcloths into the chest.

Drat.

But the drawer was deceptively deep, and Isolde knew from experience that one would need to pull the drawer almost entirely out in order to access the back of it. It was unlikely the valet had noticed the ribbon-wrapped bundle tucked at its farthest end.

Though seeing Kendall's cravats nearly touching her decidedly-private letters underscored *why* tonight's mission had been necessary.

She darted a glance at Kendall. The duke still slept soundly.

Finally after an eternity of sliding the drawer open—past His Grace's neckcloths and a small case which she guessed housed cravat pins—her letters appeared.

Truly, she should have burned them already. It was just . . . she had yet to confess the sordid tale scrawled across their pages to her parents. And the letters would be useful for that discussion.

Licking her lips, Isolde quietly, carefully lifted the packet free. Slowly, she began to inch the drawer closed, praying it didn't stick.

The letters in her free hand remained a heavy weight.

"Do you comprehend how thoroughly I loathe you?" A deep voice rumbled through the quiet.

Startling, Isolde slammed the drawer shut with a *clack*.

She whirled—the packet of letters held to her bosom like a shield—to find the duke glaring at her from his pillow, dark eyes very much alert.

Not the gaze of a man with laudanum in his blood.

"P-pardon?" she gasped.

"I loathe you," Kendall repeated, clearly enunciating every syllable. "I assume that if you are in my bedchamber at—" Here he paused to squint at the clock over the mantel. "—half-two in the morning, we have decided to forgo polite behavior and simply say what we think."

The candor of his words nearly stole her breath.

"And ye loathe me?"

"Yes." He said the word sternly, abruptly.

Well.

His low opinion came as no surprise. Isolde would say it was reciprocated.

Regardless, heat swept her cheeks, a firestorm of embarrassment, humiliation, and discomfiture. And as usual, when embarrassed, humiliated, or discomfited, she lashed out.

"I would argue, Your Grace, that constancy in polite behavior is what makes a gentleman a gentleman. If your manners wax or wane depending on the situation in which ye find a lady, are ye truly genteelly born?"

He snorted. "You are hardly a lady."

"I beg your pardon!"

"Proper behavior is rather what makes a lady a lady," he parroted back. "And all of Polite Society knows proper behavior is something *you* tossed to the wind years ago, long before you left for America."

Isolde clenched her letters tighter, hating the smug surety in his words.

Yes, four years ago, she had left Scotland to attend Broadhurst College in Massachusetts. At the time, there were no universities in the United Kingdom that allowed women into their ranks. The United States was a wee bit more progressive. Her parents had been hesitant to permit her to leave, but after much negotiation and arrangement of chaperones, Isolde had prevailed—a decision she would never regret, despite others' (i.e. Kendall's) lowering opinion.

Her time studying abroad had opened new windows in her mind and greatly expanded her understanding of the world. In fact, she had only just returned to Britain two months past.

However as Kendall so scathingly pointed out, to pursue a university education as a lady was shocking. At best, it branded Isolde as a bluestocking. At worst, she was considered a hoyden—a woman beyond the pale. Add in her ridiculous height, flame-red hair, boundless freckles, rather angular face, and inability to stem her opinionated tongue . . . well, it was obvious why she had never quite 'taken' with members of the *ton*.

Only her standing as the eldest daughter of the powerful and wealthy Earl of Hadley saved her. That and a dowry spectacularly large enough to silence even the most vociferous of detractors.

In short, Isolde knew her behavior must remain above reproach if she wished to have any standing in Polite Society.

A fact Kendall appeared more than ready to exploit.

He spread his left hand in a half circle, as if indicating the room. "Our current situation—you, uninvited, in my bedchamber in the dead of night—is yet another particularly flagrant example of your poor choices."

Isolde glared at him, her heart a trapped rabbit beneath her breastbone.

Though her mind snagged on one salient word.

"*Un*invited, Your Grace?" she asked, tone incredulous. "Do ye make a habit, then, of *inviting* gently-bred young ladies into your bedchamber of an evening? The fact would hardly surprise me. Regardless, may I refer ye, once more, tae my earlier comment about what constitutes gentlemanly conduct."

"And again, you are hardly in a position to quiz me on appropriate behavior, *my lady*." The honorific spilled from his lips with mocking irony.

He continued to glare from across the room, his dark eyes glittering.

Vividly, Isolde remembered their first encounter . . . years ago in the Duke of Montacute's garden. The meeting no one knew of save herself and Kendall.

He had appeared boyish then—dark-eyed and dark-haired—his gaze openly peering into hers. The precise opposite of his expression now.

At first, on that afternoon, she had been horrified to mistake Lord Hawthorn for John Gordon, terrified that her misstep would be reported to Old Kendall and then on to her disappointed parents.

But then, Hawthorn had smiled and flirted, easily volleying back her ripostes. He had been warm and clever and . . . unexpected.

It had been enlightening.

As had been the delicious curl of attraction that had stirred in her stomach. John never inspired butterflies; he was more brother than friend.

But Lord Hawthorn . . . well, he had loosed an entire flock of winged fluttering, battering her chest and setting her pulse to thrumming. Their too-brief conversation had spooled through her mind more times than she cared to admit. And even now, years on, she could still recall the searing press of his lips to her wrist.

She had thought of him for days afterward, wondering against reason if he would seek her out, if they would converse again.

And then came that disastrous second meeting at the opera, when Hawthorn had realized her identity, and any warmth she felt for him had died with his words—*I have no wish to associate with vulgar riff-raff.*

Now, all traces of that earnest, charming youth had been subsumed into the arrogant, haughty mantle his father had molded. Meeting one another again a few weeks past, Kendall had made his disdain and contempt for herself clear.

Though Isolde *had* recently formed a friendship with the duke's twin sister, Lady Allegra, during the lady's stay at Muirford House. Allie insisted there was good within her brother.

If so, Isolde had yet to see it.

She met Kendall's narrow-eyed glower with one of her own, her heartbeat a rapid tattoo against her ribs.

His lip curled in a faint sneer, the gaslit sconce beside the bed casting his face into planes of light and dark. "Please vacate my bedchamber immediately, Lady Isolde. I should hate to summon a footman." He shot a telling look at the servants' pull beside the bed post to his left.

Isolde feared her heart would give out. Would Kendall tell her father of this?

Hadley was an indulgent and doting parent, but invading a guest's bedchamber in the dead of night was truly beyond the pale.

"I apologize for the intrusion," she said with saccharine sweetness, dropping the duke her prettiest curtsy. "I shall leave ye to your rest, Your Grace."

Clutching her letters in both hands, she arrowed for the door.

"Dare I hope you plan to burn those posthaste?" he asked.

She froze and pivoted to look at him once more.

Kendall nodded toward the letters nestled against her palm.

Like a simpleton, Isolde glanced down at the bundle, as if surprised to find them there.

"Pardon?"

"Those letters are from Mr. Stephen Jarvis, are they not? Lord Jarvis's second son?"

Blood drained from Isolde's face so quickly, she nearly swooned.

"Ye read my letters?" she whispered on a gasp.

"I did."

"A gentleman would not have read them."

Kendall ignored her comment. "My valet was surprised to find them in a drawer allocated to me. A reading was required to ensure they were returned to their rightful owner."

"*All* of the letters? How gentlemanly of ye." She didn't even attempt to keep the sarcasm from her voice.

"Jarvis is a bad egg."

"Truly? And ye ken that . . . how? Or is your understanding merely a case of like recognizing like?"

Now Isolde knew that Stephen Jarvis was a rake of the first order. But nothing about the man had struck her as devious when first they met.

No. In fact, he had been charming and refreshingly self-deprecating.

Kendall let out a quiet huff. "I attended Oxford with Jarvis and witnessed his behavior firsthand." He flipped a hand toward the letters and then grimaced as the quick motion likely twinged his stitched shoulder. "'Tis obvious that he misled you as to his marital status and merely sought your company in order to ingratiate himself with your father. Though you really should have known better than to kiss him. A married man, no less." *A true lady would not have done so*, his tone clearly added.

Blood returned to Isolde's head, scalding her cheeks and neck.

How she hated Kendall in this moment.

Almost as much as she hated Stephen Jarvis.

Because His Grace was entirely correct, damn him.

Mr. Stephen Jarvis, an English gentleman who ran in the same social circles as herself, had been a welcome bit of home in Massachusetts. As the only British lady attending Broadhurst College, Isolde had been admitted into the upper echelons of Boston society.

Last summer, she had met Jarvis at an evening soirée. An aristocratic bachelor out to explore the world—or so he claimed—he had been polite and kind. And she had enjoyed discussing familiar places and common acquaintances. He had made her laugh during formal dinners and had been eager to discuss books and ideas. Over weeks and months, their friendship had deepened. They walked together, danced, and eventually, more than once, Mr. Jarvis had kissed her.

Isolde had been smitten. Jarvis appeared to revel in her bluestocking tendencies and celebrated the scientific bent of her mind—two things no high-born gentleman had ever done. It had been a balm to her ego, to think that she might make a match after all. Over the years, marriage had become less and less likely for herself. But Jarvis had reawakened the hope.

He was in the process of forming a company to build a railroad from Penrith to Glasgow and had begged her to entreat Lord Hadley to financially back the project. Lost in her affection for him, Isolde had agreed, and after much nagging on her part, Hadley had invested a nominal sum.

It was at that point, once Jarvis had achieved his true purpose of securing funding for his railroad, that Isolde learned the truth—Mr. Stephen Jarvis was already married to the daughter of a wealthy banker from Bristol. He had left his pregnant bride to languish in a townhouse in Bath while wooing Isolde for her father's deep pockets.

To say she had been devastated would be an understatement. She had returned home—an ashamed dog, tail wagging between its legs—desperate for the love and support of her family.

Fortunately, no one knew of Isolde's courtship and stolen kisses with a married man. However, if evidence of her behavior was uncovered, she would be ruined.

To be safe, Isolde had requested her letters back from Jarvis, correspondence which the blackguard had returned only last week. She should have burned the lot on the spot. Instead, she had stashed them here—a bedchamber used only for august visitors—until she had time to properly assess their severity, mourn her own stupidity, and confess the whole sorry tale to her parents.

Unfortunately, as Fate would have it, the letters had now fallen into the hands of the one person she would never wish to be privy to their contents.

To describe the feeling as *humiliating* was a vast understatement. If Kendall weren't already lying wounded in bed, Isolde would be tempted to put him there herself.

The situation also underscored the necessity of involving her parents immediately, much as it pained her to admit to her own indiscretions.

Her fingers curled around the packet. "And what will ye do, Your Grace, now that ye have uncovered this information? Ruin me? Sell me out to a gossip rag like the blackguard I consider ye tae be?" Isolde was proud her voice didn't quiver with the question. Her knees were already trembling enough.

He smiled at that—wide, gleaming, and terrifying. "Now . . . why would I tell you of my plans?"

Isolde's spine straightened, as it tended to do when she felt threatened. Unfortunately, such moments rendered her more reckless than usual.

She knew this, and still, she could not stem her tongue.

"Do your worst, Your Grace." She pivoted for the door. "I'll be waiting for ye."

2

MAY 1849
LONDON, ENGLAND

TWO YEARS LATER

. . . The Duke of Kendall is currently on a meteoric rise to power within Her Majesty's government. Having shed the disgraces of his father, he has become the most sought-after guest among hostesses this Season. As a boon to our female readership, the editors of this publication have heard rumors that His Grace may finally be searching for a Duchess . . .

—ARTICLE IN THE *THE LONDON TATTLER*

Tristan Gilbert, Duke of Kendall, detested balls.

He disliked hot, stuffy ballrooms filled with matchmaking mammas—their fresh-faced daughters in tow—who flocked to quiz him on the weather and the possibility of a ride along Rotten Row.

He disliked witnessing the absurd indignity of dancing, elbows flying, hair bouncing. And even worse, enduring the expectation that he himself might engage in such ludicrous behavior.

However, Kendall particularly disliked balls as they often brought him into proximity with Lady Isolde Langston. Words rose to describe her—scapegrace, virago, termagant. Truly, it was astonishing the lady was still received at all.

Thankfully, most of the *ton* followed Kendall's lead in shunning her.

Case in point, Lady Isolde stood across the ballroom, fanning her face with careless insouciance. Guests eddied around her, but few acknowledged her presence. And if they did, it was only to nod a greeting at the young woman standing at Lady Isolde's side—her sister, Kendall supposed, the lady's similar height, build, and red hair all being clues.

As he watched, old Lord Masterson tottered over to the pair—leaning heavily on his cane—and struck up a conversation. Lady Isolde replied with a polite smile, appearing oblivious to the way Masterson ogled her bosom. The man's leering raised Kendall's hackles even at thirty paces.

Though . . . Kendall's eyes narrowed . . . Lady Isolde's dress *was* rather daring. Yards of shimmering dark green satin banded across her upper arms to showcase bare shoulders and the swell of her bosom before falling to cinch her trim waist. The contrast of the luminous silk with the lady's creamy skin and vibrant auburn hair . . .

Kendall looked away, but not before seeing Masterson grin and lean in to murmur something in Lady Isolde's ear, causing the lady to flinch.

Kendall's stomach lurched.

A true lady would remain at her mother or father's side and avoid such impertinence.

Granted, a true lady would not be nearly thirty years of age, unmarried, a known bluestocking, and attending balls as if she were a débutante embarking—

"Smile, Tristan," Kendall's twin sister, Allie, hissed at his elbow. "Or at the very least, adopt a less brooding scowl."

Kendall looked down at his twin.

Only his sister had permission to call him *Tristan*, an homage to a time long past. When the two of them had raced twigs downstream and chased dandelion fluff through meadows. When he had been idealistic and sentimental. When his twin herself had been carefree and starry-eyed.

Both of them had fundamentally changed over the ensuing years. So much so, that he scarcely thought of himself as *Tristan* anymore.

Consequently, the moniker both soothed and grated in equal measure . . . all reasons why Allie continued to use it. His twin delighted in needling his ducal pride, and he tolerated her teasing as a sort of penance. Years before, his actions had prevented their father from using her as a pawn, but those same actions had also ruthlessly betrayed her trust.

And yet, Allie had somehow forgiven him for his cruelties, choosing instead to love him and renew the intense bond of their twinship.

"I cannot appear pleased to be here, as well you know." He tugged on one cuff, straightening the fabric of his shirtsleeve. "My brooding—as you put it—wards off sycophants and ambitious débutantes. I *despise* balls, and you are the only person on this planet I would humor by attending one."

"I so adore when you wax grumpy and hyperbolic," she grinned, batting her gray eyes at him. Like himself, Allie had inherited their mother's dark Mediterranean coloring, which made the contrast of her light eyes—the only positive gift from their father—even more striking. "But I thank you for the decidedly-backhanded compliment. Though if you intend to become Prime Minister one day, you should likely learn to enjoy balls more."

Kendall suppressed a grimace, as Allie had the right of it. Since their father's death, he had been so focused on eradicating the stain of Old Kendall's actions, he rather neglected entertainments such as balls.

He had always carefully guarded and cultivated his reputation. No one could say the current Duke of Kendall was not the epitome of a discerning, highborn gentleman—the sort Queen Victoria could rely upon. He kept no mistress, never gambled or caroused.

"It revolts me to have sired such a milquetoast of a man," his father had often sneered. *"You are a disgrace. No gentleman of our standing will ever admire such a boring, prudish demeanor."*

His father had not been wrong.

But Kendall chose to see such behavior as a strength. He prided himself on his ability to resist his baser instincts.

It was one of many reasons why Lord Hadley and his offspring irked Kendall so. They regularly flouted convention and appeared completely untroubled by the consequences of their behavior—such as standing unchaperoned in ballrooms or speaking their minds to monarchy.

For example, Lord Masterson had taken his leave of Lady Isolde and her sister. The women remained alone, watching the press of guests around them. No gentleman asked either to dance, well aware of the social danger of being seen as too friendly with Lady Isolde. Lady Callaghan, the wife of an Irish Peer, sailed right past the women, nose in the air. Not quite a cut direct, but close.

For her part, Lady Isolde appeared not to notice. She fanned her face and smiled at her sister, looking flagrantly radiant. As if she wished her summer-bright smile to outshine the candelabra overhead and cast other ladies into shad—

"Are you sure it is balls you dislike?" Allie asked, interrupting him once more. "Or is it merely any place that Lady Isolde happens to frequent?"

Gritting his teeth, Kendall forcibly looked away from Hadley's daughter. Clearly, his attempts to stem his youthful infatuation with Lady Isolde had not been as successful as anticipated.

Like Sir Tristan of legend, this Isolde had cast a spell over him in that sun-drenched garden long ago. A love potion that compelled him to seek her out—to watch and remember most unwillingly.

"I do not understand what you mean," he said, feigning ignorance and blinking away the sharp memory of Lady Isolde's fingertips pressed to his eyelids, of her thrumming pulse under his lips . . .

Allie grinned, far too knowingly. "Of course you can continue to deny—"

"Lady Allegra! How lovely to see you again!"

Kendall and Allie both turned as Lady Jarvis stopped before them.

Even before reading of Lady Isolde's indiscretions with Mr. Stephen Jarvis in her letters, Kendall had disliked the man's parents—Lord and Lady Jarvis. Lord Jarvis was a bombastic gambler; his wife, a social-climbing busybody.

But Kendall now knew their son's dark secrets. Once news of Mr.

Stephen Jarvis's financial crimes became public, the entire Jarvis clan would be ostracized. As it was, Kendall despised having to acknowledge an acquaintance with the family.

"Lady Jarvis." Allie dipped her head in greeting.

Kendall managed the barest of nods before looking away, pretending to study the dancers. It was the closest he could come to a cut direct without causing talk.

Out of the corner of his eye, he noticed Lady Jarvis's smile falter.

Good.

She *should* take heed. Her second son would likely find himself in shackles and transported to Australia before the year was out.

Kendall felt a spike of vindictive glee at the thought.

He had not intended to read Lady Isolde's private letters two summers ago. But once he realized that he held *her* intimate correspondence in his hands . . . well, he had been helpless to stop himself. Her spell had worked its power.

As expected, Lady Isolde's writing was as heedless and effusive as her person, providing far too much detail of her own indiscretions with the man.

However, more significantly, the letters had discussed applying to Hadley for funds to finance Jarvis's railroad venture—a request that Hadley had eventually granted.

Given Kendall's personal knowledge of Stephen Jarvis's deplorable character, the information sparked questions. Questions that had led Kendall on a merry chase—quizzing investors, hiring investigators, and gathering intelligence about Jarvis's business dealings.

The upcoming weeks would see the culmination of over a year of careful planning and plotting.

Lady Jarvis turned to Allie. "I was surprised to learn you and Mr. Penn-Leith had returned home from the Mediterranean. I understand there was a death in your husband's family?"

To Kendall's dismay, Allie had married far beneath her station in life, having fallen in love with the celebrated Scottish poet, Mr. Ethan Penn-Leith. But as she fairly glowed with happiness, Kendall tolerated her husband.

Kendall listened as Allie explained how Ethan's uncle had passed away unexpectedly, and as Ethan was the man's heir, they had returned to settle his affairs.

"It must be so lovely to be in the bosom of your family once more, Lady Allegra. Whenever my grown children return home, I rejoice in our reunion. Family brings such joy," Lady Jarvis simpered, shooting a telling look at Kendall. "Do you not agree, Your Grace?"

Only hundreds of years of good breeding prevented Kendall from rolling his eyes. Moreover, he refused to encourage Lady Jarvis with a reply. He kept his gaze firmly locked on the dancers, as if he hadn't heard her words.

Unfortunately, a break in the set landed Lady Isolde squarely in his line of sight once more.

The Honorable Mr. Andrew Mackenzie Langston and Mr. James Langston, Hadley's heir and spare, had joined their sisters. Lady Isolde appeared to be encouraging James to dance with their younger sister.

Bloody hell but the woman was a managing shrew.

Dimly, he noted Lady Jarvis taking leave of his sister.

"You behaved abominably, Tristan," Allie said on a laugh. "Lady Jarvis will never speak with us again."

"Excellent. Then my purpose has been accomplished."

"Tristan! You cannot alienate all of London. Who will be your friend then?"

"I am a duke, Allie. Dukes do not have *friends*. I have political associates and societal acquaintances. Most importantly, I have no qualms over dismissing self-aggrandizing, pompous people."

"Hah!" Allie guffawed. "Said the pot to the kettle."

Kendall grunted.

Lady Isolde was currently waving cheerfully as James led their sister onto the floor. Naturally, the lady had asserted her will in the end.

Abruptly, Lady Isolde swung her gaze around, brazenly meeting Kendall's eyes across the crowded ballroom. She raised a solitary eyebrow in challenge, as if to say, *What now, Your Grace?*

Kendall's pulse climbed.

The hoyden.

If Hadley had an ounce of spine, he would have corrected his daughter's worst impulses years—

"So when will we discuss your unhealthy obsession with my friend?" Allie asked conversationally.

Kendall jerked his eyes away from Hadley's daughter. "Pardon?"

"If you stare any more fervently at Lady Isolde, her gown will likely catch fire."

"Nonsense."

"No. *Obsessed.*"

Kendall nearly flinched as the word reverberated in his ears—*obsessed, obsessed, obsessed.*

Had he truly stooped to obsession?

No. That would not do.

He closed his eyes, taking in slow breaths and counting out seconds . . . *one, two, three* . . . forcibly casting Lady Isolde from his mind.

Eventually, his ludicrous physical attraction to her would dissipate. Even in the legend of old, the love potion had worn off in due course. Until then, Kendall merely needed to strive harder to ignore Lady Isolde's existence.

"I care nothing for *that* woman," he finally said to Allie. "My sole desire is to see our father's memory obliterated from history."

"Still on that, are you?"

"Forever. My own star will shine so bright, the world will forget that our sire ever existed."

Kendall *would* become Prime Minister.

Lady Isolde *would* be forgotten.

And the events he had set in motion with Stephen Jarvis would be another stepping stone on the path to victory.

"WHY DOES KENDALL always stare at ye?" Mac asked. "It's as if he be memorizing your face before painting a portrait."

Isolde shrugged at her younger brother's words.

Though christened Andrew Mackenzie Langston—after their father and paternal grandfather—he had been called Mac since birth.

"I cannot say." She half rolled her eyes. "Kendall despises me and feels the need tae ensure I know it?"

She certainly could not tell her brother the more honest truth: *Well, ye see, once upon a time before he knew who I was, he flirted with me and kissed my hand (and wrist) most ardently. And then, years later, he read my intensely private correspondence that I invaded his bedchamber to retrieve . . .*

Mac's eyebrows lifted, clearly doubting her. "A man does not look at a woman he despises as often as Kendall stares at yourself. Pa even asked me about it after the theater last week."

"About Kendall's staring?"

"Aye."

"Truly? How odd. Well, Papa cannot be too concerned, as he has said nothing tae myself. I care nothing for Kendall." Words that were not entirely true. Kendall inspired a great many conflicting emotions in her breast—attraction, confusion, irritation. "I'm more anxious that Mariah has an enjoyable evening."

She nodded to where their youngest sister danced with James. At nineteen, this was Mariah's first Season, and both Isolde and her mother intended it to be a successful one.

In the far corner of the ballroom, their other sister, Catriona, smiled shyly up at her betrothed, Lord Barnaby. Unlike Isolde and Mariah, Catriona was petite, blond, and demure—much to their mother's long-suffering delight. Barnie returned his beloved's look with a besotted one of his own. Nearby, Lord and Lady Hadley were speaking with Lord and Lady Alderton, Barnie's parents. They were likely discussing the wedding, which was to be held at St. George's in Hanover Square in seven weeks.

Truly, it was high time *one* of the five Hadley children—Isolde, Mac, James, Catriona, and Mariah—married. Lady Hadley was in alt, and Isolde rejoiced that sweet, kind Catriona had found a gentleman who matched her reserved temperament.

Best of all, Catriona's upcoming marriage had diverted Lady Hadley's attention away from Isolde's own unmarried state.

Isolde had yet to convince her mother that she was unlikely to marry. At least, not within her own social class. Isolde's height, education, creeping age, and 'unconventional beauty' (as Lady Hadley charitably termed it), ensured most gentlemen of the *ton* gave her a wide berth.

"Maybe I'll tell Ma that Kendall seems tae have taken a fancy tae ye," Mac rocked back on his heels, a taunting smile on his lips. Tall with reddish-blond hair, her brother was a perfect blend of both their parents.

"Ye wouldn't dare." Isolde narrowed her gaze. "Mamma would never let ye be, asking how ye ken that, wanting proof of your theories. Ye know how she is. She operates on facts, not fantasies. And ye have no facts at the moment."

"Aye," Mac grinned, utterly unrepentant, "but given the outrage on your face, it would be worth it. Kendall might be the most boorishly boring gentleman in England, but he is still a duke. And Ma well understands his eligibility."

"*If* Kendall stares at me, I am sure it is merely to catalog my many faults."

"Yet it is a fact, Sis—the duke cannot tear his eyes off ye."

Isolde fanned her face, looking away before Mac wound her up any further.

Honestly.

Brothers.

Of course, her gaze immediately collided—yet again—with Kendall's. She gave His Grace a rather pointed lift of her eyebrows and tapped her fan against her left ear lobe. If Kendall understood the traditional language of fans, he had hopefully received her message: *Please leave me be.*

"Resorting tae fan conversations, I see," Mac chortled. "I stand by my assertions."

Kendall whipped his gaze away, presenting Isolde with his impressively handsome profile—patrician nose, forehead neither too high nor too low, soft-looking lips. With his olive complexion and sharp Mediterranean features—both courtesy of his Italian mother—he appeared an exotic panther amid pale house cats.

"And now ye be staring, too," her brother continued.

"Nonsense. I'm merely contemplating the tragedy of Kendall."

"The tragedy?"

"Aye. That so much male beauty is utterly wasted on an absolute reprobate of a human being."

"Male beauty?!" Mac crowed. "Aye, I think I might need tae talk to Ma about this, after all."

Isolde sighed as her brother doubled over with laughter, shoulders shaking. Heads turned their way, including predictably, Kendall's.

James finished the set with Mariah and handed her off `to another gentleman of their acquaintance for a spirited reel, before walking toward Mac and Isolde.

At least five women turned to watch James's progress across the ballroom floor. At twenty-seven and twenty-five years of age, respectively, Mac and James were also two of the more eligible bachelors on the marriage mart.

"Ye tell Isolde what we heard at Brook's today?" James asked as he joined them.

Both her brothers eschewed membership at White's—the other prestigious gentlemen's club in London—due to its more conservative politics, preferring the more liberal Whig atmosphere of Brook's.

Kendall, naturally, reigned supreme at White's.

"No," Isolde said. "What did ye hear?"

"'Tis about Pa and his investments."

"*Och*, shut it, James," Mac warned.

Isolde huffed a laugh. As if *that* would temper her curiosity.

"Give over, Mac," she said. "Ye know ye will tell me eventually. Might as well forgo my nagging from the start."

Mac shot James an aggrieved look.

"Fine," Mac said to her, "but ye cannot go running tae Pa over it. Ye must keep this a secret."

"I will absolutely go tae Papa, if necessary. Ye ken that." Isolde adored their father, just as he adored her.

"Aye, but in this, ye cannot. I don't think he wishes us tae know, or he would have said something afore now."

"I'm well and truly worried now. Tell me."

"Promise ye won't tell Pa."

"No."

"Isolde," said with warning in his tone.

"Mac."

Her brother rolled his eyes.

"Ye might as well tell her," James said, conversationally. "Ye ken she'll get it out of us eventually."

Mac let out a heavy sigh. "Very well."

He leaned down to whisper in Isolde's ear.

I have said it before and I will say it again—I dislike how Kendall watches and studies our Isolde. Why? What treacherous plans does he spin? And how many times must I poke holes in His Grace's pride before he heeds the warning and leaves us all be?

        ——PRIVATE LETTER FROM LORD HADLEY TO LADY HADLEY

What do you think of this one, Isolde? There is some opalescence along the right edge." Lady Hadley handed Isolde a rock from the pile stacked on the table before them. "Could it be something new? Or is it just another bit of ammonite?"

Isolde tilted the rock into the morning sunlight, giving every pretense of appraising it.

Her mother's lifelong adoration of mineralogy was well known. This particular group of rocks had been collected last summer on a holiday to the Dorset coast.

Family lore asserted that Isolde's parents had fallen in love over rocks. Lady Jane Everard, daughter of the Duke of Montacute, and Andrew Langston, Earl of Hadley and grandson of a wealthy Scottish industrialist, had first bonded over their shared passion for rocks and minerals. Hadley had even read geology as a course of study at St Andrews University in Scotland.

Her parents' love of science had inspired Isolde's own educational aspirations. But instead of geology and minerals—the exploration of things past—she relished mechanics and physics. Or rather, things that were forward-looking, that aimed to better people's lives in the here and now.

"Do you ever tire of rocks, Mamma?" Catriona asked from her chair beside the hearth, pulling a needle through her embroidery.

Unlike Isolde and their mother, Catriona adored more traditional female pastimes—namely embroidery and lace-making—and identified with their mother's heritage, her accent deliberately as English as Lady Hadley's.

Catriona would make Lord Barnaby the best of wives.

"Do ye ever tire of shopping for ribbon and thread, Cat?" Mariah countered from the window seat where she was curled up with a book.

Mariah was somewhere between her sisters—loving books, learning, and Scotland—while not entirely eschewing the occasional embroidery project.

Lady Hadley smiled at her daughters. Nearing her fifty-fifth year, Isolde's mother retained the elegant beauty of her youth, despite the silver threading through her auburn hair. Often, Isolde wondered if looking at her mother was akin to seeing herself twenty years into the future.

The four Hadley women were gathered in the drawing-room of the family townhouse in Mayfair. Late morning sunlight weakly shone through two large windows, clouds threatening rain. The dressmaker was due soon for another round of fittings for Catriona's trousseau and wedding gown.

But none of those thoughts occupied Isolde's mind at the moment. No.

Instead, she could not stop spinning Mac's revelations round and round in her head. She had spent the night with her stomach in knots, tossing and turning until nearly dawn.

According to her brothers, Stephen Jarvis had been accused of fraud. His supposed company—linking the English railway at Penrith with its Scottish neighbor in Glasgow—had been an elaborate ruse. There was no railroad. Instead, Jarvis had been using the funds from recent investors to pay out profits to past investors while pocketing a nice percentage for himself in between.

Though appalling, Jarvis's crimes were not Isolde's primary concern. He deserved any punishment that might come his way.

The real issue came from Hadley's financial involvement with Jarvis—a relationship that Isolde had practically foisted upon her father.

Hadley had been the first credible investor in Jarvis's fledgling company—an enormous feather in Jarvis's cap and an association that he had widely touted. Given that Hadley was famous for his business acumen, other nobles in the House of Lords had jumped at the chance to invest as well, trusting in Hadley's stellar reputation as a savvy businessman and honorable gentleman.

And now, the entire scheme had been exposed to the light of day— tumbling down like a house of cards and causing many in Lords to lose large sums of money.

Worse, rumors swirled that Hadley was in on the ruse. That he had profited along with Jarvis.

Mac said it was nonsense. Yes, their father had invested initially, but that was the end of it. Hadley had hundreds of investments at any given time, and occasionally, a bad one slipped through the cracks. With Jarvis, Hadley was as much a victim as anyone else.

But, James had added, though their father was widely liked and admired, he also had his detractors. A gentleman did not remain an outspoken member of Lords for over thirty years without collecting enemies along the way. And those lords claimed to have evidence— solicitors' papers and personal testimony—supporting their father's complicity.

There was even talk of impeaching Hadley, a formal process by which a member of the peerage could be accused, tried, and gaoled for crimes like fraud.

Isolde felt genuinely ill.

Her relationship with Jarvis had sparked this predicament. If she had just been less arrogant—less naive and trusting in her own discernment—she would have seen Jarvis for the reprobate he was. Or, at the very least, she would not have pressured her father so relentlessly to invest with the man.

Not that her brothers knew of Isolde's *personal* involvement with Jarvis.

No, that information remained the purview of the Duke of Kendall and her parents—to whom she had confessed the whole, sordid tale immediately after leaving Kendall's bedchamber on that night two years past.

"Ye are correct. There is a wee bit of opalescence in this one." Isolde handed the rock sample back to her mother. If Lady Hadley noticed her daughter's distracted state, she did not mention it.

Isolde was desperate to speak with her father. To ascertain how truly dire the situation was. To understand what could be done to rectify it.

But Hadley had left earlier that morning—"a meeting with my solicitor and then a stop in at Brook's"—and had yet to return.

When a door shut below them, Isolde held her breath, straining to hear her father's heavy tread on the stairs. But only the murmuring sounds of the butler instructing a footman in some matter reached her ears.

"Lady Alderton asked if you are content to spend your honeymoon at their estate in Cornwall, Catriona." Lady Hadley handed another rock to Isolde for inspection.

"Cornwall?!" Aghast, Mariah set down her book—a poetry collection by Nathaniel Hawthorne, an American writer Isolde had grown to love during her time in Massachusetts. "Barnie is taking ye tae *Cornwall* for your honeymoon? Not Paris or Italy?"

"That was rather Lady Alderton's concern, as well," Lady Hadley said dryly.

"Let me guess," Mariah said, tone scathing. "Ye will be staying in a seaside hut. . . . one that comes with whistling wind and a resident sheep or three."

Catriona continued to sew, entirely unperturbed. "You know I do not seek a flamboyant life, Mariah. I have no desire to go abroad. I am merely eager to marry my Barnie and begin our years together, whether that happens in Cornwall or Paris or the wilds of Nova Scotia, I truly do not care. As long as we are together, we are content."

What would it be like, Isolde pondered, to be so sure of one's love? To look into the eyes of a gentleman and think—*You . . . I'll take you.*

"I am glad you are content then." Lady Hadley smiled at her daughter. "You know your father and I only want your happiness. And you and Lord Barnaby seem particularly well-suited."

Thankfully, Lady Hadley did not look at Isolde as she spoke.

Isolde's own unmarried status worried her mother. For a brief window of time, Isolde had wondered if Stephen Jarvis might be her soulmate, but in that, she had been mistaken. And now, it had been years since a gentleman had inspired any sort of flutterings within her.

Unbidden, the image of Kendall sliced through her mind—the intensity of his dark eyes as he gazed at her from across the ballroom—

Snick.

Another door shut below.

Isolde tilted her head to listen to the low murmur of voices drifting up the stairwell, straining to hear her father's bass.

But, no.

The dressmaker had arrived.

IT TOOK ISOLDE until after dinner to finally corner her father in his study.

Lord Hadley looked up from his desk at the *click* of the door latch.

Like his wife, Lord Hadley had aged with grace. Tall and broad-shouldered, his blue eyes—so like Isolde's own—retained the mischief and humor of a much younger man.

He stood as she entered, a smile on his lips that quickly turned to a frown when he saw her expression.

"What is it, Izzy?" he asked.

Only her father called her *Izzy*, a nickname borne of late-night conversations and long cuddles on a winter's afternoon.

It struck her anew—

How she adored this man!

She had loved him as a wee girl perched atop his shoulders as he went about business on the family estate in Scotland.

She had loved him when he readily agreed to support her studies at Broadhurst College, gruffly kissing her forehead and promising to write as she boarded a ship for America. And then, he had welcomed her home with celebration when she had returned from Boston two years before, heartsore and furious over Jarvis's deception.

And she would love her father forever . . . in his steadfast devotion and readiness to defend her against critics of her age or education.

Perhaps that was why she had yet to marry. Simply put—every other man paled in comparison to Lord Hadley. And Isolde couldn't bring herself to settle for less than the kindness and love that her parents shared.

Unbidden, tears welled in her eyes.

Isolde never cried.

And yet, knowing she had caused her father harm. That he might be suffering due to her poor judgment of character. That he could, right now, be exploring ways to save himself from a gaol sentence . . .

This man who had always been her hero and champion.

"Izzy?" Hadley rounded his desk, brows drawn down. "What the devil has happened?"

Without waiting for her reply, he pulled her into his arms.

And then she was crying in earnest, face pressed against his neckcloth, hands wrapping around his waist. His familiar smell—woodsmoke, sandalwood, and whisky—surrounded her. The scent of comfort and home.

"Izzy, ye must tell me what has happened," he murmured, pressing a kiss to the top of her head. "I can't recall the last time I saw ye have a good *greit*, and now I be proper *worrit*."

The rumble of his brogue only made Isolde's tears fall harder.

"I f-failed ye," she hiccupped in his chest. "Mac t-told me about Jarvis and the ch-charges against ye."

Her father stilled, and then a soft laugh vibrated through his body. "Is that all then?"

"Is that all?!" She pulled back, expression surely aghast.

"The way ye were *greiting*, I feared ye were hurt or possibly increasing."

"Increasing? Papa!" Isolde pressed palms to her flaming cheeks. "I might be unconventional, but I'm hardly so senseless to propriety."

Retrieving a handkerchief from his waistcoat pocket, Hadley wiped away her tears before handing her the handkerchief for her nose.

"How can ye be so *blasé* about this situation with Lords and Jarvis?" she asked.

Hadley shrugged and turned toward a cabinet in the corner.

"Come." He pointed to the pair of chairs before the fire. "Sit. I'll pour us some whisky."

"Ye ken we'll need whisky for this conversation? How is it *not* serious then?"

"*Och*, the whisky is less for the conversation and more for yourself." He tilted amber liquor into two tumblers. "Ye could use a wee dram, I think."

Isolde sat, still swiping at her damp cheeks.

Hadley brought her a tumbler with a finger of whisky.

For the record, Lady Hadley did not approve of her husband serving their daughters strong spirits. Which explained why Lady Hadley rarely learned of the frequency of its occurrence.

Her father settled himself into the leather armchair opposite Isolde with an audible *oof* and took a healthy swallow of his own drink.

"Now, this business with Jarvis—"

"Is it as dire as Mac implied?"

"Perhaps. Time will tell," Hadley hedged. "My adversaries in Lords feel the need tae make their voices heard. Every ten or twenty years, they bring trumped-up claims of some sort against a Scottish peer. It's practically a rite of passage for us Scots. Lord Melville faced similar accusations years ago."

Isolde had to wonder at her father's presumed calm. Was it merely part of his attempt to reassure her? Surely the wrinkles stacked on his forehead hinted at deeper concerns.

"But the charges of fraud against ye . . ."

"False, as ye well know. I have had no part in Jarvis's profiteering from others' investments."

"Yes, but if they bring articles of impeachment. If they force ye tae defend yourself on the floor of the House of Lords. To present evidence that ye didn't know of Jarvis's deception—"

"Then I shall do so. There are hints that the physical evidence against me—ledgers and some correspondence—appears rather damning from the outside, but I have faith that truth will triumph." Hadley took an unconcerned sip of his whisky.

Isolde couldn't share her father's nonchalance. She had read enough of history to understand that Truth did not always prevail. Generally, Truth required action and a well-planned counter-attack in order to carry the day.

"My greater worry at the moment," Hadley continued, brow knitting, "is Catriona's upcoming wedding. Alderton is a bit of a stickler, and he has voiced concern over this turn of events."

Isolde pressed a hand to her stomach, as if that would somehow calm the nausea churning there.

Catriona and Barnie.

How could she not have anticipated that connection?

"Is the wedding likely tae be called off?" she asked.

"Possibly. Alderton made it clear tae myself last night that he refuses to permit his heir to marry into a 'family of disgrace,' as he terms it."

Isolde's chest felt wedged beneath a boulder.

"I should never have encouraged Mr. Jarvis's suit. This whole affair began with my poor decisions." She drained her whisky in one long gulp, setting throat to coughing.

"*Och*, Izzy, ye take too much upon your shoulders. I could have denied your request with Jarvis. But ye ken I like tae invest when the prospect looms bright." Hadley shook his head. "All will come right in the end. In the meanwhile, dinnae *fash* yourself."

"How . . . can I . . . not? I was . . . the catalyst," she managed to say between gasping coughs. "If I hadn't nagged ye about Jarvis and vouched for him. If I hadn't made the looming returns *seem* bright—ye would never have invested in the first place."

Anxiety buzzed under her skin, wasps swarming and eager to sting. What was to be done?

"Izzy, despite the guilt ye feel, I am a man who owns his decisions. Could I have researched Jarvis and his plans a wee bit more afore giving him money—"

"But ye didn't, because ye trusted myself."

"It seemed a sound investment at the time. To be honest, I had been exploring building a similar railroad. Then the opportunity with Jarvis landed, and it was simpler to pass off the minutiae of managing it to him. By the time I realized Jarvis had been such a blackguard to yourself, it was too late for my investment tae be returned. So I chalked it up to a lesson learned and moved on."

"But now Jarvis's fraud has implicated yourself."

"Aye, as I said earlier, something like this was bound tae happen eventually. There are too many in Lords who are jealous or who wish to promote their own preeminence by taking a swipe at mine. How else is Kendall tae convince the Queen he has the mettle to become Prime Minister?"

Kendall's name dropped into the conversation with a nearly audible *thunk.*

"Kendall?!" Isolde could hear the outrage in her voice. "What does Kendall have tae do with this?"

"He is leading the charge, as it were. He was the first to bring forth accusations against Jarvis and then myself. Now, he is rallying votes for impeachment."

Kendall was the source of all this?

Oh!

Isolde pressed a hand to her stomach again, fearing she would be sick in truth.

A miasma of regret and horror and fury flooded her veins.

So . . . her father's situation *was* entirely her fault in the end.

Kendall had read her correspondence with Jarvis. Consequently, he knew that Hadley was Jarvis's first credible investor. And Kendall, the blackguard, had used that information as the starting point for his own investigation.

Guilt and fury pricked her skin.

Of course, the duke's irrational hatred of their family would reach such heights. He would see Hadley gaoled on trumped-up charges. He would destroy Catriona's happily-ever-after.

How dare he!

The bastard!

Isolde had heard the expression 'to see red,' but she had never actually experienced it.

How odd.

Hadley's study very much appeared bathed in a scarlet hue. She rather hoped it would be the color of an arrogant duke's blood.

Kendall would pay for his ungentlemanly behavior and unwarranted attacks on her family.

Isolde would see to it personally.

Mr. Stephen Jarvis, son of Lord Jarvis, has been gaoled on charges of embezzlement and fraud with regard to his railway venture between Penrith and Glasgow. Moreover, a growing faction within Parliament—led by the Duke of Kendall—is demanding Lord Hadley explain his involvement in this affair . . .

—ARTICLE IN *THE LONDON TIMES*

As a duke of the realm, Kendall's days were regimentally organized—meetings with solicitors, estate managers, members of Parliament, Ministers of State, and even occasionally, Queen Victoria herself.

Thankfully, he had four men-of-business and five secretaries—not to mention a team of clerks and stewards—to assist him in managing the lot.

Currently, the secretary who oversaw his daily diary, Mr. Adam

Ledger, was seated before Kendall's ponderous oak desk, outlining the duke's engagements for the day.

The study in Gilbert House, the London residence of the Duke of Kendall, was not quite as opulent or large as the one in Hawthorn, the family seat in Wiltshire. But Kendall appreciated the efficiency of the room—a desk with a large window behind for light, two chairs for secretaries in front of said desk, a large cabinet clock for the time, and a hearth for warmth. Practical. Efficient.

"After your luncheon with The Chancellor of the Exchequer at noon," Ledger was saying, "Your Grace will have drinks at White's with Lord John Russell. He will await you at three o'clock in the library after his audience with Her Majesty." The secretary made a neat pencil mark in the book he held, pushing his spectacles up his nose.

"Excellent." Kendall tapped his fingers on the desktop. For the past year, he had been courting favor from Lord John. The older statesman had proved an excellent tutor in governance and methods for consolidating power.

"Mr. Cartwright"—another secretary—"has drafted a list of potential questions for Lord John." Ledger slid a sheet of foolscap across the desk.

"Good." Kendall pulled the paper toward him, noting Cartwright's points—*proposed enclosure act, militia ballot suspension, the ongoing potato famine in Ireland* . . .

Morning sun streamed from the window at Kendall's back, bathing the room in cheery light. He pulled out his watch, noting the time and comparing it with the wall clock opposite his desk.

Every Monday, his butler sent a footman to the Royal Observatory in Greenwich with a chronometer to ensure all the clocks in Gilbert House were precisely in line with official London Time.

Ledger adjusted his spectacles again. "After the meeting with Lord John Russell, I have arranged—"

A peal of feminine laughter echoed down the hallway outside the study door.

Kendall's finger-tapping increased.

"Continue." He motioned toward his secretary.

Ledger swallowed. "I have arranged another brief meeting with Mr. Grierson and Mr. Fletcher. They will attend Your Grace here at Gilbert House."

"Regarding the impeachment motion against Lord Hadley in the House of Commons?" Kendall perked up.

"Yes, Your Grace. I understand they wish to discuss methods for moving forward."

"That is good."

More than good. Due to a quirk in British law, impeachment articles against a member of the House of Lords could only be brought by the House of Commons. The House had to vote in favor of impeachment and then deliver their verdict to the House of Lords. From there, Lords would appoint prosecutors, call witnesses, and act as jury in evaluating the actions of their fellow Peer.

Once Kendall's investigations had uncovered the depth of Hadley's involvement with Jarvis, he had begun rallying support in Commons for an impeachment vote. Grierson and Fletcher were his staunchest allies in this pursuit.

Kendall *would* see Hadley prosecuted. Legal papers and personal testimony indicated that the earl had committed wrongdoing.

Men like Hadley, with their liberal views on commerce and uncaring attitude toward social mores, were a stain upon the entire British aristocracy. Impeachment would not remove Hadley from Lords nor affect his peerage title, but it could result in imprisonment for a time. Even the issuing of articles of impeachment would significantly damage Hadley's reputation and power.

And any reduction in Hadley's liberal influence would only further Kendall's conservative political goals.

As if to mock the notion, another burst of laughter filtered in.

Kendall gritted his teeth.

Lady Isolde had flounced through the front door of Gilbert House not an hour past. Rather . . . she had not *literally* flounced, but the bounce in her step—and murderous glance she shot his way as she followed Allie into the small drawing-room—had called the adjective to mind.

Since then, the nonstop murmur of female voices and an occasional laugh had emanated from behind the closed door.

All in all, Lady Isolde would be much easier to ignore if the bothersome woman were not Allie's closest friend. But with his sister's return to London two months past, Lady Isolde had become a fixture in Gilbert House.

It was enough to drive a sensible man mad.

Ledger produced another sheet of paper. "Cartwright also compiled a list of potential opponents and possible adverse effects of pursuing articles of impeachment against Lord Hadley . . . items to perhaps discuss with Grierson and Fletcher."

Cartwright was nothing if not diligent with his lists. Kendall appreciated that in the man.

Mmm, Cartwright's points were salient—*potential backlash from other Peers due to Kendall's involvement in the impeachment, economic retaliation from Lord Hadley himself which could harm the dukedom's financial assets, damage to Kendall's own reputation . . .*

The murmur of Lady Isolde's melodic voice carried down the hallway and set all the fine hairs on his arms flaring to attention.

How was a man to even *think* with that termagant in the house?

"This evening, Your Grace is engaged to attend the salon of Sir Robert Sorenson, where Mr. Charles Darwin will be presenting a lecture." Ledger glanced toward the door. "I understand Lady Allegra Penn-Leith will accompany you, as she is in residence."

"Yes, I believe so. I will confirm with my sister."

Once Lady Isolde departed.

His twin's friendship with Hadley's daughter aside, Kendall very much appreciated that Allie had returned to English soil. His sister's bright presence made Gilbert House feel less like a mausoleum.

Her husband, Ethan, was still in Aberdeen, seeing to the affairs of his late uncle's estate. However, Allie had opted to remain in London, both to spend time with Kendall and to assist him as a social hostess. Lady Whipple, their aunt, usually acted as his hostess, but her health was in decline, and so she had not come to London this Season.

"Is that all, Ledger?" Kendall asked.

"Not quite, Your Grace. Do you still wish to meet with your fencing master tomorrow morning?"

"Yes." Fencing, boxing, horse riding, and other forms of physical exertion kept Kendall sane. Exhausting his body cleared his thoughts as nothing else could.

"Very good. Additionally, Cartwright has compiled the roster you requested." Ledger slid yet another sheet of foolscap across Kendall's desk.

Eligible Ladies of the Ton was written across the top in Cartwright's precise handwriting.

Ah, yes.

As Kendall had recently passed his twenty-ninth birthday, it seemed rather time to begin searching for a wife in earnest. The dukedom required an heir. But first, he needed to narrow the field.

Ledger cleared his throat. "I spoke with Marshall"—the secretary in charge of managing Kendall's social engagements—"and he is at the ready to issue dinner invitations to any young lady, and her parents naturally, who you wish to consider. With Lady Allegra in residence and acting as hostess, such invitations will be expected."

"Excellent. I will review the list this evening and apprise Marshall of my decisions."

"As you wish, Your Gra—" Ledger flinched at the sound of a particularly loud burst of mirth from the small drawing-room.

Kendall closed his eyes, breathing slowly through his nose.

It was unfortunate that women like Lady Isolde existed.

But to have to tolerate her inside his own home . . .

He longed for the day he forgot Lady Isolde Langston walked the earth. For a time when he could go weeks and months without seeing or hearing her.

However, she was like the persistent moss that plagued the north roof slates of Hawthorn—encroaching, omnipresent, and nearly impossible to eliminate.

The giggling laughter continued, propelling Kendall to his feet.

"You are dismissed, Ledger," he called as he strode out of the room.

Allie and Lady Isolde both jumped when Kendall burst through the door to the small drawing-room.

The two women were curled into a sofa before the fireplace, shoes scandalously abandoned on the floor and feet tucked under their skirts.

Sunlight from the window opposite the hearth illuminated Lady

Isolde's hair, turning it to red flames. Annoyingly, the vibrant color contrasted strikingly with her fair skin and the printed ivory muslin of her day gown. And then he was annoyed even further that he had noticed such a ridiculous detail.

Obsessed, whispered through his brain.

No!

He gritted his teeth.

His sister pressed a palm to her bosom. "Tristan! That was rather . . ." She waved a hand to indicate the door. ". . . *vigorous* of you. Whatever is the matter?"

"Must you be so loud and indecorous?" Kendall's words were meant for his twin, but as he was still staring at Lady Isolde, they appeared to be for her.

"Me, Your Grace?" Lady Isolde mirrored Allie with a palm to her bosom, drawing Kendall's eyes (irritatingly) to *notice* said bosom and further stoking the furnace of his ire.

Allie swiveled her head between Kendall and Lady Isolde. "Yes. We were both laughing, Brother. Why should you harangue my guest?"

Kendall pinched the bridge of his nose, slowly counting to ten. It was a trick he had learned long ago to manage his temper. To force his pulse to slow and his thoughts to still before saying or doing something impulsive.

"It is rather difficult for a man to think," he finally said through clenched teeth, "with such an unholy racket echoing through the house."

"Laughter?" Allie deadpanned. "You mean the sound of laughter?"

"Yes!"

A long beat of silence.

"I see," Allie said slowly, though her cadence indicated she absolutely did *not* see. "And you would therefore like us to . . . ?" She trailed off to a question mark.

"Cease laughing!" he snapped.

Allie exchanged a look with her guest.

Lady Isolde put her hand over her mouth. To stifle, Kendall was quite sure, yet more laughter.

Damn woman.

His sister rose to her feet and marched toward him.

"Enough. *Basta!*" she said in Italian with a clap of her hands. Their Venetian mother had ensured they both learned her native tongue alongside English as children. "You do not come in here and embarrass me in front of my friend."

Allie punctuated each word with a small push on his chest, forcing Kendall to back away. She kept pushing until he found himself standing in the entry hall.

"You may return when you can be civil," Allie said in sharp Italian, underscoring her command by slamming the drawing-room door shut.

The room beyond erupted in giggles.

Kendall stood in the hallway, shoulders heaving, breaths labored, thoughts fiery and raging.

He, a venerated Duke of the Realm, had just been forcefully ejected from his own drawing-room.

His twin was the *only* person in the world he would permit to treat him in such a fashion.

Sometimes he hated that his love for her rendered him powerless and capitulating. He wanted to pound on the door. He wanted to throw a porcelain vase, or twenty.

He should summon his fencing master a day early and run the man ragged.

Instead, he pivoted for the stairs and his bedchamber.

Hysterical female laughter trailed in his wake.

AN HOUR LATER, Kendall strode down the stairs, intent on his lunch with The Chancellor of the Exchequer.

A slim hand snagged his elbow.

"A word, Tristan." Allie dragged him into his study and shut the door.

She faced him, hands on her hips, eyes crackling with fire.

Knowing his twin as he did, a thorough dressing down was in Kendall's immediate future.

"I'm nearly late," he snapped. "Say what you must."

Allie's gray eyes narrowed at his tone. "I would like you to cease being uncivil to Lady Isolde."

"No." He straightened the cuffs of his coat sleeve. "Now if that is all, I have a busy schedule to—"

"*No?!* Do not be curt, Tristan. You love me, remember?" She pointed a finger at his face. "That means you do not treat me like a bothersome underling. I require more information."

"More information?"

"Yes. You are practically carved of ice when dealing with other members of the *ton*. But my friend walks through the door, and you become a raging Italian lion."

"Precisely. Because she is not, in fact, good *ton*. As I have said repeatedly, she and her entire family are a blight on Polite Society."

"Is that why you are actively seeking to ruin Hadley?"

Kendall frowned. How did Allie know—

"Lady Isolde informed me of your plot to bring articles of impeachment," his twin continued.

"My affairs with Lords are none of your concern, Allie." Kendall tried to sidestep her and reached for the door handle.

She jumped in front of him, blocking his path and pushing him back into the room. "Of course your dealings in Parliament are my affair! What happens there affects more than just men. You are determined to pave over our father's memory with your own, but what happens if you find yourself similarly disgraced? What about our family name then, the family name I also bear?"

Kendall paced back to his desk, folding his arms and half-sitting on the sturdy wooden top. "I will not permit that to happen."

"How? Again, I require specifics, not vague promises. Though you might wish otherwise, you cannot control everything and everyone."

"Will you let it be, Allie?!" Kendall threw up his hands. "I haven't the time or desire to outline details for you. But trust that I have always held *your* interests and the interests of the Gilbert family name foremost in my mind!"

Thank goodness his sister was the only person who truly loved him. Managing even one person's affections was exhausting.

"Truly? Because I fail to see what we Gilberts gain from this pettiness with Hadley. Despite your own opinions, Hadley is well-liked, both by Peers and the public."

"His politics are rubbish!"

"Hadley is a Whig and Liberal. You are a Tory and Conservative. All of Lords is split along a similar divide, and yet no other Peer commands such vitriol from yourself."

"No other Peer is as outlandish as Hadley."

Kendall stared at his sister. The window light raked her face, painting it in patches of light and dark.

"Your current choices are precarious for a man who aims to become Prime Minister," Allie said. "You risk alienating many."

"Hadley wields his ebullient bonhomie to garner public support and point the country away from time-honored ideals," Kendall retorted. "Dismissing him will show I have the mettle to *become* Prime Minister."

"I'm not sure that is a sound viewpoint." She shook her head, expression baffled. "And why Hadley, specifically?"

"You weren't here, Allie. You didn't watch Hadley, with Sir Rafe at his side, systemically decimate the dukedom's finances. Were it not for our mother's salt mines, we would be destitute at the moment."

"Hadley did that? To our sire?"

Kendall nodded, a sharp up-down motion.

"And did he continue after Old Kendall's death?"

Silence.

Ringing, damning silence.

"I see." Allie stepped away from the door, walking toward him. "So Hadley attacked Old Kendall's investments as retribution for his cruelty toward Sir Rafe. And once you inherited, Hadley stopped, as you are not part of that battle. And yet, you still seek his downfall? His ruin?" She spread her arms wide. "You are going to have to clarify this for me, Tristan. You stayed at Hadley's home two summers past when Ethan was courting me and even recuperated there for several days after your gunshot wound. You may not respect or admire the man, but you have always tolerated him and seemed content to leave the past in the past. What changed? Did you invest with this Jarvis fellow, too?"

"Of course not! The man is a snake and always has been."

"So what is it?"

"I would rather not discuss it." Kendall ground his teeth. His aversion to Hadley was personal and, quite frankly, rather humiliating.

"*Tristan*," his twin said, aggravation in her tone.

"*Allie.*"

She mimicked his stance, folding her arms. "My twin sense is telling me there is a story here."

"We don't have a twin sense."

"Hah! You are entirely wrong on that score." She tapped a finger to her chin, gaze narrowing.

Kendall forced himself not to squirm.

"Ah." Slowly, understanding dawned in her eyes. "Hadley has humiliated you. Publicly. Pricked your formidable pride, as it were."

Damn his twin for knowing him so well.

"*Dimmi tutto,*" Allie said in Italian, beckoning with her hand. A universal sign for *tell me all*.

Sighing, Kendall pushed off the desk and pivoted to stare out the window.

Sometimes having a twin was a royal pain in the arse.

"You know I will get it out of you eventually," her voice reached him from behind. "Or I can ask others, but I think you would greatly prefer to tell me yourself."

Kendall supposed that was true, too.

Bracing his hands on the desk, he told his twin the truth. "Over the past two years, Hadley has made a point of embarrassing and degrading me at every turn."

"Provide an example, if you please."

He sighed again, loud and annoyed. "Your need for specifics—"

"Tristan."

"Very well. One example. I introduced a bill in Lords last summer." Standing upright, he spoke quickly, hoping to divest himself of the tale as one might a plaster—one sharp motion to remove the bandage. "It would have enabled landowners in the Cotswolds to more readily enclose their fields, and I had gained widespread support. It was to have been my shining moment. But then Hadley made it his mission to quash the bill. He gave a rousing speech on the floor of Lords, denouncing me as a crusader for the nobility and mocking my attempts at leadership. Peers laughed. It was . . . mortifying in the extreme. Hadley's words rendered me a laughing stock."

The burn of remembered humiliation stung Kendall's cheeks.

"So Hadley openly demeans your politics, which honestly is nearly a rule of Parliamentary debate. But from Hadley, you take offense, as it hurts your feelings."

"I am hardly so fragile, Sister. Yes, I am offended, but the larger issue is one of reputation. Hadley's mockery leads some to believe I am unfit to govern. I lose all credibility."

"And you believe attacking Hadley in this manner will regain that credibility?" Allie's tone was decidedly skeptical.

"Yes! The man and his views must be silenced if Britain intends to maintain her traditional values. And Peers need to see me as the one dedicated to those traditions."

"I see."

"I am not sure that you do." Kendall turned around to face her. "Hadley continues to oppose me at every turn. All while he is making merry with the likes of Stephen Jarvis and swindling other Lords out of their money."

"So you allege, but Lady Isolde firmly believes her father to be innocent."

"Bah! That man is no more innocent than a whore in Covent Garden."

"Tristan!"

"I speak truth, Allie. And you are hardly one to call me out for vulgarity."

"True, but I worry that the more you attempt to restore respect and honor to the Dukedom of Kendall, the more you resort to our father's unsavory tactics and reinforce his memory."

Kendall flinched. "That is a low blow, Sister."

"Is it, though? You go too far with Hadley."

"Too far? I assure you I haven't gone far enough!" Kendall's voice rose. "It is absurd that Hadley and his unruly brood of children are still received, still coddled and lauded by those of the aristocracy. It is high time people understood the truth of his behavior."

He brushed past Allie for the door.

"Now if you will excuse me, Sister, I have important meetings to attend. Good day."

. . . I still firmly believe Tristan finds Lady Isolde captivating, despite his vehement denials. I plan to give them a wee nudge and see what happens.

—PRIVATE LETTER FROM LADY ALLEGRA PENN-LEITH
TO HER HUSBAND, MR. ETHAN PENN-LEITH

Isolde knew her current situation was yet another example of impulsivity.

One akin to the impulsivity that had landed her, and by extension her father, in a quagmire with Jarvis. Impulsivity that had led to Kendall's accusations—threatening Hadley with a gaol sentence, and as a complication, potentially dissolving Catriona's betrothal to Barnaby.

As Isolde was the one responsible for her family's current woes, it made sense that she should resolve them.

The scientist within her understood that the best solutions always involved going straight to the source of the problem.

In this case, Tristan Gilbert, Duke of Kendall.

If Isolde could convince Kendall to back away from his inquiry—to relinquish his ludicrous vendetta—then perhaps these rumblings of impeachment would die down.

And so Isolde currently sat in the library of Gilbert House, awaiting Kendall's arrival. In the duke's preferred armchair, no less.

Generally, Isolde—fearless and reckless though she may be at times—would not have dared be so bold.

However, Allie had insisted.

"I love my brother," she had said only an hour earlier, "but he is being obstinate and pig-headed in this matter with Hadley. Deep down, Tristan is a loving person. He needs to be fostering friendships at present, not adding to his count of enemies. Perhaps your pleading will reach him where mine has not."

Isolde was unsure on that score. If Kendall wouldn't relent for his sister—whom the man adored—why would he listen to Isolde, whom he detested?

"But . . . why must I meet with him alone?" she had asked.

"I know my brother," Allie replied. "If I am in the room, he will simply ignore you. I want him to be forced to listen to your words. However, I promise to remain close for propriety's sake."

Isolde had grimaced but acquiesced. At this juncture, she was willing to try anything. Kendall could scarcely hate her any more than he already did. And she had experienced a wicked thrill in her breast at the idea of tormenting the ill-natured duke.

Most importantly, Allie sat in the music room next door, ready and willing to assist.

Isolde took a sip of His Grace's fine Glenturret whisky which she had poured for courage. Rain pattered against the two tall windows opposite, gray skies shrouding the corners in shadows.

Heavy footsteps sounded in the central hallway outside the door.

Taking in a deep breath, Isolde forced her shoulders to ease and her face to become impassive. She had brothers and, therefore, instinctively recognized that nonchalance would be her most effective weapon.

She had just finished arranging her skirts and slouching into the chair-back when the door *snicked* open.

Pausing just inside the doorway, Kendall didn't notice her at first, curled into the worn armchair before the hearth.

Naturally, this gave Isolde a chance to study the duke as he consulted his pocket-watch, a book tucked under his arm.

He was still dressed for his club: immaculately pressed coat, precisely-tied neckcloth, silk waistcoat embroidered with metallic gold thread that glinted in the dreary light. As usual, his gray hair was militantly pomaded and styled, not a strand out of place as he tucked his pocket-watch away.

Marble, Isolde mused, had more chance of rumpling than the Duke of Kendall.

All of which explained why his yelp of surprise upon finally seeing her—a startled flinch and lift of the book he held—was so deliciously satisfying.

"Your Grace." Isolde nodded her head politely.

It galled her to pretend such obeisance, but as she wished him to consider her petition . . .

Kendall's nostrils flared as he slowly lowered the book. "How did you—"

"Lady Allegra," Isolde supplied. "Your sister is through there, likely listening at the keyhole." She indicated the music-room door immediately to the right of the hearth.

"Indeed I am!" came Allie's muffled voice.

Kendall glared at the door, a muscle twitching in his jaw, before bringing his eyes back to Isolde.

"You should have greater care for your reputation, Lady Isolde," he *tsked*, words cold. "But given your past behavior and our current situation, I doubt you will grant the subject the solemn study required."

"Thank you for your advice, Your Grace." Isolde's returning tone was saccharine sweet and, unfortunately, entirely insincere.

Drat this man and his ability to overset her. Maintaining composure in the face of his scorn was a nearly Herculean task.

Kendall tossed his book onto a side table beside the door—*The Philosophy of the Inductive Sciences* by Mr. William Whewell. She recognized the unique yellow-and-blue leather banding on the spine even from a distance.

Isolde's eyebrows rose at his decidedly-ambitious choice of reading material. Mr. Whewell's theories on scientific method were not for the faint of heart. She would know; she had spent an entire term devoted to understanding the mathematics behind them at Broadhurst.

How did Kendall find time for rigorous analytical study amid all his political scheming?

Fortunately, she successfully crushed the wave of interest and curiosity that threatened to rise.

The duke crossed his arms, feet planted wide. "Say what you must, my lady, and then get the hell out of my library." That muscle in his jaw jumped again.

"Manners, Your Grace." Isolde mimicked his *tsking* noise, unable to stem her tongue. "I should think that a student of Mr. Whewell—" Here she paused to shoot a pointed look at the book he had discarded. "—would be capable of deducing the reason for my presence." She gave him a wee smile. "The scientific method and all that."

Isolde *knew* she was a fool to taunt him. She wished to inspire cooperation, not engender more vitriol. But there was just something about *this* man that provoked her. That enjoyed jabbing at his cold exterior, willing it to shatter and spill turbulence into the space between them.

"No," he replied.

"No?" She frowned. "Meaning . . . ye refuse tae even guess?"

"Noooo." He drew the word out, as if speaking to a particularly lack-witted child. "I will not stop my investigation into your father's business dealings."

Oh.

He did not elaborate further.

Isolde settled further into her chair, propping her chin on her knuckles with deliberate insouciance. "I would appreciate more information."

"I do not have to explain my actions to one such as yourself."

"Your Grace, perhaps ye would consid—"

"If you have truly studied Mr. Whewell's work"—he mimicked her telling look at the book in question—"then consider this an exemplary situation in which to utilize his scientific methodology—deducing my reasoning for yourself."

Isolde hated his smug expression.

She preferred blackguards to be monolithic and blessedly un-paradoxical. Yet, Kendall remained stubbornly multi-faceted—both an absolute arse of a man *and* interestingly well-read and intelligent.

Worse . . . here she admitted a painful truth to herself . . . were he a different person—one *not* impossibly conceited and dedicated to destroying her father—she would likely fancy him.

Unbidden, she remembered that first meeting in Montacute's garden. How attraction had swirled, weaving like gossamer between them and fluttering with each syllable.

And then, once more, she had to quash the memory.

"So if that is all," the duke continued, "I must once again demand you vacate my home."

Isolde ignored his request. "We both know ye don't like me, Your Grace."

He snorted.

"I don't ken what I did tae earn such disdain."

"Shall I compose a list?" With deliberate boredom, he flicked open his pocket-watch again and studied the time. "Though given the breadth of what must be cataloged, it will likely take what is left of the day, if not more."

Isolde sat up slightly and waved a careless hand, refusing to permit his words to sting. "Precisely. Your argument is with myself, but as ye cannot wage war against a mere woman without being branded a cad, ye be choosing tae attack my father instead. I'm asking ye to stop. If your quarrel is with myself, then address me."

"Lady Isolde, my dispute is squarely with your father." He snapped the watch case closed and returned it to his waistcoat pocket. "How typical of your own conceit to assume that any action I undertake involves yourself. I cannot say I ever devote an iota of cranial energy to thinking upon you."

Isolde's eyebrows winged upward in disbelief. The man studied her like a mathematician studied an unfathomable equation, far too often and too studiously for his claimed apathy to ring true.

"Mmm, why do I doubt your sincerity?" She reached for the tumbler of whisky, taking a healthy sip before rotating it slowly in her fingers, permitting the amber liquid to catch the light.

"Is that . . . is that my Glenturret Scotch?!"

Isolde found the outrage in his voice utterly delightful.

"Scotch?" she asked, affronted. "I don't know what ye can mean. This—" Here she lifted the glass. "—is *uisge beatha*, the breath of life . . . or whisky to those who don't speak Gaelic. Though I suppose a *Sassenach* like yourself *would* call it Scotch." She took another sip. "It is quite excellent, which is not surprising as it was brewed in Scotland. Were ye tae mend fences with my father, he might send ye whisky that is superior tae even this."

His eyes flared and his chest heaved. Kendall took a step toward her before appearing to forcibly restrain himself.

"Tread carefully, Lady Isolde." His words cracked, a whip striking air. "Do not goad me into summoning a footman. I would take far too much pleasure in watching you be forcibly tossed onto the street."

"Tristan Gilbert! Don't you dare!" Allie called through the keyhole.

They both looked toward the music room door.

Helplessly, Isolde's eyes skimmed the lines of his profile—nose, lips, jaw—hating how the whole ignited a low hum in her abdomen and made her itch to trace the contour with a fingertip.

You loathe him, she reminded her wayward body. *He is a boorishly arrogant man in an attractive shell who is endeavoring to ruin your father and harm your family.*

He brought his gaze back to hers.

"Come now, Your Grace." Draining the last of the whisky, Isolde set the tumbler aside. "If I have learned anything from my father, it is that every proposed transaction has a finite price. A point at which the anticipated rewards are deemed worth what is sacrificed. So what compensation would be sufficient for yourself?"

His reply was immediate. "Hadley's imprisonment and the utter and complete humiliation of your family."

Rolling her eyes, Isolde pushed to her feet.

He followed her every move—a wolf studying its prey.

"Ye know that isn't what I was asking. Permit me tae try again: What will it take for ye to let this matter with Jarvis go?"

"Nothing. Nothing will persuade me."

"Are ye quite sure?" Isolde slowly walked toward him, her skirts swishing like quiet breaths.

And with each step she closed between them, he tensed.

As if he were steeling himself against . . . something.

How very interesting.

Was that *something* herself?

He *had* appeared attracted to her once upon a time. Before he knew she was the daughter of the Earl of Hadley. He had even kissed her hand—fervently, reverently—like a man under a witch's spell. That kiss had felt like a promise. Of future strolls through moon-lit gardens, of whirling dances, of whispered words in hushed corners. Even eight years on, Isolde could easily recall the burn of his touch.

Surely that attraction had melted with the force of his disdain. Like others, he was certainly tabulating her problematic features: height (too tall), hair (too red), skin (too freckled), and conversation (too opinionated).

But maybe attraction still hummed under his skin . . . an electrical awareness of her proximity.

Could she use his potential attraction against him?

She darted a glance at the table where Mr. Whewell's treatise lay abandoned.

Mmm, perhaps she should do as Kendall had demanded and apply the scientific method to this situation. A wee experiment on Sir Isaac Newton's Third Law of Motion, as it were. To see if an action on her part might elicit an equal and opposite reaction in the duke.

"Are ye quite sure ye have no price, Your Grace?" she asked again.

Kendall swallowed as she approached, his Adam's apple rolling up and down.

"Yes," he rasped, but the ferocity in his gaze betrayed him.

Again. Did she find his reaction merely interesting? Or . . . scintillating?

"Truly?" Isolde tilted her head. "There is nothing ye might desire from myself?"

Lifting her hand, she dragged her fingers across her décolletage with deliberate casualness, as if merely brushing away a spot of lint, fingertips grazing the collarbones visible above the muslin of her fichu.

A man who truly detested her would scarcely notice the simple motion. He would turn away on a huff, point toward the door, and order her to leave.

Kendall, however . . . did none of those things.

Instead, his eyes dipped down, as if helpless against the thrall of her trailing fingers, tracking their progress with fervent concentration.

That Adam's apple made another up-down journey as he swallowed. Audibly.

So, he was . . . not unmoved.

Glee rose in Isolde's chest as she took one step closer.

But she had failed to calculate her own attraction to him.

Abruptly, only two feet of space separated them. Had she ever been this close to the Duke of Kendall?

The scent of his cologne—something exotic, knee-weakeningly male, and no doubt, absurdly expensive—engulfed her. Wee details assailed her senses—the light amber streaks in his dark brown eyes, the gray night whiskers stubbling his tanned cheeks, the breadth of his shoulders so near.

And most disturbingly, how easy it would be to tip her head back, lean upward, and press her lips to the pulse that thrummed in his neck.

Isolde inhaled sharply.

At the sound, Kendall flinched and stepped back, his gaze flying to hers. A red blush climbed his cheeks and tinged his ears.

"Get out," he all but snarled.

He did not, however, turn away from her. Nor cease his study of her face.

Well . . . Isolde had wanted to test her hypothesis. She was fairly confident she had her answer.

"As ye wish, Your Grace."

She curtsied then, graceful and lingering, forcing him to watch her dip and rise.

Straightening upright, she walked past him, close enough for the bell of her skirts to brush his shins, close enough for them both to feel the heat of the other's body.

"We are not through with this conversation, Duke. This is merely my opening sally."

Hand on the door knob, she paused to look back at him. His gaze shot from her waist to her face, the flush on his cheeks deepening.

"Consider yourself warned." She closed the door behind her with a decisive *click*.

. . . I grow more concerned over this issue with Stephen Jarvis. Correspondence has surfaced between myself, Jarvis, and a solicitor in Manchester. Though I know the innocence of my own words there, when viewed through the lens of Jarvis's crimes, they could be seen as incriminating. Kendall, of course, has seized upon them to bolster his claims of my wrongdoing. How I long for the day when I can safely forget that the damned Dukedom of Kendall exists.

—PRIVATE LETTER FROM LORD HADLEY
TO SIR RAFE GORDON

K endall stared at the closed library door.

What the bloody hell had just happened?!

After several days of social engagements, he had been looking forward to an evening at home, reading Mr. Whewell's book and conversing with Allie.

Instead, he had found Lady Isolde curled like a cat in his favorite chair, her hair a flaming beacon against the printed blue-and-green muslin of her day dress.

The sight of her had been . . . jarring.

Worse, he feared that when he closed his eyes to sleep, he would still see her elegant hand tracing a leisurely line across her collarbones and calling his male attention to the curves of her lithesome body.

But the most egregious, most infuriating offense had been the *knowing* in her gaze. She had acted deliberately, drawing out his baser nature in order to tease and torment. As though she knew she had cast a love potion on him all those years ago and now delighted in torturing him.

As if he needed any further reason to detest her.

His pulse still raced, heart pounding like he had gone a bruising round with his fencing master.

But then, *that woman* always invaded his blood like sloe gin bolted too quickly—exhilarating but almost instantly nauseating.

For not the first time, he pondered how it was possible to be simultaneously so captivated and yet so repulsed.

While Lady Isolde had been away at university in Massachusetts, he had been able to resist his earlier infatuation. To cast it aside as a youthful folly. *Out of sight, out of mind* as the adage went.

But the two years since her return . . .

He swallowed, turning away from the library door.

Enough.

He had to overcome this relentless physical pull toward her. It was unacceptable.

The soft murmur of Allie's voice carried from the entry hall as she ushered her ill-choice of a friend out the front door.

Lady Isolde laughed, musical and trilling, like a bloom sprung in winter.

With a low snarl, Kendall snatched up his book—devil take her for recognizing Whewell's book and knowing the man's work—and poured himself two fingers of Scotch.

Savoring the burn of the alcohol, he sat in his preferred chair. The leather was still warm from her body, dammit.

Worse, the smell of her lingered . . . lemons and sunshine and laughter.

The scent of happiness, he supposed.

He detested it.

That . . . that . . .

Harpy?

Witch?

Shrew?

Fortunately, the English language did not lack words to describe a belligerent woman.

Sipping his drink, he settled on *hell-cat.*

That hell-cat would not win. Not this battle.

Kendall had fought too long and too doggedly to reach this point. His own meteoric rise to power was well underway, and he was rapidly amassing support in Parliament to serve Hadley his comeuppance.

But first . . .

The front door clanked closed.

Allie flounced into the library, a pleased-as-Punch smile on her face.

"That went rather well, I think." She crossed to a hidden cabinet in the bookcase beside the window, pulled it open, and poured herself some of his whisky.

"There is no Scotch for you," he growled. "Lady Isolde drank your share."

"Nonsense." She waved off his comment. "If you are going to be miserly, I'll merely ask Ethan to request another bottle from Hadley."

Allie sank into the matching chair opposite his own, expression cherubic.

Kendall glared at her.

She sipped her Scotch, staring at him over the rim of the glass and slurping loudly simply to be obnoxious.

Had all of womankind set out to vex him today? And to drink his library dry, to boot?

"I had lengthy meetings today with Lord John Russell and Lord Palmerston," he said. "We discussed foreign policy in the Crimea, the ongoing famine in Ireland, and the problem of civil unrest in Paris."

"Mmmm," she replied.

"Lord John has even begun hinting that he will recommend me for a Cabinet position next year, assuming he is still in office."

"That must be very exciting."

Kendall took in a fortifying breath. "The point is that my days are full of important matters, conversations and decisions that affect the lives of multitudes around the world. It is why we must insist that those who would join in this governance adhere to a strict standard of behavior. There is strong evidence that Lord Hadley has violated these strictures. We in Parliament will hold him accountable. Therefore, you will cease assisting your friend in her naive defense of her father, Lady Allegra."

"*Uffa!* Lady Allegra, is it?" She lifted her eyebrows. "And employing your *duke* voice?"

"My what?"

"Your *duke* voice," she said offhandedly. "It's grim and autocratic and holds a rasping edge of threatened violence. Like you are one mishap away from ordering a miscreant to be flayed alive." She pretended to shiver. "I am sure underlings rush to do your bidding when you use it."

Kendall downed a healthy swallow of his Scotch, the burn of alcohol merging with the glow of anger in his belly.

"I am most serious, Sister," he snapped. "As a member of my household, I cannot permit—"

"You are merely upset because Lady Isolde bested you today."

"She did not—" Kendall paused at Allie's knowing grin. "Or rather, I am not—"

"Furious? Raging?" she smirked. "Regretting that I returned to London?"

"Possibly." He stared her down for another long moment, fingers drumming on the arm of his chair.

It was unnerving what loving a person did to him. How could he be simultaneously so irritated with his sister and yet still eagerly seek her company?

Thank goodness his personality stifled all other friendships. It was all he could do to control the one with his twin.

"Can we please move on to discussing your list of potential brides?"

Allie asked. "You really should know better than to leave such things atop your desk."

Silence for a long moment.

Kendall sent up a prayer to whatever patron saint of patience his Catholic mother might have revered. "Need I ask you, once again, to stop interfering in my affairs?"

Predictably, Allie rolled her eyes and ignored his question. "Lady Alice Churchill-Spencer? Lady Caroline Cavendish? Such ladies are dull as dishwater. You will be bored within half an hour."

Kendall flicked a loose string off his trouser leg. "That is for me to decide."

"Do you know who will never bore you?"

"Do not say—"

"Lady Isolde."

"Hah! Because I would always be waiting for the woman to sink a dagger into my back."

"Please. Isolde would go for the heart. Subterfuge is not her style." Allie gave a careless wave.

"Were I to ally myself with such a lady—and I use the term *lady* very loosely here—I would lose any chance to become Prime Minister. Lady Isolde is barely received. Her Majesty will not accept Lady Isolde at court. Consequently, I will not jeopardize my goals by associating with her."

"Would you like to hear my opinion?"

"No. As I keep saying, I desire neither your opinions nor your meddling. I would appreciate, for once, a modicum of compliance."

His sister uncurled from the chair, setting her empty tumbler on a small table.

"Poor Tristan. You know me better than that." She crossed to him and pressed a kiss to his cheek. "I think, despite all your protestations, you might enjoy the challenge Lady Isolde brings. Unlike every other woman in Town, she does not see you as a title to be won. She couldn't care less that you are Kendall. And after a lifetime of flattery and deference—of false emotion and fawning attention—it must be both frustrating and invigorating to have a beautiful woman treat you with disdain." Allie turned for the door but called over her shoulder. "Think upon it, Brother."

The shutting of the latch echoed off the library walls.

On a growl, Kendall tossed back the rest of his Scotch.

Allie was wrong, of course.

Lady Isolde—despite her attempts to haunt him—was a ghost of his past.

And as he had done with his father, Sir Rafe, Hadley, and any other individual who had ever tormented him, Kendall would vanquish her, too.

KENDALL DID NOT have to wait long for Lady Isolde's next volley.

It came the following day in the form of a lengthy, two-page missive tucked into his waistcoat pocket—courtesy of his sister, no doubt.

Kendall sat in a private dining room at White's, waiting for three MPs from the House of Commons to arrive. The MPs had been supportive of his proposed impeachment of Hadley, though they still had reservations given the earl's political clout. This luncheon was Kendall's chance to secure their backing and assistance. White's had been a deliberate choice of venue, as none of the gentlemen had been voted a member. Only an invitation from the Duke of Kendall himself could gain them entrance—a subtle reminder of all the other ways in which the duke might assist if only they would ally themselves fully with his agenda.

However, the men were five minutes late.

And when Kendall tugged his pocket-watch from his waistcoat to check the time against the clock on the mantel, Lady Isolde's note tumbled out.

Irritated, he snatched it off the carpet and snapped the sheets of foolscap open.

Lady Isolde's distinctive handwriting was as impetuous as he remembered from her hidden letters, which recognition only further stoked his ire. The wretched woman made a performance out of every *y* and *g,* looping and curling the tails of the letters with dramatic verve, as if each tiny drop of ink required celebration.

Scowling, he read:

I will begin my argument with Aristotle's Rhetoric, *with which I assume you are familiar. If you are not, permit me to explain. In* Rhetoric, *Aristotle introduces his* pisteis, *or persuaders—ethos, pathos, logos—and defines them as tools that one may use when arguing a point. I gather you are a man of science; therefore, I suppose you will find an argument based on* logos, *or logic, to be most appealing.*

Kendall glowered at the page. Both at Lady Isolde's ridiculously condescending tone and equally ridiculous well-read mind. With a frown, he flipped to the second page:

Logical Reasons the Duke of Kendall
Should Cease His Personal Vendetta against
Andrew Langston, Earl of Hadley

1. Lord Hadley is innocent of all charges, which a thorough examination of the facts surrounding the case would easily prove.

2. The Dukedom of Kendall risks financial repercussions from Hadley's business enterprises, should the earl choose to pursue retribution upon his impeachment.

3. His Grace could anger neutral Peers in Lords by bringing spurious accusations against a Peer of good standing and impeccable reputation.

4. Even if Stephen Jarvis is found guilty of criminal business practices, it is a false equivalence fallacy to assume that Jarvis's crimes also belong to Lord Hadley.

Kendall scanned through the rest. Her list contained *sixteen* points. She had even provided justification for the number—*I chose 16 as it correlates with the Greek* phi *and Euclid's golden ratio of 1.6—the alignment of which underscores the logical validity of these arguments.*

Naturally, the letter was signed, *A Concerned Friend,* masking the impudent woman's identity.

Friend, his arse.

Irritation lit beneath his sternum.

How dare she lecture *him* on logic and reasoning.

His fingers itched for a pen. She wanted a logical argument, did she? Well, he would happily deliver one.

LORD HADLEY WAS troubled.

Isolde knew her father and his moods, and she had no recollection of ever seeing such a tightness around his mouth, as if every muscle there had frozen. Though he made a pretense of shrugging off this matter with Kendall and Lords, she noted the uncharacteristic sharpness in his voice when speaking with Marshall, their butler. Not to mention the conspicuous number of gentlemen regularly escorted into his study—Lord Lockheade, Lord Mansfield—followed by the low murmur of intense conversation.

Even Uncle Rafe had come to Town, theoretically to meet with his solicitors on a business matter, but the hours he spent closeted with her father suggested otherwise. Rafe was not a blood relation, but the close relationship between their families meant Isolde and her siblings had always called him *uncle.*

Worse, Lord Barnaby had been notably absent over the past week. Given that Catriona and Barnie had been inseparable merely ten days ago, Isolde found the development worrying. The wedding had not been called off, but Catriona picked at her food and rushed to the window every time the front bell rang, eager to see who was calling. The resigned slump in her shoulders when she realized the person at the door was not her beloved . . .

It nearly broke Isolde's heart.

She wanted to rage at Kendall. To storm Gilbert House and pound her fist against his broad ducal chest until he relented.

But even more, she was furious with herself. If only she had taken care to truly assess Jarvis and his motives. If only she had burned their correspondence before letting it fall into Kendall's hands. Though her letters only documented the fact of Hadley's investment with Jarvis, they had provided Kendall with a map of where to begin his own investigation.

Isolde would see this righted.

Unfortunately, His Grace had yet to respond to her entreaties.

A week after her visit with Kendall, Isolde sat with her mother, Catriona, and Mariah, sorting through ribbon and lace samples for Catriona's wedding bonnet. They all proclaimed excitement, but Catriona's wan complexion and Lady Hadley's false cheer rather dampened the atmosphere.

They all turned as the drawing-room door *snicked* open, and Marshall entered carrying a silver salver.

"This just arrived for you, Lady Isolde." With a flourish, the butler lowered the platter, revealing a slim package wrapped in brown paper and twine.

Lady Hadley glanced up from a pile of cream ribbon. "Gracious. From whom, Marshall?"

"I cannot say, my lady. It was delivered via street urchin."

"Street urchin?" Catriona sat back in alarm, dropping the fine Belgian lace in her hand.

Tentatively, Isolde lifted the parcel from the offered tray.

"Is it a book, Isolde?" Mariah asked, curiosity lighting her gaze.

It certainly felt like a book.

"Was there a note, Marshall?" Lady Hadley asked.

"No, my lady."

"Perhaps it is inside," Catriona offered, leaning forward.

Isolde already had a strong suspicion as to who had sent the package. No need to let her mother, Mariah, and Catriona see its contents. They would hound her for answers.

"That will be all, Marshall." Isolde dismissed the butler with a nod. "I shall open it later," she said to her family, setting the package on a side table.

"Open it later?! Are ye mad?" Snatching the parcel off the table, Mariah danced away from Isolde's grasp.

"Mariah." Isolde's voice held a warning. "It isn't for yourself." Standing, she lunged for the book.

Her sister darted out of reach, ripping at the paper.

"Mariah!" Their mother rose to her feet. "Such behavior is most unladylike!"

Of course, Mariah heeded them not at all. Underscoring, yet again, why Isolde hid her private correspondence from her siblings. Racing around the room and dodging all of Isolde's attempts to claim the parcel, her sister succeeded in unwrapping the book.

Mariah read the title and froze, a scowl creasing her brow. "What the devil. Who would send ye this, Isolde?"

"Mariah! Language!" Lady Hadley rose and firmly removed the book from her youngest daughter's hand, before glancing down at the title herself. "Mrs. Sigourney's *Letters to Young Ladies?* That is an unexpectedly fastidious choice of gift." She handed the book to Isolde. "Surely all our acquaintance know you would deride such pedantry."

Isolde forced a laugh, scrambling for an explanation. "Ah, now I recall. I requested a copy from the bookseller on Berwick Street."

"You wished to consult an etiquette guide?" Her mother frowned. "At this juncture in your life?"

"Aye," Isolde replied brightly. "As ye said, I enjoy scoffing at just such a thing. I . . . I thought we could read it of an evening and mock its absurdities."

Her mother blinked, obviously sensing subterfuge in Isolde's claim, but as the book and her reasoning were blameless, Lady Hadley could voice no objection.

"As you say," her mother finally replied. "Mariah," she turned to her youngest daughter, "you will come with me. We have matters to discuss."

"Mamma!" Mariah rolled her eyes. "It was only a jest."

"Regardless, you are out in Society now and such behavior is beyond the pale." Her mother turned for the door, beckoning. "Come. If you are not careful, I shall have you read Isolde's new etiquette guide in earnest."

The door closed behind them.

Silence settled in their wake, leaving Isolde and Catriona to stare at one another.

Turning, Catriona bent over the lace and ribbon again, picking through it woodenly.

Isolde held what she suspected to be Kendall's 'gift' stiffly at her side, the book's leather binding heavy with portent.

"It will come right, Cat," she said softly. "Ye will still marry your Barnie. We will all see tae it."

Her sister nodded, but Isolde did not miss how Catriona bit her quivering lip.

Isolde walked over to the window, fighting against a tightness in her own throat.

Damn Kendall and his machinations.

Hands tingling with nerves, she opened the book, tilting it into the light. A quick shuffle of the pages revealed no note.

No. His Grace had been careful.

The blackguard had underlined passages on *excessive volubility* and *meekness to social superiors*, emphasizing the deference a lady should demonstrate when interacting with a gentleman.

She slammed the book shut and tossed it atop the window seat.

Rubbish.

Both the text and the man himself.

She would make the Duke of Kendall see reason.

He would rue the day he crossed swords with her.

The Chancellor has moved quickly to try Mr. Stephen Jarvis for his crimes. As the result of his trial dramatically impacts the rumors of impeachment surrounding Lord Hadley, Parliament is eager to learn the truth of Mr. Jarvis's failed railroad venture. The trial date will be announced within weeks. We predict that Peers will face gaol or transportation before this affair is resolved . . .

—ARTICLE IN *THE LONDON TIMES*

Two days later, Kendall nearly barreled into Lord Hadley while stepping out from under the portico of St. George's after Sunday services.

That he and Hadley shared the same parish church in Mayfair irritated Kendall to no end.

That Hadley should pretend to piety and godliness was even more upsetting.

Kendall successfully ignored the rogue voice whispering that he himself only attended church to underscore his suitability to serve as Prime Minister.

Would that thoughts of the earl's daughter were so easily banished.

"Hadley." He nodded stiffly at the man.

"Kendall."

Kendall moved to sidestep around his enemy.

Hadley stepped to the right and blocked him.

Though nearly twice Kendall's age, the earl still matched him in height and breadth.

In summation, the man had presence.

"May I help you?" Kendall asked in his chilliest *ducal* tones.

"Aye, in fact, ye can." Hadley folded his arms across his chest. "I'd like a word."

Kendall said nothing, merely waited for Hadley to say what he wished. The less Kendall spoke—the more aloof and stern his appearance—the more power he retained. It was a lesson learned from Old Kendall. His sire might have been a monster, but he was an effective one.

If Hadley felt the impact of the tactic, he didn't show it. "I don't like yourself. And I ken well that ye don't like me."

Kendall barely stifled a snort at *that* understatement of matters.

"But we don't need to wage war, yourself and I," Hadley continued. "We could choose tae end this nonsense before innocents are wounded."

"Innocents?" Kendall scoffed. "There are no innocents here, unless you are referring to those of our Peers who foolishly invested in your fraudulent venture."

"There are absolutely those who will be irreparably hurt by our actions. Though I say *our* generously. We both know *ye* be the one forcing this farce of an investigation tae continue."

Though he wished to remain impassive, Kendall couldn't stem a rather affronted furrowing of his brow.

"I must disagree with your assessment of my actions, Hadley. I am merely following facts gleaned from my investigation. And the facts at the moment point to your own criminal activities." Kendall brushed an infinitesimal speck of lint from his shirt sleeve, hoping his unconcerned tone would rankle.

Given that Hadley's jaw tensed, he rather suspected that it did. The Scot's legendary reserve appeared to be splintering.

"Ye know that for the lie it is."

"Do I?" Kendall gave him a wan smile. "Are you calling into question my honor as a gentleman?"

The thread of menace in Kendall's words *had* to be clear. More than one lethal duel had its origins in conversations similar to this.

Not that Kendall would ever stoop to dueling the likes of Hadley. Such melodramatic exhibitionism was well beneath the purview of a Duke of Kendall.

"Nae, it's not your status as a *gentleman* I call into question, Your Grace." Hadley said the words blithely enough, but his unspoken intention was clear—Kendall was either a liar or an imbecile.

Kendall mimicked the earls' nonchalant stand. "You only wish a cease-fire because you know I am right. That you have been dishonest with your fellow Peers, and now you fear the consequences."

That muscle in Hadley's jaw twitched. "As I alluded earlier, my family and I are finding your spurious accusations challenging for a number of reasons. None of which I need tae explain to yourself, Duke."

"Hah! You, rightly, worry that a cell in Newgate might—"

"Andrew! There ye be!"

Both men turned as Sir Rafe Gordon bounded down the church steps to them.

Kendall forced his hands to not clench into fists.

"Kendall." Sir Rafe tipped his hat. "Pleasure tae see ye again."

Kendall said nothing in return. His half-brother was the very last person he ever wished to encounter—particularly not on the steps of a house of worship—and he therefore took no pleasure in the occasion.

It was bizarre, at times, seeing this man. Sir Rafe looked uncannily like Old Kendall—long-limbed, gray-haired, keen-eyed. But where their sire had emanated cruelty and disdain, Sir Rafe exuded warmth, kindness, and . . . Kendall searched for the right word . . . contentment.

How their father had sired and reared such a man—living together at Hawthorn for nearly three decades as they had—Kendall would never understand. On the surface, Sir Rafe appeared to be the antithesis of their father.

However, Kendall had doubts as to the sincerity of Sir Rafe's altruistic demeanor. Past events spoke to a streak of heedless apathy within the man.

"Rafe," Hadley nodded to his friend. "Kendall's being obstinate, as usual." The earl's words sounded like a complaint, the way one might telltale to a parent.

Sir Rafe looked to Kendall, his eyes widening as a parent's would. "Is that so?"

"Aye. He won't listen tae reason."

"*Och*, I think you're being a wee bit too hard on the lad, Andrew."

Kendall disliked his brother even more for his defense. It was an olive branch offered *far* too late.

And *lad*?! He was nearly thirty, for heaven's sake.

"If you gentleman will excuse me, I have matters to attend." Kendall gave the most cursory of nods, pivoted, and walked away.

He thought he may have heard Sir Rafe call after him, but the clatter of carriage wheels on the flagstone street drowned out the sound.

The encounter with Hadley revealed two indisputable facts.

First, Hadley was worried, as he knew there was some truth behind Kendall's claims.

And second, Kendall was winning their war. Hadley would not have approached him otherwise.

Instead of backing down, Kendall needed to step up his attacks.

He would speak with Ledger tomorrow about contacting certain newspaper editors he knew to be sympathetic.

All of Britain would hear of Hadley's perfidy.

FOUR DAYS LATER, to Kendall's approval, the *Times* ran a scathing article about Lord Hadley.

In terse terms, the author outlined the accusations against Hadley and the growing momentum in Parliament for the wealthy Scot to answer questions about his involvement with Stephen Jarvis. It even hinted that an impeachment vote might be forthcoming within the next month.

Though giddiness was not an emotion Kendall cultivated, the thread of childlike delight that suffused him had to approach the sentiment.

Even hours later, the lightness remained, swelling his lungs as he escorted Allie to the annual evening soirée of the Marquess of Lockheade. Lord Lockheade was a staunch ally of Lord Hadley, but Kendall understood the importance of attending *ton* functions.

Tonight, in particular, promised to be entertaining. The evening was to feature a private performance by the 'Swedish Nightingale' herself—Miss Jenny Lind. Therefore, the entirety of Polite Society would be in attendance, including the Queen and Prince Albert.

Fortunately, Lockheade House was a sprawling affair in Belgravia with a similarly sprawling ballroom to accommodate the crowd.

Kendall and Allie arrived ten minutes late to the soirée—courtesy of his sister's uncooperative coiffure—and found themselves seated four rows behind Her Majesty. Regrettably, their position gave Kendall a rather unencumbered view of Lord Hadley and his brood sitting two rows ahead and to the right.

Most significantly, it placed Lady Isolde squarely in his line of vision, the flickering gaslight illuminating her elegant profile.

As usual, he tensed at the mere sight of her . . . as if his senses required fortification against the visual ambush.

Tonight perhaps more than usual.

The lady wore a gown of gold silk that dipped daringly off her creamy shoulders and echoed the amber highlights in her coppery hair—yes, he was noticing, devil take it. Lady Isolde watched Miss Lind's performance with rapt attention—lips parted, breaths rising quickly, fingertips pressed against the pearl necklace at her throat. Kendall noted at least three other young men staring, as well. Gentlemen may avoid Lady Isolde, but that did not stop them from feeling the pull of her siren song.

Truly. She was a torment to noblemen everywhere.

Kendall dismissed Allie's opinion—that he found Lady Isolde appealing because, unlike other ladies, she did not curry his favor or covet the title of Duchess. That he saw her as a challenge to be conquered, as it were.

As if his behavior were so predictable.

And yet, Kendall remained riveted by Lady Isolde's profile, watching expressions chase to and fro as she listened to Miss Lind perform a particularly formidable aria from Verdi's *The Corsair*.

Oddly, Lady Isolde frowned occasionally . . . once, twice, three times.

He sincerely hoped it was due to remembering the book he had delivered to her. With any luck, the entire exercise had left her outraged and spitting fire. He smiled at the thought.

"I was unaware you enjoyed opera so, Brother," Allie whispered in his ear. "You are practically beaming with delight."

Blinking, Kendall glanced down at his sister.

"Yes, well." He swallowed carefully. "Miss Lind is remarkably talented."

Allie lifted her eyebrows and then turned her attention back to the raised dais.

For his part, Kendall tried to focus on Miss Lind, but his traitorous gaze drifted back to Lady Isolde.

She had moved from fingering the pearls at her throat to absently drawing the tip of her index finger across her neckline. Vividly, Kendall recalled that moment in his library not even a week past.

There is nothing ye might desire from myself?

Her question haunted him, flitting through his memory at inopportune moments. Like now, for example.

His baser self—the one bewitched by her love potion—desired things of Lady Isolde he refused to let his conscious mind entertain.

And yet, as Lady Isolde dragged that fingertip with infinite slowness across her collarbones, he struggled to keep a single coherent thought in his head. Blood pulsed against his eardrums, thudding in time to Miss Lind's *vibrato* and turning the room unbearably warm.

Cease staring at Hadley's daughter, he ordered his wayward eyes. *Look away.*

And yet, he watched helplessly as that solitary fingertip traced a leisurely trail up the side of her neck, pausing in the shadowed hollow beneath her earlobe. The precise place, in fact, where a lover would press a trembling kiss.

His lips burned at the thought.

Her finger began to retrace its path, holding him powerless in its thrall.

Until, with casual insouciance, Lady Isolde turned her head and boldly looked at him.

Kendall nearly flinched in surprise.

The *awareness* in her eyes unmoored him.

She *knew*, the harpy.

She knew he watched her. And she understood precisely how her seemingly mindless actions affected him.

That damned finger of hers continued its downward slide—throat, shoulder, collarbones—before pausing once more on her pearl necklace.

Enthralled, Kendall raptly followed its course for another three seconds before recalling himself.

He jerked his gaze back to hers. She smirked and arched an eyebrow before facing the stage once more, her hand dropping to her lap.

Kendall clenched his own fists on his thighs.

Damn her.

Damn her and her entire bloody family.

THE IMAGE OF Lady Isolde's slim hand still haunted Kendall's dreams three days later.

She was an enchantress, he decided. She had cast her spell upon him and would now drag him to his doom. It felt insurmountable, at times, how one solitary, theoretically unremarkable woman could so consume his thoughts.

As a boy, Old Kendall had insisted that his heir study with the estate steward at Hawthorn. Kendall had spent hours reviewing tenant contracts and land sales. Oftentimes, the steward would task him with retrieving a document from the muniments room, the archive next door to the steward's office.

There, wooden drawers lined all four walls of the room, stretching from floor to ceiling. And each and every drawer, shelf, and crevice held parchment. Contracts and deeds of sale extending back centuries, cataloging the endless movement of tenants, land, and merchandise through ducal lands. The room nearly overflowed with bureaucracy. Finding the correct contract in the chaos was a mixture of divination and pure doggedness.

Like the parchment in that muniments room, Lady Isolde stuffed Kendall's thoughts to bursting. Would the cure also require mystical intervention? Or would a ruthless organization of his mind do the trick?

Kendall was pondering that very idea as he retreated to his library to fetch Whewell's publication. Despite its association with Lady Isolde, he enjoyed exploring the man's ideas.

But when he reached for the book on a side table, he noticed that three other books had been placed on top of it.

A bit of cream foolscap poked out from the cover of the topmost one.

Kendall tugged it free.

Lady Isolde's expressive handwriting assaulted him.

> *As I fear* logos *has not been persuasive, permit me to move on to* ethos. *If my logical arguments will not convince you to correct your current course, then perhaps the reputation and words of consequential men will sway you. They have much to say on the topic of peace, forgiveness, and healing.*

Kendall tossed the note aside and picked up the books.

The Common Book of Prayer.

A Pilgrim's Progress, and . . .

The Holy Bible?

Frowning, he noticed torn bits of paper jutting out along the Bible's gilt binding.

He opened to one of her tattered-edged tabs. A passage was underlined on the page.

Paul's Epistle to the Romans.

Live peaceably with all men.

He turned to the next.
Ephesians, this time.

Let all bitterness, and wrath, and anger be put away from you. And be ye kind, tenderhearted, forgiving one another.

There was another note scribbled beneath that one:

I find God to be the final authority in matters such as this, do you not?

Scowling, Kendall dropped the book onto the table.
The Bible?!
This was hardly a religious matter.
No.
He could think of a much more relevant source for their current situation.

"ANOTHER BOOK FOR you, my lady," Marshall announced as Isolde sat at a small desk in the morning room, seeing to her correspondence.

Marshall presented Isolde with a paper-wrapped parcel atop his silver platter. She looked from the package to the butler and back down again before picking it up.

"Thank ye, Marshall." She nodded at him, grateful that her mother's staff were too polite to ask questions. However, the butler's eyebrows did raise slightly as he closed the door behind him.

Of a surety, her odd packages would be the subject of much conjecture in the servants' dining hall this evening.

Matters with Alderton and her father had not improved. Isolde heard her parents talking in low, anxious tones late at night when they thought the house asleep. Lord Barnaby had not been to visit his beloved in over two weeks. Catriona arrived at breakfast each morning with red-rimmed eyes. Isolde was fairly certain her sister had lost nearly half a stone in weight since their father's impeachment inquiry began.

All due to Kendall's malicious vendetta.

Tentatively, Isolde unwrapped the twine and paper.

A copy of Machiavelli's *The Prince* tumbled into her hand.

Of course, Kendall would find inspiration in an Italian Renaissance text devoted to instructing new princes on brutal ways to maintain dictatorial power.

Shaking her head, she opened the book, fanning through the pages. As with his previous reply, Kendall had not included a note.

However, at the beginning of chapter six, she found a message scrawled in confident black ink.

I prefer a rather different authority on governance.

Naturally, chapter six detailed the importance of a prince conquering a new land through his own skills and resources.

How typical of Kendall to be so cruel, so uncaring of the harm he inflicted on others.

Isolde stared at his words for far longer than was necessary.

In all their interactions, she had never once seen his handwriting.

Against her better judgment, she touched her finger to the ragged ink. His penmanship was bold to the point of arrogance . . . rather a microcosm of the man himself.

Now, how to respond?

8

The Duke of Kendall continues his rise to power. This week alone, His Grace will dine with both the Queen and the Prime Minister. His campaign to see justice served in the case of Mr. Stephen Jarvis and Lord Hadley has shown mettle, leading some to speculate that His Grace will soon be appointed to a position within Her Majesty's government.

—EDITORIAL IN *THE LONDON TATTLER*

Kendall found Lady Isolde's reply to his latest fusillade waiting atop his bedside table the next night.

Blast his twin and her eagerness to assist her friend.

He unfolded the foolscap with an angry flick of his fingers, bracing himself for the swooping curlicues of Lady Isolde's handwriting as it set forth her asinine requests.

She did not disappoint.

As logos *and* ethos *have seemingly failed to sway you, I call upon Pathos and appeal to your decency as a human being. Do you think, Your Grace, that you could find a beating heart within your ducal chest? I know you dislike my father and myself. But your actions do not injure us alone. As you may know, my younger sister, Lady Catriona, is betrothed to Lord Barnaby, Alderton's heir. They are a love match and deeply suited to one another. Your spurious accusations have rendered Lord Alderton wary of a union between our families.*

Kendall snorted.

Good. Excellent.

Alderton *should* be wary of uniting his line with the ilk of Hadley and his brood.

These past two weeks, I have watched my beloved sister grow listless and melancholic as she fears her marriage will be called off. I beg you, Your Grace: Have a heart. Consider the tearful innocents who are currently caught in the artillery barrage you have launched upon our family. Lady Allegra insists you are not a man like your father—cruel, tyrannical, and pitiless. That you possess scruples and a soul. I value your sister's opinions, but I have yet to see evidence of her claims. Consider seizing this opportunity to prove that you are cut of a different cloth than your sire.

Kendall crumpled the note in his fist, a growl in his throat.

He successfully quashed the gnat-sized buzz of conscience that pointed out the truth in Lady Isolde's words. That he was, perhaps, ruining the prospects of a blameless young lady.

It explained Hadley's confrontation in front of the church.

That said, how *dare* Lady Isolde compare him to his father! Her characterization of Old Kendall was entirely accurate. He had been a viciously callous man focused on his own selfish needs.

Unlike that bastard, Kendall had the good of Queen and Country at the forefront of his thoughts. He *did* consider others, specifically the world into which his future children would be born. He did not wish his son to suffer the stench of a sire's behavior. His son would be proud to call him *father*.

But in order to reach that goal, occasional . . . . mmm, not *ruthlessness* . . . *complications*, perhaps? . . . arose. Such was the nature of all ruling power. Inevitably, some innocents would find themselves on the wrong side of the fight. That had always been the nature of war.

If Hadley—and by extension, Lady Isolde—wished to protect Lady Catriona, they should have behaved in a more civilized manner. Hadley should not have joined Jarvis in defrauding innocent investors. In all truth, the earl should not have permitted Lady Isolde to pursue university studies in the United States in the first place. And Lady Isolde, alone in Boston, should not have begun a relationship with Stephen Jarvis, *kissing* a married man and then dragging her father into Jarvis's financial schemes.

The actions of Hadley and his daughter created the mire in which they floundered. They had no one to blame but themselves.

Kendall was merely the messenger. The solitary hero brave enough to stand up to Hadley's economic might and insist the earl answer for his behavior.

Like an engine, Kendall's efforts to amass votes for Hadley's impeachment required the proper amount of stoking. But once it gained a full head of steam, the forward momentum of the whole would propel Kendall to victory.

He could practically taste his triumph.

This week, Lord John Russell had asked Kendall for his opinions on the proposed Turnpike Act. Even better, Allie and Kendall were to dine with the Russells in two days' time.

When he looked to the future, Kendall saw more of the same— more veneration, more power, more accolades. All things which would push the memory of his father into history's background.

Yes, his path forward was bright and clear.

Kendall could not wait to traverse it.

"YOU NEED TO call off your dogs, Tristan." Allie slumped against the squabs opposite him in the ducal carriage.

"My dogs?" Kendall replied dryly, rapping the ceiling to tell the coachman to begin driving.

"Yes, your minions in Commons who are howling for Hadley's impeachment. I don't think Lord John is enamored of the idea."

He and Allie were returning home after dining with Lord John Russell and his wife. Kendall had taken the opportunity to finally broach the topic of the charges against Hadley with the man.

Lord John had been hesitant to take sides.

However, Kendall knew Lord John did not approve of Hadley's more outlandish policies and ideas, specifically the education of his daughter at Broadhurst College. But being Prime Minister *and* leader of the House of Commons—Lord John was not a titled Peer himself and therefore did not have a seat in Lords—his support was invaluable to win.

"Truly?" Kendall's brow furrowed. "I found our discussion encouraging."

The carriage rocked as it merged into traffic, causing his shoulder to bump against the window at his side.

"Lord John is a seasoned politician, Tristan. He was very careful not to tip his hand."

Kendall huffed out a breath. "Though I do not wish to be rude, Sister, you do not understand British politics. Another week, and I anticipate having the votes needed in Commons to impeach Hadley and thereby force a trial in Lords."

Triumph was close. Kendall could feel it rising in his chest, taste its electric thrill on the back of his tongue.

The carriage rumbled around a corner. A group of young bucks, soused and staggering, called something unintelligible from the pavement.

"But why?" Gaslight from street lamps filtered through the window, mottling Allie's face. "You currently risk isolating yourself within the *ton* and—"

"I am Kendall." He fixed her with a stern look. "I was isolated the moment I was born. To be a Duke of the Realm is to live above and apart from others."

"That is our father speaking."

"No, it is truth. I made no friends during my time at Oxford. Other gentlemen made merry, played cricket, and took ladies rowing along the Thames. No one knocked on my door with an invitation to join them. My arrival was always met with silence and staring until I took myself off again."

"Perhaps," Allie conceded. "You can be rather prickly at times."

Kendall looked out the window, noting the dark shop windows rolling past, breathing through the ache that lingered when he thought of Oxford.

Most gentlemen made lifelong friends at university. It was where the bonds that built an empire were formed.

But every effort Kendall had made—which admittedly had not been many—ended in futility. In short, he was not a particularly likable chap.

His sister sighed.

"Love was in short supply for both of us growing up," she said. "It has rather stunted our abilities to relate to others as adults. It is why you cannot maintain a civil conversation with Lady Isolde, and yet clearly wish to kiss her at the same time."

Kendall gaped at his sister for a solid ten seconds.

He knew because he counted them.

"What did you say?" The words left his mouth on a whispered rush of air. His emotions abruptly sailed past the islands of Irritation and Fury and landed on Incandescent Astonishment.

"Kissing," Allie chirped. "You and Isolde."

The word *kissing* assaulted his mind like cannon fire. Images exploded with each beat of his heart.

Boom. The press of his lips to that shadowed place beneath Lady Isolde's ear.

Boom. The lift in her body, hungrily rising to meet his mouth.

Boom. The feel of her waist as he pulled her against his chest.

Kendall could scarcely breathe through the onslaught.

"You are not denying it, Tristan. You fancy her. All your rage and protestation—" Allie swirled her index finger, indicating his person. "—is mere pretense. You are desperately attracted to her but too mired in ideas of tradition and revenge to act on that attraction. Hence all the growling and anger." She tapped her chin. "I cannot imagine it is healthy for your—"

"Are you *quite* done?" he interrupted, voice arctic and chilly.

"No," his sister answered breezily. "I will never be done until I see more of the kind, loving twin I knew as a child."

"Our bastard of a sire effectively erased that soft boy two decades ago." When Tristan had lost his mother and twin sister—the only two people to ever show him genuine affection—in one horrid blow. "Such events change a person forever."

Allie studied him for a long moment. "I fear I must respectfully disagree, Brother. I think you *permitted* those events to change you in order to protect your heart. The tenderness and goodness of that boy still exist."

"Do not spin candy floss tales of my presumed latent benevolence, Allie. You will be disappointed."

"I don't think that I will. Though they seem like opposite ends of a long spectrum, love and hate reside quite closely to one another."

Kendall fought the urge to roll his eyes at her lecturing.

"Imagine emotions like water filling a pitcher—the more emotion you feel, the more water the pitcher holds." Allie mimed lifting a jug. "Love and hate elicit similar degrees of feeling. Therefore, they fill the pitcher to the same level. And as such, they can be easily transmuted from one to the other. It is how lovers can go from adoration to hostility within minutes. The true opposite of love and hate would be an empty pitcher. A sentiment devoid of emotion. Indifference."

Allie pantomimed dumping the contents of the pitcher on the floor of the carriage.

"You claim to hate Lady Isolde," she continued, "but I'm not entirely sure that is the emotion she inspires in you. It's why you and I both detest our father to such a degree. We were supposed to love him, and we had a lake-full of desire waiting to do just that. Yet he was a cruel, violent man who thrived on the pain of others, his children in particular. And so, naturally, your concept of love and acceptance is warped."

Kendall snorted and peered out the window, attempting to block the truth in his sister's words.

"No, do not turn away from me," Allie insisted, her fingertips pushing on his knee. "I hate that Mamma and I were forced to abandon you. That love became nearly non-existent in your life and compelled you to equate power with love. But I can promise you, were Mamma here today, she would tell you that true love and happiness come from caring for others and accepting their love in return."

He swallowed. Thoughts of their mother always left him equal parts grief-stricken and furious.

Therefore, he rigorously avoided the topic.

"For some, happiness resides outside hearth and home." Kendall clenched his fist, slowly turning back to look at his twin. "For some, power *is* happiness. Power that allows one to make a difference. To affect true change—for a dukedom, for a kingdom, for millions even. Who are you to judge that?"

"In this, your perspective is wrong." The carriage rocked again, forcing Allie to grasp the velvet-covered bench for support. "I fret that one day you will wake alone atop your horde of power and gold, wondering what the point of life was. That you will realize far too late that joy comes from the love we share and the love we give. You won't arrive at happiness—at contentment—any other way."

Allie was wrong, of course. To Kendall's purview, love was messy and ungovernable—two things he stringently avoided.

He drummed his fingers against his thigh. "And I suppose you think Lady Isolde is the woman who will help me realize these truths?" His voice dripped with sarcasm. "Honestly, Allie, a scullery maid would make a better bride."

"That will be for you to decide, Tristan. But I urge you to change your course before it is too late. Before you make a choice that cannot be undone."

Thursday next, Sir William Hooker will present a lecture on the Royal Botanical Society's preservation plans for tree species within Kew Gardens. Specifically, he will discuss a pair of newly arrived cedarwoods from California which are to be installed near the Great Pagoda. Interested parties are to contact Sir William directly for a ticket to attend.

—ANNOUNCEMENT IN *THE LONDON TIMES*

I solde feared she was approaching the edge of a cliff. Metaphorically speaking, of course.

Kendall's plans for impeachment had been gaining momentum. His relentless attacks in newspapers and Parliament were taking a toll.

Isolde resorted to harassing her brothers to learn the particulars.

Mac said the evidence incriminating Lord Hadley was damning. A trial date had been set for Stephen Jarvis in three weeks' time. James learned that Alderton had spoken with his solicitors about canceling the marriage contract between Lord Barnaby and Catriona. Their sister hadn't left her bedchamber in over twenty-four hours.

Frantic worry took up a steady drumbeat in Isolde's chest. She hated the haggard concern on her father's face—dark circles sagging under his eyes—and her mother's increasingly desperate attempts at cheer. She hated hearing Catriona's weeping in the dead of night and the echoing silence of their townhouse, devoid of callers.

Isolde's world felt poised on a precipice, and the slightest jolt could send everything scattering like spillikins. Catriona would lose her Barnie. Hadley would be gaoled. And the damned Duke of Kendall would relax in his library armchair, smirk in triumph, and begin plotting his next campaign to destroy innocent lives.

Isolde pondered all this as she sat in the Palm House of Kew Gardens outside London, listening to Sir William Hooker deliver a lecture on plans to preserve past and future trees.

"With the successful removal of the lucombe oak from its original position in the middle of the Syon Vista," Sir William was saying, "we have turned to creating a plantation of Great Sequoia from California. The young trees are still in their pots near the Old Palace, awaiting final placement in the garden, which we hope to commence next week."

He continued on, discussing the preferred habitat of the giant redwoods. Isolde lifted her eyes to the palm trees and other tropical plants surrounding her.

Outside, a crisp breeze bent the bushes and treetops, but inside, the air was calm, warm, and humid. The Palm House was a true marvel of modern engineering. Made entirely of steel and glass, the building had only been finished the year before and now housed exotic flora from around the world.

"Someday, the palms around us will soar to the ceiling," Sir William had said at the beginning of his lecture, "and visitors will dine on the coconuts they produce."

Mmmm. If her entire family removed to California, Isolde mused, would the scandal with Jarvis haunt them there?

Though, even then, she would still have to live with the guilt and consequences of her heedless actions.

Her father was to have accompanied her this afternoon. An avid naturalist himself, Hadley loved nothing more than talking botany with the likes of Sir William. But the clamor in Parliament and the crisis with Alderton kept Lord Hadley firmly chained to his desk.

The two-hour ride to Kew after luncheon—her maid, Fiona, asleep opposite her, the carriage jolting side to side—had given Isolde some much-needed time to think.

She had to arrive at a plan, anything to stem the current cataclysmic slide of her family's fortunes. Or rather she *had* formulated a plan, but trapping Kendall in an iron cage until he relented did present some logistical challenges.

Now, seated at the lecture, Fiona shifted restlessly at Isolde's side—the poor girl likely counting down the minutes until she could renew her flirtation with Michael, the groom who waited with their carriage near the Old Palace. Had the maid's presence not been needed to maintain propriety, Isolde would have sent Fiona back to the coach to wait.

As if echoing the girl's restlessness, a hiss of whispered words flew between a group of society matrons and their young charges seated behind Isolde. She knew them all by sight, Lady Callagher in particular—the sort of gossiping ladies who necessitated Isolde keep a maid clamped to her side. Why were they here? A botanic lecture was hardly riveting entertainment.

Though, as Isolde scanned the room, she noted an unexpectedly-high number of young women in attendance.

The whispering behind her increased. Isolde couldn't tell what had them so excited—of a surety it was not Sir William's cedarwoods—but she was rather certain she heard one of them mutter Hadley's name.

Botheration.

Fiona looked at her, askance.

Isolde gave a subtle shake of her head.

A slight glance to the right—four rows ahead and to the far end—enlightened her. The tall gray head and stern profile were unmistakable.

Kendall.

Of course, he would be here, listening to Sir William with rapt attention. Of course, a bevy of eager claimants for the title of Duchess of Kendall had trailed after him. And, of course, they would be gossiping about the vendetta between Kendall and Hadley.

As usual, the duke was pomaded and starched into a near parody of aristocratic nobility—stiff shirt collar and dark cravat under a black frock coat. Did his hair ever lay out of place?

The image of Kendall sprawled across the guest bedroom of Muirford House—hair mussed and tumbling across his brow, shirt unbuttoned and chest exposed—arrowed through her mind.

Isolde closed her eyes against the intrusion. Which helped not at all, as now she saw the scene in even clearer detail on the back of her eyelids.

Enough.

Yes, Kendall was empirically an attractive man. Any number of scientific tests could attest to that simple fact. But handsomeness alone—without kindness, honor, or good humor—was nothing more than an empty shell. Or in Kendall's case, a shell filled with arrogance, conceit, and selfish ambition.

Isolde looked away from the duke and clasped her hands firmly in her lap.

She hadn't a clue how to force the man to capitulate, though her imagination continued to supply creative ideas.

Could she push His Grace off an obliging bridge in the gardens? Was there a damaged tree she could fell atop him? Perhaps she could coax the stiff breeze outside into assisting her.

Unfortunately, Isolde knew she could not make a scene. Not here. Not with so many gossiping mouths in attendance.

Sir William finished his lecture to polite applause, Kendall included. The duke stood, frock coat flowing into neatly pressed lines to the back of his knees, and approached Sir William, obviously asking follow-up questions. Or, more likely, pointing out the flaws in Sir William's lecture and how the mighty Duke of Kendall would see them corrected.

"Come." Isolde motioned to Fiona before the other ladies could hail her or make deliberately barbed comments within her hearing.

Besides, Isolde wished to see the California cedarwoods before returning home.

She and Fiona exited the Palm House, bracing themselves against the wind. Though not precisely cold—it was summer after all—the breeze battered their skirts and bonnets. They turned left, following the path toward the old palace and the potted Great Sequoias. After a stretch of walking, they paused for Isolde to admire a large *ginko biloba* tree and to permit Lady Callagher *et al.* to pass along the path.

Fortunately, Fiona found a stray cat to occupy herself as Isolde circled the trunk—hand holding her bonnet to her head—studying the unique bark and semi-circular leaves fanning along each branch, while also effectively hiding herself from prying eyes.

Once Isolde was sure the pack of title-hungry admirers had moved on, she motioned for Fiona to leave the cat be and continue with her toward the Old Palace.

They had scarcely walked fifty paces up the path when Kendall's familiar gray head appeared in front of them. His Grace had paused to study a rhododendron bush covered in vivid purple flowers.

Isolde hesitated, briefly considering skirting off the path once more to avoid His Grace, but then her chin notched higher. The gaggle of busybodies was no longer in sight. And she needed to seize the chance to sway Kendall's opinion.

"Your Grace," she intoned, stopping at his side.

His gaze whipped to hers, lip curling in distaste.

She detested that she had to tilt her head up to meet his dark eyes.

She detested even more the zing of electrical charge she inevitably felt in his presence.

"Must you follow me everywhere I go, Lady Isolde?" He rested a palm on his walking stick, his frock coat snapping in the wind. "Such recalcitrant behavior *should* be beneath you."

Oof!

"I did not know ye would be in attendance today, Your Grace."

"Of course not," he scoffed. "The answer to your petition is still *no* and will always be *no*."

"I haven't asked a question."

"Merely anticipating another pathetic plea on behalf of your father. It won't happen. I will see justice served."

Isolde loathed the arrogant surety in his tone.

Perhaps she *would* find a convenient bridge after all, consequences be damned.

"Justice?!" she hissed. "Your actions have nothing to do with justice, Your Grace, and everything to do with this vendetta you have concocted against Hadley."

"I believe you are confusing the word *vendetta* with *victory*, my lady." A gleam lit his eyes. "*My* imminent victory, that is."

The bastard.

He was needling her and reveling in her seething reaction, aware that she couldn't slap his smug ducal face for fear of social reprisals.

Isolde knew she should leave. Turn around, return to her carriage, and concoct a more stealthy plan.

Unfortunately, *restraint* and *self-control* had never been her fortes.

"Despite what the voices in your head say, Your Grace, ye are not, in fact, victorious in this matter."

"Oh, but I think I am," he replied silkily, leaning toward her. An unhelpful gust of air ambushed her with the scent of his cologne. "Desperation nearly vibrates off your skin."

Oh!

Isolde glared, wishing her gaze were that of a gorgon and could freeze him to stone.

Only then did she realize: Fiona was watching their exchange with an almost unholy glee.

Och, Isolde did not wish to provide more fodder for her servants to feed the Mayfair gossip mill.

"Fiona, please sit on the bench there." Isolde pointed to a bench a few paces off the trail. "I wish a more private word with His Grace."

Dutifully, Fiona sat.

Isolde turned up a side path that appeared to lead to some sort of outbuilding, Kendall following at her heels. Thankfully, the stray cat found Fiona again, diverting the maid's attention.

After walking thirty paces, Isolde whirled and fixed the duke with her haughtiest stare. Weeks of frustration over this man's actions boiled to the surface.

"Enough, Your Grace." She snatched a bonnet ribbon off her cheek where the wind had plastered it. "If ye won't stop harassing my father, if ye haven't a care for my sister and her prospects, if ye won't listen tae my pleading, then let us cease this dance." She flicked her fingers, as if shooing away a nuisance. "I shall merely have to find a more cunning way tae force your capitulation."

"Such as boring me to death with your futile begging?" Dark humor touched his lips. "As I said, desperation is hardly a flattering look on you, Lady Isolde." He stepped toward her.

"How have ye convinced anyone that ye are a true gentleman"—she matched his forward step—"not to mention a duke?"

"Back to that, are you?" Another step closer.

"It seems particularly relevant just now."

They were practically nose-to-nose. Near enough for Isolde to see the fan of faint wrinkles bracketing his eyes like a sunburst.

A loud burst of sound drifted on the breeze—Lady Callagher's strident voice and a chorus of giggles drawing nearer.

Damnation.

The women had lost their quarry and doubled-back in search of the duke.

Isolde glanced in the direction of their voices, alarm ringing in her blood. Kendall mimicked her looking, no doubt reaching the same conclusion.

To be caught standing toe-to-toe with the duke, both of them arguing like fishwives . . .

Kendall tilted his head toward the outbuilding farther up the path, its door swung wide over the gravel. Isolde followed him up the walk. As they neared the building, she realized the structure was built into the side of the hill. The door stood at the end of a tunnel-like entrance, chiseled out of the mound like an ancient burial cairn.

Why had she followed him here?

It was infuriating . . . her uncontrollable need to poke and prod this man until he was as raging and helpless as herself. Until the turbulent Italian half of his nature erupted, burning away the chilly English.

Kendall paused beside the open door, tugging his hat further down on his head to prevent the wind from making off with it.

"Say your worst, Your Grace, and then let me be." Isolde pressed an arm across her waist.

"And miss my chance to gloat? I think not." The duke's eyes thrummed with glee. "How delightful to discover that the fierce Lady Isolde cannot stand to be bested."

"Ye have hardly bested me, Your Grace," she said through gritted teeth. "I simply haven't found the time to sharpen my dirk. We Scots are always ready tae spill a *Sassenach*'s blood."

"Is that so? You think me such an easy mark?" He smirked and, once more, stepped toward her.

It was as if they were magnets unable to resist the pull of the other's magnetic field.

He stood so close, Isolde could see herself reflected in his pupils. So close, the brim of his hat and the curve of her bonnet nearly touched.

She rather forgot to breathe.

A burst of female laughter sounded from somewhere behind them, causing Isolde to startle.

"Do you suppose Kendall went this way?" a voice called.

Kendall winced. "Oh, for the love of—" He bit off an oath.

Before Isolde could muster a word of protest, he wrapped his large hand around her wrist, tugged her into the dark interior of the building, and pulled the door partially shut, hiding them both from view.

Cool darkness engulfed her.

Of all the overly-dramatic—

Isolde yanked her hand from his warm grasp, hating how the press of his fingers lingered.

"Really, Your Grace," she whispered. "I didn't know your need tae crow victory was so pitiable."

Weak sun drifted through the half-open door, the only source of illumination. Kendall loomed, cast into sinister planes of light and dark.

"You would prefer that gaggle of title-hunting ladies see us together?"

Isolde ignored the thread of truth in his words. "I would prefer your head on a pike."

"Is that so?" he asked on a low rumble.

"Aye. Give me another week tae arrange it."

Voices rose again outside, female and excited.

Isolde stilled. Kendall turned his head toward the door, light rimming the stern lines of his profile.

"Did . . . see . . . he go?" drifted on the breeze.

After what felt like an eternity, the voices faded up the path.

Glaring up at the duke, Isolde shook her head. "This war is not yet finished, Your Grace. Ye shall not win."

"I believe I already have, my lady." The pomposity of his bass voice abraded Isolde's nerves.

Och. The blackguard.

"Enough, Your Grace!" Her words emerged in white-capping syllables. "Ye torment my family, ye accuse my father falsely—"

"Nonsense! I will lead this country through tradition and decorum and serve justice to those who—"

"I tire of your delusions. I'm leaving."

"Running away, you mean?"

"Devil take y—"

Crash!

They both jumped as a strong gust of wind clanged the thick oaken door shut.

Isolde barely stifled a screech.

Hand at her heaving bosom, she glared at the duke.

"Good day, Your Grace," she spat. "May you rot in Hell!"

His soft rolling laugh reverberated off the damp bricks, sending gooseflesh chasing her spine.

Fumbling in the dark, Isolde found the door handle and pulled.

It was to be her dramatic exit.

Instead, the door didn't move.

. . . what I know of her. Hair the color of sunset, blue eyes. A smile that rivals the sun. Smells of Tuscany in spring. The daughter of a Scottish earl or duke. Clever and educated. Has set my heart to beating once more.

—NOTE PENNED SEVEN HOURS AFTER TRISTAN'S ENCOUNTER WITH THE MYSTERIOUS BEAUTY IN MONTACUTE'S GARDEN— WRITTEN, STUDIED, AND THEN CAST UPON THE FIRE.

N^{o.} That was Kendall's first thought.

"It won't open." Lady Isolde's words were breathless in the shadowy interior.

He hated the intimacy of her voice. How the sound conjured the velvety darkness of a bedchamber.

"Allow me." He batted her hand aside. Surely the door was merely stuck, and Lady Isolde hadn't the strength to open it.

The handle turned in his grasp, but the door remained firmly shut, refusing to give.

No! The door cannot be locked.

What the devil sort of place was this?

They could not be trapped in here alone. It was bad enough to be seen speaking with each other.

But if they were found together like this . . .

Kendall couldn't even finish that thought. Such a catastrophe would upend every goal he had spent the last decade working toward.

Frowning, he crouched down to examine the lock.

Damn and blast!

"It's a self-locking Chubb mechanism," he growled, standing once more.

He could feel Lady Isolde behind him, radiating tension.

"What precisely does that mean, Your Grace?" she asked.

"Ah, have I found a topic that the all-wise Lady Isolde does not already know?"

"Please don't be an ass and render this situation more difficult than it needs be."

Just standing alone in a dark place with this woman was already more difficult than it needed to be. The scent of her filled his nostrils, and the faint rustling of her skirt sent lightning skittering across his skin.

"It means, my lady," he bit out, "that the door can only be opened with a special key designed for this particular lock."

A long moment of silence met his pronouncement.

"No!" she breathed in horror.

On this one thing, they were in agreement.

"No, no, no!" she whispered again, frantic terror in her voice.

She tugged on his elbow, the pressure of her fingers scalding.

"Mind your hand, woman!" Kendall flinched, shaking her touch free.

It was bad enough to be enclosed together in this oppressively small space. But to withstand the feel of her as well?

Impossible. A man could only endure so much before breaking entirely. And Kendall greatly feared what would tumble free if the reins of his control slipped where Lady Isolde Langston was concerned.

"I want to see this lock for myself!"

"Be my guest." He stepped back and mockingly motioned for her to look her fill.

Lady Isolde bent to study the lock. Light filtered in through the door jamb, rimming her bonnet, the slope of her pert nose, and the bell of her bulky skirts.

Swallowing, Kendall turned away, squinting to examine the interior of the space.

What was this building? They appeared to be standing in a hallway that disappeared into darkness. Perhaps there was another exit.

Placing one hand on the wall, he slowly walked into the shadows, carefully testing the floor with a foot before stepping. The farther he moved from the door, the colder the air became. The flagstone sloped downward, and eventually his right foot encountered a descending stair.

"Your Grace?" Lady Isolde's panicked voice whisper-called to him. "Kendall?!"

He looked back. A Lady-Isolde-sized cutout stood before the door. As he had done, she placed a hand on the wall and began tentatively walking toward him.

"I am here," he said. "You need not come this way. I fear it leads to an ice house. There will only be the one door—the one behind you."

She stopped. "Oh. I suppose that is why this building is constructed into the hill. The earth is an excellent insulator."

Kendall returned to her.

Dread tasted of soot in his mouth.

What were they to do? They had to escape before someone found them together.

"We can't call for help," she noted. "Anyone could come."

Anyone . . . like the bevy of ladies and their mammas who had already rushed past.

"But surely my maid, Fiona, will realize what has happened soon," Lady Isolde continued, voice unnaturally high. "She will fetch Michael, the groom waiting with the carriage. They will search and find us. Together, they can . . ." Lady Isolde drifted off as she undoubtedly reached the same conclusion Kendall had.

The maid and the groom would have to ask for the key. Someone else, aside from servants, would have to know about this incident. But who? Sir William? A housekeeper at the old Kew Palace?

And how much would Kendall and Hadley have to pay to purchase silence and discretion?

Kendall pinched the bridge of his nose, breathing in and out, counting the breaths until he could speak without bellowing his rage at . . . something. The wind for trapping them together? Fate's cruel jest?

"What are we tae do?" she asked.

"We wait," he replied, dread tasting acrid on his tongue. "The door was ajar, so perhaps a servant was here and will return soon."

"Aye." Her head nodded in the faint light. "And if the door is fitted with a costly, self-locking mechanism, someone must wish this space tae be well-tended. Surely they will be by tae check."

Kendall detested the thread of admiration he felt at her astute deductions, at the sense that her mind worked similarly to his.

No good would come of such comparisons.

He merely needed a way out of this hellish predicament.

KENDALL PROWLED THE perimeter of the hallway, his large body absorbing more than its fair share of space.

Isolde hated that she couldn't look anywhere without the heat of his simmering rage blistering her skin.

Shifting, she adjusted her shoulder blades where they leaned against the brick wall beside the door.

Kendall paced the visible section of the hallway like a caged wolf. The overwhelmingly masculine smell of his cologne—dark amber and sandalwood—assaulted her with each flip of his frock coat.

He had already spent an inordinate amount of time inspecting the door hinges and the locking mechanism itself.

"The hinges won't budge," he announced after an hour of prying at them with a Barlow pocketknife. "The screws are inset in the door jamb, and the pins in the hinges are forged into place. The door itself is far too thick to batter through with sheer force."

The angry defeat in his voice had abraded Isolde's frayed nerves.

They were well and truly trapped.

Kendall had resorted to broody pacing after that.

Every now and then, he would pause, lift his watch into the light filtering through the door jamb, and announce the time in stern ducal tones.

Three hours. They had been trapped together for three hours.

Aside from Kendall's clipped calling of the time, they hadn't spoken to one another in over ninety minutes.

Isolde kept to her space on the wall, her feet aching from standing. She had briefly sat down, but Kendall had been unable to pace with her long legs blocking the hallway. And regardless of how minor or inadvertent the touch—a sweep of her skirt, the brush of her hand—the man recoiled as if she carried the plague.

Her bonnet and his hat and walking stick rested on the floor just inside the door. And though the space hadn't seemed particularly cold when they first entered, Isolde could feel the chill creeping into her bones. Fortunately, she wore a pelerine—a loose, shawl-like garment that covered her shoulders—but it would hardly provide sufficient warmth once nighttime descended.

She tried not to dwell upon that fact. Or how the light around the door jamb dimmed with each ducal proclamation of the hour.

Fiona *had* to have realized by now that Isolde was not returning. Would she raise a hue and cry within Kew itself? Or would Fiona discreetly return to Mayfair to inform Lord and Lady Hadley? Isolde could hardly say which option she preferred.

Kendall strode back to the door, stopping opposite Isolde and matching her stance—shoulders leaning against the wall, arms crossed.

The faint light illuminated one side of his face, leaving the other in shadow and turning his eyes into glittering obsidian.

"Your family will assume I abducted you," he said, voice gravelly. "If you don't return home tonight, that is what they will fear has happened. Fiona last saw you in my company, after all."

Isolde let the thought bounce around her mind.

"Or that you and I eloped," she couldn't help but say, just to entertain herself with his reaction.

Kendall did not disappoint.

"Do not be absurd, Lady Isolde," he growled. "No one would believe such lunacy." He punctuated the comment with a slow, scathing perusal of her person.

Isolde couldn't help but laugh in return. "But ye abducting me like some nonsensical Drury Lane farce is somehow *more* believable?"

"Yes," he snapped.

"I suppose ye did kidnap your sister from Italy, so there is a history of such behavior."

Kendall squeezed his eyes shut, jaw clenched.

Isolde hoped he was praying for patience.

"My history with my twin is none of your affair, Lady Isolde."

"Except, perhaps, your wee penchant for kidnapping," she needled. "I do believe I am feeling rather abducted at the moment. Ye did drag me in here."

He pinched the brow of his nose, a sure sign—she now knew—that her words were taking a toll.

"What I mean," he said with condescending patience, "is that others are more likely to perceive me as a criminal, eager to hurt Hadley, rather than a lovesick swain carrying on a besotted secret courtship with a woman like yourself."

Well, when he put it that way . . .

"A woman like myself," she repeated slowly. "That unattractive, am I?"

The duke grunted, that muscle in his jaw flexing as he gritted his teeth. "It is not your physical appearance I find disagreeable, Lady Isolde. As well you know."

Interesting.

But then, her experimentation had already hinted at this.

"Just my engaging personality?" she asked sweetly.

"More like your hoydenish behavior."

"And so ye abduct me . . . why? Tae what end? Hold me for ransom? Blackmail?"

"You act as if those accusing me of such actions will be thinking rationally. The impeachment vote against your father looms large. Every faction in Parliament will use the ammunition at hand to malign their opposition, even a trumped up abduction charge."

"Are ye sure we're still speaking hypothetically, Your Grace? Ye appear tae have given my abduction quite a bit of thought."

Isolde had the deep satisfaction of watching Kendall turn to look at the door and suck in a deep breath, as if reining in his temper. His Adam's apple bobbed up and down the olive skin of his throat.

He was slowly unraveling—neckcloth loosening, night whiskers stubbling his chin. His gray hair had belligerently escaped its pomade, and it now slumped around his ears and curled onto his temples. In short, he was becoming more Italian by the minute.

With agitated hands, he jerked his pocket-watch free, checking the time again.

Only ten minutes had passed.

"I need out of here," he muttered, running a hand through his hair and mussing it further. He appeared nearly haggard.

Isolde felt a pang for his distress.

"My father will come," she said. "He would turn the world over tae find me. Never fear. We shall be rescued."

"Yes, but what will be the outcome of that rescue?" he nearly snarled.

Isolde did not misunderstand his meaning.

If they were caught here by the wrong person—a gossip, perhaps, with sufficient societal clout to cause waves—they would be forced to marry.

The thought rendered Isolde nauseous.

"Hadley is discreet. He wants a . . . a"—her tongue stumbled over forming the syllables—"*marriage* between us even less than yourself."

Kendall snorted. "I sincerely doubt that is possible."

Isolde narrowed her eyes at him, ignoring the sting of his remark. "Well, ye will simply have tae take my word for it then. Besides, it is significantly more likely a servant of Kew will find us first, do ye not agree?"

In answer, the duke pinched the bridge of his nose once again and remained incredibly still for a frighteningly long time.

You are dearly missed, my Izzy. Your mother and I breathlessly await
your return. Never doubt our love for you.

—PRIVATE LETTER FROM LORD HADLEY TO
LADY ISOLDE LANGSTON AT BROADHURST COLLEGE, BOSTON

My father will come.

Even hours on, Lady Isolde's words taunted Kendall.

What would it be like to be so arrogantly confident in others'
affection? To simply *know* that you were loved?

The worst part? Kendall did not doubt Lady Isolde's words. Hadley
would come for her.

Kendall could give a treatise on the earl's faults—and heaven knew he
had on multiple occasions—but he could not disparage the way Hadley
openly adored and cared for his wife and children.

As for Kendall, it would be days before anyone missed him. His
coachman would have returned to Gilbert House by now, assuming

Kendall had traveled home by other means. Allie might wonder where he had gone, but he doubted his twin would become concerned too quickly. She would merely surmise he had chosen to stay at his club for the night.

And even once people realized he was truly missing, they wouldn't be genuinely worried, supposing he would return home when ready.

In short, it was a rather dispiriting revelation, though hardly a surprising one.

Night had long settled over the ice house. Kendall could no longer see his watch, but he guessed the time to be approaching midnight.

Lady Isolde shifted across from him.

They had both slumped to the floor around sunset, each leaning against an opposite wall, their feet stretched past one another on the flagstone. He could see little of her now, just the general shape of her body and the poof of her skirts beside his knees.

Kendall kept his feet carefully angled, desperate to avoid any physical contact. Fighting the spell of his attraction to Lady Isolde was difficult enough from a distance, but feeling the burn of her touch and resisting the sharp cut of her wit and intelligence . . .

If he was to escape this debacle with his sanity and reputation intact, he had to minimize the battering of his defenses.

Cold seeped up through the floor and drifted along the hallway. He tucked his gloved hands into the pockets of his frock coat.

"Why do ye hate my father so?" Lady Isolde asked, her voice a silken rasp in the darkness. The sound raked along his skin and set all the fine hairs on his forearms flaring to attention.

"I do not hate your father."

A guffaw met his pronouncement. "Please. Spare my unbelief."

"It is true. I have no quarrel with your father, per se. I merely abhor any Peer who violates our laws."

Kendall could practically feel her eyes rolling. "We both know that tae be a lie. A man can seek justice without spitting vitriol. There is more to the story."

"I have no intention of discussing this topic with you."

"Why?"

"I am not obligated to provide you with a reason." Resisting her meant *not* being lured into an intimate conversation.

"Mmm," was her only reply.

She shifted, lifting one knee over the other and accidentally dragging her foot up his shin in the process.

He hissed at the scalding contact.

"Pardon," she whispered.

She likely couldn't see his answering twinge of pain.

Hours. He had endured *hours* of this torture. The smell of her perfume, the rustle of her feet, the soft *shush* of her hands across her skirts, the occasional brush of her leg or arm.

It was Kendall's personal definition of Hell.

Worse, he was learning all manner of things about her.

When she was amused or exasperated, Lady Isolde made a snuffling noise somewhere between a huff and a snort. He kept telling himself it was irritating, but he was terrified that part of him found it rather . . . *damnation* . . . adorable.

She didn't fill the air with mindless chatter, as if needing the sound of her own voice to dispel the quiet. Instead, she sat in the hush with him, content to dwell in stillness.

And though they were faced with a decided crisis, she hadn't devolved into hysterics or drowned him in recriminations. No. Rather, the lady endured their unwilling captivity with an admirable stoic verve.

Lady Isolde shifted again, voice echoing softly in the quiet. "So if ye won't speak of my father, then perhaps ye will explain why ye dislike myself tae such a degree? I understand that I am not tae everyone's liking—that ye find my education and upbringing distasteful—but there are other similarly unconventional ladies amongst the ton. I am hardly singular."

Kendall begged to differ on that point. Lady Isolde was utterly unique, for better or worse.

The silence stretched a little too long.

"Your Grace?" she prompted.

"I am merely collecting my thoughts."

He could hardly tell her the truth. That he both liked and loathed her in equal measure, just as Allie had observed.

He had to push her away. Because if Kendall let Lady Isolde too close, he feared he would toss all good sense—his hopes and aspirations—to the wind and chase after her like a stag in rut.

In particular, a conversation such as this was rather high on the list of *Things to Avoid with Lady Isolde*.

"Ye won't be answering that question either, will ye?"

Kendall grinned at the exasperation in her voice.

"*Och*, and now ye be smiling, Your Grace. I can see your fine teeth glinting even in the dark."

He only smiled wider.

"Am I sport tae ye, then?" she asked.

"No, Lady Isolde. Unlike my father, I do not torment women for entertainment."

"Truly? Because I should like it noted that I am feeling decidedly tormented at the moment."

"Is that so?"

"Aye."

He laughed at that. At the sheer petulant annoyance in her voice.

"A Frustration of Dukes, 'tis what ye lot are," she grumbled.

"Pardon?"

"The collective noun of dukes. A Frustration. Ye ken how a group of crows is called a murder? Or a pack of lions is a pride—"

"Yes, I am well aware of what a collective noun is, my lady."

"Dukes are a Frustration." She gave her signature sniff. "Or perhaps a Smugness? An Arrogance?"

"Have you read *The Book of Saint Albans*?"

"*The Book of Saint* who?"

"*Albans*. I must admit I am surprised you do not know the work. It's a late medieval text on courtly manners, and according to most research, written by a prioress."

Silence for a beat.

"That is tae be commended, I am sure," she finally said. "But I am unclear as to how that relates to a Smugness of Dukes. Unless ye were merely wishing tae give a *demonstration* of said moniker—reveling in my ignorance—in which case, well done. Bravo." She clapped, the sound echoing off the walls.

Kendall was helpless to stop another grin, hating the way delight licked his chest. Damn this woman and her quick wit.

He knew he should stop speaking. Every exchange between them eroded his resolve.

And yet, his foolish mouth opened.

"*The Book of Saint Albans* is the origin of most collective nouns in the English language," he explained. "The book contains a long list of them, such as a gaggle of geese or a pod of whales. But the authoress did become fanciful when naming groups of people."

"Fanciful?"

Kendall couldn't help but notice—just by the sound of her voice—how she leaned in.

"Yes. A Poverty of Pipers, for example. A Blast of Hunters. A Superfluity of Nuns. Or my personal favorite—a Complaint of Wives."

"That *would* be your favorite." Her dry words drifted through the dark. "Is there one for husbands?"

"No, but there is one for Scots."

"I am almost afraid tae—"

"A Disrespect of Scots," he helpfully supplied, tone far too chipper and deliberately vexing.

She kicked him. Hard. The toe of her walking boot hitting his anklebone.

"Ow!" Kendall pulled his leg back with a yelp.

"*Och*, I do beg your pardon, Your Grace," her sugary voice sailed across to him. "Was that a Scot disrespecting your *Sassenach* self?"

He rubbed at his injured ankle. "Indeed, it was."

"I have brothers, Your Grace," she snorted, that snippet of sound he liked far too well. "Ye would be wise tae remember that fact."

Quiet reclaimed the space.

Kendall rubbed his nose and wiggled his toes, willing warmth into them. The night was not so cold that he feared for their health, but the air had passed into uncomfortably chilly at least an hour ago.

Lady Isolde shifted again, leaning forward and pulling her knees close to her chest, her hands tucked against her ribcage. She turned her face toward the door, permitting the faint moonlight to gently trace the contours of her elegant profile.

He closed his eyes against the sight.

She was so still, he wondered if she had finally fallen asleep.

But then her voice reached him, small and weary. "No one will come until morning, will they?"

He hated it, the note of fear in her tone. It seemed wrong, somehow, to live in a world where Lady Isolde succumbed to despair.

Until that moment, he realized he had always thought of her as existing beyond the natural forces of nature. That, of course, she would gallivant off to university in Massachusetts and return blazing with life. Of course, she would shrug off the *ton*'s scorn, as if it mattered not. Of course, she would be immune to feelings of anxiety or fear.

Lady Isolde wrote the rules of her life, rather than contort herself to others' whims.

She shifted again, as if restless. Only then did Kendall realize what he should have long ago—

She was shivering.

"You are cold," he said, not a question.

Her only answer was to rub her hands up and down her arms.

Damnation.

They would need to share body heat in order to stay warm.

He was going to have to . . . to . . . *hold her*, wasn't he?

His body both recoiled and yet slavered at the thought.

Heaven help him.

Hadley would likely take a claymore to his head if he discovered his daughter and arch-nemesis cuddled together.

But even then, Kendall decided that touching Lady Isolde was wiser—not to mention more tolerable—than watching her suffer.

He refused to examine *why* his brain reached such an illogical conclusion.

Biting back an oath, Kendall did what needed to be done.

"Here now." Crouching, he crossed to her. "The night will only become colder. Let us combine our body heat."

"Y-yes."

Kendall settled against the wall beside her, feet stretched in front of him.

"My s-skirts can be a b-blanket for your legs," she stammered.

Smart woman.

"And my frock coat is wool and wide enough for us both," he added.

She nodded, her head shadowy in the moonlight slipping underneath the door.

With a shaking hand, Lady Isolde set her skirts on his thighs. Kendall pulled the bulky, voluminous weight of them across his legs, instantly grateful for the extra warmth.

Gritting his teeth, he spread his right arm behind her shoulders, holding the side of his frock coat open in invitation.

Before that moment, Kendall would have said Lady Isolde was as loathe to touch him as he was to touch her. That she would lean against him tentatively, avoiding as much of his body as possible.

But he should have known that this woman would never behave as expected.

With a hiccuping sigh, she melted onto his chest, the weight of her body sagging into his as if boneless. Her cold nose pressed into his collarbone, as she reached to pull the tails of his coat around her hips and shoulders.

It was at that moment Kendall realized the gravity of his mistake.

Bloody hell.

The delectable *feel* of her, soft and pliant against him. His body lunged at its leash, his hands tingling with the desire to explore the fine texture of her cheek, the curved nip of her waist, the silken weight of her hair.

Torture. Plain and simple.

Swallowing, he tentatively allowed his right hand to rest on the most convenient place—her right hip bone.

"Thank ye," she murmured against his pectoral, pulling her knees to lean against his thighs. "Ye be so warm."

He nearly laughed at that.

Warm? He was in Hell. His skin was afire, each point of contact pulsing like hot coals. Could blood actually boil?

He held impossibly still, terrified that if he moved, the heat scouring his veins would lick outward and compel his hands to move, to caress.

Take strength, man! he encouraged himself. *Think upon your goals. Of the life to which you aspire.*

Lady Isolde stirred and Kendall had to fight the impulse to hold her firm, to snarl that she should not—*could not*—move.

Instead, she adjusted her head, pressing her ear against his chest.

"Your heart beats so fast," she whispered. "Surely that cannot be healthy."

Kendall couldn't stem his mirthless laugh this time.

Healthy? No, indeed it was not.

"Go to sleep," he ordered instead.

She gave that snuffling snort he liked far too well. Worse, he felt it as much as heard it.

And for a minute or two, he thought she had finally obeyed him. Her body melted further and her breathing deepened.

But then her voice whispered, "Oh! Ye be afraid of the dark."

"Pardon?"

"I feared the dark too, as a wee girl. My heart would race so. Just like this." She tapped his sternum beside her cheek. "But Papa would tell me a story and chase the *bockies* away."

"The what?"

"*Bockies* . . . the bogeymen."

"Your father would do that? Sit at your bedside and tell you stories?" The very thought felt foreign. That an earl as powerful as Hadley would traipse up to the nursery and concern himself with a daughter's childish anxieties.

"Aye. It's how I know he'll come for me. So ye shouldn't be afeart." She patted his chest, but the motion was sloppy. Lethargic. "Papa will always come . . ." Her voice drifted off.

Kendall sensed the moment sleep claimed her in earnest. Her head sagged forward, lungs expanding in a gentle rhythm.

He remained awake, feeling the involuntary twitching of her body, the warm puffs of her breath.

A lock of her flame hair had escaped its pins and tumbled across the black wool of his frock coat. Pale moonlight twined through the amber strands.

It was apropos, he supposed, that her fiery hair reflected the tumult of her personality. But how odd to hold her in repose. To know, definitively, that she was capable of stillness.

He shook his head.

What would the morrow bring?

Or rather, how much money was he going to have to pay in order to hush over this incident?

Neither he nor Lady Isolde had done any wrong. He had not compromised her virtue. She, for once, had not acted indiscreetly.

They had simply met with an unfortunate accident.

But if their situation were discovered by the wrong person, no degree of virtue or integrity would matter.

Surely, Hadley was intelligent enough to realize this. That the whole affair needed to be handled with discretion and secrecy.

God willing, a servant would find them as he or she went about morning chores. That was easily dealt with.

Kendall clung to that hope.

Because even as he held Lady Isolde's sleeping body cradled against his chest, he could scarcely breathe through the thought of any other outcome.

WARM. ISOLDE FELT so warm.

No. Scratch that.

Her front felt warm, as if she were curled close to a roaring fire. But her spine was chilled. Was she dreaming of the hearth at Muirford House?

Sleep-addled, she cuddled closer to the source of heat, sighing into its comfort.

Two facts trickled through her brain.

One, the warmth was muscled.

And two, it had a heartbeat.

Isolde frowned.

That hardly seemed right.

Slowly, her tired brain flickered awake.

Memory rushed in behind.

Ice house.

Trapped.

Duke of Kendall.

Heaven help her.

She was curled around Kendall like a *numpty*-headed *loonie*.

His heart beat a steady rhythm under her ear and his arm snaked around her waist, snugging her close.

It felt . . .

Well, it felt safe. Kind. Gentle.

Words she would have never associated with the duke before this moment.

But then, the entirety of his reaction to their circumstance had been unexpected.

Yes, he had ranted a wee bit as gentlemen were wont to do. But once that had passed, he had offered her succor. Kendall had noticed her shivering and had showed compassion rather than disdain. He had wrapped his arm around her and held her body with . . . well . . .

Tenderness.

That was the only word to describe it.

Kendall held her as if she were the most precious thing. A possession to be cherished.

Allie insisted there was good within her twin. And for once, Isolde believed her.

Now, huddled against him, her head tucked into the hollow between his shoulder and chest, Isolde felt protected. Secure.

Like all would be well if only she could remain here, safe in the strength of his arms.

How odd.

That *his* would be the embrace that brought comfort in a moment of trial.

Granted, it didn't hurt that the man smelled divine—sandalwood and soap and something expensively masculine. Could Isolde ask Allie what cologne he wore?

His lungs lifted in deep, even breaths.

Isolde knew she should pull away. She was fully awake now and daylight had crept into the wee hallway.

But . . .

Just one minute more, she thought.

What harm was there in resting for a while longer? After all, it would be rude to awaken Kendall.

With that thought, she closed her eyes again.

THE SOUND OF a key in the door lock jolted Isolde awake.

"—check every outbuilding before moving farther afield," a man's voice said.

Kendall stirred under her head.

Isolde pushed off his chest as the door opened and sunlight streamed into the corridor. Wincing, she shielded her eyes, blinking into the brightness.

As her eyes adjusted, a sea of faces greeted her.

A rotund man with a set of keys in his hand.

Her father, Hadley, beside him.

Allie with her arms crossed at her waist.

Uncle Rafe, hands in his pockets.

Sir William Hooker and Lord Alderton, both with eyes wide and aghast.

And beyond them, several men dressed in the distinctive blue coats of the Metropolitan Police Force or *Peelers*, so called after Sir Robert Peel who founded them.

She rather feared she saw a journalist or two milling in the background.

"Well, they have been found," the man with the keys said to Isolde's father.

"As I have been insisting, my brother would not kidnap a lady!" Allie looked up at Hadley. "I know you have a low opinion of Kendall, my lord, but he is hardly a criminal."

Isolde thought she heard Kendall snort, but surely she was mistaken.

Pushing to standing, she met her father's gaze. He looked . . . haggard . . . unshaven, coat rumpled, dark circles under his eyes. Never had she seen the Earl of Hadley appear so shaken.

Behind her, she felt Kendall rise as well.

"Gentlemen," the duke intoned.

Isolde spared a glance at him.

Oddly, Kendall resembled her father—gray whiskers on his jaw, hair akin to a haystack, neckcloth loosened. The duke stared at Hadley, something burning in his dark gaze.

She swallowed and looked forward.

"Well, Hadley," Alderton announced, "I should hope that you will be seeing another daughter wed." The earl looked to Isolde. "And soon."

Isolde's heart stopped in her throat.

No!

Kendall remained grimly silent at her back.

She met her father's gaze once more.

"Come, lass," Hadley said gruffly. He reached out a hand and pulled Isolde into his arms, hugging her tightly. "Let us take ye home."

KEW GARDENS SCANDAL! This morning, the Duke of Ken-dall was discovered locked inside an ice house with Lady Isolde Langston, eldest daughter of the Earl of Hadley. Rumors are already swirling as to why, precisely, the two were together. Was it an illicit tryst between lovers? Or, as some are claiming, was it an abhorrent kidnapping attempt by Kendall and another volley in his war against Lord Hadley?

Only time will tell.

—ARTICLE IN *THE LONDON TATTLER*

Hours later, Isolde watched her father pace before the hearth of the drawing-room in their Mayfair townhouse.

Lady Hadley sat between Mariah and Catriona on a sofa to the right, studying her husband with concern. Mariah remained wide-eyed, but Catriona dabbed at her cheeks every few minutes with a sodden handkerchief.

Mac and James sat in two chairs opposite them.

Uncle Rafe stood beside the hearth, a shoulder leaning into the mantel.

Seated in a chair facing them all, Isolde had never felt so wretched. A tingling numbness had begun to spread from her fingertips to her scalp, rendering her lightheaded and nauseous.

Shortly after her arrival at Broadhurst College, Isolde and her chaperone had stumbled across a den of ribbon snakes in the woods. Dozens of serpents slithering into a Gordian knot of astonishing size.

Now, a similar tangle of fearsome creatures had taken up residence in Isolde's abdomen, coiling around her stomach and twisting through her entrails.

"What is tae be done then, Pa?" Mac asked.

Catriona sniffed, stifling a sob.

Lord Alderton had made his position clear: Isolde's disgrace was a Lucifer match to a powder barrel—the spark that destroys the whole. His lordship would not permit an alliance between his heir and the family of a compromised lady.

Isolde feared she already knew the answer to Mac's question. The writhing tightened in her gut.

"Aye," James nodded. "Do ye ken Isolde will have tae marry Kendall?" Her brother shot her an apologetic look.

"As I keep saying," Hadley said, his pacing unbroken, "I willnae permit any alliance between our house and that monster."

It was telling of her father's distress that his accent had slipped into that of his youth.

"But, Kendall didn't kidnap Isolde in the end. The gentleman is innocent," Uncle Rafe said. "This is merely a most unfortunate accident."

"That . . . that—" Hadley paused, clearly searching for an epithet he could use in the presence of his wife and daughters. "—*scoundrel* is anything but innocent. He would confine us all to Newgate if given the opportunity. Dinnae assign any modicum of conscience or goodness tae your brother, Rafe. Ye of all people know what the duke is capable of."

That isn't quite true, Isolde wanted to say.

Yes, the duke's actions with regard to her father's impeachment were reprehensible, but Kendall was not merely one side of a coin.

He had been kind, even in the face of their captivity.

Or, if not *kind* precisely, at least . . . accommodating.

Her gaze caught Rafe's and read the same sentiment there.

This Duke of Kendall, for all his faults, was not a man like his father.

"But if Isolde doesn't marry Kendall, Alderton won't permit . . ." Mac trailed off, his gaze turning to Catriona.

"*Och*, I will pay Barnaby to elope with Cat to Scotland," Hadley said. "They are both of age and can marry without a guardian's permission."

"Andrew," Rafe said, reproach in his tone, "ye ken that Barnaby won't defy his father."

"Then he isnae worthy of my daughter!" Hadley snapped.

Catriona sagged into their mother, shoulders heaving in silent tears.

Isolde merely breathed through the coils banding her chest.

Slowly, over the past several hours, she had unraveled the sequence of events that had occurred while she was locked away with Kendall.

Fiona had been bewildered when Isolde disappeared. The maid had witnessed Isolde exchange heated words with Kendall, sat on the bench as directed, and petted a cat. But when she looked up again, Isolde and Kendall were gone. Fiona had waited for ages for Isolde to reappear, but eventually the maid had returned to the carriage and Michael the groom, reporting what had happened. After all, Fiona had overheard His Grace state that his victory over their family was imminent.

Alarmed, Michael immediately left for Mayfair, where they laid the whole at Hadley's feet. Isolde's father had wasted no time in calling upon Gilbert House, Rafe in tow. There, the men learned from Allie that Kendall hadn't returned home from Kew Gardens either.

Given the long history of bad blood between their families, Hadley was convinced Kendall had kidnapped Isolde in an act of petty cruelty.

Allie insisted that her twin might have his faults, but he would hardly behave so viciously. There had to be some other explanation. Rafe was in agreement.

But Hadley refused to back down. With Allie at his heels, he called upon the director of the Metropolitan Police force, reporting that the Duke of Kendall had kidnapped Lady Isolde Langston against her will.

From there, events spiraled. Lord Alderton heard of the accusation and immediately joined in the hunt, intent on uncovering the truth.

Hadley had wanted every train and road in England searched.

Rafe and Alderton insisted they begin with Sir William Hooker and the environs surrounding Kew, just in case there had been an accident.

And thus . . . Isolde and Kendall had been discovered.

"Will ye call Kendall out in a duel then, Papa?" Mariah asked. Isolde disliked the quiver of excitement in her sister's voice.

"A duel?" Hadley paused his pacing. "Bah! As if I would stoop tae such a low. Kendall is no gentleman and deserves no such concession from myself. Nae, I'll content myself with raiding his coffers and paupering his dukedom, as I did to his father."

A wee frown dented Isolde's brow. She had never heard of this. Her father had waged economic war against Old Kendall? Did the current duke know?

Somehow, Isolde suspected he did.

No wonder the duke was so hellbent on annihilating her father. Isolde was merely a pawn caught between their battling wills.

"Regardless if Isolde accepts Kendall," James said, returning to his original argument, "surely the duke must offer for her if he wishes tae salvage anything of his own reputation."

"I hope Kendall does offer for her," Hadley snorted. "It will give me tremendous satisfaction tae toss the duke out my front door, preferably with my boot!"

"I'll gladly assist ye in that," Mac agreed, a particularly threatening expression on his handsome face.

Her menfolk would find themselves gaoled or worse if no one intervened.

Isolde exchanged a glance with her mother.

A quiet sorrow rested in Lady Hadley's gray eyes, as if her heart were breaking. As if she already mourned the outcome of this scandal.

Her mother's expression said what Isolde already knew.

There was only one solution that would see Alderton appeased and Catriona married to her love. Only one solution that would rectify the misfortune Isolde's own involvement with Stephen Jarvis had brought upon them all.

Only one way to ensure that her brothers' and Mariah's future marriage prospects were not tainted. That her father's legacy shone bright and unspoiled.

If the Duke of Kendall proposed, Isolde would have to accept him.

KENDALL HADN'T SET out to get drunk.

Truly, he hadn't.

Usually, he modulated his drink, refusing to indulge in the loss of control that drunkenness could bring.

But if the events of any day would compel him to find solace in a bottle . . .

Moreover, he needed something to block the memory of holding Lady Isolde in his arms. But no matter how much he drank, he could feel her yet pressed against his side, the scent of lemons filling his nostrils.

Damn her.

Damn *him* for being so arrogant.

No—

Damn *Hadley* for creating this farcical tragedy by bringing half of London to discover them.

Kendall sat in his private study, the one directly off his bedchamber, a fire burning low in the grate. He liked this room, partly because his father had eschewed it and partly because its placement between the bedchamber and dressing room meant that servants would struggle to listen at the lock.

In short, it allowed him to brood in privacy. To curse his Fate and Scottish earls and womankind in peace.

Allie discovered him there, three sheets to the wind.

"Lord Hadley," Kendall said, saluting his twin with a bottle of brandy, "is a cretin."

"Is he now?" Allie plucked the bottle from his fingers.

"Give me that!" He reached for the brandy, but misjudged the distance and nearly toppled out of his chair.

Allie pushed him back into his seat with a firm hand to the shoulder. He slumped against the leather.

"I think you have had enough, Tristan." Setting the bottle on a sideboard, she returned to the fire, taking the seat opposite him. "And yes, Hadley behaved indiscreetly. He refused to heed my defense of you."

"Imbecile," Kendall belched. "Now you see why I . . . why I . . ." He frowned, his sodden brain searching for the right words. "He . . . he must pay."

"I've never seen you drunk."

He squinted at her.

"You are less morose than I would have expected," she continued, conversationally.

"Th-thank you?" he hiccupped.

"You are going to have to offer for Lady Isolde. But I think you already reached that conclusion." She pointed at the brandy bottle on the sideboard. "Hence, the drunkenness."

Indeed, Kendall had come to that realization about two seconds after seeing the sea of faces outside the ice house.

Curse Hadley and his eagerness to believe the worst of a Duke of Kendall.

He ignored the tiny voice whispering uncomfortable truths in his ear. That his own attacks on Hadley had influenced the earl's assumptions. That in the past, when at his angriest, Kendall might have entertained the thought of kidnapping Isolde as retribution.

The brandy, thankfully, had been effective at silencing that pesky voice.

"You are backed into a corner, Brother," Allie continued. "Yes, Hadley was wrong to assume that you had abducted his daughter. However, if you do not offer for Lady Isolde, they will say you ruined her on purpose—an unsporting, vicious volley in this war you have launched against her father."

Kendall stared morosely into the fire, head lolling against his chair. "If I don't . . . If I don't marry her, I will become . . ." He searched his pickled brain for the right word. ". . . no one."

"Yes. You will be *persona non grata* in the *ton*. No longer received."

"And even if I *do* marry her, I will never become . . . become Prime Minister." The very thought had his hand twitching for the bottle again. "Her Majesty . . . does not like Hadley's liberal politics . . . or Lady Isolde. She is too educated, too opinionated, too . . . Lady Isolde-ish to be received at Court."

It was one of a hundred reasons why Kendall had rejected courting the woman in the first place.

"Yes," his twin agreed, compassion in her voice. "No matter what decision you make now, your political prospects are grim."

"My future . . . 'twas so bright . . . so close," he whispered. "And now it is all . . . all . . ." He gave up searching for the word and instead made an exploding motion with his hands.

"Yes. I am so sorry, Tristan."

Silence stretched for a moment. Coals settled in the grate, sending a shower of sparks up the chimney.

He turned his head where it rested on the back of his chair, eyes blearily trying to bring his sister into focus. "No . . . comfort, Allie? No, *it will come to r-right*"—he hiccupped again—"or, *Brother, you shall c-conquer this too?*"

His twin tucked her feet underneath her, red skirts spilling onto the floor.

"You should know me better than that, Tristan. I have never been one for false platitudes."

He sighed and pressed two fingertips against his brow bone, attempting to stem the pounding that had taken up residence there.

Silence reigned again.

Kendall stared at the mesmerizing flames licking the grate.

"Was it . . . w-was this inevitable, do you s-suppose?" he asked after a while, unable to stem his hiccups.

"What do you mean?"

"Can a Tristan ever escape the s-spell of an Isolde?"

Allie laughed, a startled burst of sound. "Is that what you think has happened here?"

"Sometimes," he whispered. "She is madness in my blood, Allie. I loathe it . . . I want . . . I want her gone. But now, that madness has cost me . . . everything." He spread his arms wide, enunciating slowly, forcing his sluggish tongue to form the words. "Every goal. Every dream. Every hope. Gone. I am just l-like the Tristan of legend."

"While that is vividly melodramatic to be sure, I have to disagree with your conclusions. We both know you have a tendency toward obsession. You decide a situation must unfold in a specific way and then charge ahead, intent on that vision."

He frowned, lifting his head and fixing her with his bleary gaze. "Pardon?"

"Oh come, Tristan. Ethan has told me about your behavior with his sister-in-law—"

"Viola . . . Viola Brodure?"

"Yes, and how you fixated on using her talent, along with Ethan's poetry, to further bolster your own political clout. And then, you moved on to kidnapping myself and focused on utilizing my marriage as a stepping stone to power."

Kendall's brandy-soaked brain could scarcely absorb her words. "Your point?"

"You have spent the years since our sire's death zealously focused on furthering your own reputation and consolidating political power. This latest contretemps with Hadley has had a similar aim."

"Yes. A dream that is now rubble." Anger dissipated a bit of his drunken fog. "Again, what is your point . . . aside from rubbing s-salt in my wounds?"

"You become consumed by a sort of mania. Once you decide on a goal, you cannot be swayed from it. Remember the skiff in the boathouse of Hawthorn growing up? The one you were so insistent you could repair? You spent an entire summer at the pond, trying to make the boat seaworthy again."

"Try? I s-succeeded!"

"You did. But when you obsess, Tristan, you miss what is truly important. You ignored me that summer. And in the end, it was our last together. I would have given anything to have that time back."

Guilt rose in Kendall's chest. Yes. He, too, would have given anything for more time with his twin that year.

"Though unwillingly, you display a similar fixation for Lady Isolde," Allie continued. "She calls to you."

"I do not want her as my duchess!"

"But that is my point, Tristan. You are so focused on resisting her, you miss the beauty you could have together."

At Allie's words, hypothetical scenes crowded his mind. Isolde smiling at him from down the dinner table at Hawthorn. Isolde laughing on his arm as he escorted her into a ballroom. Isolde sliding a hand around his neck to tug him down for a kiss—

The images should have been comforting, hopeful even.

But they sent a flight of anxious wings battering his ribcage.

He didn't *want* that life.

He didn't want to love and accept Lady Isolde. She was too chaotic, too vibrant, too . . . too . . .

Uncontrollable.

Yes.

That was it.

The emotions Lady Isolde awakened in him were simply too much. They were messy and difficult, and he could not control them. If he gave into them, she would *rule* him, body and soul.

And Tristan Gilbert, Duke of Kendall, hated relinquishing control.

"I recognize that love has been scarce in your life up to now, Brother," Allie continued. "But there is still time to learn to love and be loved in return."

Aggravation flared at her words.

"I know how to l-love, Allie." He glowered at his sister.

"I do not doubt that you love me." She stood and crossed to him, pressing a kiss to his cheek. "But I think that sometimes you could use help in showing it a bit more. Moreover, I am not entirely sure you see *yourself* as lovable."

Kendall flinched, the truth of Allie's words landing with a nearly audible thwack against his psyche. "What is *that* supposed to m-mean?"

"Just something I wonder. That perhaps you equate political power— admiration and deference—with love because it is the only way you can conceive of people liking you for yourself."

Kendall gaped up at her.

"Think upon it," she called as she exited the room.

He had no intention of thinking upon anything.

He wished to remain drunk and mourn the loss of the life he had spent the last decade cultivating.

He wanted—

Kendall paused, looking at his trousers.

With a trembling hand, he removed a long strand of glimmering auburn hair from his thigh.

The solitary hair felt indicative of this debacle. Of all the ways Lady Isolde invaded his thoughts, weakening his will until the whole crumbled.

With a grimace, he dropped the hair onto the carpet.

The only silver lining he could see?

Old Kendall was likely looking up from Hell, apoplectic that his heir would have to offer the role of Duchess of Kendall to one of Lord Hadley's offspring.

Kendall hoped his sire choked on the horror of it.

SCANDAL ROCKS KENDALL! Dedicated readers of this publication will know that the Dukedom of Kendall is no stranger to scandal. The previous duke's bigamy trial appalled Polite Society thirty years past. And now his son has shocked a new generation with his own flagrant behavior, spending a night closeted with Lady Isolde Langston. We can only hope that, for their families' sake, a marriage between the two lovers is imminent.

—ARTICLE IN *THE LONDON TATTLER*

The next morning, Kendall presented himself on the stoop of Hadley's townhouse—dread roiling his stomach and an unrelenting demon pounding against his temples.

His mind felt detached from his body. Someone else's hand gave his hat to Hadley's butler. Someone else followed the man into Hadley's study. And it was a stranger who stared at Hadley standing grim and furious behind an enormous oak desk similar to Kendall's own.

Only then, did Kendall note the other man in the room—Sir Rafe.

It took all of Kendall's breeding not to recoil.

This had to be the very definition of hellfire. Forced to grovel for forgiveness before the two men in the world, after his dead father, whom Kendall despised the most.

Of course Sir Rafe would be here. His half-brother, yet again, a catalyst in one of the most traumatic and dreadful moments of Kendall's life.

The point at which one existence was brutally severed and a different one thrust upon him, most unwillingly.

Kendall pushed back the old memories that threatened to surface.

Leave it, he ordered himself. *It is in the past.*

"Kendall," Hadley said by way of greeting.

"Hadley." Kendall forced sound past his stiff lips.

His heart raced in his chest like a mad beast. Was this akin to the battle terror soldiers felt before engaging the enemy?

He rather thought it was.

Allie's words from the night before haunted him—*I am not entirely sure you see yourself as lovable.*

No, he did not.

But then, the two men in this room ensured he was constantly reminded of that fact. Such had always been their way. To make it clear that no one could love a boy sired by a monster such as his father.

"Say what ye need tae say and then remove your sorry carcass from my house," Hadley snapped, eyes narrowed in fury.

Kendall stilled at the earl's words. A small frown dented his brow. Why was Hadley not gloating?

This was the man's moment of triumph. The point at which he dashed all of Kendall's future hopes and raised his daughter to a duchess's coronet.

But as he pondered the man, Kendall realized that Hadley looked more like a caged dog waiting for the order to kill. As if he longed to tear Kendall limb from limb.

He glanced toward Sir Rafe, but his brother's expression was carefully blank. A trick no doubt learned at their father's knee.

"I believe you know my intentions here, Hadley." Kendall pushed the syllables off his numb tongue. "Though entirely accidental, your eldest daughter and I were discovered in a compromising situation. Despite your lowering opinion, I am a gentleman in all respects. Therefore, I formally request Lady Isolde's hand in marriage."

"No." Hadley pointed at the door. "Now get the hell out!"

Kendall stood, stunned and blinking.

Had Hadley . . .

No?

But . . .

Kendall looked to Sir Rafe again but found nothing there to explain Hadley's response.

"Lady Isolde will be ruined." Kendall could hear the bafflement in his tone.

"Aye, no thanks tae you," Hadley returned. "But ruined is better than marriage to a brutish man who will turn her life into a living nightmare!"

"Andrew," Sir Rafe reproached quietly. "Have a care."

"*Och*, I will have a care over this *eejit's* dead body!" Hadley jabbed a finger at Kendall.

"Is this also Lady Isolde's opinion?" Kendall's brows drew down in confusion. "She refuses my suit?"

What was Hadley's game here?

"Aye!" Hadley spat.

"I don't know," Sir Rafe said at the same time.

Kendall looked between the two men. "Well, which is it? As this moment will define the remainder of Lady Isolde's life—as well as my own—I should like to hear from the lady herself."

"No," Hadley repeated. "I am her father, and she will abide by my decision."

That seemed . . . . unusually heavy-handed for the earl.

Kendall's frown deepened, his mind racing to connect the dots.

Why would Hadley bring him to this point, only to toss him out on his ear?

It made no sense, unless . . .

"Was this your plan all along?" Kendall asked, voice rising. "Publicly accuse me of kidnapping your daughter—which truly is an appalling breach of conduct—and then humiliate me further by refusing my suit and blackening my name? Thus ensuring I am declared *persona non grata* among the *ton*, like my father, and destroying my political clout." This *had* to be a gambit on Hadley's part. The puzzle pieces slotted too neatly into place. "I have long known you to be a scoundrel, Hadley, but this is cruel, even for yourself. Is your hatred of me so strong, you would see your eldest daughter ruined and banished out of spite?!"

Hadley turned a rather alarming shade of red. If the earl had been an engine, steam would be billowing out his ears.

"Cruel? Hatred?" the earl repeated, tone low and menacing. He rounded his desk, barreling toward Kendall.

They were of a height, he and Hadley. But the older man had to have an additional forty pounds of pure muscle on his frame.

"Yes," Kendall squared his shoulders. He would not be intimidated by this Scot. "You are renowned for your adoration of your wife and children. And yet this—" He motioned to the space between them. "—appears the very opposite of love. Why would you see your daughter disgraced in such a fashion when other solutions exist?"

"Do ye even ken what love is, boy?!" Hadley roared in Kendall's face. "You, who were raised by that abomination of a father! You, who have done nothing but plague us all with your damn high-handed conceit and petty need for revenge over slights that—"

"Andrew!" Sir Rafe pressed a hand to his friend's shoulder, urging him back. "He is goading ye. Let it go." Sir Rafe locked eyes with Kendall, the white scar on his cheek pulling tight. "He's not worth it."

His brother's words knocked the air from Kendall's lungs as sure as a pugilist's fist.

The syllables taunted him.

Not worth it, not worth it, not worth it . . .

The past reared up. Another time. Another place. A different man with Sir Rafe's face and a whip in his hand.

"Get up, you miserable milksop." His father delivered a swift kick to Tristan's belly. *"You are bleeding on the carpet, and we both know you are not worth its price."*

As he always had, Kendall breathed through the pain and then buried it deep.

Hadley shook his friend's hand free and fixed Kendall with a baleful stare.

"I love my daughter more than life itself, boy," the earl rasped. "'Tis why I will fight tooth and nail to spare her the heartache of marriage to a man like yourself. We all know how your father treated his wives—"

Kendall's tether snapped.

"I am *not* my father! The comparison offends me more than I can express. In case you have forgotten, Hadley, Sir Rafe and I share the same sire! I have never and *will* never disrespect a woman, wife or no. But then, you have *always* conflated me with my father. We are not, in any respect, the same sort of gentleman! Perhaps, you should begin seeing me in that light."

"If ye want me to see ye differently, then ye need to behave differently!" Hadley cracked. "Drag your carcass out of Old Kendall's shadow!"

"Gentleman." Sir Rafe stepped between them. "I believe we have veered off track. There is the matter of Lady Isolde to address."

Grunting, Hadley turned back to his desk. "I have already said my piece with regards tae that, Rafe. I will be damned if I ever call this man my son." He gave Kendall his back, staring out the window.

Kendall clenched his fists, unsure what to do.

He didn't wish to marry Lady Isolde any more than Hadley wished him as a son-in-law.

And yet . . .

"Before I bear the dishonor and ignominy of having ruined an earl's daughter, I would like to hear from her own lips that she will not have me. As I said, I do not harm women, and it pains me that Lady Isolde will suffer for an innocent mistake," Kendall all but growled. "As the brunt of this disgrace will fall unfairly on her, I want to ensure that this is, indeed, her choice."

Silence reigned for a long moment.

Sir Rafe looked between Hadley and Kendall, a grudging sort of respect on his face.

"I will fetch Lady Isolde." Sir Rafe crossed to the door.

The clock on the mantel ticked away the seconds.

It felt rather like the countdown to a firing squad.

Kendall clenched and unclenched his fists.

Finally, the door reopened, admitting Sir Rafe and Lady Isolde.

Her blue gaze flew instantly to Kendall's.

I should loathe the very sight of her, he mused.

And yet . . .

He couldn't help but notice how the cream muslin of her dress contrasted with the pale softness of her skin and the gleam of her hair.

The purple smudges atop her cheekbones indicated a night as sleepless as his own. Worse, she had been weeping. The red rimming her eyes could mean nothing else.

But weeping . . . why? Over the prospect of ruination? Or having to become his wife?

It was nearly unfathomable at this juncture—at the point his life disintegrated into a pile of dust—that he *still* found her beautiful. That an infinitesimal part of his soul sighed in relief that finally—*finally*—she might be his wife.

"Ye called for me, Papa?" Lady Isolde said to Hadley.

The earl turned, and the look of love and desperation he gave his daughter hitched Kendall's breath.

Hadley pointed at the duke. "I need ye tae tell this man tae go to the devil, Izzy."

Kendall's mind snagged on the nickname.

Izzy.

It spoke of late-night cuddles and firelit giggles. Of love given and received.

Of a reality he had never experienced.

ISOLDE PRESSED A hand to her midriff, willing her stomach not to rebel.

She had been sitting on the edge of the sofa in the drawing-room, her mother's hand tight in her own, listening to the raised male voices in her father's study.

Kendall had arrived promptly on their doorstep this morning. All of them understood the purpose of his visit.

How Isolde detested this—her sisters' weeping, her brothers' ranting, the sorrow in her mother's eyes.

And now, standing in Hadley's study, the anguish etched on her father's expression.

"P-pardon?" she asked her father.

"I need ye tae send Kendall away with a flea in his ear." Hadley pointed again at the duke.

Isolde paused, looking between her father, Uncle Rafe, and Kendall.

She knew her father was opposed to a marriage between herself and the duke.

But was she not going to be permitted to even speak with Kendall? To hear his proposal for herself?

"I should like to speak with Lady Isolde alone, if possible," Kendall said, his shoulders rigid and lips scarcely moving.

"Nae," Hadley snapped.

"Of course," Isolde said at the same time.

Her father glared at the duke, color rising along his collar.

"Papa," she said, "ye ken that I must speak with His Grace myself. It is how things are done."

"Izzy," Hadley rasped, hand lifting as if he would reach for her, anything to stem the rushing tide of this situation.

Isolde feared her heart would crack in her chest.

"Come, Andrew." Rafe motioned for Hadley to leave. "Let us give Kendall and Lady Isolde a moment to discuss their possible future."

Gritting his teeth, her father followed.

"Five minutes," he hissed to Kendall. "Any more and I'll personally toss ye into the street!"

The men filed out, the study door clacking shut. Briefly, Isolde wondered if her coffin lid might make a similar sound when closed.

Finally, she properly studied her prospective bridegroom.

Gracious.

He appeared a wreck.

Yes, he was starched and pomaded as usual. But there was a haggard droop to his eyelids and a faint rash on his neck, as if a razor had been scraped too roughly over his skin.

More to the point, his famed hauteur was notably absent. Instead, he seemed nearly an automaton, so stiff was his bearing.

"Ye wished tae speak with me, Your Grace?" she managed to say.

Her words shook him from his stupor.

He spared a fleeting glance for her before audibly swallowing.

Then, Kendall did something Isolde would have considered unthinkable even five minutes past—

He ran a shaking hand through his gray hair, disheveling the lot and completely undoing his valet's efforts. A lock tumbled across his forehead and curled against his temple, half covering one eye.

Disheveled looked good on him, she noted. It took his appearance from *sternly controlling* to *dangerously rakish.*

"I don't . . ." he began, licking his bottom lip. "That is . . ."

He swallowed again and darted her a second glance that was, well, hesitant. Unsure, even.

Oh.

Hesitant and *unsure* looked even better on him.

Was this the softer man that Allie knew? The one that Isolde had glimpsed in the ice house?

Letting out a deep breath, he spoke again, "Despite the accidental nature of our entrapment, the consequences remain the same."

"Aye."

"I have respectfully requested your hand in marriage, Lady Isolde. Your father has denied that request."

"I suspected as much."

"But as I fear you will bear an unfair portion of this decision"—*deep breath*—"I wished to put the question directly to yourself."

He said the words woodenly, gaze locked on the floor. But he fidgeted as he spoke—his hands clasped before him, then behind, then finally shoved into his trouser pockets, as if helpless to know where to put them.

"And what . . . what question was that?"

She needed to hear him say the words, she realized. To know that there would be no misunderstanding.

No turning back.

He lifted his head, dark eyes meeting hers, shoulders squared, expression clear and intent.

"Lady Isolde," his voice quiet but firm, "will you do me the honor of becoming my wife?"

She saw it then, buried deep in his soft brown eyes—

The faintest glimmer of that earnest boy in Montacute's garden. The one who had flirted with her, volleying ripostes and winning her laugh. The one who had kissed her wrist with such electric fervor.

She had liked that boy very much.

And so, it was almost to that boy she replied.

The only response she could give that would save her own honor and that of her family.

Straightening her spine, she met the duke's gaze.

"Yes, Your Grace"—her heartbeat a deafening roar—"I will marry ye."

14

The Duke of Kendall has suffered a spectacular tumble from grace. Though rumors swirl that he will soon marry Lady Isolde Langston, the stench of indiscretion will haunt the dukedom for years. The Queen has made her displeasure known, describing both His Grace and Lady Isolde's behavior as reprehensible.

Regardless, the investigations Kendall set in motion continue. The trial for Mr. Stephen Jarvis will begin next week, and the impeachment vote for Lord Hadley is still outstanding.

—ARTICLE IN *The London Times*

Kendall scarcely saw his bride-to-be in the two weeks leading up to their wedding.

Most of his time was spent with solicitors, hammering out the marriage contracts with Hadley. The earl was ruthless in protecting his daughter's interests. And Kendall was too stunned, too numb to do anything but concede to Hadley's demands.

Kendall expected that someday he would feel profound shame for his lack of spine, but for now, it was all he could do to breathe through each day.

Everything tasted of a funeral pyre—ash and destruction.

One by one, gentlemen who he had considered friends—or at least friendly colleagues—sent him polite notes severing their acquaintance: Lord John Russell, Lord Palmerston, Lord Aberdeen . . .

The list went on.

Kendall was a sinking ship that others abandoned in panic, eager to escape the wreckage.

No invitations arrived at Gilbert House. At least, none from Peers whom he respected.

A visit to White's brought wide-eyed stares and whispered conversations as he passed.

Kendall did not return.

He ceased his daily meetings with his secretaries, as there was now no diary to discuss.

Not even the commencement of Stephen Jarvis's trial cheered him.

Instead, Kendall exhausted himself with his fencing master, attempting to purge the despair in his veins.

Once a week, he darkened the entry hall of Hadley's townhouse to visit his betrothed.

There, Kendall sat opposite Lady Isolde in Hadley's well-appointed drawing-room, Lady Hadley pouring tea as they aimlessly talked about the weather—*Hadn't the wind been chilly of late? Would the wisteria blooms endure?*

Generally, his betrothed looked at her hands or the fire or the window, her expression dull and un-Isolde-like. As if, like him, she struggled to accommodate the abrupt change in their circumstances. But also, like him, she was polite and congenial and faintly . . . warm. Traits that were similarly un-Isolde-like but more positive in nature.

Lady Isolde was every whit as beautiful—auburn hair framing her face, waist trim in her neatly-pressed gown—and he found himself staring even more intently, memorizing each tiny thing. A patch of freckles beside her right ear formed a near-perfect circle and the tips of her eyelashes gleamed red-gold. Some appendage always had to be in motion—a bouncing foot or tapping finger. And despite her distress, that snuffling noise he adored remained.

Could his attraction form a viable foundation for marriage? A marriage in which—if he and Isolde negotiated a truce—they might eventually reach a sort of tentative friendship?

He felt a trace of hope at the thought.

Mostly, however, Kendall sat in the quiet of his library—the Library of Shame as he now thought of it—reminding himself that getting drunk at ten in the morning was probably ill-advised. The mantel clock ticked relentlessly, a cruel memorial to the days when time had mattered.

It was simply unbearable . . . witnessing every last goal and aspiration crumble to dust.

But then, he had always known this would be the result, were he to marry Lady Isolde. The circumstances of their marriage aside, allying himself with her scandalous reputation ensured that his own character and prospects suffered. It was why he had so stringently resisted the love-potion-fueled temptation of her.

Yet, had he succumbed *before* ducking with her into that ice house, he would have courted her properly. And so when faced with the loss of reputation and political clout, he could have claimed her heart as compensation.

Now . . . he had neither reputation nor Lady Isolde's affections. Though again, that faint hope glowed, suggesting that perhaps attachment and regard might grow with time.

Allie's staunch presence proved a balm.

His twin joined him in his Library of Shame, occasionally distracting him with raucous tales of her growing-up years in Italy and reading him humorous letters from her husband, Ethan.

Kendall would reply with appreciative syllables.

But Allie did permit one unwelcome caller to disrupt his wallowing.

"I am not at home to persons such as you," Kendall grunted as the butler led Sir Rafe, hat in hand, into the library. "Please leave."

"I will. Once I've had my say." His brother looked around the room with interest. "Do ye still keep liquor in the hidden cabinet like our father?" He nodded toward the bookcase to the right of the window—the one where a panel of false book spines pulled out to reveal a small cavity.

Kendall hated this. Hated that Sir Rafe probably knew Gilbert House better than himself. That he shared so much history with his half-brother, and yet . . . none at all.

"No," Kendall lied, folding his arms across his chest. "I've filled it with the bones of my enemies."

Sir Rafe managed a wan smile, the upturn of his lips tugging on the white scar stretching from his temple to his cheekbone. He paced over to the window.

"I like the new drapes." He touched the blue velvet that Kendall's housekeeper had changed two summers past.

"I'm told the color compliments the similarly-new carpet. Now, why are you here?"

His brother turned back to him, eyebrow raised, rotating his hat in his palms. "Several years ago, I purchased an estate along the coast north of Inverness. It is a lovely old place with expansive sea views from nearly every window. Dunhelm Castle, it is called."

Kendall merely stared at the man, unsure how this fact pertained to anything.

Sir Rafe did not misunderstand Kendall's annoyed confusion. "I am returning there in a fortnight and will remain in residence for the remainder of the summer."

A long beat of silence.

"And you took the time to inform me of this . . ." Kendall trailed off.

"Because I wanted ye tae understand that ye are welcome at my door. Should ye ever decide tae visit."

Kendall blinked.

That would never happen.

And so he said as much: "That will never happen."

"As ye wish." Sir Rafe turned his hat again. "I ken that the events of the past week have been upsetting, for both yourself and—"

A bark of caustic laughter escaped before Kendall could squelch it. "And so you couldn't ignore an opportunity to gloat in triumph?"

"Nae, ye may hold myself in low esteem, but I am hardly that sort of gentleman. I wanted tae offer ye an olive branch." That same wan smile touched Sir Rafe's lips. "I have always, and will always, consider yourself tae be family."

"We both know that to be a lie." Kendall's tone dripped acid. "I recall someone recently stating I am not *worth it*. No gentleman willingly welcomes those he deems *unworthy* into his home, much less his intimate life."

The hat in Sir Rafe's hands stilled. "I . . . I must apologize for those words, Kendall. They were spoken thoughtlessly in the moment, and I have regretted them ever since. I most certainly did not mean them."

"How typical of you," Kendall sneered. "Breezily speaking your truest thoughts and then ignoring the very real consequences of them."

"Again, I apologize for my lapse. I recognize that our heartless sire kept ye isolated. Ye were only permitted a few weeks at Eton before he called ye home—"

"No thanks to yourself!" Kendall snapped. "Again: Words. Have. Consequences." He enunciated each syllable with militant precision.

Sir Rafe acknowledged the hit, his head rearing back.

"Ye were allowed tae go to Oxford," his brother said, "but ye made no friends. Not a one."

Ye made no friends.

The harsh truth in those spare words lashed Kendall's psyche. The past week had definitively proved that, aside from his sister, there was not a single other human being on the planet who cared a fig for his continued existence.

"Get out!" Kendall strode toward the door, intent on calling a brace of footmen to drag his brother to the street. "I refuse to be so mocked and humiliated in my own home!"

"Ye made no friends because Kendall chased off anyone friendly to yourself," Sir Rafe's voice called from behind. "Your lack of friends had nothing tae do with yourself, and everything to do with our father's desperate need for control."

Kendall stilled, chest heaving.

What idiocy.

Surely, that was a falsehood.

Frowning, he turned to look back at his brother.

Sir Rafe continued, "Old Kendall knew that the friends I made at university—Hadley being chief among them—were my ultimate source of strength. And it was those relationships, those friends, that caused our father's downfall in the end. Our sire was a vicious, malevolent man, but he was not an unintelligent one: He learned from his mistakes with me and ensured that you never formed alliances outside of himself. Your *protection officer*"—he leaned on the descriptor with heavy mockery— "guaranteed it. Kendall deliberately kept ye isolated and alone."

Kendall's thoughts turned inward.

Memories rose.

Laughing over dinner with a gentleman, only to have the man shun him two days later.

Inviting another potential friend to go rowing along the Thames, only to have the man fail to arrive at the appointed time.

Talking animatedly with an interesting gentleman each day before lecture, only to have the man be called abruptly home after three weeks.

An endless stream of unanswered letters and unreturned social calls.

Over and over, such events occurred until Kendall abandoned trying to make friends altogether.

He had always assumed it was his title and stiff personality that others found repellent. Both were barriers to any sort of true relationship.

And yet . . .

His brother's words made . . . a plausible, terrible sort of sense. Such actions were precisely what their father would have done.

A miasma of long-buried emotions churned in Kendall's abdomen— grief, loneliness, rejection.

Sir Rafe watched Kendall with quiet patience. With *compassion*, he realized. The emotion on his brother's face was compassion.

"Do not believe the lies that man told ye," Sir Rafe said. "Ye can overcome the horror of your upbringing. Ye *can* find peace and joy and even love in your life. As I have told ye in the past, the measure of a man is greater than mere political power."

The words abraded the ends of Kendall's nerves. He had heard enough. "That is your opinion. Careless words, again."

"No," his brother shook his head, "it is a fact. I have always looked upon ye a bit like a son—"

And there it was—the end of Kendall's tether.

"You have *never* been a father to me," he spat, voice low and vibrating with rage. He pointed at the door. "Get out."

How dare this man enter his house to deliver a pathetic excuse of an apology and unsubstantiated theories, capping the whole with a lecture.

And then to imply that he had been any sort of father-figure . . .

Sir Rafe nodded. "At the very least, think about visiting. I shall extend the offer to Lady Isolde, as well."

Wrenching the door open, Kendall pointed into the entry hall. "Get. Out!"

KENDALL WAS STILL fuming several hours later when Allie found him slumped into his favorite—though *favorite* was far too-cheerful a word for his mood—library chair.

"I am not forgiving you for permitting that bastard of a brother of ours to speak with me," he said without preamble.

"He merely wished to extend an invitation. There is no harm in that."

"No harm?!" Kendall's voice rose.

He hated speaking with Sir Rafe. It always left him . . . unmoored.

Kendall deliberately kept ye isolated and alone. Sir Rafe's words still hung in the air. And when combined with Allie's suggestion that Kendall saw himself as unloveable . . .

Rubbish.

Or rather, it wasn't rubbish. It was all likely true.

But it was rubbish to think upon. What was the point? The fact of his sire's cruelty was long established.

Kendall had survived. And he would have his revenge once he obliterated his father's memory. Or he *would* have. That dream was dust now.

Loss swamped him anew.

He was rather sure he could feel a headache forming behind his eyes.

"Enough, Tristan," Allie sighed. "I do not wish to argue with you."

Kendall squinted at his sister. She appeared more . . . subdued than usual. Something was wrong.

"What is it?" he asked.

"You know something is troubling me." She met his gaze, a soft smile tugging at her lips. "Twin sense." She tapped her temple. "You *do* have it."

He made a rolling motion with this hand.

Allie didn't make him wait. "I've been thinking lately . . . you have a choice before you right now, Brother."

"A choice?"

"Yes. You are grieving the loss of the world you knew. Mourning the future you thought to have."

"Your point . . . aside from rubbing salt into my wounds?"

"I hate seeing you in such pain. It hurts." Allie rubbed the heel of her hand against her breast bone. "But I know from my own past that pain can be a catalyst for change . . . a good sort of change."

"Good? How is pain *ever* a good thing?"

"Obviously, the pain itself is not"—she rolled her eyes—"but the fruits of the pain do not have to be negative. 'Tis part of the reason I permitted Sir Rafe to speak with you. Our father was a terrible man, but Sir Rafe let hatred and pain change him for the better."

"So you claim."

"No, I think that anyone looking in on Sir Rafe's life would see a man who is loved and loves in return. A man happy and content with his lot."

"But he is nothing and no one. The bastard son of a duke. A man who has all but retired from Polite Society. How is that success?"

"To echo Sir Rafe's own words, power is only one measure of success. There are other criterion."

Kendall knew this. He wasn't an imbecile.

"But I don't *want* other criterion. I want power. I want revenge. I want Iso—" Damn his ungovernable heart for battling to insert Isolde here. He inhaled. "But my dreams are now turned to ash."

"Then be a phoenix, Tristan. Rise from the ashes."

Rise from the ashes? He would prefer to return to the heights he had already summited.

"And remember, no matter what our father may have taught you— no matter your prior experiences—you *are* worthy of love. You are *capable* of love." She paused. "In short, you are all sorts of lovable."

Kendall snorted. "Being capable of love will in no way ensure I can build a real marriage with Lady Isolde."

"Nonsense! Let the pain you are feeling now work on you. Let it push you to become a better man."

"A better man?" He fixed her with a baleful glare. "Am I not sufficient as I am?"

Allie sighed. "A softer man. One of more heart. Gentler. Kinder. The sort of man that the boy Tristan admired. The man he might have become without our father's monstrous interference."

Kendall lolled his head against the back of his chair. "As I have said too many times to count, Allie, that tender-hearted boy is long dead. Quashed under the heel of our father's brutality. He lives only in your fanciful memories."

"I disagree. You reverted from *Kendall* to *Tristan* for me. I think it is time you rediscovered that boy for yourself. The Tristan I know would be a caring husband to a wife."

Wife.

As in, husband and wife.

Himself and Lady Isolde.

It still felt surreal.

That Kendall would marry her. That he would take her to his bed. That she would be the mother of his future heir.

That five years from now, it would be Isolde's blue eyes that met his at the opposite end of the enormous dining room table of Hawthorn.

The sensations banding his lungs felt impossibly contradictory.

Horror over how thoroughly his life had deviated from its intended course.

But also . . .

Perhaps . . .

Did he feel that same minuscule thread of hope? Of anticipation?

Lady Isolde would be his *wife*!

He would know her intimately—her thoughts, her routines, her mannerisms. Hers would be the voice to greet him first most mornings. The one to perhaps inquire about his day.

And, not insignificantly, he would finally see her hair tumbled in all its glory, learn the feel of her skin, the taste of her lips—

The naive boy he had been that afternoon in Montacute's garden would have crowed in triumph. Ecstatic to finally make this lady his wife.

Perhaps . . . in some unforeseen way . . . this marriage wouldn't be the Greek tragedy he feared.

"Allie—"

"And don't bollocks things up with Isolde." His sister frowned. "Or rather, when you do inevitably bollocks things up, remember to apologize. In order for your marriage to work, you will need to learn how to swallow your formidable ducal pride and say *I'm sorry*."

Kendall glared at his sister. "I know how to apologize."

"That's good!" She grinned. "Because something tells me you are about to get a lot of practice at it."

15

. . . How shall we bear it, my Jane? To watch our bonnie Izzy marry that tyrant with an ice-pick heart? I feel I am living a father's worst nightmare—to knowingly hand over a daughter to a man who will mistreat her.

—PRIVATE NOTE FROM LORD HADLEY TO LADY HADLEY

Please, Izzy," her father murmured. "Please reconsider this course of action."

They sat side-by-side on the sofa in the library—each with a tumbler of whisky in hand—watching the fire burn low.

Tomorrow morning, Isolde would wed the Duke of Kendall via special license—a joint wedding with Catriona and Lord Barnaby, who had graciously agreed to share their wedding day.

Tomorrow night, Isolde would be living somewhere else entirely.

She swallowed back the tears which threatened once more.

All she did was *greit* these days.

"I would do anything tae spare ye this," Hadley continued. "I fear ye don't understand the deep repercussions that await—layer upon layer of—"

"I don't repent of my decision, Papa," she whispered.

And even given everything—the unknown repercussions her father dreaded—she still had no regrets.

Marriage to Kendall remained the only solution. The only way to right the harm that her heedless actions had caused.

"Catriona will wed her Barnie tomorrow, along with myself and Kendall. So there will be genuine happiness and celebration," Isolde added, once again feeling relief that, with her betrothal to Kendall, Lord Alderton had agreed to go forward with Barnie's marriage to Catriona. After all, Alderton's grandchildren would now be first cousins with the next Duke of Kendall.

And how much easier to celebrate the day with Catriona. To let her sister's delirious joy carry them through.

How odd . . . to be happier for her sister's wedding than for her own.

Lady Hadley had been the one to propose joint nuptials. "We have already prepared so much for Catriona's wedding. Why not celebrate Isolde at the same time?"

Catriona's eyes had lit with delight. "Oh! I should adore that!"

Lady Hadley had exchanged another of those sad smiles with Isolde over Catriona's head.

But Isolde had understood what her mother left unsaid.

It was difficult enough for Isolde to marry Kendall—*marry Kendall!*—but to have to smile and pretend cheer for the well-wishers in attendance . . .

Or worse, endure comfort and pity, as if the event were more funeral than wedding.

Lady Hadley was resigned to Isolde's marriage. As the daughter of a powerful English duke, her mother understood the rules of their world better than most.

Her father, however . . .

"I can think of no one I would like ye tae marry less than Kendall," he said, relaxing into the sofa beside her. Isolde feared that additional gray had appeared overnight in his hair and whiskers. Her poor father had aged a decade in mere weeks. "Are ye sure there isn't a footman in the house ye fancy more? Anyone at all ye could elope with? It breaks me tae think of ye tethered to a blackguard like Kendall, Izzy. I willnae . . ." His voice broke. "He's powerful, and I willnae be able tae protect ye. He will own yourself, and I fear—"

"Hush, Papa." Isolde placed her hand over his. "All will be well. I know I tend to act rashly, but I have carefully weighed all other outcomes. For myself and His Grace. For our family and Catriona. This course is the correct one."

Granted, Isolde had received some encouragement in her decision.

Every day since Isolde's betrothal, Allie had called at Hadley's townhouse, and more than once, their conversations had devolved to her twin.

"I know I am repeating myself," Allie had said just two days past, "but a caring heart rests beneath Tristan's stern exterior. He was the brother who would hug me close until the terror of a nightmare faded. The one who would read me stories when I was unwell. He merely needs to remember the person he once was. I think you will help him rediscover that boy."

"Do ye ken that tae be possible? He so greatly dislikes myself."

"Give him time." Allie hugged her tight. "And remember: We shall be sisters! Can you imagine? You shall have to visit often."

The thought of Allie as a sister cheered Isolde immeasurably.

She recounted details of her conversation with Allie for her father, ending with, "No one knows Kendall better than Lady Allegra, and she assures me he has an honorable heart—"

"Oh, Izzy," her father choked. "Do not assume it is *honor* that drove Kendall tae offer for your hand. He has tae marry ye, or face the wrath of Lords."

"Papa, ye ken that isn't entirely true. His Grace has made an effort tae visit me and take tea with myself and Mamma." Kendall had remained reticent and stoic throughout, watching her intently with his dark eyes. But he *had* visited. "Those actions are not selfish in nature. Kendall does take care tae be seen as a gentleman."

"*To be seen,*" her father repeated. "That is the key phrase there. What Kendall does behind closed doors, where actions are not seen, however—" He drifted off ominously, face twisting in misery. "Please, Izzy. I can name other solutions beyond this one."

He was correct, of course.

But Isolde knew this was the only choice that saved the family honor. That would see her brothers and sisters well-married. That would gain her father an ally in Kendall, rather than an enemy. After all, now the men were tied by blood, and any missiles they figuratively launched at each other would potentially harm the children of Isolde's union.

Her marriage was the only way to bring peace.

Jarvis's trial for fraud was already underway. The jury would likely hand down a verdict within the next few days. Her father's impeachment still hung on a knife's edge. Mac had confided earlier that a vote in Commons could go either way.

"I ken that, Papa, I do. But I am choosing this path," she replied firmly, pushing back her own misgivings. "And ye have ensured my future is well-guarded."

That was true.

Hadley had been ruthless with the marriage contracts.

"I have," he agreed, swirling his whisky. "Your dowry is ample; however, Kendall receives none of it outright. Everything will go to yourself and your . . . children."

Her poor father nearly choked on the word *children*.

She took in a slow breath, trying very hard *not* to think upon the making of said children. As an educated woman well-past the years of naiveté, she knew how a man and woman conceived a child.

It was simply impossible to imagine Kendall as the man in that scenario.

Or rather, she *could* picture Kendall in some dimly-lit bedchamber— and had many times in the days since their betrothal—but in all her imaginings, he was never tender or affectionate.

No. Other adjectives surfaced. Cold. Clinical. Unfeeling.

Words that *did* accurately describe him.

Though . . . Kendall had been none of those things when he held her in the ice house. Briefly, she relived the breadth of his chest, the tender press of his arm around her.

Isolde would happily spend more time with that caring man.

Anxiety fluttered in her stomach. And maybe . . . a wee bit of hope.

Perhaps with patience on her part, she could coax more warmth to Kendall's surface, as Allie suggested.

"All will come right, Papa," Isolde said, hoping if she said the words enough, she could will them into being. "Catriona is deliriously happy, and tomorrow will be a joyful day. Ye shall see."

Her father grunted, tossing back his whisky.

Isolde, of course, did not say the day would be a joyful one for herself.

But knowing her decision ensured those she loved remained safe . . . that would be reward enough.

WHEN KENDALL HAD imagined his marriage—albeit a moment he had rarely envisioned—it had always been a staid affair. Polite applause. Restrained guests. A solemn ceremony followed by an intimate breakfast at Gilbert House or Hawthorn.

The bride in question had *always* been a woman of reserved elegance and impeccable behavior.

His actual marriage, however, involved none of this.

At the moment, he found himself seated beside his new bride—a woman whose behavior was anything but reserved—in the Earl of Hadley's ballroom-turned-dining-hall, listening as raucous Scots toasted the newly-married Lord and Lady Barnaby.

Scarcely anyone spared a glance for the new Duke and Duchess of Kendall, seated quietly beside one another at one end of the table.

Kendall remembered little of the ceremony itself. Just the dreadful finality of his decision. The tremor in Lady Isolde's hand as he slid a simple gold band onto her left ring finger. The fleeting press of his mouth to hers.

It lingered with him still—the lift in her chest, the petal softness of her lips . . .

He took in a steadying breath and reached for his wine glass.

The only positive aspect of his marriage would be having Lady Isolde—no, Isolde, Duchess of Kendall—in his bed.

Would she welcome him there, he wondered?

Thoughts of her—thoughts he had spent years holding at bay—had kept him awake the previous two nights, restless and rather fevered with desire.

He would never force her. The very idea of Isolde stoically enduring the consummation of their marriage was so distasteful, so repugnant . . .

No.

Even as a boy—when he was still Tristan—he had regarded the act of sexual union as something more than a base urge to be slaked. Touch and affection were so rare in his life, that the notion of accepting them from a woman's hand . . . the vulnerability of the moment, the intimacy . . .

The prospect had felt laden with importance. Reverence, even.

His sire had found Tristan's prudishness repulsive. He wanted his son to flaunt his virility—to swive his way through London and then swagger into White's, boasting of his conquests.

To that end, Old Kendall had marched Tristan to a brothel in Covent Garden on his sixteenth birthday. For himself, Tristan had been apprehensive and, well, curious. He was a sixteen-year-old boy, after all. He had faced the evening hoping to discover connection. To feel . . . well, not *love*, naturally, but something akin to it. Gentleness, perhaps. Tenderness.

Instead, the whole affair had been unspeakably tawdry.

The girl his father forced him to . . .

And she *had* been a girl, surely no older than Tristan himself, but skilled and experienced . . . with eyes so *old*, so seeing, he still shivered to remember them.

For her, he had simply been a client. A purchaser of her wares. Yet one more faceless man to whom she sold her body. Another jangle of coin in her purse for food in her belly and a roof overhead.

An act that Tristan believed would be transcendent and loving became violating instead—of his body, of his dignity. His skin crawled at the memory.

He had vomited into the chamberpot afterward.

And then gave the poor girl another coin for not informing his father.

After that night, he had vowed he would never again exchange anything—money, power, protection—for a place in a woman's bed. He refused to purchase a woman's body in any fashion. Future liaisons would be freely given.

Of course, that vow extended to his own wife, as well.

Kendall dared a glance at Isolde beside him. She studied the merriment around them, the food on her plate untouched. Occasionally, she would pick up her fork and push a morsel of wedding cake around the perimeter.

"Are you well, Duchess?" he asked.

She startled . . . at his nearness or hearing herself referred to as *Duchess*, he could not say.

"Of course." She forced a smile. But not her true one . . . the radiant smile that never failed to arrest his lungs.

She set down her fork and folded her hands in her lap.

He hated seeing her like this, he realized. So unlike the spirited woman he knew from Montacute's garden, his library, the soirée, the ice house. That lady was practically a force of nature. A whipping breeze of energy and vitality that, quite literally, could steal his breath.

How could he bring her back?

A moment later, Lady Hadley approached to claim Isolde, stating it was time to change into her traveling costume. Kendall and Isolde would leave straight away for St. Catharine's Dock where Kendall kept his steamship, the *SS Statesman*, berthed.

He watched Isolde trail her mother across the room. Guests stopped them, wishing his bride well and embracing her, bestowing brief kisses upon her cheek.

Never had Kendall seen it so clearly . . . the vast web of love that surrounded his new bride. What would his life have been like had he been raised with such unconditional affection?

It hardly mattered now, he supposed. He would always remain an interloper within his bride's family—a witness to the warmth they shared, but never a part of it. Instead, he would be seen as a destroyer of love. As the monster who had tainted their happiness.

It was yet one more misery to bear.

Kendall rose, intent on changing his tailcoat for a traveling frock coat.

But he had only taken three steps before Hadley accosted him.

"A word, Duke," he said, nodding for Kendall to follow him into a hallway off the ballroom.

"Hadley." Kendall kept his expression neutral as he faced his new father-in-law.

Folding his arms, the earl fixed Kendall with a steely-gaze, his blue eyes so reminiscent of his daughter's. "I don't know what your game has been these past months. Ye have hounded me at every turn and now this." He waved a hand toward the ballroom.

"Your point?" Kendall asked.

"I never cared about this mess with Jarvis. That is merely business. But my Isolde—" The earl's voice broke. His chest heaved. "In her, ye have taken something of mine I value more than my name and my freedom. More than my lucre. More than life itself." Hadley closed the distance between them, his eyes drilling Kendall. "If ye hurt her, damage one hair on her head, or put a shadow of a misery on her face—"

He paused, giving Kendall a truly terrifying look—the sort of expression many an Englishman had likely seen on a Scot poised to deliver a killing blow.

"I dinnae fear Newgate, Duke." Menace laced Hadley's words. "Choose wisely."

And with that, the earl pivoted and returned to his guests.

In the end, Allie was the only person in attendance to share kind words. As Kendall watched Isolde tearfully hug her parents goodbye, Allie wrapped her own arms around him.

"I leave tomorrow for Scotland and Ethan. Write to me, Tristan." She reached up to press a kiss on his cheek. "And in the meantime, hope for good things. Apologize when you are wrong. Let the pain forge pathways of love in your heart. Believe you can be a better man—one that the boy Tristan would have liked to become."

But given the hollow ache in his chest, Kendall wondered if such optimistic change was possible.

16

Lord and Lady Hadley saw two daughters married this morning. Lady Catriona Langston wed Lord Barnaby, eldest son of the Earl of Alderton. Meanwhile, Lady Isolde Langston married the Duke of Kendall. We wish both couples every happiness.

—ARTICLE IN *THE LONDON TATTLER*

The agonizing silence inside the duke's opulent town coach clawed at Isolde's already frayed nerves.

Opposite her, Kendall appeared the very definition of ducal power and affluence—fitting, she supposed, for their nuptials. But his ruthlessly pomaded hair, starched neckcloth, and pressed frock coat felt more like armor than clothing. As if he needed to protect the softness his sister swore rested inside him.

Or perhaps that was merely Isolde's own fanciful thinking.

The weight of his gold band sat cold and unforgiving on her left hand.

They both watched the world roll past the carriage window . . . ladies strolling along the pavement, hawkers calling their wares, humanity going about a sunny London afternoon. People whose lives had not just been upended.

Isolde took in a steadying breath.

Kendall was her husband.

Husband!

Isolde knew he possessed an inner warmth. She had caught glimpses of it beyond Allie's assurances. She *had.*

She clung to the hope of that warmth with both hands.

"It was a lovely ceremony and breakfast." She attempted to begin a conversation. Anything to thaw the taut silence between them.

"Yes," he replied softly, his gaze not meeting hers. But his hand opened and closed to a fist on his thigh. The only hint that agitation roiled beneath his calm exterior.

Armor, indeed.

Oddly, Isolde found it a wee bit heartening. They were both struggling to adjust to their new reality.

"I understand we are tae board your steamship?"

"Yes."

He said nothing more.

Surely, he would need to respond in more than monosyllables at some point, right? Granted, it would help if she asked a question that could not be answered with a simple *yes* or *no.*

"What will our itinerary be once aboard, Your Grace?" she asked.

He continued to gaze out the window.

"Kendall," he finally said. "Not, *Your Grace.*"

"Pardon?"

"As my wife, you will refer to me as Kendall."

Wife. She was this stern man's *wife!*

And—

"Kendall," she repeated like a *numpty.* "Not . . . not Tristan?"

Though even as she asked the question, she knew it to be wrong. The man before her would never be *Tristan.*

"No." Finally, he looked at her, his expression unreadable. "Only two people—my mother and my sister—have ever been granted permission to refer to me as *Tristan*. I do not expect to extend the privilege again."

Oof.

Well, that certainly made her position in his life clear, did it not?

"And our itinerary aboard your ship?" she repeated.

"We shall sail clockwise around the Isle of Great Britain, occasionally stopping to re-provision—Cornwall, Wales, Cumbria and so on." Noticeably, he did *not* mention Scotland, though surely they would round the whole of her homeland in circumnavigating the island. "The thought of visiting Paris or Rome, where we would encounter other English nobility this time of year . . ." His voice drifted off.

Isolde understood only too well his meaning.

Neither of them wished to spend their days deflecting pointed looks and barbed comments from their peers. To don cheerful faces and pretend their marriage had been a joyous event.

"Aye," she agreed. "A leisurely cruise around the coast of Britain sounds lovely."

And it did. Quiet. Remote.

Kendall nodded, and she noticed the tiniest softening of his countenance. As if her approval mattered to him.

His reaction emboldened her tongue.

"Will we stay in harbor inns along the way?" she asked. Allie had mentioned once that her brother's ship did not have proper sleeping cabins.

"My steamship underwent a refurbishment last year," he replied, stretching his long legs across the carriage interior, his shoes brushing against the silk of her skirt. "I had a string of small cabins combined to form a proper bedchamber and bathing room. Therefore, we shall not need to stop at local inns. I will ensure you are comfortable throughout the journey."

His words were gently said.

But Isolde snagged on one fact only—

A bedchamber. Singular.

No doubt, it was sumptuous.

A place where they would have all the time in the world to . . .

She broke off at the thought.

Her stomach tumbled and rolled, the snakes writhing once more. And when the carriage wheels rocked over a particularly uneven stretch of flagstone, she feared she might be sick.

Do not think upon it.

She pressed a hand to her belly, willing the nausea to subside.

Would she truly lie with this man tonight? No matter his physical attractiveness, she desperately wished to know him further before engaging in such intimacy.

Kendall shifted, his hand methodically straightening a crease along the thigh of his trousers.

"I must ask, given the unexpected . . . nature . . . of our nuptials," he began, gaze fixed on his knees, "do you wish to consummate our marriage this evening?"

Isolde felt her jaw sag at the unforeseen question.

Had he read her mind?

"Is refusing an option?" she couldn't help but ask.

"I am not in the habit of forcing unwilling women into my bed."

"I have made commitments to yourself, Kendall." Squaring her shoulders, Isolde forced the words past her nervous lips. "I will always do my duty."

He snorted, lifting his dark eyes to hers.

"I do not want your *duty*," he leaned on the word with sardonic asperity, surprising her with his directness. "I want your willing participation. I want your enthusiasm, Duchess."

Duchess.

Despite her shock at Kendall's bluntness, she couldn't help but feel a jolt at the moniker.

And her *willing participation? Enthusiasm?*

The very syllables conjured a slew of images—the varied ways she could enthusiastically participate with him.

Heat flooded her chest and sent a blush scouring her cheeks.

Kendall watched the whole with his typical impassive gaze, as if her answer mattered not at all to him.

Well.

If he wished her to be a *willing* partner in the event of consummation, he would need to be less Kendall-ish.

Perhaps appear more enthusiastic *himself* at the prospect.

"In that case, I should like a reprieve," she replied, unable to keep the relief from her voice.

"You need not appear so alleviated. Is the thought of marital relations with myself so abhorrent?"

"Nae," she rushed to say, willing her fiery cheeks to cool. "It is simply that this is all . . . so sudden. And it would be nice to take a wee space of time to . . . to know one another better afore . . ." She let her meaning drip off the end of ellipses.

Before *enthusiastic, willing participation* as it were.

She swallowed. Loudly.

"As you wish," he replied, turning to look out the window once more.

Lovely.

She had clearly disappointed him.

Isolde had brothers and, therefore, knew enough of the male ego to recognize a frustrated man when she saw one.

It was simply . . .

How could she make love with a man who was essentially a stranger?

Silence stretched between them, trembling and fraught.

But, she had to wonder . . . if she did go to his bed . . . would it help uncover the kinder version of him she had glimpsed in the ice house?

Biting her lip, Isolde asked the next question burning her tongue. "If I delay consummating our marriage, will ye simply look elsewhere for pleasure? Your mistress, perhaps?"

Those dark eyes whipped back to her, turbulence churning in their depths.

"As a proper wife, you should not ask such a question. A proper husband would never answer it," was his terse reply.

"We both know I am not like other wives, Kendall. It is why ye have found marrying myself so distasteful."

"I also find the prospect of paying women for pleasure distasteful. So it appears we are at an impasse on this matter."

Hmmm.

This entire conversation was . . . unexpected.

Kendall would not force her to his bed nor *pay* a woman for services rendered. But a willing woman—a lonely widow, perhaps?—might be a different matter altogether.

The thought of him seeking comfort in the arms of another lady . . .

Isolde frowned. She was rather sure a wee sliver of jealousy lodged in her heart.

How ludicrous.

"What if I wish to stop in Scotland, Your Gr—Kendall?" she asked, desperate to change the direction of her thoughts.

Again, he turned to look out the window, expression once more impassive.

Isolde stared at his profile. The man was a geometric puzzle—the isosceles triangle of his nose, the slightly acute angle of his chin, the parallel lines of his cheekbones and jawline.

She wanted to crack him apart.

"Scotland?" he repeated. "Why?"

Isolde could not suppress a huff of astonishment. "Because Scotland is my home. That is reason enough, is it not?"

He continued to contemplate the streets of London outside the carriage window, sunlight dappling his face.

"At the very least," she continued, "I should like tae call upon Sir Rafe and Lady Gordon at Dunhelm Castle. It is so lovely there this time of year, and Uncle Rafe expressly invited us to—"

"*Uncle* Rafe?" Kendall's eyes whipped to hers.

"Aye, not a true uncle, of course. But Uncle Rafe and Aunt Sophie have always felt like family. I should like to visit them if only for a day or two as—"

"No," he said, sharply.

"No? Why not?"

"Because you are my wife, and I do not wish you to maintain an acquaintance with *that* family."

"*That* family!" Isolde repeated, jaw certainly flapping open now. "Rafe is *your* family. He is *your* brother and received into Polite—"

"I will never call that man anything other than a disgrace!" Kendall snapped.

At last!

Isolde had broken through the duke's icy, English hauteur—removed a chink of that formidable armor.

"I am eternally grateful Sir Rafe changed his own surname from Gilbert to that of his mother—Gordon," Kendall continued. "'Tis the only intelligent thing the man has ever done. You said you will do your duty by me, Duchess. And part of that *duty* is severing contact with ilk like Sir Rafe Gordon!"

"And my own flesh-and-blood family?" Leaning forward, she punctuated her words by poking his knee with her fingertip. "Will I be required to sever contact with them, as well?"

Kendall caught her hand, wrapping it in his much larger palm and sending heat licking up her arm. Isolde froze at the unexpected contact.

"If I thought Hadley would tolerate it, yes." He matched her leaning, dark eyes drilling into hers. Color tinged his cheeks. "I would be delighted to forget that man is now my father-in-law."

Oh!

"Does such rancor mean you will continue to pursue this outlandish impeachment case against my father?"

Glancing down, Kendall frowned, as if puzzled that he held her hand. He released her and sat back, folding his arms across his chest. The muscles in his sleeves bunched and caused Isolde to wonder what the motion would look like were he in his shirtsleeves . . . or perhaps with no clothing at all.

Vividly, she remembered the firm heat of his chest under her cheek, the faint puff of his breathing lost in sleep. How simple it would have been in that ice house to lift her chin and press her lips to the underside of his jaw, the crook of his neck, the alluring hollow where his clavicle—

Willing participation . . . his words.

Isolde blushed anew.

And how paradoxical, to be so frustrated with this man and his rigid view of their life and world, and yet find her heart racing from the lingering sensation of his hand encircling hers.

"The impeachment is already well under way, Duchess," Kendall said, "with or without my presence. The verdict on Jarvis's trial will be handed down in the next day or two. The decision there will likely influence the vote in Commons, assuming it arises within the next week. There is little I can do at this juncture, other than recuse myself if the case is brought before Lords."

"But ye will not aid my father in any material way?"

Kendall snorted. "One could argue that Hadley trapped us in this quagmire"—he motioned at the space between them—"in order to force my hand. To compel me to call off my dogs, as Allie says. So, no. I will not help Hadley. But as I said, events have already moved beyond my control."

"Events *you* set in motion."

"There is a fine line to walk here, Duchess. I need to distance myself from Hadley's disgrace as much as possible."

"To protect your own interests?"

"Yes," he snapped, "which you would be wise to heed, as my interests have now become *your* interests and, most importantly, those of our future children. As I have already said, your allegiance belongs to me now. The sooner you accustom yourself to that fact, the more smoothly our lives will proceed."

"Accustom myself to severing acquaintance with lifelong friends? At your decree?"

"Precisely. I am pleased that your expansive university education has finally permitted you to grasp the nature of your new life. I will always command your allegiance, from now until your last breath."

"Like hell you will, Kendall!"

"I will not have my duchess cursing like a fishwife!"

"Like. Hell," she enunciated, sharp and staccato. "Ye will never cleave me from the bosom of my family."

"Your loyalty is mine," he growled through his teeth.

"Nae, it is not," she replied in an equally savage tone. "Ye will *never* be my first choice. I will always choose my family over yourself. My loyalty is theirs forever."

"No, it is not!"

"Oh, but it is! They love me. You do not. They will always love me. You never will. I would choose them a thousand times over your sorry self. Because they are deserving of my love and affection." Her voice cracked with unshed tears. "Because they will never abandon me. And as such, I will never abandon them. I cannot say the same of you!"

Kendall sat back, as if her words had dealt him a blow. His expression shuttered.

"That might just be your cross to bear, Duchess. I did not want you. I did not wish for your hand. You would *never* have been the bride of my choice," he said through clenched teeth. "But you are *mine* now. The sooner you accept the realities of your new situation—the sooner you yield to it—the better."

And with that, he stared in silence out the window once more, allowing the rocking jangle of the carriage to fill the space between them.

17

Mr. Stephen Jarvis has been convicted of fraud and embezzlement of investors' funds. A jury handed down the verdict yesterday evening. The question remains: How will Mr. Jarvis's conviction affect the impeachment vote of Lord Hadley in the House of Commons?

—ARTICLE IN *The London Times*

Kendall had bollocksed things up with Isolde.

He knew it even as the sharp words had arrowed from his mouth in the carriage.

He knew it as he endured the tense silence of a meal aboard the *SS Statesman* that first night, the clinking of cutlery on Sèvres china filling the fraught quiet.

He knew it later that night, as he bunked in his secretary's small cabin, naturally permitting his duchess to have the opulent bedchamber and bathing room. Thankfully, there was ample room aboard ship, as no secretary or man-of-business had accompanied them. Just his valet and Isolde's maid.

Kendall understood he needed to apologize to his wife. But how? Life as a duke did not prepare one for humility. Or change, for that matter.

Without Allie to guide him—to act as Mentor to his words—surely he would only bungle any attempt, thereby necessitating further apologies. The whole would become a Catherine Wheel he could not escape.

In short, the entire endeavor felt futile, so why begin?

And yet, as the days passed aboard ship, the silence between Kendall and his wife grated—an ill-fitting shoe he desperately wished to reshape.

He busied himself with his ship, speaking with Captain Woodbury and generally absenting himself from his new wife's side. She, too, was grieving what her future might have been. Perhaps, she merely needed space to adjust to her new life.

Isolde appeared content with her own company. She read on the sofa in the bedchamber or stood at the starboard railing, watching the coastline slide past.

Kendall would pause as he crossed the deck to study her then. How she would lean her weight into the wind, closing her eyes as if communing with seabirds or summoning merfolk. At times, she would even dangle her bonnet from its strings, allowing the breeze to unravel her hair and send streams of flame arcing over her head.

And he would stand stock-still, a captive yet again of her ethereal beauty.

But she scarcely spoke.

He did attempt conversation.

"I received word in port earlier today that Stephen Jarvis has been convicted of fraud," he told her over a dinner of roasted lamb.

Kendall had inwardly rejoiced at the news. The man deserved every punishment.

"Oh," was Isolde's uncaring reply.

She cut into her lamb.

"Transportation and five years hard labor."

"I am glad justice is served," she said without a trace of gladness.

He considered drawing breath to apologize, but her expression—flat and lifeless—halted the words in his throat.

How could a mere apology ignite a spark again in her eyes?

Of course Kendall would darken the light of a woman like Isolde. Perhaps he was more akin to his father than he recognized—a destroyer of vitality.

Allie's words would not let him be.

Let the pain forge pathways of love in your heart.

Believe you can be a better man—one that Tristan would have liked to become.

The boy Tristan would have despised the Kendall he had grown to be.

And yet . . .

As Kendall watched Isolde stroll up and down the deck, wind trailing long tendrils of coppery hair in her wake, he couldn't help but imagine what his younger self would think of his marriage.

Tristan would be disappointed at the forfeiture of his goals—his dream to obliterate Old Kendall's memory.

But . . . that same boy would rejoice to marry Isolde. To call this vibrant creature his own—the only woman, unsuitable or not, he had ever thought to marry.

Yet as the days passed and the coastline swept by . . .

The white cliffs of Devon glittering in the sunlight.

Cornwall with its charming villages clambering up basalt cliffs.

The wild bays of Wales with green mountains rising beyond.

Cumbria's rolling hills and deep estuaries.

Kendall couldn't help but feel a fragment of that lost boy surfacing.

The boy who had spent hours reading about far-off lands and dreaming of adventures in the jungles of Brazil or the Orient.

The boy who had curled on his mother's lap—him nestled into one arm and Allie in the other—and listened to stories of her childhood in Venice, the clipped rhythm of her Italian lulling him to sleep.

The boy who had raced Allie to the lake beyond the parterre gardens, shouting and laughing over who could reach its banks first. Allie inevitably won.

But then his twin had always shone more brightly than himself—more talkative, more charismatic, more . . . loveable, he supposed.

Do ye even ken what love is, boy? Hadley's words drifted through his mind.

No. Kendall did not know what love was . . .

Well, he knew that he loved Allie. He knew that he had loved his mother.

But that love was different. It had grown with him from his earliest memories. Allie and their mother were, quite literally, part of the muscles and sinews that supported both his bodily frame and spirit. And even then, he would have destroyed his relationship with Allie had his twin not been determined to mend it.

However, outside of his womanfolk, not once had anyone else loved him of their own accord, no matter Sir Rafe's tale of their sire's interference. The old duke had been dead for six years, and Kendall still had no friends.

And so this beginning with Isolde felt like the whole of his life. Fruitless. Hopeless.

Isolde had made that clear, after all.

I would choose my family a thousand times over your sorry self. Because they are deserving of my love and affection.

The implication being, of course, that Kendall himself was not. Not deserving of her love. Not meriting her affection.

And yet, the love-potion-spell of his wife intensified its hold on him.

He would be talking to Captain Woodbury about restocking their coal supply for the evening, and Isolde would step onto the deck. And Kendall's breath would catch anew.

This luminous creature was his wife. His *wife!*

Surely, someday he would know the feel of her lips, the give of her body in his arms . . .

Apologize, whispered more than once through his mind. *Grovel if you must.*

And still . . . he said nothing.

It was utterly unlike him—to vacillate, to wallow in uncertainty without a clue as to how to move forward.

Allie said he viewed himself as unlovable. She was not wrong.

When no one in your life had ever loved you for yourself . . .

Occam's Razor, as well as the whole of the scientific method, could easily draw conclusions from that fact. Sometimes, the proof *was* in the pudding, as it were.

And so he endured Isolde's cold behavior—monosyllabic dialogue, careful politeness, the painful lack of warmth.

Because for him . . . he had never known anything else.

ISOLDE WAS SLOWLY going mad.

Initially, the silence between herself and Kendall had felt necessary. They had both experienced a tremendous shock. Taking time alone to adjust to the change in their fortune seemed a wise course of action.

But after a week of tense nothingness, she had nearly reached the end of her tether.

Isolde knew Kendall cared for his sister, but perhaps that love was all his frozen heart could summon.

His chilly demeanor and cool replies to her basic questions—Will we stop in Plymouth? *Yes.* Can we explore the harbor in Aberystwyth? *No.*—made Isolde's place in his affections clear.

As did the conversation she overheard between the duke and Captain Woodbury about her father and the vote in Commons.

Kendall had prevailed in the end.

The evidence from Jarvis's trial convinced the House of Commons to vote to impeach her father. Kendall's laugh of triumph upon reporting the news had spoken volumes.

In Liverpool, Isolde sent a telegram to her father in London, unable to stem her anxiety.

Hadley's reply had done little to assuage her concerns: *All will be well with me. Worry not.*

Worry not?!

Were all the men in her life intent on vexing her?

She had no expectation that her marriage would magically evolve into a loving union.

And yet . . . Isolde could feel Kendall's eyes upon her at the oddest times—as she paced the deck or sat reading near the stern. But then that had always been his way. Stare and judge but never actually speak.

It was maddening.

His words from the carriage continued to dance a merry jig through her brain.

I want your willing participation . . . your enthusiasm.

Such treacherous syllables, those words—each one a whirlwind spinning havoc in her mind.

Because . . . those syllables led to questions.

How willing a participant did he wish her to be, not just in their marriage bed, but in their life?

What precisely did he mean by *enthusiasm*? Synonyms comprised a throng in her brain—passion, eagerness, ardor. At night, entwined with him. By day, walking at his side.

How delusional was he to demand such energy of feeling without conceding an ounce of his own ducal pride?

Willing participation required mutual respect, tender feeling, and vulnerability. Things she began to doubt Kendall capable of in any real way. Moreover, if he wished her to eagerly welcome him into her bed, he would need to learn to apologize.

And grovel.

Smiles, laughter, compliments, and congenial conversation would also assist.

All the things Kendall categorically did *not* do.

And yet, despite his chilly demeanor, Isolde found herself unable to stop studying him. As if like her mother with fossils, Isolde, too, craved finding a gleam of opalescence in her new husband—some hint of treasure buried within.

Her efforts provided a few glimmering insights.

For example, Kendall walked the deck of his ship with ease, his weight carefully balanced, his shoulders loose-limbed and strong. An athlete's grace, she realized. Her husband was a man comfortable in his own skin.

Also, his gray hair was unruly. Though his valet would pomade and style it each morning, by mid-afternoon, the ocean humidity and constant breeze tousled his hair into a delicious mass that tumbled across his forehead in boyish waves.

And though Kendall was demanding and autocratic, he was never cruel. He barked orders and expected immediate compliance. But when a nervous midshipman mistakenly replied, "Yes, my lord," instead of "Yes, Your Grace," Kendall didn't belittle the lad. Instead, he dispassionately corrected him and repeated his request.

As they worked their way north, Isolde hadn't cared too much where they stopped. The ship re-provisioned at regular intervals, docking in Bristol and Liverpool to restock coal and the kitchen larder.

But when the bonnie hills of the Highlands rose in the distance, Isolde's heart soared. The green slopes and craggy cliffs sang in her blood—*home, home, home.*

However, each of her requests to go ashore was met with the same answer.

"May we explore the Isle of Arran?" she asked as they restocked in Ayr.

"No." Kendall looked to the island. "The winds are not favorable."

The next day, as the sun shimmered on the water—

"*Och*, look! I believe that is the Isle of Islay in the distance. Come, let us explore it."

"No, I fear the harbor is not deep enough for the ship's draught."

As they continued north, Isolde only glimpsed the charming village of Oban, nestled between the Isle of Mull on the west and the dramatic slopes of Ben Cruachan on the east. The town sat at the bottom of the Great Glen, a series of valleys and lochs that started with Inverness on the north and neatly divided the Highlands in two.

On the whole, it felt as if Kendall wished to complete their honeymoon as quickly as possible and banish her to one of his ducal estates. Heaven knew many an aristocratic wife had endured just such a fate.

But if this was to be Isolde's only taste of freedom—her one chance to visit the glens and lochs of her beloved Scotland—then she intended to make the most of it.

The isles of the Hebrides—Skye, Uist, Lewis and Harris—stretched endlessly north and west, luring her with promises of lands to explore.

Kendall be damned.

As they sailed into the Rough Bounds—a pocket of western Scotland that even Highlanders themselves considered wild—Isolde decided to seize the reins of her Fate.

She had always found the Rough Bounds romantic and evocative. They stretched from the top of the Isle of Mull at the south to the shores of the Isle of Skye in the north. The area was spottily inhabited, as the Highland Clearances had seen many of residents evicted over the past thirty years. Most had immigrated to America or moved south to work in the bustling factories of Glasgow and Manchester, leaving the area depopulated and desolate.

From the deck of the *SS Statesman*, the coast appeared lushly green, untamed, and deliciously inviting. They passed by the quaint Isle of Canna—as an obliging map in Isolde's bedchamber informed her. There, a well-maintained white house nestled into the dunes of a protected inlet, gleaming white sand and turquoise water stretching before it. Sunlight flitted through the racing clouds overhead, bathing the whole in dappled light.

Standing at the rail of the ship, Isolde could only describe the scene as idyllic. She simply had to know who lived there. A shepherd, perhaps? Or more likely, the keeper of the island. This was MacLean land, she knew—owned and maintained by the laird—and his lairdship would assign a clan member to see to the island.

Surely, the owners would welcome a visitor . . . such was the Highland way.

Kendall would veto the prospect of a visit.

But Isolde was done asking her husband's permission. This was *her* life, devil take it, and she was going to live it.

To that end, Isolde spoke with Captain Woodbury of her wishes. The captain glanced around the deck—presumably looking for Kendall's gray head—before warily agreeing.

He instructed two midshipmen to lower one of the tender boats so she could row herself ashore. The ship would circumnavigate the island and pick her up when they returned.

"What are you doing?" Kendall barked, glowering as the rowboat swung over the side of the ship and descended toward the water. He strode across the deck to her, his long legs eating up the planks in quick strides.

Isolde tied her bonnet more tightly to her head and tugged on her leather gloves. She had already changed into sturdy boots and a dress of superfine wool.

"I am rowing out tae the house there." She pointed at the island. "It looks enchanting, and I should like to visit the owner, as my family are acquainted with Clan MacLean. It is all settled with the captain. Of course, I do not expect ye to accompany me. Ye may enjoy a respite from my suffocating presence." She smiled up at him, perhaps a wee bit too cheerily.

Kendall paused, his expression darkening. "Rowing a boat on the ocean is a far cry from navigating a skiff across a pond at Hadley House or whatever your prior experience may be."

"I am well aware of that fact, Kendall. Despite your lowering opinion of my abilities, I am observant and astute. Mac, James, and myself spent our summers rowing to and fro across Montrose Basin. Why, we rowed from the Bridge of Dun, down the River South Esk, and across the Basin to the North Sea itself just two months past. A distance that is substantially farther than the one from this ship to the shore there." She pointed at the white house. "My arms are strong and my determination stronger. I shall not remain a spectator aboard this ship, watching the shore pass me by."

Watching Life pass me by, she might as well have added.

Kendall glared at her for so long, Isolde was unsure if he would reply at all. It was the most she had said to him in one go since that awful conversation in the carriage on their wedding day.

"Be that as it may, this is most ill-advised, Duchess. I do not like the look of the clouds in the sky there." He nodded to the dark mass gathering on the southern edge of the horizon.

"*Och*, everyone knows clouds blow from west tae east in the Highlands. Those clouds will stay tae the south. Even Captain Woodbury believes so. And if a squall does come through, we are sheltered here in the Inner Hebrides from the open ocean, regardless. The waves off Scotland are tame in comparison to the punishing surf of other coasts, like New England. Moreover, once I pass into the sheltered harbor there—" She pointed to where the headland curved inward to a deep crescent, waves gently lapping at the sandy beach. "—the sea becomes nearly glassy. So ye see, all will be well. Ye needn't do anything but stop for myself when I return in the afternoon."

She smiled at him again. Her brightest smile. The one that had ensured Cook always slipped her warm shortbread as a lass.

Kendall's frown deepened.

He looked from her face to the white house and then back again.

"You are truly determined to visit whoever lives there?" He shook his head, as if the very idea were mad.

"Aye. 'Tis the way of Highland hospitality. And I should dearly like an adventure."

He sighed. "You will wait before getting into the boat."

"Pardon?"

"If I am to accompany you, I need to change my trousers and footwear into something more suitable."

"Ye will be . . . accompanying me?"

"Yes. Though I oppose this harebrained idea, I cannot in good conscience permit my duchess to row herself ashore alone."

Isolde bristled. "I just assured ye I am a most accomplished boatwoman."

"Be that as it may, I must guarantee your safety. If anything were to happen, we both know your father would accuse me of your murder." He gave her a sardonic look. "I'd rather go down with the dinghy."

And with that shot, he walked off, calling for his valet.

18

LORD HADLEY IMPEACHED! Late yesterday afternoon, the House of Commons voted to bring articles of impeachment against the Earl of Hadley. We will provide more information the moment it is received.

—ARTICLE IN *THE LONDON TIMES*

The boat was a mistake.

That was Kendall's only thought as he pulled on the oars.

It had taken nearly thirty minutes to change his attire—his valet had insisted on switching out his waistcoat and coat, as well as shoes and trousers—and then a series of swells rolling in from the Atlantic had made launching the small rowboat somewhat precarious.

By the time Kendall began pulling on the oars, the southern clouds had become rapidly-approaching westerly clouds. The sky had grayed, and the series of swells had morphed into chaotic waves, lapping and tugging at the oars. The small dinghy dipped and rocked.

Kendall should have told Isolde *no*. He should have remained firm and unyielding. Ordered the sailors to return the rowboat to its place and refused to relent.

But . . .

She had *smiled* at him.

The wide, joyous smile that glowed with her essence.

The smile that he was honest enough to admit he adored.

The one that had been painfully absent since their betrothal and marriage.

Thank heavens she did not yet know its potency against his resolve. Because he feared he would do quite a bit to receive more of such smiles.

As it was, Kendall simply could not refuse her request.

A larger wave approached from his left, causing the boat to pitch sharply. He pulled hard against the oars.

"Veer a wee bit tae port," Isolde called over the wind.

As Kendall was the rower, his back was to the land. He could not discern what lay ahead of them.

Isolde had proved herself a capable sailor. She had been calling instructions for the past while.

However, she could not see the rain sweeping across the ocean from the west behind her. It had already struck the *SS Statesman*. From what Kendall could tell, the captain had ordered the anchor weighed to assist the ship in combating the weather. If Woodbury had any sense, he would sail around to the more sheltered leeward side of the island to wait out the storm.

If Kendall had any sense himself, he would not be in this tiny dinghy with his wife.

He angled the prow to the left as instructed, taking a wave head-on.

It was the only way to navigate seas such as these—face the wave. If a boat ended broadside to the surging sea, it could easily become swamped.

Kendall pulled on the oars, willing the boundary into the protected harbor to approach faster, but the frothy water hampered his efforts.

"Can you swim?" he yelled as he fought to keep the rowboat steady over another series of swells.

His wife looked affronted. "O' course. I'm a strong swimmer. Can ye?"

He nodded in reply.

"Hard starboard!" she called.

Kendall obeyed.

The truth hit him then—

He trusted her.

It was a rather startling realization.

He trusted Isolde's perspicacity and judgment. Her ability to keep a cool head and think rationally through a difficulty, just as she had in the ice house.

Though he denigrated her unconventional experiences, they had formed her into a lady of courage and pluck.

Isolde, Duchess of Kendall, had a spine forged of steel. Nothing— not even the Hebridean Sea—would best her.

Admiration welled upward and expanded his ribs.

The waves rose and fell, but he and Isolde found a rhythm. An ebb and flow—his muscles rowing, her voice guiding them.

"Port!"

"A wee bit starboard!"

The headland and the sheltered inlet beyond drew nearer. Once they passed into calmer waters, the rowing would become easier. They would reach the beach. The owner of the small house would welcome them into a warm parlor, and they would all toast their adventure with whatever whisky this isle produced.

Kendall surprised himself by smiling at the thought even as he battled through another white-tipped wave.

With him at the oars and Isolde guiding the boat, they would make it ashore. They would.

Bloody hell. Despite the peril, he felt good. The burn in his arms, the new-found harmony with his wife, the clarity of the task before them—

The rain hit with a gale force, blinding them both.

Kendall's hat blew off, flying skyward. Isolde held the brim of her bonnet to her face, a shield against the drenching water.

She yelled something, but the wind whipped it away. She gestured to the right and he steered that way. She pointed left, and he followed.

Tense minutes followed, waves lapping over the side of the boat. They were taking on water.

Slowly, they passed into the inlet, the headland providing shelter from the worst of the storm.

The *SS Statesman* rocked ominously in the more exposed ocean, smoke belching upward. Hopefully, Captain Woodbury was preparing to steam off to find a more protected place to anchor.

Kendall pulled at the oars. Though less choppy in the inlet, the sea still made steering perilous.

Neither of them saw the rogue wave. Barreling in from the north, it scooped up their paper boat of a dinghy with ease.

The boat flipped with astonishing force, tossing both Kendall and Isolde into the ocean.

Helplessly, his arms reached for his wife as the frigid water of the Atlantic swallowed him whole, waves pushing him down, down into the cold, dark depths.

Summoning all his will to hold panic at bay, he paused for a moment, waiting for the natural buoyancy of his body to indicate which way was up. With a powerful kick upward, he broke the surface.

Waves buckled around his head and rain drenched his cheeks. Shaking water out of his eyes, he scanned the surrounding ocean.

Searching for the only thing that mattered—Isolde.

He didn't see her.

The rowboat bobbed about twenty yards off, overturned and drifting away on the current.

But he still couldn't see *her*.

He kicked toward the boat, grateful they had at least made it into the inlet where the sea wasn't nearly as rough.

"Isolde!" he yelled. "Isolde!"

He paused, trying to listen, but heard nothing beyond the roar of wind and waves.

"Isolde!"

Where was she?

Was she hurt?

Terror seized him.

Diving underwater, he opened his eyes, hoping for a flash of white petticoats or coppery hair. Any sign she was near.

But only the murky deep greeted him.

Panic bloomed, sending jittery terror through his limbs.

He had to find her.

She could not have gone far. But what if another rogue wave or treacherous current had—

His lungs protested the lack of air.

Pushing upward, he broke the surface again.

"Isolde! Where are you?!" he screamed.

Turning in a circle revealed nothing new.

The boat still bobbed upside-down on the waves. Beyond the sheltered inlet, the storm appeared to be gathering force. He could no longer see the *SS Statesman* through the sheets of rain.

But . . . Isolde?

Where had she gone?

She was too strong, too full of life, too fiery . . .

A wave pushed him under.

Gasping, he surfaced again.

"Isolde!"

Treading hopelessly, he spun around once more but saw no gleam that might be her head.

No!

He simply couldn't lose her!

Diving again, he scanned the water, desperation a hammer punishing his ribs.

No flash of white.

No red hair.

He surfaced, drew a breath, and dove again.

Find her! Find her! pulsed through his brain.

She had to be caught, her long skirts snagged on some treachery underneath the waves.

He ignored the thoughts that whispered horror . . . *she should have surfaced by now . . . she has been underwater too long . . .*

Kicking upward, he gasped for air once more. A terrifying mixture of *panicdespairgrief* banded his chest and rendered breathing more difficult.

You are panicking, a dispassionate part of him noted.

A Duke of Kendall never panicked.

And yet—

How could he *not* panic?

"*Isolde!!*" he screamed into the wind.

The surging sea answered.

He ducked under the swell of a wave.

"*Isolde!*" he cried again upon surfacing.

Nothing.

No!

No!

She couldn't be gone.

Not now.

Not like this.

Not with the two of them chilly and silent and unreconciled.

"Isolde! Isolde!"

His breathing became chaotic, arms aching and pulsing with fire. Salt water and exertion turned his voice hoarse.

The rain felt like tears on his face.

Exhausted, he leaned onto his back and tried to catch his breath, letting the bitter waves wash over his face.

"Isolde," he whispered.

A sob left him.

And then another.

He should have listened to Allie.

He should have apologized to Isolde and groveled for forgiveness.

He should have held his wife, kissed her, told her that . . . that . . .

Bloody hell!

How ghastly to realize *now* the depth of his adoration . . . as he faced the horror of losing her before their life together had truly begun.

No!

His Isolde could not be gone.

He could not *permit* her to be gone.

She was his. He would find her.

Pulling on his reserves of strength, he kicked upright, took in a deep breath, and dove again.

The watery depths had not changed.

No glimmer of white. No flame-red hair.

His lungs burned, urging him upward.

But desperation held him under.

Find her! Find her!

Regrets pummeled him with each swell of the waves.

I never held her.

I never apologized.

I never kissed her.

Regret. Regret. Regret.

He broke the surface, sobs heaving his chest, great mourning gusts he could not control.

Tristan.

His name sailed by, threading through the wind.

And then again . . .

Tristan, Tristan . . . where are you?

Who called him?

An angel?

His mother, perhaps?

He supposed he *was* that far gone.

Floating on his back once more, he let the waves pummel his body.

"*Eccomi,*" he whispered in Italian. *Here I am.*

He was a boy, racing down the stairs of Hawthorn into his mother's waiting arms.

Tristan! Caro!

Allie clinging to him, sobbing goodbye before the carriage took her and their mother away.

Tristan! Don't leave me.

"I'll find you," he promised.

I'll find you.

Isolde! Isolde!

Tristan! Come back!

He wanted to return.

To become Tristan once more.

To be Tristan with his Isolde, love potion be damned.

"Isolde," he gasped.

Tristan.

Just once. Just once to hear his name on her lips.

Waves topped his head, and he let them push him under.

I need to fight.

That was his thought as he sank into the deep.

Fight. Fight.

But to what end? His Isolde was gone.

He would never be *Tristan* to her.

Not in this life.

But perhaps in the next. Perhaps he could find her there . . . as he had in Montacute's garden, sunlit and laughing, teasing in her blue eyes.

His lungs howled for air, the pressure unforgiving.

Tristan! Don't ye dare!

Something snagged on his hair. Then his elbow.

He opened his eyes in astonishment.

A flash of pale arm dragged him upward.

He kicked, breaking the surface.

And met the blue gaze of his furious wife.

"Tristan! Ye *eejit!*" she called. "Don't ye dare drown!"

Hand firmly around his wrist, she began dragging him toward shore, kicking her legs and paddling with one arm.

Strong. So strong.

She was alive.

Alive.

So very alive!

He wanted to weep for the sheer joy of it.

For the relief of seeing her bedraggled red head.

Isolde. Isolde.

Her name sang through his blood.

He wanted to shout *hallelujah*, to chant hosannas of gratitude.

Instead, he summoned the strength remaining in his cold limbs and joined his wife in swimming for the beach.

THE *EEJIT* HAD almost drowned.

Isolde was furious as she methodically stroked for shore, Kendall swimming weakly at her side.

Why had he not saved himself? Why had he remained in the waves? To find her?

She had *told* him she was a strong swimmer. How typical of his arrogance to doubt her! To stubbornly search for her.

But why had Kendall behaved so recklessly? Had he no care for his person?

Selfless was not a word she ever expected to associate with the Duke of Kendall. Nor the word's kinsmen—*concern, empathy, warmth* . . .

The rowboat had flipped, and she had surfaced underneath it, finding a wee pocket of air protected from the battering storm. Treading water, she had taken advantage of the reprieve.

She knew from experience—this was hardly the first time a rough sea had forced her to swim—that her skirts could be both a blessing and a curse. The fabric was naturally buoyant, helping her to stay afloat. But the volume of them was prone to snagging or tangling her legs. And the corded horsehair of her petticoats—needed to create the fashionable bell of a modern silhouette—would eventually become sodden and drag her down to a watery grave.

So she had quickly untied several of her underskirts, permitting them to sink to the ocean floor, and tossed off her bonnet before ducking out from underneath the boat to join Kendall.

Isolde had assumed she would find him stroking for shore.

Instead, the idiot was bobbing thirty feet away, needlessly diving. She had called to him, but it wasn't until she switched from *Kendall* to *Tristan* that he had appeared to heed her.

Thank goodness she had reached him in time, snatching a fistful of hair and then his arm, pulling him to the surface.

Isolde pushed back thoughts of *what if.*

What if she hadn't been able to help him?

What if she hadn't found him?

What if . . .

What if . . .

The possibilities left her nauseous.

She and Kendall might not see eye-to-eye—heaven knew how he disliked her—but she would never wish him harm. He was not an evil man. Just . . . difficult and unyielding.

Glancing to the side, she saw that Kendall was keeping pace with her, matching each of her strokes with his own. Though the uneven splash of his arms betrayed his exhaustion.

Fortunately, the ocean calmed as they drew closer to the beach.

Her lungs burned, pain prickling along her chilled skin.

Tired.

She was so tired.

And then . . .

Kendall stood up, his chin just above the ocean surface.

At last!

They had reached shallower water.

Without saying a word, he wrapped a hand around her elbow, permitting her to rest her muscles for a moment as he doggedly sloshed toward shore. How he had any strength left, she could not fathom.

His gray hair was plastered to his forehead, his lips blue from cold. And yet his clenched jaw spoke of determination.

Isolde shivered.

"Almost there," he said, voice hoarse.

At last, she felt the give of sand beneath her own feet. Standing upright, she staggered forward, the angry sea pushing against her spine as if eager to eject her onto dry land.

Her legs were jelly, chilled and wobbly from the cold water.

The wee white house contrasted with the sodden dune grass behind it, sturdily braced against the wind and rain.

Staggering out of the surf and up the beach, Isolde collapsed onto the white sand. Rolling onto her back, she breathed in wretched gasps, the rain peppering her frigid skin. Thankfully, the storm did not feel nearly as fierce on land.

Kendall dropped beside her, mirroring her pose. Air whooshed in and out of his lungs, synchronizing with her own.

His hand found hers lying on the sand, his cold fingers tucking her palm against his.

The danger of the past hour washed over her.

They had almost died, nearly dragged to a watery grave.

A sharp burning sensation crept along her limbs, her chilled body coming back to life.

Violent shivering wracked her. From the tremor in Kendall's hand, he was experiencing the same.

With a groan, he rolled onto his hands and knees before pushing himself to standing.

He reached a hand down and pulled her upright. They both staggered in the sand and nearly went down again. But Kendall wrapped an arm around her waist and held her firm.

"C-come," his deep English voice rasped in her ear. "L-let us hope these islanders have a warm f-fire to welcome us."

They stumbled up the beach, over the dunes, and all but sagged against the front door of the house.

Only then did Isolde notice the shuttered, dark windows.

Kendall's knock yielded no answer.

Unable to help herself, Isolde huddled against him, her arms still wrapped around his waist, her cheek pressed to his shoulder. He trembled under her hands, cold wracking his large body. But his reciprocal arm around her own waist was tight and strong.

"B-blast it all!" He looked down at her. "You w-will catch your d-death in this."

He was right. They would both catch their deaths if they didn't get out of the cold and wet.

Her hand shivering violently, Isolde tried the door handle.

The door swung open on well-oiled hinges.

"Hello?!" Isolde called, pushing away from Kendall and stepping into the house, relishing the instant relief from the weather. "Is anyone at home?"

Kendall followed her, closing the door behind them.

"Hello?" she repeated.

Only the sound of their sodden clothing dripping on the rush mat in the entry vestibule greeted them.

A glance showed the house to be as she had anticipated. The arrangement of rooms in a white house was always the same.

A central hall with a staircase ascending.

A parlor to the left with a large hearth for cooking.

A dining room to the right.

A cold larder and scullery along the back of the house.

And upstairs, surely two bedrooms, one to either side of the stairwell.

The house appeared cozy and lived-in, the owners likely away to visit relatives or gather supplies on the mainland.

"No one is home," Kendall said, his voice practically in her ear.

Isolde jumped at his closeness.

"Aye," she nodded, glancing up at him.

He appeared . . .

She frowned.

He stared at her with quiet intensity, his dark eyes studying her face as if he feared she would bolt. As if he wanted to pull her back into his arms for safe keeping.

Which as a thought was . . . was . . .

Bizarre.

It was bizarre.

Had the ocean addled his thinking?

Or was the dim light merely playing tricks on her eyesight?

"We need to find dry clothing," he said. "And then build a fire to warm you."

Her frown deepened.

What an odd way to phrase that.

Not a fire to warm 'us,' but a fire to warm 'you.'

Where was the terse, unfeeling Kendall she knew?

More to the point, he had yet to utter one recrimination.

Not a single, *You hare-brained idiot! You almost killed me!*

Instead, as he bustled around the small parlor to the left of the front door, he appeared almost frantic to find blankets or spare clothing.

"Up-upstairs," she chattered, pointing to the central staircase. "Th-there will be b-bedrooms."

He started up the stairs, hand on the rail to pull himself upward. But then, he turned back and offered her a hand.

"Can you climb?" The solicitousness in his voice gave Isolde pause.

Because the man currently looking down at her—his hand extended, brown eyes concerned and . . . and *worried*—only bore a superficial resemblance to the duke she had married eight days past.

Her eyes dropped to his palm, stretched out to her almost in supplication. In pleading.

She lifted her eyes back to his, again noting the concern etched there.

What the hell had happened to him out on that ocean?

19

There were indeed two bedrooms upstairs, Tristan discovered.

Isolde pointed out that it appeared a family of sorts lived here—father, mother, and several older children.

One bedchamber had two single beds and a trunk of adolescent clothing. As was typical of a cottage so far north, the bed frames were actually floor-to-ceiling boxes built into the eaves. Three sides of each bed were wood panels with the fourth side—the one facing the room—covered in heavy wool drapes. On a stormy evening, the sleeper could pull the fabric tight, trapping in heat and keeping out drafts.

The second bedroom had a similar box bed—a larger matrimonial bed for two persons built into the eave opposite a solitary dormer window. Two pine kists flanked the window. One of the trunks held wool trousers, lengths of tartan to wrap a kilt, linen shirts, woolly jumpers, and a spare coat. The other bore petticoats, women's underthings, and several woolen dresses.

Tristan grabbed trousers, a shirt, wool stockings, and a thick jumper that looked large enough to fit him. He retired to the children's bedroom, leaving Isolde to change her own clothing in the larger bedchamber.

His poor wife trembled from cold—gray-blue lips and fingers, freckles stark against the pallor of her cheeks.

But she was alive.

She lived!

The euphoria of finding her had yet to wane.

Now . . . he needed to build a fire to warm her. And then locate some food for her belly.

With shivering hands, he stripped off his sodden jacket and trousers, toweling his skin dry with a blanket from one of the beds.

As he dressed in the borrowed clothing—buttoning the shirt and pulling the trouser braces onto his shoulders—he could hear Isolde's movements. A shuffling noise. The lid of a pine kist closing.

Somewhere out on that ocean, she had become the axis of his world. And now, every atom of his body was attuned to hers . . .

His fingers fumbled in their haste to dress himself and return to her side.

He felt . . . scrubbed raw. Like the newly-birthed lambs of Hawthorn in spring, tottering on unsteady legs and blinking into the brightness of this vast, unknown world.

What now?

The thought winged about in his head, as if held aloft by tiny sparrows.

What was he to do?

Apologize, Allie's voice came back to him. *Swallow your ducal pride and say* I'm sorry.

He nodded as if listening anew.

Yes. He would do that. Why had the idea felt so impossible?

Now, it seemed a simple thing. He had behaved like an ass; he wished Isolde to be happy. *Ergo* . . . he would apologize.

Then what?

Let the pain forge pathways of love in your heart.

Believe you can be a better man—one that Tristan would have liked to become.

Damn and blast.

Easy for Allie to say. But how did one *become* a different sort of man? And could he change enough to earn Isolde's regard?

The task of reforming his person overwhelmed him, the sheer impossibility of it.

He could feel his habitual frustration rising.

His cold hands slipped in pulling on his stockings and a curse escaped his lips.

The trousers were a mite short, the shirt too large around, but the thick stockings warmed his feet. He had just pulled on the heavy jumper—a sort of knitted coat that buttoned up the front—when his wife called.

"C-could ye assist me?"

Just the sound of her voice . . .

Tristan closed his eyes at the joy of it.

Swallowing, he crossed the small hallway and pushed open the door to the matrimonial bedchamber.

Every thought in his head evaporated.

His wife stood with her back and shoulders to the door.

Her *bare* back and shoulders.

She had removed her bodice, skirt, and corset cover, and now stood clad in only her drawers, chemise, and corset.

All of it wet, clinging to her skin.

Beautiful.

So beautiful.

Her hair tumbled from its pins, and she had pulled the vivid mass over her right shoulder, using a towel to wring the water out of it.

Breathe, Tristan reminded himself. But as with the wild ocean they had narrowly escaped, the simple task proved a challenge.

She looked over her shoulder at him, eyes the color of a June sky.

Rain lashed the window to his left and cast shadows on the brown-and-russet tartan drapes of the box bed.

The dim light illuminated the gooseflesh pebbling Isolde's skin.

"You're cold," he said and then promptly hated himself for stating the obvious.

"Aye," she shivered, setting down the towel and presenting him with her back once more. "But I cannot undo my laces without assistance."

Finally, Tristan noticed the problem. Her corset laces were a tangled mess at the small of her back—wet and snarled and impossible to untie by feel alone.

"Will ye help me?" Again, she glanced over her shoulder at him, gaze tentative, as if she expected him to deny her assistance.

It stung.

That she assumed the man he had been that morning would have refused such a simple request.

He had never been such a monster. But she obviously did not know that.

How was he to change her opinion of him?

He had never sought a lady's good opinion. Or fostered a friendship with someone who liked him simply for . . . himself.

Perhaps he truly was an *eejit,* as she had said. To think that a woman as vibrant as Isolde would ever look on him with anything approaching affection.

The hope was likely dead before it even began.

"Of course," Tristan murmured, stepping close and frowning as he tried to suss out untangling the jumble of cord.

She faced the wall once more, clutching the front of her corset to her bosom.

Neither of them said a word, the sound of the wind and his fingers tugging on the sodden laces filled the rain-pattered quiet.

But his hands were stiff and numb. Every few moments, he had to pause and blow on them, willing warmth back into his veins.

The frequent pauses gave him far too much time to ponder the beauty of her back . . . the sharp press of her shoulder blades, the tawny freckles dotting her pale skin. The strand of amber hair lying across the base of her neck, dripping seawater onto her shoulders.

His lips ached to kiss the drops off her skin.

He tugged at the corset strings.

The drawstring along the neckline of her chemise had loosened, sagging and exposing the creamy pearls of her spine.

Lifting a hand, he traced the air over each vulnerable bump, his finger only half an inch above them.

So delicate.

So fragile.

So tenuous.

A testament to how close they both had come to death.

I would have died for her.

The very thought rocked him back on his heels.

But . . . it was truth.

He would have died to save her life.

He nearly *had* died.

Because . . . it would be simply unbearable . . . living in a world where her light—her bright, joyous light—no longer existed.

Worse than losing power in Lords.

Worse than failing to expunge his father from history.

Tristan had already suffered both of those calamities, and they paled in comparison to the imagined prospect of losing Isolde.

Forcing his hands back to the task, he continued to loosen the Gordian knot of the laces.

His mind traveled a similar path, thoughts untangling into vivid clarity.

What a bloody fool he had been.

Winning her affection would prove a difficult road.

Impossible, perhaps.

But if he were willing to die for her . . .

Then surely he could fight to prove himself a gentleman worthy of her love.

Like the frigid Atlantic churning outside the window, another tidal wave swept overtop him.

Metaphorical but no less powerful.

It cascaded through his veins, invading muscle and bone, shattering the rigid control that a lifetime of Old Kendall's cruelty had wrought.

And behind that cleansing water . . . swirling and eddying in its wake—

He felt chaotic and messy and fervent and . . . and wanting.

So. Much. Want.

It swamped him. A vast sea of *wantwishdesire* so wide and so deep it was all he could do to breathe through the rushing tide.

Eyes closing, he swayed forward, his hands stilling in their task, a knuckle pressing against the corset cover.

Like that long ago day of their first meeting, he wanted a lifetime with her.

In a flash, he realized the spare, final truth.

He had fallen.

From the first moment he had turned and laid eyes on Isolde in Montacute's garden—

That had been the beginning of the end.

He had never stopped falling.

Every claim he had ever made to dislike her had been a lie. Lies upon lies he had told himself to somehow bury the truth—

She was the woman for him.

She always had been and always would be.

He loved her.

How he loved her.

Her fire, her intelligence, her vivacity, her strength.

Hallelujah they were married!

On a deep breath, he continued with his task, tugging a lace free.

He wanted all of her.

Her laughter, her adoration, her heart.

He wanted her face to light with happiness when he entered the room, or every time her eyes opened to his of a morning. He wanted her to run to him after days spent apart, as eager for his company as he was for hers.

He wanted to make her laugh until her sides ached, to bathe her in joy, to keep her safe within the arc of his care.

And for the first time in . . . ever . . . a different future crystallized.

In this future, he and Isolde cuddled together in a warm bed, her face pressed to his chest, shoulders shaking with hilarity. Or they were sitting before the fire of an evening, talking philosophy and reaching for books to support their arguments.

A child intruded on the scene. And then two. And then four . . . girls with ragged red braids, boys with torn trousers and sticky fingers.

Tristan wanted that.

He wanted to drink in love and hope, like a child gulping down lime punch on a hot summer's day. To drown in adoration of her and the life they would make together. To fill her days with devotion.

A marriage of true minds.

To become one.

The longing for that future burned in his blood, an agony of yearning so acute, he trembled.

Pulling the final lace free, he swayed forward, helpless with the need to press his lips to her nape. To express with his body the hunger scouring his heart.

Thankfully, he paused before actually touching her.

But his lips hovered there, over the first pearl of her spine, aching to taste her skin.

She stilled, surely able to feel the heat of his breath.

And he hated it. The tense wariness she displayed in his presence.

A wariness of his own making.

Somehow . . . someway . . . he had to become a better man for her. A man sufficiently worthy of her heart.

Swallowing, Tristan stepped backward. Wrenching his sodden limbs from the ocean had been easier.

"I think you can manage from here." The rough growl of his voice reverberated.

Startled, she glanced over her shoulder.

Her haunted expression struck him anew—a lock of hair clinging to her cheek, the wide openness of her blue gaze, the charm of her freckled skin.

Want. Want. Want.

"Thank ye," she whispered. "Thank ye, Kendall."

Kendall.

His father's name clanked between them like an anvil.

"Tristan," he rasped. "My name is Tristan."

He pivoted and left the room.

ISOLDE STARED AT the doorway Kendall—ehr . . . Tristan?— had just vacated. Her eyes wide as saucers.

Something had changed in him.

He had been so focused and so . . . *something* . . . behind her. Intent? Judgmental?

And had he . . .

Had he nearly *kissed* her neck?

She could still feel his breath against her chilled skin.

And that look he had given her just now—

Haunted and . . . if she had to name it . . .

Hungry.

So terribly hungry.

She shivered and *not* from the cold.

Moreover, it appeared she was to call him *Tristan.*

What had caused this abrupt shift in his behavior toward herself? Had he hit his head when the rowboat toppled them? Was he fevered?

Frowning, she finished dressing—toweling off and donning the simple underthings and woolen dress of the mistress of this house— before braiding her hair into a thick rope that hung to her waist. She would need to loosen it at some point to dry fully. But for now, she was content that it no longer dripped down her back.

A quick glance outside showed the storm had worsened. Rain battered the glass windowpanes and wind flattened the dune grass into horizontal sheets. Thank heavens they were out of the elements.

She found Tristan downstairs building a fire in the hearth. Despite the pampered life he had certainly lived, he knew how to lay peat and arrange dry grass so the flame from a Lucifer match would catch.

He looked up when she entered the room.

"Thank ye again for your assistance," she said, running her palms down her skirts.

Slowly, he stood, staring at her the entire time. That same dark intensity in his gaze.

"Of course." His voice was still hoarse from the sea water.

How odd to see him clothed in homespun wool trousers and a loose knitted jumper. Not a trace of London finery remained. Gray whiskers rimmed his jawline and his hair stood on end.

He appeared . . .

Well, he looked . . . *lost.*

Earnest and wary.

A trapped wolf, tentative and primed to startle at the first hint of danger.

Perhaps a part of him remained out to sea.

His eyes flitted up and down her body, no doubt taking in the equally haphazard nature of her clothing. His eyes lingered on her feet and ankles, clad in thick woolen stockings. The bodice fit her well enough, but her skirt and petticoat stopped mid-calf. Few women were as tall as herself.

In summation, Isolde was currently displaying far too much leg and ankle for propriety. Thank goodness only her husband was here to witness it. Though given how he appeared to forcibly drag his eyes away from her legs, perhaps even that was of concern.

Well, His Ducal-ness would simply have to manage.

Breaking his gaze, she spun in a circle, taking in the room.

The parlor was a homey place. A large cooking pot hung from a hook over the fire, ready for whatever food Isolde could find in the cold larder. A worktable sat before the front window, and a large hutch with dishes rested against the back wall. A pair of Orkney chairs—one large and one small—dominated the room, sitting proudly before the hearth. Woven of rushes, the chairs stood nearly at the height of Isolde's shoulders, their hooded tops curved to trap every last morsel of heat from the fire. They seemed a pair of hunched monks, muttering prayers.

Tristan rotated as well, his eyes focused on herself rather than the room.

His attention was . . . confusing.

"I'm going to explore and see what provisions there are." She motioned toward the room at the back of the house. "The storm may take a wee while to pass."

In the cold larder, Isolde found red lentils, onions, a salted side of cured ham, and a bottle of excellent whisky from Talisker on Skye.

"You are very fortunate, Your Grace," she said with mock severity when she re-entered the room, arms laden, "that I know how tae cook." She shook the burlap sack of lentils at him.

He frowned. "That is a rather odd thing for the daughter of an earl to have learned."

"Nae. I enjoyed spending time in the kitchens as a lass, and I had tae do some cooking for myself while at university in the States. This—" She pointed to the ingredients, setting them on the worktable. "—will make a lovely supper."

Tristan located a fresh spring out the back door in a rear courtyard—a small space ringed by a series of even smaller outbuildings—and filled the cooking pot with water, setting it to boil. Isolde chopped the onion, adding lentils and a healthy chunk of cured ham to the pot.

For his part, Tristan laid out their sodden clothing to dry before the fire, draping her skirt and his coat over a drying rack. He carefully opened the case of his pocket-watch, gently dabbing seawater out of the gears.

"Is your watch salvageable?" she asked, nodding toward it as she tossed a laurel leaf into her makeshift soup.

"Perhaps." He shrugged. "Though given that I have yet to see a clock in this house, I shan't be able to reset the time regardless."

The unconcerned tenor of his words snagged her attention. Heaven knew the Duke of Kendall had an obsessive sense of time. Vividly, she recalled his endless pacing while trapped in the ice house, voice militantly announcing the hour. Would he be so *blasé* tomorrow without a clock marking the passage of each minute?

And yet, as she studied him bent over the watch—its gold casing glinting in the firelight—he didn't look like the Duke of Kendall from the ice house. Instead, he appeared a scholar tinkering with a mechanical curiosity—an inquisitive expression on his face.

She looked away, unsure what to make of it or the confused tangle his expression made of her emotions.

Isolde stirred the soup, before crossing to the hutch and pouring a healthy finger of whisky into two pottery mugs. She handed one to Tristan as he set his watch aside, motioning for him to sit in the larger of the two Orkney chairs. She settled into the smaller, pulling it closer to the warmth of the peat fire.

"Are you warm?" His voice reached her like that of a disembodied spirit.

She glanced toward his chair, but only his legs and fingers cupping his mug were visible. The rest of him was tucked into the curved hollow of the chair back, hiding his face.

She sipped her whisky. "Aye, finally. Yourself?"

"Tolerable."

"I imagine the owners of this cottage will return sooner rather than later," she said. "They haven't prepared the house for a long absence."

"Agreed."

The fire popped.

Tristan said nothing more.

Isolde stifled a sigh.

It appeared he had reverted to single-word answers. Whatever had occurred on the ocean had not loosened his tongue.

Isolde sipped her whisky, enjoying how the liquid suffused her veins with a languid heat.

They had both sailed a wee bit too close to death today. And as the tension of their near miss ebbed, her eyes drooped in sleep, her body bobbing away on a dark current.

She came to with a start at the weight of something settling on her lap.

Tristan's hands . . . quietly draping a tartan blanket over her legs.

"Thank ye," she whispered, astonishment in her voice, head lifting to meet his gaze.

He merely studied her with those earnest eyes, so open and un-Kendall-like.

"Would you like more whisky?" He motioned to her cup, now sitting on a side table.

Isolde blinked up at him.

"What happened?" The question tumbled from her lips.

"Pardon?"

She pulled the blanket closer. "Why are ye being so kind tae myself?"

"Do you not like my demeanor?"

"Nae. I ken that . . . or rather, it is . . ." *Lovely. Unexpected. Unnerving.* ". . . different," she finished lamely.

"Different?" His brows drew down.

"Nice. Genial," she quickly amended. "Attentive."

Silence.

They stared at one another for a long moment.

He has the loveliest eyes, she thought. Chocolate brown with flecks of caramel gold that glimmered in the firelight.

"Nice. Genial," he repeated slowly. "Two descriptors you do not typically associate with myself."

A statement. Not a question.

She floundered, unsure how to reply without offending him.

He held out a staying hand. "You needn't answer."

Turning, he stirred the lentils in the pot and retook his seat.

Isolde looked from the fire, to his long legs stretched toward the hearth, and then back to the fire again.

Perhaps she should have had him refill her whisky mug after all.

"Why . . ." She paused to lick her lips before continuing, "Why have ye decided tae be more . . ." She searched for the right word. ". . . amiable?"

Nothing.

And then, his voice low—

"You were underwater for so long, I feared that you had . . ." He trailed off.

They were both talking in ellipses, it seemed.

"I couldn't find you, and I realized . . ." He took a deep breath. "It made me reexamine my priorities. What I truly want from my life." A lengthy pause. "From our marriage."

Our marriage.

So . . . not merely *enthusiasm* and *willing participation* then?

Aye, she was going to need more whisky for this conversation.

"And what is it ye wish of our marriage?" she asked.

Another long stretch of silence.

"I must . . ." He swallowed, the sound audible. "I must apologize for my prior conduct. My behavior since our marriage has been . . . unacceptable, for which I am most sorry. I have resolved to do better. To *be* better."

Isolde blinked in astonishment.

Before this moment, she would have considered the phrases, 'I am sorry' and 'I have resolved to do better' to be absent from his ducal vocabulary.

"How hard, precisely, did ye hit your head when the dinghy *dooked* us into the waves?"

He chuckled, the rich sound adding to the whisky-warmth in her veins. "Not hard enough, I fear."

"I am sorry, too, for the cruel things I have said." She stood and poured another finger of much-needed whisky into her mug.

"You were merely responding to my recalcitrance."

She tilted the bottle toward him, an unspoken question in her eyes. He nodded and lifted his mug.

"Nae, I will not permit ye tae take all the blame on yourself." She finished pouring his drink and set the bottle on the floor beside him. "As my mother always says, it takes two to quarrel."

"No, that simply is not the case here, Iso—"

He broke off as she leaned forward and placed her pointer finger over his lips.

"Hush," she smiled. "Let us not argue about this, too."

At which point, she realized he had gone preternaturally still.

Both their eyes dropped to her finger on his surprisingly-soft lips.

Oh.

What had she been thinking?

An apology on her tongue, Isolde pulled her hand back.

But she had retreated scarcely an inch before his long fingers wrapped around hers.

They both stared at their conjoined hands, electric heat licking up her arm.

Slowly, so slowly, he lifted her hand to his mouth and, with infinite tenderness, pressed a lingering kiss to her wrist.

The precise spot he had kissed that long-ago afternoon in Montacute's garden.

Gooseflesh erupted over the entirety of her body—up her arms, across her shoulder blades, down the backs of her legs.

His eyes closed as if in pain, his exhale an almost moaning breath.

Bloody hell.

She was in so much trouble.

Because a man who looked at her as he had this afternoon, who kissed her wrist with such fervid reverence . . .

"Tristan," she breathed, a note of *something* in her tone that even she couldn't decipher. Warning? Pleading?

"I know . . . I won't." He moved to nuzzle her palm, bestowing kiss upon kiss, as if helpless to stop. "I would never . . . you need never fear that I . . ."

Her eyelids fluttered closed at the riot of sensations. His whiskers abrading her skin. The gentle pressure of his lips. The heat of his breath on her fingers.

It was all Isolde could do to resist sliding her hand into his hair and pulling his mouth to hers.

He was her husband.

At some point, she would kiss him. She would do significantly more than that.

But they had both had such a shock today. Their close encounter with Death had certainly affected him.

What if she kissed Tristan tonight, only to have him revert to scathing Kendall tomorrow?

No.

She couldn't . . .

To set an expectation of something that she wasn't willing to continue when this uncharacteristic mood of his passed.

She tugged on her hand, and he instantly released her.

He looked up through hooded eyes, his lungs heaving as if just pulled from the ocean once more.

Isolde took a step back, clasping her hands behind her back, digging fingernails into her palm to interrupt the phantom memory of his touch.

"Let me check the lentils," she whispered.

Isolde turned for the fire before he could answer.

It was only much later, as she lay alone, warm and comfortable in the matrimonial bed—the bed he had insisted she take—that she realized.

Tristan had never answered her question—

What *did* he wish from their marriage?

20

Tristan was fairly certain he had crawled from the ocean into his own personal version of Hell—adoring his wife and yet helpless to know how to inspire a reciprocal affection in her.

No wonder poets bemoaned the misery of unrequited love.

The ache of it tortured him. It wound through his limbs and squeezed his heart—a tentacled Kraken of *yearninghungerlonging* that gave no quarter.

And yet, he welcomed it.

The longing sizzled in his veins, sparking and hot. He lived! She lived! And some forgiving god had gifted him a second chance at her love.

Tristan passed a long night curled into one of the narrow box beds in the second bedchamber, his brain endlessly looping through the events of the day.

One moment, he bobbed in the ocean, screaming into the wind, desperate to find Isolde.

The next, he was once more unlacing her corset, exposing inch-by-inch the delicate ridge of her spine and freckled expanse of skin.

This, inevitably, led to the memory of kissing her palm.

Over and over, his senses revisited the feel of her hand under his lips—the give of her skin, the faint tremor in her palm . . . as if his touch had not been entirely unwelcome.

He had nearly come undone.

Despite his exhaustion, sleep was long in coming.

Tristan woke to wind rattling the gables and dreary daylight seeping through a crack in the bed drapes. A glance out the window confirmed the storm still raged—frothing the sea and pushing mounds of sea foam up the beach.

He dressed in the same shirt and pair of trousers, adding a worn wool coat overtop. His own clothing was still too sodden to wear.

His wife's bed was tousled and empty.

He found her dressed in the cold larder, bent over a cupboard, appearing to inventory its contents.

A blue homespun wool gown hugged her waist and ended mid-calf, displaying a rather erotic length of ankle and leg. Light from a window to her right rimmed her hair—plaited into a simple crown atop her head—turning it to liquid amber.

Her unaffected beauty stole his breath.

Want. Want. Want.

Helplessly entranced, he had to lean a shoulder against the door jamb to ensure he remained standing.

How could you not have known? a part of him wondered. *How could you not have realized before now how thoroughly you love her?*

Well, he *had* known, he supposed.

He had simply assumed it to be a flaw in his personality.

To love the daughter of his enemy—to marry a scandalous woman—would be the height of folly. And the Duke of Kendall did his utmost to avoid folly. Which was ludicrous, given the missteps that had landed them here.

He *was* often afflicted with a sort of mania, an obsessive need to obtain or achieve something.

Isolde had been a compulsion in his blood for nearly a decade.

As with so much else, Allie had seen the truth of that, too.

Isolde placed a bag of what appeared to be flour onto the worktable, brushing a tendril of copper hair off her cheek.

Ti bramo.

The Italian words drifted through his brain—*I yearn for you.*

He didn't often think in Italian, but occasionally phrases surfaced, particularly when there wasn't a similar word in English. In this case, the Italian verb—*bramare.*

To him, *bramare* felt akin to *yearning* in English but more intense. It meant to long for something with a wild ferocity. An agony of yearning that was nearly all-consuming.

The verb summed up his current state with sharp accuracy.

Ti bramo.

I yearn for you.

Bramo noi.

I yearn for us.

He shifted against the door jamb and she turned.

"Good morning," Isolde smiled. "Did ye sleep well?"

"Yes." He wanted to cross the small space between them, slide a hand around her waist, and kiss that beautiful smile in greeting.

Instead, he settled for motioning toward the cupboard. "Will we starve, do you think?"

She shrugged, setting turnips beside the flour. "The owners were certainly low on stores. It might be why they are not here at present—the need tae restock food supplies before the autumn harvests. But look!" She beckoned him forward to peer out the window. "Chickens!"

Sure enough, six hens huddled in a small coop in the rear courtyard, trying to find shelter from the wind and rain that pummeled the landscape.

"Where there are chickens, there should be eggs." Isolde grinned at him.

Tristan cataloged that image—the delight in her blue eyes, the window light accentuating the freckles on her nose and cheeks, the dainty point of her chin.

It filled his heart to overflowing.

As the day progressed, he added more images to those first ones, amassing an impressive collection.

Isolde kneading bread, a worn apron around her waist and flour smudges dotting her cheeks.

Isolde holding her stomach and laughing as he braved the pelting rain, trying to coax a hen off her roost to collect eggs for their lunch.

Isolde licking the side of her finger, catching warm honey as it dribbled from the crust of bread she had baked.

Tristan wished to capture the day in pictures—a series of paintings titled "An Ode to Love." Perhaps he would even hire the famous Sir Ewan Campbell himself to paint them.

He had sensed Isolde's eyes on him, as well.

When he turned away to complete a task—fill the heavy cooking pot with water or reach a cutting board on a high shelf—her gaze lingered. She had even watched rather brazenly as he shed his coat and stacked a supply of peat in the cold larder. Afterward, Tristan regretted not making a bigger show of flexing his muscles and bending low to pick up the weighty blocks of turf.

But all was not bliss and simplicity.

Their stores of peat and coal were sparse. If they were stranded here too many days, they would likely exhaust their ability to cook meals and heat the house. It might be summer, but isles of the Hebrides were rarely warm.

The available food was hardly plentiful—some flour, oats, onions, mealy potatoes, and a few old neeps. For meat, there was the bit of cured ham, a crock of salted mackerel, and eggs from the six chickens.

Their own clothing was still wet, specifically their shoes. The homeowners had a pair of old boots that he and Isolde took turns wearing outside, but they both required footwear. And Tristan's watch hadn't dried out enough to resume working. In the meantime, he kept dabbing at the gears, hoping to prevent salt water from corroding the whole. Granted, knowing the precise hour mattered little. The wee house felt like a space outside of Time.

Then it was evening once more, and they were seated before the fire, each sipping whisky in their appointed chair. Wind still battered the small cottage, but the rain appeared to be on the wane.

"When do ye ken the *SS Statesman* will return for us?" Isolde asked.

Tristan leaned out of his chair, but he could only see her feet draped in a blanket for warmth and her fingers wrapped around her mug.

"As soon as she is able," he replied, pulling a blanket atop his own legs. "The captain and crew will have sought a sheltered harbor to ride out this storm. But once it passes, they should return to collect us."

"Hmm," was her reply.

Silence.

And then . . .

"May I ask ye a question?"

"Of course," he replied.

"Yesterday, ye said that being unable tae find me in the waves made ye reconsider your desires for our marriage. But ye never expounded upon it."

Tristan paused.

"That . . . that is not quite a question," he said, unable to resist. "It is a statement of fact."

"*Tristan.*" She leaned out from her chair, fixing him with an aggravated look.

"I would be happy to assist you in forming one—a question, that is." He sipped his whisky. "I am a most excellent question asker—an inquisitive inquirer, if you will."

She stared at him, jaw sagging. "Ye do not ask questions, Tristan Gilbert. Ye command and give orders."

"Is that so?"

"Hah! I see what you did there. If I didn't know better, I would think this a weak attempt at teasing . . . or possibly even flirtation."

Ouch. That rather put him in his place.

"Am I that ridiculous at flirting?"

"Nae . . . but why would ye feel the need tae flirt? I'm your wife."

"And a husband cannot flirt with his wife? I missed years of flirting with you before our marriage. Perhaps I am merely trying to right past wrongs."

She leveled a finger at him. "Ye be distracting me from my question."

"Truly, you have yet to ask one."

Isolde huffed. "What would ye like from our marriage?" She shook her head, sitting back in her chair. "Is that sufficiently *question-ish* for yourself?"

Tristan sipped his whisky, stifling a laugh. "I never knew vexing my wife could be so enjoyable."

"Tristan! Your answer, please." She beckoned with her hand.

Mmm.

How to reply?

He wanted a true marriage—one of trust and love. Of respect and devotion.

"Ye be thinking far too long over there, Husband," she continued.

"Merely attempting to put my answer into words."

"The topic of our marriage requires such careful reflection?"

No, I simply don't wish to overwhelm you with the force of my affections.

"Not at all," he said aloud. "It's merely that . . . fearing you had been . . . lost, I regretted not coming to know you more fully. For example, I do not know your favorite flower, your preferred food. Or even your favorite season. I wish to right those wrongs and, hopefully, create a truer marriage between us."

She did not reply for a long moment.

Tristan resisted the urge to lean forward and suss out her expression.

"Have you ever wooed a lady?" she finally asked.

"Pardon?"

"I am practicing my question-asking skills as I have recently been informed they are lacking. Have you ever wooed a lady, Your Grace?"

Tristan blinked. "Uhmm . . . no."

"I thought not."

She said nothing more.

What the devil was she getting at?

"Am I to understand that you find my attempts to foster more harmony between us . . . inadequate?"

"Nae," she replied. "They are unexpected and possibly a wee bit unnerving—"

"Unnerving?"

She leaned forward again. "Ye must admit, ye have been rather churlish with myself throughout the entirety of our acquaintance.

This—" She twirled a finger to indicate his person. "—is a welcome reprieve. But the cynic within me has tae wonder at its longevity."

Tristan had no clue how to respond.

Because she was correct, in a way. Even *he* didn't know if he could make this change within himself permanent.

But he was determined to try.

"I wish to change," he said quietly. "And I believe that is where true change begins . . . with a desire to be different."

"And the wooing?"

"I have never wished to woo a woman."

"Never?"

Only you. Once upon a time.

"I am a duke."

"And dukes do not *woo*?" Her voice held an ironic lilt.

"Most women are so enamored at the thought of becoming a duchess, they come pre-wooed, as it were."

"Mmm, that makes a certain sense, I suppose. Though *I* certainly didn't marry yourself tae become a duchess."

That was true.

Isolde couldn't care less about his title and lands.

She would only ever see him as a man, for good or ill.

"Precisely. Hence the need for—" He mimicked her previous motion, twirling a finger to indicate her person. "—wooing."

She lifted an eyebrow. "To ensure I am a *willing, enthusiastic* participant?"

The boldness of her—volleying back his own words—knocked the breath from his lungs.

"Been thinking excessively about that, have you?" The sentence, sardonic and tinged with derision, slipped out before he could stem it.

"The first rule of a good wooing, Your Grace, is to avoid saying arse-headed things." She saluted him with her mug. "Something ye clearly are going to find a wee bit challenging."

She was not wrong.

"I'm trying to do better," he said, disliking the petulant growl in his tone.

Isolde gave him no reply. Instead, she sat back and nursed her mug.

Maddening woman.

Neither of them spoke for a long moment.

"I hate that the choice of who tae marry was taken from us." Her voice drifted out from the depths of her chair. "That we will always wonder . . . what might have been."

He snorted, soft and low.

What might have been.

Surely, he would wonder that as well, but not for the same reason. What if they hadn't been forced to marry? What if he had never come to his senses?

"I believe we always had a choice," he replied.

"Perhaps. But not good choices." A pause. "I know ye would not have married me otherwise."

In that, she was utterly wrong.

But even he understood she was not ready for the full truth.

"Do you remember our first meeting?" he asked instead, swirling the whisky in his cup.

"At my father's house party two years past, when I was introduced tae yourself and Allie?"

"No."

Though Tristan supposed that encounter had been momentous as well, seeing Isolde for the first time in six years. Her beauty and animation had bludgeoned his senses, rendering him a struck gong of longing and horror. He had stood stupefied in Hadley's drawing-room, awash in the realization that his attraction to the earl's daughter had dimmed not one whit despite time's passage.

Isolde said nothing for a while. Coals collapsed in the grate with a rustle.

"Our first meeting," she repeated, voice so hesitant he had to strain to hear. "Are ye referring tae our encounter at the Duke of Montacute's garden party?"

"You remember?"

"Aye, how could I forget? I utterly mortified myself. But I am surprised you remember me. I assumed ye had forgotten all about it."

Forgotten?! The irony. "I remember everything about you, Isolde."

Naturally, she misunderstood his meaning.

"I suppose ye have always seen the worst of my behavior," she said with a soft laugh. "Our first meeting was so embarrassing, mistaking ye for John as I did. My brothers teased me for months once they learned of it. Because, of course, I told John and, of course, he told Mac and James. Surely that was when your lowering opinion of me began. You must have thought me the veriest hoyden."

Perhaps, later, he had thought her a hoyden in an effort to save his sanity. But at the beginning? "Not at all."

"Nae?" she huffed. "Now I know ye be *bamming* me."

Taking a deep breath for courage, Tristan told her the truth—

"I thought you the most beautiful creature I had ever seen." A pause. "I still do."

She was quiet for so long, he wondered if she had even heard him.

Finally, she cleared her throat. "Mmm, much better."

"Pardon?"

"Your wooing." She set down her mug and stood up, stirring the fire which had devolved to rapidly cooling coals at this point. "Keep . . . keep using pretty phrases like that."

"That I find you beautiful?"

"Aye." She turned to look at him. "It sends shivers down my spine when ye say it . . . so matter-of-fact, as if it's patently obvious."

He frowned, setting down his own mug. "Haven't you a mirror? It *is* patently obvious."

"Please," she snorted in disbelief. "I am an overly-tall, overly-educated, outspoken lady with hair the color of maple leaves in October and skin that appears speckled with mud. Polite Society only tolerates my presence because my father is an earl, and my dowry rivaled a maharajah's treasury."

What the bloody hell?!

"Come here," he motioned.

She folded her arms. "Why?"

"Because I tire of talking to your specter huddled there." He pointed to her own chair. "And my chair is large enough for us both."

She snorted. "Aye, if I am practically sitting on your lap."

"That was the basic idea . . . yes." He raised an eyebrow and lifted his blanket in invitation. "It's simple mathematics. Two bodies in one space are warmer than just one."

"Opting for *logos*, are ye?"

"I am indeed. We cannot put more peat on the fire, as we wish to conserve our stores, therefore the room will continue to cool. Consolidating our body heat would merely be a practical application of Newton's Law of Cooling."

"Ensuring that a larger portion of our bodies' heat loss is transferred to one another instead of the room at large?"

Heaven help him but he adored her intelligence.

"Precisely." He patted his thighs. "Fourier's equation could apply specific numbers for heat transference, if you would like."

On a sigh, she draped her own blanket around her shoulders. "I *have* always admired Fourier's equation of thermal conductivity. And I suppose we have put it to good use in the past."

"In the ice house? Indeed, we did."

He slid to the left, giving her room to maneuver.

Gingerly, she draped her knees over his thighs and perched her bottom on the seat to his right. He dragged his blanket over both their legs and slid his arm around her waist, pulling her against him. She shifted her own blanket around her shoulders and used the excess to cover his chest.

As in the ice house, she melted into him, happily sinking her weight into his body, tucking her arms between them, and resting her head on his shoulder.

And as then, Tristan wanted to simultaneously sigh in contentment and groan in pleasure. Unlike then, he gave himself over to the delectable feel of her in his arms—the curve of her bosom against his ribs, the press of her thighs over his, the heat of her palm on his heart.

"This is cozy," she murmured.

"It is." Wonderfully so.

"You are deliciously warm." She burrowed further into him. "An excellent practitioner of thermal conduction."

"Thank you."

"I didn't think ye would be the sort tae *coorie* down and cuddle for a wee while."

"Neither did I, Duchess," he laughed, softly. "But I rather delight in holding you close."

21

Curled into Tristan's chest, Isolde struggled to sort through the emotions flowering like snowdrops in her chest.

What *was* she feeling precisely?

Wariness and concern quickly surfaced—both for the abrupt change in her husband's behavior, as well as questions as to its longevity.

But she was fascinated, too, by the complexity that lay beneath his stern exterior—teasing and gruff honesty.

In turn, this engendered a desire to know that complex man further.

But most of all, she felt astonishment over his calm declaration—

I thought you the most beautiful creature I had ever seen. I still do.

Isolde would hear the echo of those words on her deathbed. The shock of them—uttered so matter-of-factly in his gravelly, aristocratic voice—had obliterated every other thought from her head.

Impossible.

Impossible he had thought that of her then.

Impossible that every time Tristan had looked at her with judgment and repugnance in his gaze, he had also been pondering her beauty.

Yet, he held her now as if she were treasured.

He cradled her gently, her forehead tucked into the hollow between his shoulder and his throat, the worn wool of his borrowed homespun jacket soft under her cheek.

It had been an unusual day, the two of them focused solely on each other and what they must do to survive. And yet, Isolde could not remember when she had last enjoyed the passing hours so thoroughly. Perhaps Christmas Day with her family?

It had been bizarre to see Tristan without the trappings of his dukedom. Instead of frowning judgmentally at the humble fare she cooked or complaining about the spartan nature of their surroundings, he had rolled up his sleeves and set to. As if they were a team. Or a . . . couple.

Aye, he had been quiet. She doubted Tristan would ever be overly-talkative, like Allie's husband, Ethan Penn-Leith.

Instead, he strangely reminded her of Ethan's older brother, Mr. Malcolm Penn-Leith. The sort of man who said little but exuded calm and competence in equal measure.

Though in Tristan's case, that calm and competence were intertwined with the commanding power of a dukedom. After all, one did rather anticipate him throwing open a door and barking commands at a small regiment.

Yet, if he thought her beautiful . . . well, then she could be ruthlessly honest with herself—

She found Tristan devastatingly attractive. Any woman with a beating pulse would find him so—enigmatic, brooding, and swathed in authority. It was a potent combination.

Isolde felt as if she had ensorcelled a lion. And though delightful to have tamed a menacing beast, she was also wary of said enchantment's duration.

"If ye have always found me so lovely, why were ye *crabbit* with myself, particularly after our marriage?" She adjusted her head on his shoulder, soaking in the strength of his body, the delicious feel of his muscled arm around her.

"I was ill-tempered over our situation, not yourself specifically."

Skepticism rose along with her eyebrows. She wasn't quite sure she believed him, but she let the explanation pass.

"And before our marriage?" she asked. "Ye *loathed* me. Those were your precise words."

A long sigh rattled his chest beneath her ear. His arm around her waist tightened and his other hand came to rest atop her legs, just above her knees. His thumb absently drew circles on her thigh, sparking electrical currents with each sweep.

Surely Newtonian law could describe the sensation mathematically, but Tristan's touch scattered her wits so thoroughly, she currently struggled to remember her own name.

"I had to loathe you, Isolde. There seemed no other choice."

"No choice? That is rather unexpectedly histrionic of you." She pulled back to look at him. "I fear I require a wee bit more explanation."

His dark eyes quietly drank her in while that rogue thumb continued its leisurely debauchery of Newton's well-formed mathematical equations.

"Allie believes that *love* and *hate* are sibling emotions rather than true opposites, as they both involve similarly deep feelings."

Isolde stilled, pondering the thought. "Like a binary star. They appear independent from one angle, but in reality, they orbit one another."

"Precisely. Also, I rescind any unkind thing I have ever said about your university education."

She poked his ribs.

He squirmed, lips curving upward.

"And how does this relate tae your loathing of myself?" She rested her palm against his sternum.

"I could only loathe or admire you. That was the binary choice."

"Ah."

So what did that mean now? He had decided to admire her instead?

Her lips could not form the question, much less ask it.

As with his insistence on her beauty, such admiration felt impossible. Unbelievable.

"But even then . . ." he began.

He lifted his hand from her leg.

Isolde raised an eyebrow, a question mark in her expression.

His eyes burned into hers, amber-streaked from the glowing coals of the fire. Lion-like, she supposed.

Without breaking her gaze, he brushed the tips of his fingers across her décolletage, tracing the collarbones beneath her gown.

The press of his fingers singed her nerves, setting them to sparking.

"Even then," he repeated, eyes staring at his hand, "you knew what you did to me. How enamored I was. You tortured me."

Isolde's heart hammered against her ribcage.

She had suspected.

But that was hardly the same thing as hearing him admit it.

His fingers traced her collarbones again, just as her own had done in his library . . . and then again at Lady Lockheade's soirée.

The sparks in her chest burst into fireworks.

"It was a wee experiment," she whispered. "Tae see how ye would react if I . . ."

His hand moved to cupping her jaw. "And your conclusion?"

"Undetermined. Ye stared at me a great deal, and I did wonder if ye found me attractive." Heat rose in her cheeks at the admission and her gaze dropped to his throat. "But it seemed so outlandish a thought, and ye generally acted as if I were a leper."

He grunted and tilted her chin, lifting her gaze to his.

Isolde was quite sure she watched mathematical volumes on attraction and desire write themselves in his eyes.

And then, he leaned toward her, touching his lips to her ear and whispering so closely his syllables brushed her skin—

"If you ever believe anything I say, Isolde Gilbert, please believe this: You are a remarkable human being. You are the flash of a bluebird's wing in winter that steals my breath." He said the words gruffly, fiercely, as if he resented having to draw them from his lungs. "You are draped in bravery and grace. No pampered English miss would have donned a *selkie*'s skin and saved my hide yesterday. And instead of crumbling under the unknown of our current situation, you made soup from lentils and kneaded our bread. You scream down the wind of challenges, and I admire you all the more for it."

He dropped her chin, returned his hand to her leg, and stared at the fire.

As if he hadn't just said the most lovely thing imaginable.

As if his words didn't reverberate in her bones.

Surely this lyrical poeticism originated in his Italian self.

Isolde stared at his profile—the blade of his nose, the twin arch of his lips—trying to command her riotous thoughts into order.

"For someone who has never wooed," she swallowed, "ye are proving surprisingly adept at it."

He spared her a sideways glance before looking back to the fire. "It is no idle flattery, Wife. I recognized your strength the moment we first met in Montacute's garden."

Again, he said the words on a growl, as though their tenderness angered him. It was an echo of his prior way of speaking—as if she irritated him beyond reason.

Loathe and admire, he had said. Perhaps this was how it manifested.

"You seem . . . upset about that. About my supposed loveliness . . ."

"No." He shook his head, still not looking at her. "I am merely struggling as I always do when in your presence."

"Struggling?"

"Yes. Resisting the urge to kiss you."

Oh!

The air left her lungs in a *whoosh*.

"And given how still you've gone," his voice remained gruff, "you have not arrived at the point where my kiss would be eagerly welcomed."

Eagerly welcomed? Perhaps not.

Curiously allowed? Of a certainty.

But, of course, now she was back to staring at his lips and wondering.

Would she feel more than curiosity, were she to kiss him . . . *when* she inevitably kissed him?

She had kissed several gentlemen over the years. Jarvis had been the last, however—a cautionary tale, if ever she needed one.

And though some of those kisses had been lovely—decidedly lovely, in fact—they had never left her wanting more.

Closing his eyes, Tristan rested his head against the back of the chair, his thumb reverting to its maddening caress of her thigh.

She should kiss him . . .

And yet, Isolde hesitated.

His abrupt change still left her wary.

Less than forty-eight hours ago, he had hardly been capable of uttering a civil sentence in her presence.

So, yes, he found her physically attractive. And perhaps he had decided to label that sense of attraction as *admiration* in the wake of their near-drowning.

But a rather sizable part of her doubted that a man could change so quickly. Worse, who knew what version she would wake to of a morning—the hateful or the loving one?

She would prefer he despise her continually rather than have him murmur beautiful promises one day and then devolve back into haughty Kendall the next.

That would crush her . . . imagining what might have been.

No. She was not ready to kiss him. Not yet.

She leaned back into the curve of his arm around her waist.

"I hesitate and now ye won't even look at me?" she asked.

"Too tempting."

"Because of . . . kissing?"

"The topic currently occupies a rather alarming portion of my brain matter."

"*Tristan.*" His name emerged half chuckle, half reproach. "Now, ye are being ridicul—"

"Please can we speak of *anything* else?" he growled, eyes still closed.

"Anything?"

"Yes!"

Well, when he gave her such an opening . . .

Might as well spur him back into his Kendall persona. A test, of sorts.

She was forever conducting experiments with this man.

"Why do ye hate my father so? The true reason, if you please."

Those chocolate-brown eyes flared open, his thumb frozen on her leg.

"Hadley?" he frowned.

"Yes. He is my father, in case you have conveniently erased that fact from your memory," she said dryly.

He grimaced and returned to staring at the coals glowing in the grate.

"Come now," she prodded. "Surely there is more tae the tale than his ill-advised investments with Jarvis."

"Must there be?" His arm tensed behind her.

"Ye saw my father impeached," Isolde scoffed. "Ye hired investigators, hounded him in the newspapers, and courted votes in Commons, ensuring all and sundry understood the depths of your low opinion. No man goes tae such lengths merely to see justice served."

"Isolde—"

"In all honesty, I expected more gloating from yourself over your victories."

"Gloating?" He finally returned his turbulent gaze to hers.

His thumb began its leisurely trail over her thigh once more.

"Aye. Gloating. Ye have a history of it with myself." She continued to press the topic. "Ye said upon our marriage that ye would cease prosecuting my father. Will ye recuse yourself now that he has been impeached?"

"Yes. I will keep my word. My efforts to attack Hadley ended the day I offered for your hand."

Isolde hoped that was true.

"But what was the catalyst for it all? The accusations and rancor?"

"You are certainly determined to test my will today, Wife."

"Yes, well, that is rather the point."

"Pardon?"

"As I said earlier, I am skeptical of this change in yourself. Over the course of our acquaintance, ye have called me vulgar and unladylike. Not even eight days ago, ye stated that I would *never* have been the bride of your choice. And now, ye act as if I were the only bride ye had ever envisioned. The only woman ye have ever . . . wooed." She tapped a finger against his chest. "Ye can see how I would be confused."

"And so you ask me about your father?"

"Aye! Because the subject is likely tae spark your temper—to draw out your *Kendall* self. We both know Papa's investments with Jarvis were not the origin of your vitriol, but rather an excuse to seek revenge. Does your hatred stem from the fact that Papa targeted the Dukedom of Kendall's financial interests in revenge for your father's treatment of Uncle Rafe?"

He leaned back. "How do you know that?"

She shrugged. "Papa says things without realizing I will connect the dots, as it were. So is that the reason?"

Tristan closed his eyes again.

"Isolde." He said her name with such weariness, as if she had once again pushed him to breaking.

But, then, that had been her purpose. To discover the point where he would retreat inward and shut her out. Like pressing against a cut on one's finger to locate where it was most sore.

To find the edges where *Tristan* ended and *Kendall* began.

It appeared that she had discovered one edge—a border, so to speak—between the two sides of him.

"The problem here, Tristan, is that ye wish tae know myself better, as ye said earlier. But a true relationship is never one-sided. If ye wish tae know me, I must also know yourself. It is how friendship or marriage or any true relationship works."

He breathed in and out for long moments, eyes still closed.

"I'm trying," he finally whispered. "But this is new to me. And the answer to your question is . . . difficult. I have never had . . . that is, I do not know how to make . . ."

His voice drifted off, but she easily completed the sentence—

A friend.

He didn't know how to make a friend. Because he had never had one.

Naturally, his honesty would disarm her indignation. But then, this man had always upended her world.

Her heart ached for the quiet, watchful boy Allie described her twin as being.

"That is a very vulnerable thing to tell me, Tristan," she said softly. "As a would-be friend, I appreciate your honesty."

Finally, he opened his eyes, pinning her with his dark ones. Something tortured glittered in their depths, but when he spoke, his voice was pure, icy Kendall—

"I don't want or need your *pity*, Duchess."

It gave her chills, that voice. So cutting and cold, but when paired with the hurt she knew lay behind it . . .

"Compassion is not pity, Your Grace." She pressed her palm to his chest. "Empathy is not pity. It is one of many things ye will have tae learn in order to forge a genuine marriage between us."

She spoke truth, but part of her had to wonder if the task was simply too great.

Years of arrogant behavior could not be erased with just a few pretty words.

But if he was committed to change—to finding himself as Tristan once more—she would help him in any way she could.

And given what she had seen of Tristan so far . . .

She could tumble headlong into love with him.

"If ye will not speak with me about my father, which"—she held out a hand to stem his protestations—"I ken tae be a trying subject. For now, let us start easier. Tell me about your studies at Oxford, and I shall tell ye about mine at Broadhurst."

He swallowed and nodded in agreement.

It proved an engaging topic.

He described studying mathematics and physics at Balliol College. She recounted her own studies of engineering.

"Consider engineering tae be *physics in application*, if ye must," she quipped.

That somehow veered off into a conversation about Mr. Charles Darwin and his voyage aboard the *H.M.S. Beagle*. Apparently, they had both been avidly following Mr. Darwin's publications about the flora and fauna of the Galapagos.

Three hours passed in a blink, the fire extinguishing entirely and their limbs stiff and sore from sitting in the darkness.

And still, they talked.

Somewhere in Tristan's description of Mr. Darwin's thoughts on the geologic structure of coral reefs, Isolde drifted off to sleep.

She woke with a start at the sound of footfalls.

Tristan was carrying her upstairs, cradled against his chest as if she weighed no more than a child.

"I can walk," she murmured.

"No. Let me carry you."

Mmm, she liked the sound of that.

The feel of cold sheets under her head shook her awake once more.

"Thank ye." She burrowed under the counterpane and tucked deeper into the bed box, mourning the loss of his body's heat.

"My pleasure," he rumbled in return.

She could scarcely see him, as they had no candles. But still, she sensed him turn to leave.

Unthinking, she reached for his hand, seizing it in her own.

"Stay," she whispered. "Just tae sleep, nothing more."

"Isolde . . ."

"Ye needn't touch me if it's too difficult, but the night is cold and Fourier's equation of thermal conductivity needs more testing, I ken."

"Is that so?"

"Aye. 'Twould be for science."

"Me sleeping in this bed with you?"

"I do appreciate your intelligence."

"Well, for science then . . ."

Isolde was rather sure a smile wove through his words.

The mattress dipped beside her, and she heard the *shush* of bed drapes being pulled shut.

Her last memory was his voice at her back—

"Sleep, Wife. I shall keep you warm."

22

Another day.

Another visit to Tristan's own personal Hell.

He awoke slowly, daylight a gentle hum against his eyelids.

The sun is shining, was his first thought.

Mmm, I'm curled around a delectable woman, was his second.

Both of those thoughts sat happily in his brain until their import sank in.

A sunny day meant calmer seas. The *SS Statesman* would be returning soon.

And woman?

He tipped his chin to the head that nestled against him.

Isolde.

She was tucked against him in spoon-fashion—her back to his chest, his nose touching her neck. His arm lay over her waist, holding her fast.

Daylight slipped through the drapes behind him, bouncing a shaft of cheery sun off the walls of the bed box.

Heaven help him.

The whole was such sweet torture.

He should have refused when she asked him to stay. A man could only resist so much temptation before succumbing.

But this . . .

To awake in her bed, the one place he would choose over any other on Planet Earth . . .

He stored yet another image of Isolde for his catalog, this one entirely sensory. The press of her shoulder blades against his chest, the rise and fall of her ribs under his palm, the smell of her sleep-warmed skin.

He breathed her in.

It was simply . . . too much.

The feel of her, the longing choking his lungs.

His heart beat a staccato tattoo in his chest.

Powerless to resist, he dragged his nose across the freckles at her nape.

Soft. So soft.

With agonizing slowness, he pressed his lips to the back of her neck.

Her skin was every whit as luscious as he had imagined, warm and velvety smooth.

He inhaled sharply at the contact.

Helplessly, he kissed her nape again. The precise place he had ached to touch when he had unlaced her corset.

And then he noticed it—

Isolde was holding still.

Too still.

Awake-still.

Bloody hell.

Shame and disgust roiled through him.

Carefully, he pulled away from her, rolling to his back, a hand pressed over his eyes.

How many times had he vowed that he would not take what she did not freely offer?

And yet the second he could, he stole a kiss. A kiss she had not wanted or granted him leave to bestow.

As usual, his intelligent wife was wise to be leery of him and his intentions.

Somehow, someway . . . he had to control the Kraken of his desire. To wait until her ardor matched his own.

Patience.

He had to be patient.

To that end, he slipped from the bed box.

She said nothing.

He studied her as he stood beside the bed, a corner of the drapes held in each hand, intending to shut them again. Isolde's eyes were closed, as though she slept. But the flutter of her eyelids and shallowness of her breaths betrayed her.

Do better, he adjured himself. *Be better.*

Quietly, he drew the bed curtains closed and left the room, dressing quickly in the second bedchamber before going downstairs.

But once there, the restless longing in his blood would not subside.

Outside, blue sky and sunshine dominated—a rarity on the west coast of the Highlands.

Surely, the *SS Statesman* would return for them. Perhaps in as soon as a couple of hours, depending on where the ship had waited out the storm.

Needing to burn off his excess of energy, to quell the ache of his longing, Tristan tugged on his own boots, still damp but serviceable. He found a cap for his head—his hat having been lost at sea—and set out to explore the island. Perhaps there was another house on the opposite side? Briefly, he considered waking Isolde, but she had held herself so still—clearly not wanting his company after his indiscretion—that he discarded the notion.

Though the sun shone, the wind tugged at his hat and whipped his coat behind him. He climbed a gently sloping hill, heather and moss spongy beneath his feet, to survey what he could.

Standing atop the rise, he spun in a circle. The island was decidedly small—scarcely a mile end-to-end, he would guess, and only half as wide. The whole of it was covered in heather, gorse, and *machair*—green grassy fields—not a tree or tall bush to be had.

On the mainland, the mountains of the Rough Bounds rose, a

cottage here and there dotting the rugged shoreline in the distance. But no village. And certainly no roads leading inland.

As it had been for millennia, the ocean was the preferred highway of the Highlands. And the only source of rescue for Isolde and himself.

However, scanning the sea from his vantage point, he saw no sign of his ship. Not even a whiff of her smoke on the horizon.

Well, she would return. If not today, then certainly by tomorrow. Or, if the ship had suffered damage in the storm, Captain Woodbury would send a rescue party to collect them.

Their own island—Canna, Isolde had called it—showed signs of having had significantly more inhabitants in the past. Along the eastern edge, several houses clustered around a sheltered bay, but even at a distance, their glassless windows and crumbling roof lines testified to their abandoned state.

There were sheep, however, looking uncannily like puffy white clouds scudding across the *machair*. The keepers of the isle should be returning soon, he supposed. Like Tristan and Isolde, the storm had probably caught the caretakers off-guard and forced them to seek a sheltered harbor on the mainland until it passed.

He took a roundabout path back to the house, walking the length of the white sand beach where he and Isolde had washed up. Despite his exertions, the vibrating energy in his chest had not abated.

La bramosia. The desperate yearning still wracked him.

Fortunately, the storm had deposited several large tree trunks on the sand, many of which did not appear too waterlogged.

Well, if his ship was delayed in returning, the driftwood would provide another source of fuel for the fire. And he had a prodigious amount of energy to burn and no fencing master handy to assist him in expending it. In his current state, tree limbs would weigh but a lark's feather.

Dragging a long log behind him, Tristan returned to the house. From there, it was a simple matter to locate an axe and then a whetstone to sharpen its edge. The chickens clucked and pecked around him as he worked.

Within half an hour, the sounds of wood chopping echoed off the stone walls of the house and courtyard.

A quarter-hour later, he shed his coat. A short while after that, he tugged off his shirt and used it to mop the sweat from his brow before tossing it atop his coat.

He turned back to the axe and the task before him.

ISOLDE AWOKE TO the sound of an axe splitting wood and bright sun peeking through the bed curtains.

Frowning, she turned over, feeling the cold mattress where her husband had been.

Memories trickled in.

Tristan's body wrapped around her own, holding her tightly against his chest.

That had been . . . lovely.

She had sensed him waking up, and so she had held still, terrified to break the spell.

And then the feel of his lips at her nape.

Gooseflesh pebbled her arms just recalling the moment.

A rather embarrassing part of her hoped he would continue his caresses.

Instead, he had retreated and left the room.

She had waited, hoping for his return, but had fallen asleep instead.

Throwing off the coverlet, she pushed back the heavy drapes and padded over to the window, looking down at the wee courtyard between the cold larder and the series of outbuildings.

Mmm.

Tristan stood in the center dressed only in trousers, braces, and boots—acres of tanned Mediterranean skin gleaming in the daylight—chopping at what appeared to be driftwood.

Och, 'twas a sight as bonnie as the sunshine.

Isolde felt immensely cheered.

Dressing quickly, she darted down the stairs and into the cold larder, peering through the window there.

Aye.

The scene was even better from here.

The same arms that had held her so tenderly the night before now swung an axe with brutal efficiency, the motion smooth and practiced.

Why had a duke learned to use an axe? Surely Tristan had an army of woodsmen to do such tasks. And yet, the motion was too practiced, too fluid to be anything but the result of years of muscle memory.

Ropy sinews snaked down his arms, and the straps of his braces framed his pectorals as if they were a painting hung in the National Gallery. All the man lacked was a kilt to be considered a proper Highlander. Perhaps she could coax him into one. Hadn't she seen a length of tartan in the chest upstairs, just waiting to be folded into a *feileadh mòr*—a great kilt?

And this beautifully-formed man was her husband! For the first time, she felt a wave of gratitude that *he* was the man she had married in the end.

Isolde intended to boil some porridge and summon him for breakfast.

Instead, she fetched a wee bit of vinegar and a rag to clean the glass windowpanes. Just . . . to ensure the vista was as clear as possible.

Perhaps . . . bread would be a better option for breaking their fast.

Yes.

And if she had a view while kneading the dough . . . well, so much the better.

BLOODY HELL.

Tristan had needed this.

The steady repetition of swinging the axe, the satisfying *thunk* of steel cutting into wood, the aching burn in his muscles.

As usual, the exertion focused his thinking while the cool breeze and warm sun soothed his fevered skin. Invigorating and cleansing.

Over and over he swung the axe, feeling like a madman. As if only by exhausting himself, he might purge the worst of his longing.

Swing. *Thunk.*

Swing. *Thunk.*

He demolished one log and traipsed down to the beach for another. And then another. When thirsty, he drank from the rock-lined spring off the back door, even dumping the cold water over his head at one point.

As usual, the physical labor quieted his mind, rendering the world a far-off buzz. Nothing intruded.

No thoughts of *what if* or *if only.*

Just the sound of wind and waves and the bite of the axe.

Eventually, something flickered in the corner of his eye, a flash of white.

"Tristan!" a voice called, breaking through his trance.

He paused, resting the butt of his axe on the ground, chest heaving with exertion.

Isolde.

Waving a white handkerchief to get his attention.

His hungry eyes drank her in, as if he hadn't seen her in days instead of hours. Her hair looped her head in a crown, the same blue gown hugging her curves, the same eighteen inches of calf and ankle on delectable display.

And yet, as ever, she was the most beautiful creature he had ever seen.

The yearning within him surged to the surface, uncaring that he had just spent half a day working himself to exhaustion.

Would it never end? This dumbstruck sense of amazement and awe whenever he saw her?

"Ye must stop." She shook her head, crossing to him.

"Stop?" he repeated.

"Aye. Ye have been chopping wood like a man possessed for hours now."

He *was* a man possessed.

"And your palm is bleeding." She pointed to the axe in his hands.

Oh.

Looking down, he could see the smear of blood on the wooden handle. He lifted his right hand, staring at the burst blister on his palm.

He hadn't felt a thing.

His palms sported callouses on the pads from years of fencing and horse riding. But a blister had taken root, nonetheless.

A glance up at the sky showed the time to be at least past noon.

He looked back to his wife.

She regarded him with concerned eyes, as if he were a wild beast on a leash.

Or . . . a man who had taken unwelcome liberties with her person hours earlier.

"Come." She took the axe and leaned it against the chopping block. "Let me clean and bind the blister for you."

Tristan nodded.

How like her. To offer him care when he had neglected to do the same.

She turned toward the small pool of spring water, beckoning him. Ducking inside the house for a moment, she returned immediately with the bottle of whisky and a strip of clean linen.

With competent hands, she lifted his injured palm, cupping it in her own. Dipping the handkerchief into the water, she gently dabbed at the blood, wiping it from his skin.

Her gaze darted to his bare chest as she worked, surely noting the gooseflesh there. Not due to the cold, of course, but the sparking electricity of her touch.

Once his hand was clean, she lifted the bottle of whisky in salute.

"I thought you would give me a swallow *before* tending to my injury," he said.

"Ye hardly be hurt tae that degree." She shook her head. "Lord Lockheade is a close family friend, as I suppose ye know. However, ye may not know that his lordship is a fully trained medical doctor. He recommends using whisky tae clean a wound, as it will prevent infection."

She poured a small amount of the fiery liquid onto his hand. Tristan winced at the sting.

Blotting the wound dry, she wrapped his palm with the length of cotton, tying it in a small knot on the back of his hand.

"There," she nodded and looked up at him, still cradling his hand in hers.

The sunlight danced across her cheeks, highlighting those freckles he adored and catching her blue eyes.

"Thank you," he said, unable to remove his gaze from her face but equally unable to decipher her expression. "You always seem to be saving me from myself."

"*Och*, it's not as one-sided as that. Ye did carry me up to bed and then serve as my personal bed warmer all night."

Right.

He owed her an apology.

Likely, he would owe her a sea of apologies as time progressed.

"Isolde, I . . ." He expelled a long breath and then forced the words out. "I apologize for my behavior this morning."

She tilted her head. "Your behavior?"

"Yes. I should not have . . ."—*another deep breath*—". . . kissed your neck without your permission. I can offer no excuses other than my determination to be more respectful—"

"I took no offense at the gesture."

"Pardon?"

"Your kiss."

"But . . . ye were holding yourself so still, as though you did not—"

"Aye, I was holding still! It was so lovely, waking in your arms. And I was terrified if I moved, ye would pull away. And that is precisely what happened."

"Isolde—" His voice cracked and his jaw moved helplessly, her confession robbing him of words.

"Ye need to speak with me, Tristan. Not make assumptions and rush off. Ye might have whispered, 'Isolde, may I—'"

"But I did not ask, and I would never . . ."

"Hush. Enough." She lifted his injured hand. "I shall merely take a kiss for a kiss. And then we will be even."

And with that declaration, she pressed her soft lips to his palm, to the wound there.

A shuddering breath left him at the unexpected touch.

"Isolde," he repeated her name, this time on a rasping whisper. "May I . . ."

He couldn't finish the sentence.

Her gaze met his. Surely reading the longing—the ferocious yearning that whisked words from his lungs.

"Oh, Tristan," she breathed. "When ye look at me like that . . ."

"Like what?"

"Like ye are drowning in those waves again. Like ye will expire if ye do not touch me . . . if ye do not kiss me."

The direct statement drew a short laugh from him.

"Yes." He blinked. "*Yes.*"

"Then, let us do something about it."

Shaking her head, she dropped his palm, reached her hands around his neck, and threaded her fingers into his hair.

With a slight tug, she pulled his lips down to hers.

The sudden press of her mouth, the feel of her body rising to meet his chest, the onslaught of sensation—electricity and heat and *hallelujahatlast!*

It was simply . . .

Tristan gasped at the shock.

She startled and pulled back, but only retreated an inch before his hands circled her waist and held her fast.

"No," he growled. "More." A pause. "Please."

She smiled, that glorious smile.

He captured it with his mouth.

The give of her pillowy lips beneath his . . .

The taste of her, summer and sunshine . . .

The sound of her helpless whimper . . .

His arms wrapped around her *justlikethat,* lifting her into his body, one hand at her waist, the other between her shoulder blades.

Her own hands twined into his hair, nails raking his scalp and sending a jolt down his spine.

A guttural moan tore from his chest.

Heaven help him! He had imagined this kiss more times than any sane man should. Thoughts of her had haunted his fantasies and fanned the darkest embers of his desire.

But the reality of her mouth on his—

Would he require a lifetime of kisses to slake his hunger?

Somehow, he had walked her backward, pressing her shoulders against the sun-warmed stone of the house.

His lips left her mouth, eager to explore the silken skin of her cheeks, the tender slide of her throat, the delectable hollow of her collarbone . . .

And still, it wasn't enough.

His hands moved to cup her face, tilting her head so he could plunder her mouth once more.

Her own hands roamed his chest and shoulders, painting fire in their wake.

Want. Want. Want.

Hers and his own.

Her name fell from his lips. A litany of desire. "Isolde . . . Isolde . . ."

As if she were an enchantress, and all he could do was dumbly repeat the purpose of her spell—

Summoning him to her side.

I DIDN'T KNOW.

The words tumbled through Isolde's mind.

I didn't know a kiss could be like this.

Tristan's lips pressed to her own. His body caging hers. His chest under her palms.

He was a feast, and she had only just realized the depth of her hunger.

The slide of his broad palm from her ribs to her waist sent a shower of electrical shocks skittering between her shoulder blades.

Surely Newton had a law to describe this, too.

His kiss obliterated every other she had experienced.

How had she even considered those to be kisses? They were a child's press of lips.

But this?

This was a claiming.

Part of her still heard him demanding *more* in stern ducal tones.

Normally, she hated that Kendall voice—haughty and domineering. Yet when he commanded her to continue kissing him . . .

And kiss, they did—chasing one another's lips, nipping throats and jawlines, breathy moans punctuating the lot.

At one point, Tristan pulled back and pressed his debauching thumb to her bee-stung mouth, dragging it across her bottom lip, tracking the movement with unholy fascination.

"This mouth . . ." he whispered.

Isolde kissed his thumb with deliberate ardor.

A shuddering breath escaped him, and he rewarded her by pressing his lips to hers once more, his large hand cradling her head as he pillaged.

Heaven help her.

Any more of this and she would struggle to recall her own name.

Finally, Tristan rested his forehead against her own, breaths coming in great gulps.

"Why?" His voice was rough. "Why did you kiss me? I thought you wary of—"

"I am. It is just . . ."

She swallowed.

He waited, his lips the barest breath away from hers.

Damnation.

She was going to have to tell him.

"I watched ye. Out the window."

"Chopping?"

"Aye."

And she had. For *hours*.

Spellbound by the lithe grace of him. Studying every last inch of his body—the taper of his shoulders to his narrow waist, the way his back muscles rippled with each swing of the axe, the hypnotic rhythm of sound.

All the while, unable to forget the feel of his arms around her, the ache in her belly when he had kissed her neck.

It had set a need buzzing through her veins. Like a cup of strong coffee bolted on an empty stomach.

Her thoughts had run wild.

They were *married*. Why not kiss him? Tristan wanted her, admired her.

And she . . . well, she wouldn't mind exploring their physical attraction. Perhaps it would help to solidify this change in him.

"So you kiss me out of lust, then?" He braced his arms on either side of her head.

Oh.

Well.

And what of it?

"Ye needn't make it sound tawdry. I am permitted tae ogle your fine body." She dragged her palms down said body in emphasis. "Ye be my husband, in case ye have forgotten."

He laughed at that—a weary, pained-cousin of a laugh. "Oh, Duchess, I have not forgotten for one second that you are my wife."

"What now?" She skated her fingers upward, liking how his eyes closed in pleasure as she raked them through his hair.

"What do you mean?"

"Ye be a wee bit obtuse, Husband." She trailed her hands down his neck.

He opened his eyes.

She lifted her brows suggestively.

"I won't have you out of mere lust, Wife."

Isolde frowned.

"But . . . I believe your requirements were *enthusiasm* and *willing participation*." She pressed a hungry kiss to the hollow at the base of his throat, drawing a rumble from his chest. "Am I not sufficiently displaying those qualities?"

"I changed my mind," he rasped.

"Ye can't do that."

"I . . . I believe I can, actually."

"Tristan."

"Isolde."

"You want me!"

"Yes, but I don't want only your lust," he growled. "I want *all* of you."

Och, this frustrating, stubborn, confusing—

"Ye already have all of me, Duke!" She pushed on his chest, forcing him to take a step back. "Ye *own* me—my body, my choices, my very life. What more can ye possibly want?"

"Everything. I. Want. *Everything*," he enunciated with knife-sharp precision.

"Everything?"

"Yes." He fixed her with his dark eyes, turbulent and ravenous. "When we finally come together, I want it to be because you love me. Not because I am a duke or your husband or a muscled chest you admired in a courtyard. I want you to come to my bed because you cannot help yourself. Because it is the only way to express the vast ocean of your longing. Because you will *die* if you don't have me. I want your heart, Isolde."

"My heart?" She threw her hands in the air. "Ye be demanding my very soul!"

"I suppose . . . I suppose I am."

She tapped her sternum. "So ye require my soul, but offer me what of yourself? *Like* and *admiration*, as ye said last evening? What if I want your heart—your own soul—in return?!"

She thought to taunt him, to force him to back down from his absurd request.

Instead, he laughed. That same caustic, knowing laugh.

In two steps, he filled her vision once more.

He cupped the back of her neck and pulled her against his chest, his lips claiming hers with terrifying ferocity.

Isolde arched into him, eagerly returning the embrace.

Drawing back, he pressed his forehead to hers once more.

"You are being rather slow on the uptake, Duchess. I told you yesterday that *love* and *hate* are binaries—two sides of the same coin."

"Aye."

"*Ergo*, I had to hate you, because otherwise, I would have had to admit that I . . ."

Maddeningly, he trailed off without completing the sentence.

His mouth claimed hers once more, kissing with erotic thoroughness. She clung to him, breathless.

"In short," he growled in his gravelly *Kendall* voice, "you already *own* my soul, Wife."

His hands left her so abruptly, Isolde took an involuntary step forward.

He turned and picked up his axe in one hand. Bending, he scooped up his shirt and coat in the other.

Isolde watched him walk away, helplessly admiring the lithe stretch of his gait, the bunched muscles between his shoulder blades.

I had to hate you because otherwise, I would have had to admit that I . . . love you.

She touched trembling fingertips to her swollen lips.

Had he . . .

Was that . . .

Had the Duke of Kendall just confessed that he loved her?

23

Isolde trailed her husband inside the house, her mind a turbulent sea.

He loved her?

He had, perhaps, loved her . . . for years?

The very idea was akin to a brush fire, incinerating every single assumption she had made about this man.

She had known he found her physically attractive.

But . . . love? Genuine love?

The sort of love that waits through a day, a journey, a sickness just to hear a beloved's voice once more? Love that strokes a tired brow and listens patiently to fears and touches skin only the moonlight sees? *That* kind of love?

Tristan stood at the carved-stone basin in the cold larder, dipping a clean rag into water to rinse and towel off his body. His braces now dangled around his knees, causing his trousers to rest perilously low on his hips.

He did not look at her.

"Ye love me," she said.

"Astute as usual, Wife." His tone was pure icy Kendall.

"And ye have likely loved me for . . . years." Just saying the words aloud felt absurd.

"Yes." Clipped. Terse.

Isolde almost smiled. How typical of him, to declare his love in a militant fashion.

"When?"

He didn't misunderstand her question.

"From the very beginning."

"Montacute's garden?"

A nod. Just one. A sharp up-down of his chin.

He dragged the towel down his bare chest, sending her thoughts spiraling.

"But last night, ye declared that ye only liked and admired myself."

"I lied."

"Why?"

"To spare your disbelief. To avoid consummating our marriage out of mere lust or misplaced duty on your part."

"Ah. So we will not . . ." She rolled her hand. ". . . until I love ye in return. Until I feel as if I will *die* if I don't have ye."

"Precisely."

"Will we cease kissing, as well?"

He finally looked at her, his gaze as turbulent as the ocean outside the window. "No."

"Nae?"

He tossed the towel onto the counter beside the basin.

"No," he repeated, stern and English and oh-so-ducal.

Even as the word left his tongue, he was backing her up against a cupboard, his large hand cradling her head.

And for the third time in as many minutes, Isolde found herself kissed senseless.

Gracious, but she adored this.

Feeling this haughty, arrogant man come undone beneath her palms—current crackling between their bodies.

"I have never particularly appreciated your imperious *Kendall* voice until this afternoon," she whispered against his mouth.

"This voice?" he asked, sharp and autocratic.

"Aye," she grinned on a laugh.

He kissed the smile off her lips. "Allie calls it my *duke* voice—domineering and cold, she says."

"Your sister has a way with description."

His eyebrows drew down. "And you . . . appreciate this voice?"

"When ye be ordering me tae kiss yourself? Aye. I like it very much." She ran her fingertips over the night whiskers stubbling his jaw. "Think of all the delightful things ye could order me tae do."

A faint blush tinged his cheeks. "You will be the death of me, woman."

She laughed and gently kissed his throat.

He sighed, his shoulders relaxing under her hands. And when he spoke next, she heard Tristan.

"As I said last night, Isolde, I wish us to have a true marriage. A love match, as it were." Once more, he braced an elbow above her head, his other hand gently cupping her cheek. "I want us to forge something genuine and lasting. So I will wait until you are ready to meet me where I am."

"Ye be asking me tae trust yourself."

"I suppose that I am."

He pressed the tenderest kiss to her lips before pushing off the wall and walking into the parlor.

Isolde blinked. Her mind could scarcely process the flood of new information.

Again, she followed him, leaning a shoulder into the door jamb and watching as he pulled his shirt over his head.

"I should like such a marriage, Tristan. But as I believe we touched on last night, creating a true relationship between us—a deep connection as friends—will take time."

"I am painfully aware of that." He was back to using his *Kendall* voice again.

He tucked in his shirt with brisk jabs, pulling his braces over his shoulders. His eyes did not meet hers.

As if . . .

Ah.

Of course.

He had been emotionally vulnerable and now felt unsettled and embarrassed, acutely conscious that he had handed her a great degree of power.

She needed to tread gently.

Moving out of the doorway, Isolde picked up his jacket and held it open for him. It felt a rather wifely thing to do.

He slid his arms into the sleeves and then turned around to face her. She pressed a soft kiss to his mouth.

On a sigh, he tucked her against the length of his body, his arms holding her with reverence.

They stood like that for a long while, her cheek resting in the crook of his shoulder, gently swaying back and forth to the *thump* of his heart.

Finally, Isolde stirred and lifted her palms to his lapels, peering up at him.

His brown eyes met hers, unguarded and tentative.

"Will it . . ." he began and then paused before continuing on a swallow. "Will it be possible, do you suppose? For you to ever . . ."

"Love ye? Aye, Tristan Gilbert."

"Truly?"

Foolish man.

"The husband I have seen here in the cottage . . . attentive and candid and listening . . . *that* man would be easy tae love."

He kissed the grin off her face, as if helpless to stop himself.

"Your smiles, Duchess," he whispered. "If you only understood what they do to me."

"This smile?" Isolde smiled, wide and bright. "Now you are being ridiculous—"

He devoured that one as well.

"If ye continue tae kiss me like this, Husband, we shall never finish this conversation."

"I'm listening," he murmured, pressing his lips one last time to the corner of her mouth before lifting his head.

"As I've said, I need tae trust this change in yourself. That once we find ourselves back in Society, ye don't revert tae Kendall, at least with regards tae myself. That ye won't retreat and close yourself off again."

"Yes. That is my vow. For now, I desperately need . . . I need you to teach me how to love you."

"That I can do, Husband."

He nodded. "But where do I start?"

"Well, for myself, when I love someone, I feel accepted precisely as I am. As if I can behave as my truest self without fear of judgment or mockery."

"As I am with Allie?"

"Precisely. But in order to have that trust and acceptance, we both must share everything that we are with one another—our thoughts, our wants . . . our past and desires for our future. No hiding. No shying away from difficult topics."

He nodded.

"To that end," she continued, "I'm going to ask ye difficult questions about yourself. Your relationship with your father and mine. Your hostility toward Rafe. And in return, ye will ask me questions about myself, and I will answer them."

He sighed. "How did you become so wise on this topic?"

"I was raised in love, Tristan." She kissed his cheek. "Now, ye must be famished. I have a loaf of bread cooling and some lentils for our luncheon. And then I suggest a stroll along the beach tae see if your ship is on the horizon."

TRISTAN CLUTCHED ISOLDE'S hand in his as they strolled across the sand.

Waves lapped the beach and the cheery sun turned the water a deep aquamarine, the color of robin eggs in Spring.

But no ship dotted the horizon, even when they climbed to the top of the small rise and surveyed the isle in all directions.

And yet . . . Tristan did not mourn its absence.

The *SS Statesman* would return for them eventually. Given the ferocity of the storm, the ship's gears had likely needed adjusting and perhaps some repairs.

Similarly, the gears of his pocket-watch had finally dried, but Tristan hadn't bothered to wind it. To what purpose? Time was meaningless here.

After a lifetime of having eyes upon him at all times—his father, servants, hangers-on—it was oddly freeing to simply exist on a tiny island at the ends of the earth.

"Ye be rather silent there, Husband," Isolde said at his side.

He glanced at her. The wind had tugged long strands of her hair loose, sending them spinning behind her like a comet's tail. Fitting, he supposed, to compare her with a heaven-sent star.

"Merely enjoying the serenity of this moment. If you expect me to become a voluble sort of chap, you will be severely disappointed."

"Nae, I ken that ye will never be a *bletherer*."

He tightened his grip on her hand.

How he wanted this. All of this. Her. Them.

And kissing her . . .

Well, he was trying *not* to think of kissing her. Because once he started reliving the give of her body under his hands, the rise of her chest to meet his lips with her own . . .

Deep breath.

Yes.

Best not to think of that.

Otherwise, he would do nothing *but* kiss her and where would that leave them?

"You said you would ask me questions?" he prompted.

"Aye. I would love to hear of your experience with Uncle Rafe, my father, and your own. I ken ye dislike all three men. Where would you like to start?"

He winced.

All three tales were dreadful . . .

"You must realize you are asking me to relate some of the most humiliating and painful experiences of my life."

"Am I?"

"Yes."

"Would it help if I told a mortifying story first?"

Tristan perked up.

She dropped his hand and faced him, walking backward across the white sand, pushing strands of hair out of her face.

"Do you even feel humiliation?" he asked. "I find it almost impossible to believe."

"Well, I do have a strange ability to laugh at my foibles. And well—" Here she shrugged. "—to be rather honest, I think ye have already been central to most of my humiliating moments."

"I have?"

"Aye." She ticked off on her fingers. "Our first meeting in Montacute's garden, and then there was the business of my letters to Jarvis."

Anger lit in Tristan's chest. He caught her around the waist and pulled her against him.

"Isolde, you cannot blame yourself for that man's perfidy. He is a disgrace to gentlemen everywhere, abusing your affections and deceiving you as he did."

"I should have been more astute." She rested her hands below his shoulders.

"No. Did you not hear what I just said?"

She sighed and tipped her forehead to his chest, relaxing into him. "'Tis so lovely, being held by you."

It was, indeed.

She patted his pectoral, a small frown denting her brow. "Though I must ask, where did you learn to swing an axe like that? Ye are a duke, if ye recall. Ye don't need the impressive muscles ye hide beneath your finery."

"Impressive," he repeated. "You appear to appreciate said muscles, Wife."

She laughed in reply, a delightfully wicked laugh that utterly tested Tristan's resolve.

With a steadying breath, he tucked her hand back into his and motioned with his free hand for them to resume walking.

"The tale of your axe skills, if you please, then," Isolde said, the wind billowing her skirts behind her.

Tristan happily seized on the reprieve. This tale, at least, was marginally more tolerable to relate.

"As you likely know," he began, "Allie and my mother left when I was ten years old, once Old Kendall granted my mother a permanent separation. As heir, I had to remain with my father. Obviously, I was bereft. The two people I loved more than anyone else in the world—and the only two people who have ever loved me—were severed from my life in one cruel blow."

The memories of that final day . . . His mother's anguished, yet determined, expression. Allie's sobs, clinging to him. His own promise, whispered in his twin's ear, *I will find you. We are forever, you and I.*

Isolde nodded, "Yes, Allie has told me of it. I know why your mother did what she did—she feared for her life. Your father was cruel and violent. Uncle Rafe has spoken more than once of how horrid your upbringing with that man must have been."

Tristan's old resentment toward Sir Rafe festered.

Tugging on her hand, Tristan guided his wife around a small pool the outgoing tide had left in the sand.

"Rafe knew and yet did nothing to help." Tristan couldn't keep the bitterness from his voice.

"Rafe? What could he have done?"

Not betrayed me, for one.

He knew he would tell Isolde the story eventually. Just not today if he could help it.

"I thought we were discussing my axe-throwing prowess?"

"Mmm," his wife hummed. "Continue."

"Life after the departure of my mother and sister was difficult. My father became more morose, more prone to outbursts of anger."

Tristan would hide in the boathouse or ride his horse to exhaustion across the countryside. Anything to be where his father couldn't easily locate him.

"I started to visit the gamekeeper with some regularity. Auld Graeme, they called him—a Scot. In hindsight, I am sure my presence on the doorstep of his cottage was unwelcome. But as I was Lord Hawthorn, he could hardly toss me out on my ear. Finally, in a bid to get rid of me, he said I would have to make myself useful if I were to hang about. His very words."

"Seems like he took a liking to ye then."

"Hardly," Tristan snorted, remembering the grim-faced Scot. "Do not delude yourself, Duchess. My father employed servants as hard and cold as himself. Anyone with a heart quit their post almost immediately upon taking it. The gamekeeper tolerated me. And in return, I learned to chop wood."

"Ye became proficient."

"Perhaps." Tristan lifted his gaze to the green *machair* rimming the beach, tufts of grass rippling in the breeze. "I found the repetitive motion soothed my mind. It permitted me to cast aside my worries and heartache and just . . . be. I am named *Tristan*, after all. I had to discover something to dispel all the melancholy and hurt."

"Pardon?"

"Tristan. My name. It derives from *triste* in Italian. Sadness. Gloom. Our mother named us twins, you see. How she convinced Old Kendall to relinquish the task to her, I shudder to think. But she named us for the feelings in her heart upon our birth. *Allegra* for my sister—joy and happiness at our arrival. And *Tristan* for myself—sorrow and heartache at the pain my life would be, forever tethered to Old Kendall and the duties of a dukedom."

"How poignant. Allie has never told me this."

"My mother named us true. Allie has always been the brightest light. The day she left, I felt as if all happiness had been stripped from me. Maudlin, I know."

"Nae, losing a beloved sister like that—particularly your twin— would be devastating. And to be abandoned in Old Kendall's care . . ."

They had reached the end of the beach, where sand gave way to basalt boulders stretching along the headland.

"Yes. I cannot say I expected anything else, however. I was born to be melancholy, as I said, and—"

Isolde pulled him to a stop. "What rubbish!"

"Pardon?"

"Ye are hardly melancholic, Husband. Ye are a wee bit quiet and taciturn, but that is not the same thing as a depression of spirit."

How could he explain to her? This woman who hummed with joy and left a dour man like himself scanning the air for sunbeams in her presence.

"Aside from Allie, there has been very little cheer in my life, Isolde. And as others are fond of pointing out, I am not precisely . . . likable."

Though Isolde appeared to like him well enough. Once he had ceased being such an arse and apologized.

"Nonsense!" She took his face in her hands. "Last night, ye said the most beautiful things about myself."

"All true."

"So, I will now reply with my own thoughts. Believe these words, Tristan Gilbert." Her blue eyes echoed the sun-kissed sea at her back. "Ye are a loving brother tae your sister. Ye be a fair employer tae your servants. And most importantly, as I have noticed these past three days, a warm, kind heart beats in your chest. Ye be the sort of gentleman many would be pleased tae call *friend*."

She spoke the words so prosaically, so simply. As if they were the veriest truth.

And yet, they danced a whirlwind in his brain, struggling to settle into any sort of order.

"I don't think I shall ever be capable of the exuberance you radiate simply by breathing."

"I disagree. Ye were born into light, Tristan Gilbert. Aye, your father was a right bastard of a human being, but ye were gifted with a mother who loved ye and a sister who still dotes upon ye, no matter how surly your tongue. Your life is not destined tae be one of sorrow. Ye simply need tae relinquish your formidable control and allow happiness a wee space within."

He kissed her—tenderly, gently—his lips reverently supping on hers.

"I feel happy right now," he confessed. "Brimming with it."

And he did.

Had he known this bubbling lightness—this joy—awaited him, he would have swallowed his damn ducal pride and admitted he loved her years ago.

"Good. Let us hold on tae that happiness together." Abruptly, she grinned, wild and mischievous. "Now, I'm going to race ye back to the house. The loser has to collect eggs!"

She took off at a sprint down the beach, skirts billowing and bunching around her knees, sand kicking off her heels.

Laughing, Tristan chased after.

He caught her around the waist halfway to the house, but all thoughts of winning fled his mind when she spun around and kissed him, her helpless giggles trapped against his lips.

Eventually, they decided to collect eggs together.

Yet Isolde's ideas still rang in his mind hours later, as Tristan held her close in their bed.

Choose happiness.

Was it truly that simple, this change he sought? To search for sunlight instead of shadows when examining his hours and days?

It was a novel way of pondering his life.

He fell asleep to the sound of his wife's breathing—her shoulders tucked to his chest, his arm wrapped around her waist—wondering what words, what stories, what gifts, he could summon tomorrow to give her.

24

"Hold yourself still, Tristan," Isolde scolded. "I am nearly finished."

"I cannot believe you coerced me into this."

"Hush. Ye love me. That's why." Isolde finished adjusting the length of plaid and pushed to her feet. Standing back, she surveyed him, hands on her hips. "Well, this *is* a bonnie sight, I must say."

Admittedly, Isolde considered her husband handsome in any state of dress, but this in particular . . .

She had been correct about the *feileadh mòr.* Tristan looked splendid in a great kilt.

The red and blue of the wool wrapped around his lean hips, the whole cinched tight with a belt and a sporran hanging front and center. He currently only wore his shirtsleeves and one of the mysterious owner's homespun waistcoats. Instead of using a brooch to secure the top half of the kilt at his shoulder, Isolde left the long tails to hang behind, ending at the top of his boots.

Neither of them had gone back to wearing their own attire. Isolde's corset and bodice were too tight-fitting to easily knead bread and gather eggs. And the fine fabric of Tristan's trousers would not withstand the rigors of their island existence.

And so they both continued to wear borrowed clothing.

"You have been staring for far too long, Wife." Tristan glared at her. "And there is no mirror, so I cannot say if I look presentable or, the more probable scenario, utterly ridiculous—like an Englishman being attacked by tartan." He twisted trying to see the entirety of the kilt.

"Ye don't look ridiculous."

"Isolde."

"Tristan."

"How do I appear then?"

Mmm. Delicious? Edible?

She went with, "Magnificent. It truly is a disservice tae Scottish lassies everywhere that ye were born a *Sassenach*."

She gave a coquettish purse of her lips and pretended to fan herself.

"Is that so?"

"Aye."

"Come here, then," he ordered in that demanding *Kendall* voice he knew rendered her weak in the knees. "I need more convincing that you truthfully appreciate the kilt."

Och, he was a quick study, she would give him that.

He had been ordering her about for the past day in that voice.

Sit, while patting his knee.

Eat, setting a well-honeyed slice of bread before her.

Kiss me, pointing at his lips.

Sometimes mere minutes apart.

And in each instance, Isolde hastened to obey like a child scampering down the stairs on Christmas morning.

Now, she saucily approached him, extra sway in her hips, knowing it would earn her a thorough kiss.

Tristan did not disappoint, pulling her into his arms and bending his head to hers.

As ever, she melted into him, hands circling his waist and fisting his shirt.

Every kiss felt like the first with him—electric and thrilling. Intoxicating.

And with each one, something warm and lush unfolded in her chest. This man.

Oh, how she could come to love him. Domineering and demanding, but gentle and warm. Clever, witty, and hard-working.

Isolde knew herself to be strong-willed. It was one of the reasons she had assumed she would not marry. For her, any true marriage would require a man strong enough to match her will. One who would not be intimidated or overrun by her brash personality.

Tristan met her as an equal.

Isolde found it nearly bizarre, receiving the entirety of his attention. He had not lied about his disposition. He could be intense and obsessive, and she was now in the cross-hairs of it.

The emotions he stirred within her were not full-blown, capital-L *Love* obviously. Not yet. Such a powerful sentiment required more time to develop.

However, *giddy infatuation* would not be far off the mark.

And given the import Tristan placed on love, she would not say the words to him until she was utterly sure of her affections, no matter her own impetuous nature. He merited her honesty.

Eventually, they would escape this island sanctuary and rejoin the world. Would Tristan manage the adjustment? Or would he find it too difficult to be gentle Tristan and the mighty Duke of Kendall at once?

Pulling back, she ran her hands over his chest. "We'll make a Scot of ye yet."

"I consider that highly unlikely, Duchess," he intoned in his deepest *Kendall* voice. "However, if it earns me such a reward, I will indulge your . . . fetish? . . . from time to time."

She laughed and kissed him.

But she did insist he wear the kilt. "Just for the day."

They had settled into a bit of a routine on the island.

She made breakfast.

He chopped driftwood for the fire.

She ogled him as he swung the axe.

He demanded kisses in payment for her ogling.

They argued John Locke and the writings of modern economists, like John Stuart Mill, as they collected eggs from the chickens for lunch.

And then debated the sagacity of the philosopher Carl Marx as the eggs cooked over the fire.

Isolde had never really pondered what a perfect day would be, but passing the hours like this . . .

Well, it was nigh upon perfection.

They had been on Canna for four days now.

The proprietors of the cottage would return eventually. There were sheep to herd and crops to manage. Isolde and Tristan had already discussed ensuring monies were delivered to the owners to cover the cost of the stores they had used, as well as rent for their sojourn.

But most importantly . . . where was the *SS Statesman*?

Unless the ship had been severely damaged, or worse, why hadn't Captain Woodbury returned for them?

Tristan didn't wish to speak of it. "Either she will return for us, or she will not. Worrying will solve nothing."

But Isolde could feel the anxious tension in his arms and noted how often his gaze strayed to the sea.

While walking along the beach, Tristan's glorious kilt snapping in the wind, they did happen to see a wee sail boat skimming by the island.

Laughing, Isolde raised her hands, jumping in excitement.

The sailors waved heartily in return, spinning their caps overhead in greeting. But they did not venture close enough to hear her calls for help.

"Well, that was rather disappointing," Isolde declared as the boat sailed from view. "Why did they not stop? We were beckoning them toward us."

Tristan made a show of looking down at his kilt. "We are wearing the clothing of the island residents. I wonder if they assumed we were old friends calling hello."

HOURS LATER, ISOLDE found herself before the fire, curled into her husband's lap once more. The sun had set and twilight painted the clouds in daubs of peach and violet.

She had shown Tristan how to pull the top half of the great kilt around his shoulders, wearing it like a cloak. The plaid was long enough, he could even expand it to cover herself.

These were the moments Isolde liked best, she decided—cuddled against Tristan's chest, talking themselves hoarse before the glowing fire.

"If I had kissed you that day in Montacute's garden, would your lips have been as knowing as they are now?" he asked, his thumb pressed to her bottom lip, as if helpless against the urge to touch her.

"*Would* ye have kissed me?" Isolde sat back, astonished.

He began systematically to remove the pins from her hair.

"Tristan," she laughed, "ye be distracting me."

"I adore your hair," he murmured, continuing to remove her hairpins. "And I want to see it all. It was the first thing I noticed."

"It is the *only* thing people notice. Poor Mamma. She was devastated when I inherited her coloring. She had hoped I would appear a perfect English rose. Instead, I emerged screaming and decidedly Scottish."

"You were an angel in that garden. I could scarcely speak, your beauty stunned me so."

"Scarcely speak?! You *flirted* with me."

He raised his eyebrows. "I *attempted* to flirt with you. But you flirted most expertly in return. You clearly had more experience with the opposite sex than myself."

"Aye, perhaps. I had kissed a boy or two by that point—the primary word in that sentence being *boy*; they were hardly *men*. I was a scientist even then and had to assuage my curiosity on the subject."

"And your conclusions?" He removed the last pin, sending her hair tumbling over her shoulder. He wound a lock around his fingers, studying it in the light.

"The act of kissing was pleasurable enough but not anything I intended to actively seek out."

"Is that so?" He laced his fingers through the mass of her curls, massaging her scalp.

Isolde moaned, arching into the sensation.

"And do you still feel that way, Wife, now that you have experienced my kisses?"

She laughed. "Ye ken well that I adore your kisses. Have I not demonstrated the fact sufficiently over the past two days?"

"I feel the data on my own end are inconclusive," he replied, voice deadpan, hand cupping her jaw. "It will likely require more research."

"Is that so?"

"Yes. In fact, we should begin conducting the experiment right now."

"Tristan," she giggled as he lifted her mouth to his.

Isolde meant to ask him about his father . . . about Rafe.

But then Tristan kissed her, and every other thought vanished in the delight of her husband's lips touching hers.

THE NEXT EVENING, Tristan held Isolde before the fire once more.

He adored this, his wife snugged against his chest, her hair unbound and draping over them.

Somehow his life had shifted from a living Hell to the purest Heaven.

Their day had passed much like the one before it.

No ship, though they had seen several sailing boats at a distance.

"Eventually, someone will come," he had said, trying to reassure them both.

He could not bring himself to speak of the *SS Statesman*.

Something had happened to his ship. Too much time had passed for her not to return if she were seaworthy. The ship itself was replaceable. But the crew . . .

Tristan could not even contemplate the loss of life if the *SS Statesman* had gone down in the storm.

And still, anytime he ventured outdoors, he couldn't help but scour the horizon for a telltale plume of smoke.

If she was with him, Isolde would take his hand and quietly wait, saying nothing. No platitudes or hollow comfort.

Just her calm, understanding strength.

One of a hundred reasons why he adored her.

They had spent the day roaming the section of the island they hadn't yet explored, trying to find a boat or something they could use to cross to the mainland, but the abandoned buildings yielded little.

"If our supplies run too low," Tristan had said, "we may need to dispatch a sheep for food."

"I sincerely hope it does not come tae that."

"Me, too. I can wield an axe, but acting the butcher might be a bit beyond my skills."

They were quieter that evening, cuddled together before the fire.

Again, Tristan unpinned her glorious hair. It was a husband's delight, to see his wife's hair loose and tumbled. He ran his fingers through the mass with hypnotic repetition, admiring how the fiery strands shimmered in the firelight.

Isolde stirred against his chest.

"Tell me of Rafe," she murmured.

He let her hair drop.

She traced her fingertips down his throat.

"I struggle to understand your antipathy toward your brother," she continued. "Yourself and Allie would not exist were it not for Uncle Rafe's actions, uncovering your father's bigamy. Both you and Rafe loathe your sire, and both wish tae see his memory eradicated. Ye are similar in manner and temperament."

"You know him much better than I."

"Perhaps, but why do ye dislike him so? Is it due to Rafe's close friendship with my father?"

"That certainly doesn't help." Tristan wrapped his hand around hers, trapping it against his chest.

She said nothing, waiting patiently.

Yes. He needed to tell her.

Taking in a deep breath, Tristan freed the words.

"Six months after my mother and Allie left, my father sent me to Eton," he began quietly. "He had finally noticed my melancholia and wished to see it remedied."

Eton will form you into a man, not the disappointing milksop I endure at present, Old Kendall had sneered.

"I know for many Eton is a trial," Tristan continued. "But for me . . . it was revolutionary freedom. I had never been around so many boys at one time. They were rambunctious and loud but so full of life. My first day there, I saw a man in the visitors' area who, at a distance, appeared to be my father."

"Uncle Rafe," Isolde breathed.

"Yes, but it took me a few long moments of staring to piece it together. At first, I was merely puzzled, as my father would never come to Eton to fetch me, and I worried what terror awaited me at his hand. And then I remembered. I knew my father had two sons from his bigamous marriage—George, who was the heir, and his younger brother, Lord Rafe. George perished of drunkenness when I was about six or seven. I overheard the butler whispering to the housekeeper about it . . . how George died in squalor, penniless and friendless. But Sir Rafe, as he is now known, had moved to Scotland and embraced his Scottish mother's family."

"Aye, his mother was a daughter of the Earl of Ayr, if I remember correctly. A lovely, Scottish lady whom Rafe adored. She passed away about a decade ago."

"Well, I knew some of this at age eleven. And so deduced that the man who eerily resembled my father, though a bit younger, had to be my illegitimate half-brother. As I approached, I realized he was speaking with a boy my age."

"John."

"Yes. Sir Rafe had crouched down and spoke gently with the boy. I will never forget Sir Rafe's expression when he lifted his head and noticed me approaching. He went deathly still . . . and then smiled—the warmest, kindest expression. No one ever smiled at me like that . . . as if my very existence were a delight. At first, I wondered if he considered me a stranger. Surely, he would not smile so brightly at the boy who took his birthright. But then Sir Rafe stood and bowed, greeting me as Lord Hawthorn, before turning to introduce me to his son, Mr. John Gordon."

The moment seared into Tristan's memory . . . shaking hands with John for the first, and nearly the last, time. This boy who looked so much like himself—his nephew, but more like a long-lost brother. Unlike Tristan, who had been so ecstatic to be at Eton, John's eyes were red-rimmed, and he kept wiping his nose with a handkerchief as he leaned into his father's side.

All will be well, Rafe had whispered to John. *I love ye, son, and your mother and your siblings love ye. You will be back home with us before ye know it.*

"Sir Rafe obviously doted on John," Tristan said, "just as John adored him. The sort of father-son relationship that I had read about in Mr. Dickens's novels."

"Aye, Rafe is a loving father and husband tae his family. Though I am unsure, given all this, how ye came tae dislike Rafe so."

"Patience, Wife." He jostled her shoulder. "I expected Sir Rafe to dismiss me out of hand. Instead, he invited me to join John and himself for luncheon at a nearby inn. The entire experience was . . ." Tristan sighed. How to explain this? "You must understand. My mother and sister had been ripped from me. I had spent six months chopping wood with Auld Graeme and trying to avoid my father's angry fist. And now, I found myself seated beside my much older brother—a cheerful, kind replica of my father who asked me about myself and matched every youthful ideal of what my sire should have been.

"It is petty to say now, but I was jealous of John. Impossibly jealous. Here, John had a father—one who looked like my own—and yet was warm and caring and so unbearably gentle. And I wondered, why couldn't Fate have made me Sir Rafe's son, too? We inhabited the same family tree. I was merely attached to it at the wrong place.

"I made it my goal to become friends with John. He was sunny and outgoing, but I had hopes. In my foolish dreams, we could become like brothers. Perhaps, I could return home with him to Scotland over the long breaks. Perhaps, if I proved myself, Sir Rafe would adopt me as a sort of surrogate son."

"Oh, Tristan," Isolde breathed, her eyes glittering in the soft light. "Ye break my heart." She pressed a soft kiss to his cheek. "I am sure that Rafe would have accepted ye in a trice if he could have."

Tristan shrugged, the pain of old memories numbing his limbs. "Perhaps. I will never know. Regardless, the dream was short-lived. I had been at Eton for merely a month when my father's personal secretary abruptly arrived with orders to collect me. I was not permitted to say goodbye to anyone, particularly not to John. When I arrived home, my father met us in the entry hall, face red and eyes gleaming with rage. I was hauled into his study and thoroughly beaten with a cane."

"Tristan!"

"Allie has told you how he was, Isolde." He fixed his wife with a steadfast look. "Such behavior should come as no surprise. After battering me, my father stood over my body as I coughed blood on the floor and dispassionately related *why* I had been so punished. Apparently, Old Kendall had occasion to visit London and had there encountered Sir Rafe. My foolish older brother had boasted to our father that I had dined with him. That I was becoming friends with John. That my loyalties were already more tied to Sir Rafe than our father and would only become more so over time. I cannot imagine what possessed Rafe to goad Kendall in such a manner. Perhaps he thought to taunt our sire or to draw blood in their endless war with one another. Who knows. He clearly was unconcerned with how his words would impact me."

Isolde pushed off his chest, sitting upright. "Have ye told Rafe this?"

"Of course not," Tristan scoffed. "He is an intelligent man. I am sure he has put the whole together."

"But . . . had he known what the outcome would be for yourself, surely Rafe would have said nothing to your father."

"We shall never know. The event proved a pivotal one in my life and not for the better. After that, my father tightened the bars of my cage. A strict tutor was hired, and I was educated at home, my every move monitored. As I grew, I was required to take a protection officer along for any excursions outside our estate."

"A protection officer? Like the Queen herself?"

"Yes. Mind you, the men were less concerned about my own personal safety and more invested in relaying my every word and action back to

Kendall in exchange for a handsome wage. Eventually, I did convince my father to let me attend Oxford. Of course, the protection officers dogged my every step, making it difficult to form friendships."

And even in that, I fear my father interfered, Tristan did not add.

Isolde pressed her cold nose to the side of his throat, relaxing back into his arm once more.

"Could ye ever forgive Rafe for betraying ye? His actions might have been accidental."

Tristan ran a hand up and down her spine. "That is a difficult question to answer. Sir Rafe's careless, taunting words utterly altered the course of my life. Without his interference, I might have remained at Eton. I might have made friends." *And known camaraderie,* he did not add. "As such, I do not care to associate with Sir Rafe or welcome him into my circle. He shattered any goodwill there might have been between us. I think tolerance might be all I am ever capable of."

And yet, even as he said the words, Tristan recalled Sir Rafe's last visit.

I have always looked upon ye a bit like a son . . .

The problem, of course, had always been the same.

Tristan still wanted to like Sir Rafe. He truly did.

But he didn't trust his brother.

After all, were it not for Old Kendall's bigamy, Sir Rafe would be the Duke of Kendall now. Surely, that had to chafe . . . the thought of all the power Rafe might have had if their sire had not been such a despicable human being.

How could Tristan ever believe that Sir Rafe's motives were as altruistic as he claimed? That there was no sense of wronged vindication in his actions?

Isolde trailed her fingertips across Tristan's shoulder before resting her palm over his heart.

"I hate the hurt I feel within ye," she whispered, kissing his chest beside her hand. "I hate that ye were left alone with that monster."

"It is in the past. I thank God every day that my father is finally dead and gone."

"Aye, but the wounds he inflicted fester still."

Tristan said nothing; she was correct, as usual.

She kissed the place above his heart again. "We will heal them together, Husband."

He latched onto the hope of her words.

Perhaps through the light of her care—her understanding heart—he could repair his own bruised soul.

SEVEN DAYS.

An entire week.

That was how long they had been on the island.

Rain pattered against the window once more, drizzling and calm. So unlike the raging squalls of the week before.

Isolde touched her fingertips to the chilled glass panes, peering out to the beach.

Tristan was dragging more driftwood up to the cottage, his head ducked to avoid the worst of the rain.

Once more, she marveled at the change in him.

She had to press the heel of her hand to her breastbone every time she recalled his story of Rafe.

No wonder Tristan was so cold to his brother.

She could scarcely blame him, and she *knew* Rafe and considered him family. She knew that he had never intended the consequences of his words.

And yet, to imagine the vast well of hurt within Tristan's heart. The boy who wasn't loved. Who was abandoned by his mother and sister. The boy who ached for connection, for family. For the kind of adoration Isolde's own family felt for each other.

Perhaps Tristan didn't see it, but she did.

Out on the beach, Tristan dropped a particularly large log atop the rocks before the cottage and then turned to retrieve more.

Watching him . . . she could feel it creeping in—a fierce, possessive, adoring sort of emotion.

Abruptly she was glad he insisted they wait to fully consummate their marriage. Because she wanted to fall purposefully for him.

To know that the change in her own heart toward him was just as real as the change in his behavior toward herself, and not the product of lust or a false sense of physical connection.

Isolde turned to go heat some porridge for lunch, but something caught her eye.

She looked back at the window, squinting into the mist.

Was that . . .

Was that a boat approaching their beach?

25

DEATH IN SCOTLAND! It has been reported that the Duke and Duchess of Kendall drowned on Tuesday last in a boating accident off the west coast of Scotland. The Duke married Lady Isolde Langston not even two weeks past, and the couple were celebrating their honeymoon when a tempest overturned their rowboat. Rescuers were unable to reach them.

—ARTICLE IN *THE LONDON TIMES*

Isolde clutched the side of the masted fishing boat, staring as the port of Oban drew near. Rows of fishing cottages ringed the horseshoe-shaped harbor, the slopes of Ben Cruachan rising behind.

Most importantly, the tall smoke-stack of the *SS Statesman* loomed over the fishing boats clustered against the wooden pier.

She had felt more than heard Tristan's sigh of relief upon spotting his ship.

Positioned at the bottom of the Great Glen with the large Isle of Mull between it and the open sea, Oban's sheltered waters ensured it was a bustling stop for boats plying the canals of the Great Glen to Inverness or merely a way-station for fishing vessels, like the Loch Fyne skiff in which Isolde currently sat beside her husband.

"Nearly there," she murmured to Tristan.

Her husband nodded, stiff and straight-backed. Like herself, he appeared rumpled, unkempt, and anxious.

The sails overhead snapped in the breeze.

The caretakers of the island had been astonished to find the Duke and Duchess of Kendall inhabiting their home.

"We were attending my sister's wedding on Skye," the woman, Mrs. Thorburn, had said, red hair gleaming from underneath her bonnet as she bobbed an awkward curtsy to Isolde. "'Twas only yesterday, as we were leaving, that we heard an English duke and duchess had drowned north of Oban."

"Aye," Mr. Thorburn added. "We never suspected that ye would have found shelter in our home. I imagine they be right *worrit* about yous back in London."

Almost mutely, Isolde and Tristan had changed into their own clothing, Mrs. Thorburn helping Isolde with her corset strings.

"Such fine fabric," the woman had murmured, running a hand down the wrinkled superfine of Isolde's voluminous skirt. Without her layers of stiffened horsehair petticoats, the material dragged on the floor.

Isolde made a mental note to dispatch Mrs. Thorburn an entire wardrobe's worth of muslins and soft wool as a thank-you for their hospitality.

Once dressed, Mr. Thorburn had sailed them to Tobermory, a small fishing village on the east coast of the Isle of Mull. From there, Tristan had secured a fishing boat to sail them into Oban, where they understood his steamship had berthed for repairs.

The closer they drew to Oban, the quieter Tristan became. Was this his Kendall-self rising up, Isolde had to wonder.

But he held her hand tightly. And when their fishing boat docked, he scrambled onto the pier and reached to help her ashore.

Heads turned their way and fingers pointed as they made their way across the dusty road and to the only hotel in sight—the creatively named Oban Inn.

Tristan greeted the innkeep and requested their finest suite of rooms. "For the Duke and Duchess of Kendall," he intoned, sounding every inch the powerful duke he was.

The innkeep's eyes widened into saucers, and he hastened to lead them to their rooms.

Surely by nightfall, every living soul within a ten-mile radius would know that the missing duke and duchess had not drowned but were instead bedraggled and warming their toes before a fire in the inn's nicest suite.

The suite of rooms was indeed large—a sitting room, dressing room, and bedchamber with an imposing tester bed. The furnishings were typical of the Highlands—utilitarian, spare, and at least a hundred years old. But the rooms appeared brightly scrubbed, the linens crisp and white.

"I have ordered a bath drawn for you, followed by a warm dinner in the private dining room downstairs," Tristan declared, his tone stern and aloof.

Her husband pulled his pocket-watch from his waistcoat pocket. With a frown, he checked the clock ticking on the fireplace mantel.

"Are ye not staying with me?" Isolde glanced out the window toward the evening sun. "At least tae dine?"

"No," he said, eyes on his watch, fingers spinning the dial to set the time. "I must consult with Captain Woodbury immediately and understand the state of affairs aboard the *SS Statesman*. I am sure my cook will prepare dinner on ship. Of course, I shall send over your ladies' maid immediately to attend to you."

"Very well. I shall join ye aboard ship as soon as I am bathed and more properly dress—"

"No, I should prefer you to remain here." Snapping the watch case closed, he returned it to his pocket and finally lifted his head to look at her.

"Tristan," Isolde began, reproach in her tone. "I should like tae be with ye. To know what has occurred with your ship."

He visibly softened, face turning tender and his shoulders losing their military sharpness.

Shaking his head, he crossed to her in three large steps.

"I should worry about you if you were aboard ship, Wife. I have no idea as to the vessel's state." He pulled her against his body and kissed her lips with possessive thoroughness. "However, I know you will be safe and watched over here. Let me ascertain the shipshape soundness of the *SS Statesman* before dragging you onto it again. I will give you a thorough recounting of everything the second I know."

She ran her fingers through his hair. "Promise ye will return tae me as soon as possible? Or summon me if it is safe?"

"I promise." He kissed her again . . . and then he was gone.

THREE HOURS LATER and Tristan still hadn't returned from the ship.

Isolde sat in the private dining room, having dined and watched the sun set. The fire burned low in the grate, a simmering coal of heat.

Much like her irritation.

Oh, Isolde tried to swallow it back, to tell herself that the damage to his ship must be concerning to keep him from her side for so long or prevent him from sending for her or communicating *something*—

But was that truly the case? Or had he merely become immersed in discussions with Captain Woodbury and forgotten about his promise to her?

She knew Tristan wanted to change, but the demands of his title and his own rigid sense of duty might prove Herculean to alter.

Her husband might be engrossed in his ship, but the local laird, Sir John MacDougall of Dunnolie and his son, Mr. Alexander MacDougall, found her easily enough.

Word spread quickly in Highland communities.

"Ye be Scottish, Your Grace!" was the first sentence out of Sir John's mouth after introducing himself. He turned to his son. "Can ye believe it, Alex? A proper Scottish lass as an English duchess! No wonder she fought the sea and won."

Isolde smiled, her first true smile in hours.

Sir John exemplified the sort of Scottish nobleman she adored—brash of opinion, open of manner, and brimming with bonhomie. About her father's age, Sir John arrived in a kilt and bonnet, his graying red hair disheveled from the omnipresent wind. Mr. Alexander MacDougall was a copy of his father, only thirty years younger.

Isolde rang the bell and ordered a light supper and some whisky brought to the private dining room for the men.

"*Och*, the captain of the steamship said ye had drowned." Sir John cupped his hands around a tumbler of whisky. "And now I find ye be Lord Hadley's daughter. A much-admired Scotsman, Lord Hadley. Had we known ye were one of our own, we would have searched harder. A stuffy English duchess . . . well, that lot willnae survive the Baltic waters of the Rough Bounds. But a Scottish lass . . . I would have held out hope."

"Aye," Mr. MacDougall chimed in, sitting casually back in his chair. "The fancy steamship was damaged in the storm. Limped into harbor here in Oban about five days ago. We saw it from the house, didnae we, Da?"

"We did. Dunollie, my castle and estate, sits along the coast just north of town," Sir John clarified.

"The word spread like wildfire—an English duke and his duchess drowned in the storm. The captain couldnae do anything tae save them, he said. Watched them go down hisself." The younger man mimed holding a spy-glass.

"Then they discovered the rowboat, smashed tae bits near Kilmory. Lost things often wash up there," Sir John said as an aside to Isolde.

"And Wee Iain Swinburn found a battered tophat made in London that the duke's valet said belonged to His Grace," Mr. MacDougall added. "And then another lad found a fine silk bonnet and the torn bit of a horsehair petticoat."

"And yet no one thought tae check the island that had been our original destination?" Isolde asked with a frown.

"We should have," Sir John agreed far too cheerily. "But the captain of yon steamship was so adamant that ye had drowned. And Robbie McCann passed Canna on his way tae Skye the day after the storm. Said he saw Mr. and Mrs. Thorburn walking the beach, himself in a kilt and all, waving a greeting without a care in the world. We figured if ye had washed ashore there, Mr. Thorburn would have sailed to find a doctor for ye. No use risking our own lives tae search for bodies that may never be found."

It all made a sort of awful sense.

"Regardless, I immediately sent word down tae Glasgow of the tragedy, asking a message be telegraphed tae the duke's residence in London, Gilbert House or some such," Sir John continued.

"When was that?" Isolde asked.

"About four days past now, I ken."

Four days.

But with Allie gone to Scotland to reunite with Ethan, who had been at Gilbert House to receive the message? The butler, perhaps? If so, Tristan's servants would likely have informed her own family.

A sick worry twisted through her gut. If they assumed Isolde dead, her parents would be bereft.

A telegraph must be sent to Glasgow and then on to London immediately, informing everyone she and Tristan were healthy and well.

With any luck, the *SS Statesman* would be seaworthy. If she and Tristan left tomorrow, they would arrive in London not too many days after their telegram.

Isolde's mind whirred with thoughts and unanswered questions.

She and the MacDougall men moved on to discussing common acquaintances.

Sir John invited herself and Tristan to join them for dinner tomorrow at Dunollie House.

Isolde tentatively accepted, with the caveat that she and Tristan might be returning to London in the morning. The growing worry gnawed at her stomach.

Fortunately, Sir John was an excellent storyteller and proved effective at distracting her darker thoughts. She was laughing at a particularly funny anecdote when the door to the private dining room *snicked* open.

Tristan entered.

Or rather, the Duke of Kendall entered.

Her husband's valet had been thorough in tidying up Tristan's appearance—hair trimmed, whiskers scraped clean, clothes expensive and neatly pressed. Not a trace remained of the tousled, earnest man he had been on Canna.

Isolde was unsure if she liked the transformation or if she couldn't wait to muss him. Later. In their private bedchamber.

He froze in the doorway, no doubt taking in the scene of his wife laughing with two unknown men.

"Tristan." She crossed to him.

"Duchess," he replied, pure Kendall and more than a hint of reproach in his voice.

Isolde faltered.

Why was he upset with her?

He was the one who had left her for hours.

Or did his irritation stem from her addressing him as *Tristan* in company?

Drat.

She did not understand how to navigate this.

Isolde felt her smile turn brittle.

"Come, Husband," she said too brightly. "Allow me tae introduce our guests."

TRISTAN FEARED ISOLDE was slipping through his fingers.

She had been laughing with the wretched Sir John and his son when he entered the dining room.

Tristan's presence might have been a burial shroud for how thoroughly it dampened the atmosphere.

Not even three words out of his mouth, and his wife's glorious smile had morphed into a patently false one.

He knew he had done something wrong. That he should have somehow been more tender in that moment. But he only knew how to be Kendall when amongst other people, and he couldn't see how to soften his public ducal persona.

But what did Isolde expect him to do?

Conversation with Sir John had gone no better. The man took a slew of impertinent liberties with Isolde—calling her *lass* despite Tristan's repeated corrections, treating her as Scottish first and a Duchess of the Realm second.

Then there was the matter of his son, Mr. Alexander MacDougall. The younger Scot was not an unhandsome man. And he studied Tristan's wife far too avidly, even being so bold as to follow his father in kissing her hand upon departure.

Tristan had wanted to rip her fingers out of both men's grasp.

Isolde had scoffed when he said as much upon reaching their bedchamber.

"Now, ye are being absurd, Husband. Ye sound jealous."

"I am jealous!" He pulled her into his arms. She came, but rather reluctantly. Which merely underscored his worry.

"Tristan." She touched a hand to his cheek. "Ye cannot growl and snap at every man I interact with."

Tristan nuzzled her palm. "We might have to agree to disagree on this point, Wife."

"As I've said before, ye need tae trust me, just as I must trust yourself." She pulled her hand away. "Besides, if time permits, we are tae dine with the MacDougalls tomorrow, an evening I would find enjoyable."

She stepped out of his arms, and he resisted the urge to pull her back. To kiss her until she relaxed against him.

Instead, she folded her arms, studying him.

"I missed ye," she said. "Ye were gone so long aboard the ship, I had begun tae worry."

Ah. Was this the source of her withdrawal then?

"I am sorry if I caused you any undue alarm. There was much to sort with the captain."

"Aye, but I had tae learn the whole of what happened tae the *SS Statesman* from Sir John and not yourself."

Tristan hated that she had a valid point. He should have at least sent word to her as he had promised. Summoned her aboard the ship. Something.

Instead, he had become too involved with Captain Woodbury and neglected everything else.

"Again, I apologize," he said.

His wife nodded at his words, but the tension in her stiff shoulders did not ease. Clearly, words of apology were no longer enough.

He hated this, knowing something was off between himself and Isolde, but feeling unsure of how to correct it.

"I understand word has already been sent to London of our demise." Isolde wrapped her arms around her waist.

"Yes. Heaven knows what uproar our supposed deaths have caused." Tristan shuddered to ponder it. "I have charged Captain Woodbury with sending word at first light to your family in London and Allie in Aberdeen of our safe recovery. In speaking with the captain and examining the damage and repairs, the *SS Statesman* should be shipshape and fully seaworthy the day after tomorrow."

"That is excellent. We can dine with Sir John tomorrow and then leave for London the following morning. My family will likely be there still, what with Papa's impeachment being confirmed and the trial looming."

Tristan disliked the thread of reproach in her tone, as if she had not truly forgiven him for the slights against her family.

Damn and blast.

Time.

He needed more time with her.

More time alone. More time to talk and wander and simply . . . be. To nurture this fragile *thing* that was blossoming between them. Not necessarily to sway her loyalty to him, but to ensure that she saw himself as family, too.

"Why would we cut our honeymoon short?" He meant the question to be sincere, but it came out steel-edged and contentious.

Her shoulders tensed. "My family—and Allie for that matter—must be devastated about our supposed drowning."

"Yes, but returning to London makes little sense, particularly as Allie is in Aberdeen. Word will be sent to them tomorrow morning and will arrive days before us, given the speed of the telegraph network once our message reaches Glasgow. If you have further concerns, we can both pen letters, telling the tale of our shipwreck and rescue in full detail. But none of these facts should prevent us from proceeding on our honeymoon trip."

Where I can continue to woo you, he did not add. *Where I will have the space to learn how to be both Tristan and Kendall.*

"*Och,* my father will want reassurances beyond a few lines in a telegraph, Tristan," she clapped back. "Or even a letter, for that matter."

"Do *you* wish to return to London?" he asked, disliking the curt sharpness in his tone. "To forgo this space of time you and I have together?"

Tristan could feel the harmony they had established on the island slipping through his fingers, like the tide washing out to sea.

"I don't know." Isolde threw her hands up. "My family will be beside themselves with grief, particularly my father." She ticked off her fingers. "Over the past two weeks, Papa has endured watching me marry a man he considered an enemy, suffered impeachment by Parliament, and then was told I had drowned! I would be shocked if the whole hasn't sent him to an early grave. I cannot continue on this journey without assuring myself that he is well. That he knows—that my whole family understands—*I* am well. Do ye not worry about your sister?"

"Allie is a practical sort. A message will serve as well as my own presence and will reach her more quickly. More to the point, as I said, she is in Aberdeen with Ethan, not London. Why is a message insufficient for your father?"

He did not say the words that burned his tongue: *Why are you prioritizing your family over me?*

"How can ye *not* see it as insufficient?! I don't . . ." Isolde pinched the bridge of her nose and took in a long breath. "I don't wish to argue with ye. It sounds as if we have a day or two yet before we must make a final decision. And we are both tired and *crabbit.* Today's events have been momentous. Come. Let us summon my maid and your valet and prepare for bed."

Tristan permitted her to ring the bell and then listened from the adjoining room as Isolde chatted with her maid.

But when he finally slid into bed beside her and gathered her against him, his wife held herself stiffly before eventually rolling out of his embrace.

His arms had never felt so empty.

Time.

He had needed more time before being cast into the world like this. Time to adjust to this change within himself. Time to woo his wife properly.

He should have insisted they stay an entire month on that damn island. Maybe he would buy the thing and keep Isolde there until he found a way to earn her love.

News of the shocking deaths of the Duke and Duchess of Kendall has rocked London. The terse telegraphic dispatch describing their untimely demise would touch even the hardest heart. Black crepe drapes the windows of Gilbert House and the Earl of Hadley's townhouse in Mayfair. We all join in mourning the lives of a young couple taken too soon.

—ARTICLE IN *THE LONDON TATTLER*

The next morning, Tristan escorted Isolde downstairs to their private dining room, his wife quiet and agonizingly polite. Conversation between them was strained at best, their disagreement unresolved.

Tristan hated it.

Isolde was mute and withdrawn, and he hadn't a clue how to mend things.

As usual, his *Kendall* self had blundered and set everything to wrack and ruin.

But what was he to do?

He had apologized for neglecting her the evening before.

Though he supposed that wasn't the true problem.

He and Isolde disagreed about when to return to London, and he didn't know how to resolve it, other than to simply accept her plans and try not to be too surly.

But returning to London so quickly . . .

It almost guaranteed they would never form a true marriage. She would retreat within the bosom of her family, happy to be surrounded by those she loved once more.

And he would—

Well, he would likely return to his Library of Shame and develop a dependence on brandy or some such.

Huzzah.

Tristan simply couldn't permit that to happen.

They needed to find a solution, a compromise they both accepted.

Looking at her across the small dining table, the morning light haloing her head, firmed his resolve.

He loved this woman.

And he would fight for the future that—

An enormous cheering roar went up from the harbor.

Frowning, Tristan looked to the window.

Isolde rose. He followed, peering out to the pier over her shoulder.

A newly-arrived clipper ship was anchored in the bay—a sleek, modern boat built for speed. Passengers from the boat were being welcomed onto the pier amid clapping and shouts.

"Whatever is going on?" Tristan groused.

"I can't say." Isolde popped onto her tiptoes, squinting through the windowpane. "Perhaps, some sailor or soldier has returned—"

His wife broke off on a keening cry.

She whirled for the door, wrenching it open.

"Isolde!" Tristan called after her.

He exited the private dining room just in time to see her race out the front door of the inn.

"Isolde!" he yelled.

But she heeded him not, sprinting decidedly un-duchess-like across the road and pushing into the gathered crowd.

What the devil!

Scowling, Tristan followed, his heart beating in his throat.

Had she no sense?! She could be hurt—

However, the crowd parted for her, like Moses commanding the Red Sea, an undulating wave of people cheering and celebrating.

Above it, Tristan heard Isolde's wailing cry—"Papa! Papa!"

Hadley's tall, graying head separated from the throng.

"Isolde? Izzy?!" the Scot gasped, eyes rapt. A gusting sob left him. "Praise God! Izzy! You're alive!"

Isolde launched herself into her father's arms. Hadley wrapped her against him with fierce emotion, burying his face in her hair.

Even at a distance, Tristan could hear the earl's wrenching sobs.

The surrounding villagers reached for handkerchiefs, wives collapsing on husbands' chests, weeping. A pair of young boys raced in and out, whooping as if welcoming a conquering hero.

It was all rather . . .

Well.

Trust Hadley to make a scene.

A familiar, bespectacled form separated from the crowd, walking toward Tristan, a leather briefbag in hand.

"Your Grace." Ledger, his secretary, bowed.

"Ledger," Tristan nodded.

"I am pleased to see the reports of your demise have been inaccurate." Words said with characteristic English reserve.

"As am I."

They both turned as Hadley's voice sailed over the crowd once more.

"I cannae believe ye live. *Och*, my Izzy." The earl swiped at his eyes. "They said ye were dead! I feared my heart would break at the thought of ye gone forever."

"I'm alive, Papa." Isolde cupped his face and pressed a kiss to his cheek. "I am well."

The crowd sighed, fishwives clinging to each other, faces wet with joy and relief.

Several grizzled sailors took turns using the same bit of muslin to wipe their tears.

Tristan turned back to Ledger.

Only to find his secretary reaching for his own handkerchief.

Oh, for the love of . . .

"You, as well, Ledger?"

"Forgive me, Your Grace, but it is simply so beautiful." Ledger lifted his spectacles to dab at his eyes. "Lord Hadley was overcome with grief on our voyage north. I cannot say that I have ever seen a man so devastated. His keening at night . . ." The secretary drifted off, eyes glossy. "His lordship collapsed when I told him of Lady Isolde's demise. As I'm sure you know, Captain Woodbury sent the telegraph reporting your deaths to Gilbert House, so someone had to inform Hadley. His lordship immediately hired the fastest ship in London to take us north. Said he refused to accept his daughter's death until her body was found and vowed to search the deep if need be. And then to arrive, and find Lady Isolde is well—"

Lady Isolde.

Not Tristan's duchess or his wife.

A woman who was still identified by her connection to Lord Hadley.

Ledger sniffled and dabbed again with his handkerchief.

The man's tears were certainly not for Tristan himself.

That spare fact should not sting, and yet.

The truth was stark.

No one would be devastated at Tristan's loss.

No one would send up a keening lament over his funeral pyre.

He recognized the thought for the self-pitying one it was.

But that made it no less true.

And Tristan's next question rather confirmed his thinking. "I know why Hadley is here, Ledger. But why did you accompany him?"

"Oh, well, someone needed to see to your body, Your Grace. Ensure you were taken to Hawthorn and interred with your ancestors." The secretary straightened. "It seemed fitting for it to be myself. The last entry in your daily diary, as it were."

Of course.

Duty.

Duty and coin in Ledger's pocket.

Tristan's corpse would simply be one more matter to address, like ordering coal for the fires of Gilbert House or requesting a contract from a solicitor.

Nothing that involved emotions, certainly.

In stark contrast, Hadley continued to hug Isolde, still weeping openly and touching her hair, her chin, her shoulder . . . as if he could scarcely believe she were real.

"I did send word of your demise to Lady Allegra in Aberdeen," Ledger continued. "I sincerely hope we can dispatch a message today to assure her of your safe arrival. I anticipate she will be beside herself with grief."

"I have already seen it done, Ledger." A letter to his sister had departed at first light, as well as one from Isolde to her family.

"Excellent, Your Grace."

The villagers lining the dock whooped once more.

"My Izzy lives!" Hadley bellowed to the crowd, his arm around Isolde's waist. "Let me treat ye all to a dram or four tae celebrate her safe return."

The throng roared its approval, every one streaming toward the Oban Inn, Hadley and Isolde in their midst.

They swept right past Tristan where he stood with Ledger—sailors hooting and women spinning one another in a jig.

No one looked in their direction. Specifically . . . not Isolde.

Her red head turned left and right, accepting well wishes and congratulations, but not once did she scan as if seeking for him.

Look back, Tristan willed. *Look back and see me. Remember the island. Remember that I am here.*

But she did not.

Instead, she rested her head on her father's shoulder, sinking into his love as readily as she had sunk into Tristan's own just yesterday.

She did not turn to search for him.

No.

But Hadley did.

As the pair reached the door's inn, the earl swiveled his head, unerringly finding Tristan's gaze.

Hadley's eyebrows rose and a faint smile touched his lips, but it was difficult to discern the earl's expression at a distance. Fury? Gloating? Triumph?

Regardless, Tristan felt it as sharply as a rapier strike. Yet another jab in the never-ending war between himself and the Scot.

For her part, Isolde skipped into the inn, deliriously happy to be in her father's care once more.

Tristan utterly forgotten.

He knew it was unfair. Melodramatic, even.

Isolde had experienced a shock at Hadley's unexpected arrival.

She *did* feel a vague sort of fondness for Tristan himself. He knew this. Even so, her affections paled when held beside the vastness of Tristan's love for *her*.

And more significantly, her own tremendous love for her father.

The unevenness stung.

Tristan could feel bitterness and resentment creeping in. The same gnawing emotions that gripped him whenever he watched Sir Rafe interact with his son. The same feeling he had experienced on his wedding day, observing Isolde with her family.

As ever, he remained a silent observer to a wellspring of love and happiness. Never a partaker.

He hadn't a clue how to inspire such reciprocal emotions in others. It was like another Chubb lock, this one leading to an iron safe labeled *Love and Acceptance*. And once again, he didn't hold the correct key.

He was a thousand ways a fool.

Creating a truer relationship between himself and Isolde would not overshadow her deeper affections for her family.

He would always come second in her heart.

Isolde had informed him of this on their wedding day, had she not?

Ye will never be my first choice. I will always choose my family over yourself.

She had been honest with him from the beginning.

He had simply hoped that he might change her mind. That he could earn a measure of that loyalty and love for himself.

That someday, she might choose him instead.

Pain and longing ached in his chest, sending jittery energy down his limbs. He wanted to rage. To chop wood or fence or *something* until he dropped from exhaustion.

This was why, he realized. Why he employed a *Kendall* self at all.

He donned the mighty Duke of Kendall as a shield, protecting the soft Tristan parts of him.

But he had loosened that shell and invited Isolde inside.

He had confessed he loved her.

Placed his small, wounded, barely-formed heart in her hands.

But her palms were already overflowing with others' hearts whom she loved. Others who commanded more of her attention, more of her care.

And now—

Now, he didn't know how to stop hurting.

Isolde hadn't betrayed him. Of course, Tristan celebrated the happiness she felt at seeing Hadley again.

It was merely a stinging reminder of where he stood in his wife's affections. Where he would likely always stand. Hadley and her family would always come first.

And moreover, Hadley's sharp glance had said the rest of the story— the earl would ensure Isolde always preferred himself.

Tristan should have consummated their marriage when he had the chance. What a fool he had been to insist on waiting.

If he had made Isolde his wife in truth, there might be a babe growing within her belly right now.

His child. Their child.

Anything to tether her more firmly to himself.

He flinched away from the ugly thought. To so use the life of an innocent child.

Tristan swallowed and looked away from the inn door.

He disliked the emotional claws clinging to his shoulders—jealousy, self-pity, irritability—spectral demons ravenous for his soul.

Unfortunately, recognizing their existence didn't magically exorcise them.

He had promised Isolde that he would be different once they left the island. That he would not return to his Kendall ways.

And yet, his querulous mood insisted, *she* needed to change, too. If she wanted him to remain Tristan where she was concerned, then she needed to *treat* him like Tristan. As if he were a person who mattered to her.

If their marriage were to become a true one, they both needed to focus more fully on one another.

But for now . . .

He consulted his watch. There were still many hours in the day to fill.

"Come, Ledger." Tristan motioned to his secretary while pivoting for the *SS Statesman*. "Tell me all that has occurred in London over the past two weeks. Leave out no detail, particularly as it relates to Lord Hadley and his impeachment."

HOURS LATER, TRISTAN'S mood had not improved.

Ledger had come amply prepared with information from Parliament and the goings-on there.

As Tristan already knew, Commons had voted to impeach Hadley. The Articles of Impeachment had then been delivered to Lords, and the House of Lords had granted Hadley bail until the trial.

"They are still mulling over a date for the trial, as Parliament is set to adjourn at the end of July," Ledger said over a luncheon of fluffy Scottish baps and ham. "They may well wait until next spring to bring the trial. As we both know, Hadley is generally well-liked, and the faction supporting him is pushing for a delay."

"Hoping that support for the prosecution will die now that I have married Hadley's daughter."

"That is my assumption, Your Grace."

The familiar acrimony rose in Tristan's chest—the frustration and rancor that had initially spurred his dogged pursuit of Hadley.

Why should Hadley be permitted to use money and friendships to buy his way out of accountability on this matter? There were legitimate questions regarding his activities—incriminating letters between Hadley, his solicitors, and Jarvis—that required answers. The sort of information that a trial would bring to light.

Granted, the morning's events had not endeared Tristan to his father-in-law. The earl's knowing gaze—that he was deliberately thwarting Isolde's affections for her husband—still rankled. A glance out the porthole of the ship toward the Oban Inn showed the festivities to be ongoing.

But Tristan also recognized that destroying Hadley would not spur Isolde to transfer her loyalties to himself.

No, it would almost assuredly do the opposite.

So what were Tristan's options?

He could publicly ally himself with Hadley and glean whatever droplets of affection Isolde sent his way.

His soul shrank from the idea. That he would permit love for his wife to own him to such a degree. To supplant all integrity.

What should he do?

He reached for the cup of ale beside his plate.

Ledger cleared his throat, toying with his fork. "I did receive a letter earlier this week from Lord John Russell, passing along a request from the committee in Commons overseeing Hadley's impeachment. They asked for additional corroborating evidence of certain pertinent facts, particularly relating to the incriminating letters from Hadley's solicitors. The provenance of the letters isn't crystal clear, so the committee wishes to use Your Grace's sterling reputation as a guarantee of veracity. Lord John indicated that Your Grace should likely recuse yourself given the new familial tenor of your relationship with Hadley. Lord John stated he would support you in not providing incriminating evidence against your father-in-law."

Tristan paused, mid-swallow. He slowly lowered his tankard.

"How did you reply?"

"I was unsure what to do." Ledger pushed his glasses up his nose. "And then news of Your Grace's supposed death arrived."

"I see."

"So the issue remains outstanding. How would Your Grace like me to respond?"

A faint twist of something—dread? anticipation?—curled in Tristan's stomach.

Yes, what was he to do?

"The requested information is true to the best of our knowledge?" he asked.

"Yes, Your Grace."

Tristan drummed his fingers on the tabletop.

Withholding the documents would deny the committee important information.

But if he released it, he would be in open opposition to his father-in-law. Something he had promised Isolde he would not do.

Yet . . . a petty part of Tristan still longed for Hadley to receive his comeuppance. If Hadley truly was innocent, then proving his claims shouldn't be difficult. He would have his day in court. In the meantime, Tristan wished to ensure that all relevant facts were presented.

He reached a decision.

"Return to London and have the requested documents sent to the committee. Just ensure it is done with the utmost discretion and secrecy," he informed Ledger. "I would greatly prefer that news of this does not reach Hadley's ears, much less become public."

"Yes, Your Grace."

An hour later, Tristan had given his secretary an additional list of tasks to perform and then put the man on a packet boat bound for Glasgow and on to London.

From there, Tristan summoned his valet and dressed for dinner.

Isolde sent him a speaking look when he finally joined her and Hadley in their private dining room at the Oban Inn.

"Ye were missed, Husband," she greeted him with reproach in her voice.

Hadley's faint grunt and baleful glare negated her sentiment entirely—the earl had not missed Tristan's company in any fashion.

Tristan longed to kiss Isolde in greeting, to wrap her in his arms and never let go.

Instead, he settled for holding his hat in his hands and staring at the tense set of his wife's mouth from across the room.

"Hadley," Tristan nodded at his father-in-law.

"Kendall," Hadley said stiffly in return.

Neither of them spoke another word. Tristan could not trust himself to speak politely to the man. And given the stern set of his brow, Hadley likely felt the same.

They walked the half mile to Dunollie House north of town, where they were to dine with Sir John and Lady MacDougall. Isolde alternated between taking her father's arm and Tristan's, as if desperate to sooth the animosity between them. Or at the very least, prevent her father and husband from coming to blows.

Dunollie House was less a grand estate and more a genteel farmer's abode. In fact, Tristan was rather sure that Thistle Muir, Ethan Penn-Leith's ancestral home, was more luxurious. Dunollie Castle, a derelict, medieval ruin, loomed over the more recently-constructed house.

Sir John and his son were just as presumptuous and irritating as the night before. Only this time, they had Hadley as an audience. While the men tried to impress Isolde with their volubility, Tristan conversed with Lady MacDougall and nursed a glass of sherry, praying for dinner to be announced soon.

But the sound of his wife's laughter echoed through the shabby drawing-room, and Tristan found himself turning to look at her every other minute, noting the radiant happiness on her face.

A happiness he had no hand in creating.

"Let me show ye the Brooch of Lorn, Hadley," Sir John said. "'Tis a brooch that belonged tae Robert the Bruce himself."

They all dutifully followed Sir John across the room, where he pulled a wooden case from a cupboard. Inside, a silver brooch mounted with a large milky-white charmstone lay nestled on a bed of blue velvet.

Sir John lifted the jewel reverently, cradling it in his hand.

"'Tis a rare sight. It remained in my family for centuries before it was looted by the English. *Sassenachs* taking Scottish heirlooms as usual." He spared a glance for Tristan with those words. "But it was returned tae our family about twenty years past when General Campbell discovered it hidden in an old chest. Even Queen Victoria herself had tae stop and inspect it. Held it in her wee hands just like this." Sir John cupped the brooch between his palms.

Hadley whistled. "An admirable piece of history, Sir John."

"May I hold it, as well?" Isolde asked, smile bright.

"O' course, lass!"

Tristan watched as Isolde cradled the brooch in her hands, Hadley leaning in for a closer inspection.

She did not lift her head to look at Tristan, to ask if he would like to see the brooch, too.

As on the street that morning, she did not look his way at all.

Again, it was Hadley who raised his head and shot Tristan a look. This time he had no trouble interpreting the earl's smugly triumphant expression.

Tristan turned to study the art over the fireplace—a Highland scene painted in an indifferent hand—unable to recall the last time he had felt so miserable.

Would this interminable evening never end?

After tucking the brooch safely away, Sir John offered Isolde his arm to lead her into dinner. "We are so few this evening, we needn't fuss over ceremony and bother with precedence."

Though the man hadn't looked at Tristan as he spoke, it was a deliberate snub. As a duke, Kendall should have been first through the door, his wife on his arm.

Instead, Isolde smiled radiantly and crooked her hand into Sir John's elbow.

Hadley offered his own arm to Lady MacDougall, leaving Tristan and Mr. Alexander MacDougall to follow them into the dining room.

Tristan stared at Isolde's lovely auburn head, wishing with everything in his soul that they were still tucked safely away in that cottage on the island.

Any doubts he had about his orders to Ledger had fled.

Watching Hadley so knowingly commandeer Isolde's attention and affection underscored the futility of Tristan's hope. With Hadley standing between them, Tristan would never develop a truly loving relationship with his wife.

After all, why would she choose him?

ISOLDE STARED INTO the drawing-room fire, listening to the laughter rumbling from the dining room.

She and Lady MacDougall had left the men to their port.

"*Och*, they appear tae be having a right lovely go of it," Lady MacDougall said, eyes drifting fondly to the door before focusing again on her embroidery.

Isolde supposed that was one way of putting it.

Another burst of merriment erupted, Tristan's bass chuckle notably absent.

A block of ice was warmer than her husband's behavior this evening.

Isolde wanted to howl in frustration.

She had seen shades of Kendall yesterday, but today Tristan had entirely withdrawn into his ducal self. With her father and the MacDougalls this evening, he had reverted every whit to the haughty Duke of Kendall.

Not a trace of Tristan in sight.

The change in his behavior was precisely what Isolde had feared. That the second they found themselves in Society, he would become Kendall once more.

Ye possibly haven't been as attentive tae your husband as ye should, a wee voice whispered through her mind.

It was just . . .

Her father's arrival had caught her so off guard. And the intensity of his distress had overwhelmed her. Hadley thought she had died. Isolde could summon tears just remembering how he described the agony and grief of his journey north.

Isolde had admittedly forgotten about her husband for an hour or two. The entire town of Oban, as well as her father, had wanted to hear the story of her miraculous escape from the sea.

But when she managed to slip out of the inn's taproom to search for Tristan, it was to find he was aboard the *SS Statesman* again, closeted with his secretary, Ledger.

Clearly, he hadn't missed her company enough to come looking for her, either.

Her father had been less sanguine. "Does Kendall even know ye be alive, Izzy? He hasn't bothered to check on ye or even greet myself. I cannot imagine how ye managed a week alone on a scarcely-provisioned island with him."

"He was kind and caring while on the island, Papa. We worked together tae survive."

Hadley's scowl more than expressed his opinion of her statement. "It pains me more than I can express tae see ye search for good in that man."

"There *is* good in him, Papa."

"Ah, Izzy. Your kindness fair breaks my heart."

Isolde had bit her tongue.

To his credit, her father had been polite to Tristan. Well, Hadley had basically ignored the duke, but knowing the anger on her behalf that roiled under her father's polite facade, Isolde admired him for his forbearance.

A few minutes later, the laughter in the dining room died down, and the men joined the ladies in the drawing-room. Instead of crossing to claim a seat beside her, Tristan ceded the space to Hadley and stood unspeaking by the fireplace.

Isolde tried to catch Tristan's eye, to force him to truly look at her. But when he finally did turn her way, his gaze was flat and unreadable.

And then her father touched her arm and asked a question, claiming her attention.

Isolde chewed her lip, hating this trapped feeling, torn between her father and her husband. Tristan was like the Kendall before their marriage, appearing utterly disinterested in her. Behaving as if she mattered not at all.

She hadn't a clue how to thaw her husband's icy exterior. Clearly, this cold distance between them had originated in her insistence they return to London and her family there. But instead of talking to her—reaching out—he had cut her off and withdrawn.

And now the space between them had expanded exponentially, and she hadn't a clue how to stem it.

Deliberately, she took Tristan's arm as they walked back to the Oban Inn. His muscles tensed under her touch, and he smelled like Kendall once more—exotic and expensive and intoxicatingly male. Isolde longed to bury her nose in his throat, loosen his neckcloth and shirt buttons, and kiss his mouth swollen.

Drat him.

Had her father not been walking beside her, she would have said as much to her husband. Anything to crack his *Kendall* shell and bring Tristan back.

As they neared the harbor, Tristan paused and turned to her.

"I shall leave you both here, Wife." He pressed a dispassionate kiss to her hand. "I am sure your father will see you safely to your rooms in the inn."

"Ye aren't coming with me?"

"No. I wish to ascertain if the overnight accommodations aboard the *SS Statesman* are suitable for a lady."

Isolde doubted the duke had ever before uttered such a flimsy excuse.

Clearly, he knew an argument was brewing between them and wished to avoid it.

Fine.

She would let him have the night to simmer. But tomorrow, there would be a reckoning.

Pushing upward, she pressed a kiss to his cheek.

"I shall see you at breakfast, then," she murmured, stepping back.

"Of course." A glimpse of Tristan flashed in his eyes, there and gone again.

Worse, Isolde hated the self-satisfied look on her father's face as he bid Tristan good evening and led her away.

27

KENDALL FOUND! The saga surrounding the Duke and Duchess of Kendall continues. Their Graces, presumed drowned and deceased, were instead discovered healthy and well in the seaside village of Oban, Scotland. However, we have learned that Lord Hadley had already departed for Scotland, intent on recovering their bodies. We can only hope that his lordship experienced a joyous reunion with his daughter.

—ARTICLE IN *The London Times*

Isolde slept poorly.

Though it had only been a week, she had grown accustomed to the luxurious warmth of Tristan's body curled around hers at night.

She arrived in the private dining parlor scratchy-eyed and yawning, eager to see her husband.

Hadley was already in the room, dining happily on sausage, blood pudding, and eggs.

Tristan, however, was absent.

"Good morning, Izzy," her father said cheerily, standing to kiss her cheek and pull out a chair for her.

Isolde forced a smile she did not feel and began dishing her own plate.

Would her husband attend breakfast? Or would she have to board the *SS Statesman* and run him to ground?

They were married, for heaven's sake.

How could they forge any sort of true marriage if he retreated inside himself the second a hiccup occurred?

Hadley was rather quiet, as if sensing the rising choler of her temper.

Finally, the dining room door opened, admitting Tristan in a rush of sea air. He appeared as starched, pressed, and ducal as ever.

Naturally, he did not apologize for his tardiness. *A Duke of Kendall would never stoop to excuses*, Isolde could almost hear him intoning in his aristocratic English baritone.

Instead, he gave a sparse greeting and then sat opposite her father at the round table, leaving Isolde as the lone bridge between the men.

The three of them ate in agonizing silence for a few minutes. Tension poured into the room, suffocating Isolde's lungs—coal gas awaiting a spark to combust.

Finally, Hadley set down his fork and dabbed at his mouth with his napkin.

"As I mentioned yesterday, your mother and siblings left London last week for Muirford House," her father began, looking at Isolde. "I have spoken with the captain of the clipper ship. He thinks it a fine idea to sail up the Great Glen and then on tae Montrose around the coast of Moray. Your mother and the rest will be anxious tae see ye, Izzy."

Isolde stilled, just as Tristan's head snapped to attention.

She met her husband's turbulent gaze, before turning to her father. "I don't believe Kendall has decided where we will go next, Papa."

Or rather, she and Tristan hadn't come to an agreement on where they would next journey. Returning to London was less of a concern now that Hadley had arrived.

Her father spared a glance for Tristan. "Aye, well, His Grace can sort himself out while ye come with me tae Muirford House."

"Papa," Isolde said, reproach in her tone.

"My wife's place is at my side, Hadley." Tristan threw his napkin down on the tabletop. "Even you know as much."

The derision in Tristan's tone provided the spark needed to ignite her father's temper.

"Two weeks." Hadley braced his hands on the table. "Ye have had my Izzy in your hands for two *bloody* weeks, and ye nearly killed her. By my reckoning, *Your Grace*"—he leaned on the honorific with scathing sarcasm—"ye arenae worthy of Isolde's keeping. Ye can have her back when ye have proven your ability to properly care for a wife!"

"The law would state otherwise," Tristan snapped. "Isolde and I are married and therefore—"

"The law can go hang!"

"Yes, all of Parliament currently debates your casual relationship with legalities, Hadley. Your association with Jarvis has clearly shown—"

"There isnae a sheriff in all of Angus who will demand I return Isolde tae your care, Kendall." Menace laced every one of Hadley's syllables. "If ye want my daughter, ye will need tae raise an army and storm Muirford House. And even then, ye will drag her most unwillingly from her family, just as ye did two weeks ago in London!"

Tristan clenched his hands into fists.

"Enough!" Isolde hurtled to her feet, hands spread wide, as if she would separate the men.

Hadley and Tristan rose as well.

Her father's chest heaved, his nostrils flared . . . a bull prepared to charge.

Tristan, however, had turned to ice—white-lipped, chilly, unreachable.

"Despite your lowering opinion of me, Hadley," Tristan clipped, "I *will* never force my wife to do anything or abide anywhere she does not wish. If Isolde desires to return with you to Muirford House and stay for the rest of her natural life, I will not stop her. Her choices will always remain her own."

Tristan rounded the table for the window, but not before he spared the briefest flicker of a glance for herself.

And in that look, Isolde saw it all.

Resignation. Surrender.

He would not fight for her.

He would not fight for them. For their marriage.

The one time she wished him to be the commanding Duke of Kendall, spewing decisions and making arrogant demands . . .

Tristan didn't.

He was abdicating the field, as it were.

Her stomach sank to the soles of her feet.

Without saying another word, Tristan faced the windowpanes, shoulders stiff and unyielding.

Isolde turned back to her father, hating the gleam of triumph she saw in his eyes.

"Glad that's decided then," Hadley said, holding out a hand. "Come, Izzy. We have packing tae do."

She hesitated, too stunned by the change in Tristan to think clearly.

With a gentle hand under her elbow, Hadley urged her toward the door.

Isolde spared one last look for her husband before following her father out of the room.

The stark image of Tristan framed against the window burned behind her eyes as she climbed the stairs, her father a few paces behind.

Where had the husband who loved her gone? The one who had trembled with adoration and kissed her with such holy reverence?

Why would Tristan say nothing—do *nothing*—to keep her?

Why would he not fight—

The truth lit her mind in a crackling bolt of illumination.

Och.

She was such an *eejit*.

Tristan *expected* her to leave him.

Because everyone he had ever loved—or even viewed with fondness—had abandoned him.

His mother.

His twin, no matter how unwillingly.

Rafe.

The list was agonizingly short.

Tenderness ballooned in her bosom.

Tristan did not expect her affection or loyalty because he had shockingly little experience with those emotions.

She shut the door to her suite and turned to face her father.

"I'm not leaving with ye, Papa," she said with quiet firmness.

"Pardon?"

"I will be staying with my husband."

"With Kendall?" Outrage tinged his voice.

"Aye," she replied with a thread of irony. "He be the only husband I claim."

"But . . . why? Wouldn't ye prefer to be with your family?"

Gracious.

How to answer that?

Her father misread her hesitation.

"He has threatened ye with violence if ye disobey him." Hadley's brows gathered like a thundercloud. He turned for the door. "That bastard—"

"Papa!" Isolde caught his elbow. "Tristan has *never* threatened me in any way."

"Tristan?!"

"Aye. That is his Christian name."

"Ye dinnae call him Kendall?"

"Not anymore."

Her father's frown deepened, and he studied her for a long moment, as if trying to make sense of her mood.

Comprehension dawned.

He grimaced. "Izzy, ye must understand . . . sometimes the act of . . . of marriage—" Here he rolled a hand, ruddy color climbing his throat. "—can cloud one's thinking. It can make ye feel a connection that simply isn't there."

Well.

That was certainly . . . interesting.

Her father thought she was addled from the ardor of Tristan's husbandly attentions. In the annals of uncomfortable conversations between father and daughter, this topic had to rank among the most fraught.

Isolde breathed through the heat flooding her own cheeks.

"I don't think ye have been listening attentively, Papa." She placed a hand gently on his forearm. "Just now, Tristan stated quite clearly that he would never force his wife to do *anything* against her will. Particularly not . . . *that*."

Her father reared back. "Ye mean ye haven't . . ."

"Nae."

Not for lack of desiring *that* on her part. Though she did not clarify the point—fraught conversation and all.

Hadley pivoted and walked over to the window, unconsciously mirroring Tristan two floors below.

How odd.

Her father and Tristan were so alike in many ways—loyal, fierce, devoted—and yet so dissimilar.

Would there come a time when they could breathe the same air and not be at one another's throats?

"I cannae believe he hasn't—" Hadley shook his head. "Does Kendall not find ye—"

Thank heaven he did not finish that sentence. Nothing good would be at the end of it.

Mmm, how to explain the situation to her father without betraying her husband's confidences . . .

"Tristan wishes us to know one another better before we . . ." Isolde took in a deep breath.

"And yourself?" Hadley turned back to her. "What do ye wish, Izzy?"

"I wish tae know him better, as well. I am determined tae make a true marriage of this, Papa."

"With Kendall? I've seen gentlemen treat *dogs* with more kindness than he's shown yourself over the past day."

Well.

He was not wrong on that score.

"I won't offer excuses for Tristan's behavior. But we did have a wee bit of an argument just before ye arrived, Papa. We haven't had a chance tae discuss it since then, and so the whole has been festering. I perhaps have not been as attentive and considerate of him, either."

"Oh, Izzy," her father sighed, "as I've said, it breaks me tae watch ye search for good in that man. Ye be sailing straight into heartbreak."

"Perhaps, I am. But I have tae try, Papa. He is attempting to become a better version of himself. For example, Tristan has sworn off his persecution of ye and, the past twenty-four hours excepted, has been attentive to myself."

Her father snorted. "A tiger doesn't change its stripes."

"Perhaps, but I have to believe that such change is possible. I ken ye see Tristan as the reincarnation of his father, but ye forget that he is Rafe's brother and John's uncle. That the same gentle, noble blood that flows in their veins also runs in Tristan's."

"Izzy—"

"I know ye don't believe me, not yet, but he *is* a worthy man, Papa."

"Do ye love him then?"

Och.

That was the question, was it not?

She had scarcely passed a week of knowing Kendall as Tristan. An exhilarating week, yes, but seven days were hardly sufficient to declare one's undying passion.

True love—the sort her parents shared, the sort that sacrificed and pledged unwavering devotion—took more time.

Isolde found Tristan fascinating, clever, and unbearably attractive. His laughter and keen observations lit delight in her chest. Surely those were the seeds of love. But if and when love arrived in truth, she would tell Tristan first. Not her father.

"Scratch that." Hadley made a sharp motion with his hand. "Of course, with your tender, affectionate heart, ye will come tae love him. The bigger question remains—is a man such as Kendall even capable of loving anyone outside himself?"

Tristan's expression—yearning, ragged with adoration—rose in Isolde's memory . . .

She had to swallow back a tightness in her throat.

"Oh, Papa," she whispered. "I don't think ye have anything tae worry about on that score."

ISOLDE HAD LEFT.

Tristan stood ramrod-still in front of the window of the private dining parlor, afraid if he so much as twitched a muscle, he would shatter.

His wife had left.

She had taken her father's hand and walked out the door.

The pain was every whit as awful as he had anticipated. Needles lacerated his chest with each breath.

Perhaps he should have fought for her.

But . . . how?

Her loyalty remained with her father.

Nothing Tristan said or did would ever triumph over that fact.

This entire situation underscored *why* he had spent nearly a decade fighting his love for her. Because the scenario had played out as he had foreseen from the beginning.

He had surrendered to his emotions for Isolde.

She had not returned his affections.

And now he was left in jagged shards, forced to watch her sail away, taking his soul with her.

The agony of it serrated his breathing.

The door clicked open behind him.

Tristan ordered his body to turn around, to address whomever had just entered. But his muscles refused to obey.

It was likely only a servant come to clear the breakfast dishes.

The door *snicked* shut and a rustle of skirts drew near. Isolde's distinct smell of lemon and cheer filled his nostrils.

Oh.

"Come to say goodbye, Wife?" He forced the words past lips numb with misery.

In response, she ran a hand up his spine and through his hair, certainly undoing his valet's efforts not an hour earlier.

The unexpected touch felt akin to a knife's edge.

Tristan flinched, pivoting to glare at her.

His wife glared in return.

And then she proceeded to untie his neckcloth.

"Isolde." He recoiled from her reaching hands.

Unfortunately, his heels hit the wall behind him.

His wife did not retreat.

No.

Instead, she closed the distance between them and pressed her glorious lithe body against his.

She grasped his head firmly between her palms . . . . and kissed him.

A drugging, intoxicating kiss that set his blood to pumping and left his hands aching to touch her.

But Tristan knew.

If he touched her—if he returned her kiss—he would crumble. He would beg and plead and promise her anything if only she would stay with him, be with him, accept the burning fire of his love—

Pathetic milksop, his father's voice rang in his ears.

Undeterred by his lack of response, his wife broke off the kiss and continued to tug at his neckcloth. "Though I appreciate how attractive ye be in all your ducal finery, Your Grace, I like ye more disheveled and wanting under my palms."

"Isolde," he growled, trying to catch her hands, anything to stop their torturous caresses.

"And I'm going to keep kissing yourself until ye kiss me back." She leaned up, intent on his mouth once more.

He dodged, her lips finding the underside of his jaw.

"No," he all but snarled.

"Nae?!"

"I refuse to give you a goodbye kiss and then watch you leave with your father."

Finally, he managed to capture her wrists and halt her scorching exploration.

He glowered into her ocean-blue eyes.

"*Och*, ye be in fine *Kendall* form. A true marriage, ye said . . . ye want a true marriage between us. In a true marriage . . ." She paused, her eyes glistening. "In a true marriage, Tristan Gilbert, we choose one another. Full stop."

His chest collapsed, all bravado evaporating.

She seized the advantage and pressed upward once more, kissing him so softly, so tenderly, Tristan felt his heart crack.

"But," he breathed against her mouth, "you left with your father."

"Aye, to tell him I would be staying with yourself. He deserved tae hear my decision in private."

A terrifyingly incandescent hope exploded in Tristan's chest, clogging his throat. He dropped her wrists, his palms grasping her trim waist.

"Let me repeat, just in case ye didn't understand," she continued. "I"—*kiss*—"pick"—*kiss*—"you."

As if finally given permission, his arms slipped fully around her, crushing her body to his chest.

Blood roared in his ears. He pressed his lips to her hair, her temple, the delectable dip beneath her ear.

"But . . . you said," he whispered into her skin, voice hoarse, "you said you would always choose your family over me."

"Aye, and ye declared I would never have been the bride of your choice. Did ye mean that?"

"You are the only bride I ever wanted. The only one I ever envisioned."

"Precisely. We have both said things we didn't mean." She framed his face between her palms once more. "I know ye feel that no one has ever wanted you for yourself. That as Tristan, you are not sufficient alone. But I choose ye just as ye are."

Tristan shook his head, expression surely as baffled as he felt. "Why? Because you are my wife?"

Isolde laughed, the glorious, effervescent laugh that sang happiness to his soul. "It isn't out of duty or obligation, if that is your concern. I choose yourself because being with you is akin to champagne bubbles in my blood—intoxicating and heady. Because if I were tae leave now, I would miss ye ferociously. Because you, Tristan Gilbert, bring me such happiness that—"

Tristan captured the remainder of her words with his lips. Euphoria cascaded through him, fireworks exploding in his veins.

"You are truly remaining with me?" he managed to say, though it was a trial, as his lips refused to leave her skin. "I didn't mishear? This isn't a dream?"

"Aye," she murmured on a soft moan, arching her back to grant him greater access to her throat.

Tristan eagerly obliged.

"As I've said before, we need tae trust one another, Tristan," she continued, urging his head upright. "To trust that we both are committed tae this. To us." She pressed the softest kiss to his mouth. "We need tae believe the best of each other's actions and behaviors."

"I'm sorry." He pressed his forehead to hers. "I'm sorry I doubted you after your father's arrival. I should have had more faith. I should have—"

"Enough," she laughed. "No recriminations. Just trust. Trust that I care for ye. Just as I trust your love for myself. Trust that we are two souls endeavoring to become one."

She *chose* him . . . his Isolde.

Tristan wanted to weep for the sheer joy of it.

Her fingers threaded into his hair, pulling his mouth back to hers.

Bloody hell, how could he ever get enough of her?

They kissed for long intoxicating minutes, until they were both breathless and desperate to be closer.

"Husband," she gasped, "must we continue tae wait to consummate our marriage? I fear ye shall be the death of me otherwise, I yearn for ye so."

Any thought of protest fled Tristan's mind.

She belonged to him.

Just as he belonged to her.

A union of two souls into one, as she had said.

He had wanted to wait . . . to know for a surety that she loved him. To hear her say the words.

But as he drowned in the feel of her body against his, the pull and lift of their deepening kisses, his resolve crumbled to dust.

He could scarcely breathe through another day without making this woman his wife in truth.

"No more waiting, my love," he whispered into her ear. "Tonight. I promise."

28

Ah, Jane! Our Izzy lives! I can scarcely comprehend the happiness of it. Alas, she has chosen to remain with Kendall instead of returning home with myself. I cannot say I understand her decision. Kendall appears somewhat altered since their marriage, but I doubt His Haughty Grace can ever change sufficiently to be worthy of our lovely lass.

—PRIVATE LETTER FROM LORD HADLEY TO LADY HADLEY

T*onight.*

The word thrummed in Isolde's brain.

Tonight. Tonight.

The woman she had been three weeks ago would be shocked to know her thoughts now.

That she would be eagerly wanting—no, begging, pleading!—for the Duke of Kendall to take her to his bed.

And yet, she could scarcely think of anything else, the anticipation was so keen.

Nightfall could not come quickly enough.

After a rather lengthy hour of reconciliation in the private dining room, she had helped Tristan set his neckcloth and hair to rights. Her own coiffure had required similar repairs.

And even then, only a complete *eejit* would be unaware of what had transpired.

Isolde appeared thoroughly kissed, lips red and plump, while the skin on Tristan's neck was deliciously abraded.

Hadley's faint frown when they emerged spoke volumes. As did the way his eyes dropped to Tristan's solicitous palm resting on the small of her back before lifting to her surely radiant smile.

Tristan bid her farewell with a lingering kiss on the cheek.

There were matters he needed to discuss with Captain Woodbury, and Isolde wished to spend more time with her father before he departed on the clipper ship the following morning.

"I shall see you at dinner," her husband promised.

"Aye," she smiled in return.

His returning gaze was pure Tristan—gentle, worshipful, awestruck—and she adored him all the more for it. Infatuation bubbled through her veins, rendering her light-headed.

"Hadley," he nodded politely, taking his leave.

Isolde watched Tristan's long, sure strides retreat, admiring the broad set of his shoulders, the confident swing of his arms.

Tonight.

Finally.

Her father cleared his throat at her side.

Isolde tore her eyes away from her husband.

Hadley's expression could best be described as puzzled.

"I cannot say I ever expected tae witness such softness in Kendall's demeanor," he said, his own gaze drifting up to where Tristan still walked along the pier. "I suppose he does have something of a heart."

"Papa!" Isolde laughed, taking his arm.

"Though whether Kendall can maintain such affection . . . *that* remains tae be seen."

ISOLDE ENJOYED A lovely day with her father.

They walked up the coast north of town, scrambling over the ruins of Dunollie Castle and admiring the view across the inlet to the Isle of Mull. Sir John and Lady MacDougall joined them, lending the excursion a festive air.

However, dinner with Hadley and Tristan proved strained. But both men summoned their best behavior, and the whole didn't revert into a shouting match, so Isolde considered it a step—albeit a rather wee one—in the right direction.

And then it was nightfall once more.

Isolde bid her father farewell, as he would be departing at first light on the clipper ship.

Her maid helped Isolde change into a nightrail and plaited her hair before being dismissed.

A portion of Isolde's mind stood aside, marveling that her hands actually trembled. Not with virginal nerves, but with feverish anticipation, eager for her husband's arrival.

Tristan quietly entered from the adjoining dressing room. He wore a colorful silk banyan, the nightshirt he had donned their first night in Oban notably absent.

With a giggling laugh, she ran to him, wrapping her arms around his neck. "I missed ye. I missed us."

He pulled her tight against the muscled length of his body, and she breathed in the heady scent of cologne and warm male skin.

"You are the loveliest thing." He pressed his face into her hair. "I feel utterly unworthy of you."

"Nonsense."

He pulled back, brown eyes open and sincere. "Are you sure of this, Wife? I will never—"

Isolde grinned, took his face in her hands, and kissed him hungrily in reply.

She expected him to be as eager as herself, hands grasping, desperate for more, more, more.

Instead, he quieted her kisses, refusing to be drawn into mindless passion.

He touched her with hallowed reverence, as if she were a treasure of infinite value. As if he were a pilgrim paying homage . . . overwhelmed and awestruck.

Each caress became a vow, a promise.

I honor you.

I treasure you.

I love you.

Isolde felt worshiped. Cherished. Beloved.

Light-filled and awestruck.

The incandescent beauty permeated her heart with such joy—

Emotion clogged her throat and stung her eyes.

The veneration in his hands and lips awakened feelings deeper than mere lust—connection, belonging, harmony.

The beginnings of a deep and abiding devotion. A chrysalis waiting to transform into the fluttering beauty of true love within her heart.

The promise that, with patience, love would eventually arrive.

Lying in his arms in the aftermath—her back to his chest—she wanted to express some of this to him.

But before a syllable could leave her mouth, Tristan tucked his face between her shoulder blades.

A shuddering sob wracked his body.

TRISTAN TRIED TO control his weeping. Truly he did.

What sort of pathetic idiot *wept* after consummating his marriage?!

He blamed his emotional Italian mother.

It was just . . .

The whole had been so luminous, so transcendent. A wonderstruck hosanna of love and connection and tenderness . . .

He hadn't known such purity could exist in the act of marriage. That the tawdry and traumatic encounter he had been forced to endure as a youth could become, in a different situation, something so nearly holy and sacred.

Yet alongside the wonder and reverence, a sense of desperate terror lurked.

Making love to his wife had profoundly deepened his adoration of her. Even now, he trembled at the thought that she may never return his affections.

She had said she could perhaps come to love him . . . that day of their first kiss on the island.

But if she never did—if she never came to love him fully—could he continue to adore her? Or was hope so intertwined with love that, without one, the other would wither and die?

Please let her learn to love me in truth, he silently pleaded. *Just this one person. Just this once. Please let her become fully mine.*

Another sob ripped from his chest, emerging from a churning wellspring of anguish and heartache. Of terror and hope.

Damn and blast.

He needed to stop, to cease these unmanly tears and—

Isolde turned in his arms.

He expected her to say something. To ask if all was well. To express consternation at his weeping.

Instead, she gathered him close, her arms coming round his shoulders, pressing his head into the crook of her neck and running her fingers soothingly through his hair.

She uttered not a sound.

Clutching her, he released the dam of emotion constricting his lungs, the whole emerging as terrible, gusting sobs.

Fear that he may never earn her love.

Fury for his father's abusive behavior that robbed him of love.

Anguish for the lonely, abandoned boy he had been.

Heartache for the young man, unloved and unwanted.

Anger at all those who watched Kendall's savagery and did nothing.

And finally—it arrived as a quiet pin-prick of light—forgiveness for himself. For being unable to break free from Kendall. For permitting his father's cruelty to continue in some measure in Tristan's own behavior.

And his wife—his glorious, extraordinary wife—held him through it all.

Until her tears joined his.

As if she bore silent witness to his grief, understanding without a word spoken.

It couldn't be love on her part. Not yet.

But in that moment, it felt close enough.

THE FOLLOWING DAYS and weeks were the happiest of Tristan's life.

Despite his lingering fear that he might never earn Isolde's heart, a bond had clicked together in their marriage—like a belt buckle snapping into place, holding two separate halves together.

As he and Isolde had nowhere to be and time to spare, they decided to linger on their journey, declaring it a honeymoon in truth. He rather forgot he even owned a pocket-watch.

It took them three days to finally leave their suite in Oban and board the *SS Statesman*.

From there, they plotted a meandering course northward, exploring whatever they wished.

And with each stop, Tristan collected more images of his duchess.

The flash of her shapely ankles as she scrambled over the ruins of Iona Abbey.

The giddy delight of her awestruck expression as they stood in Fingal's Cave on the Isle of Staffa, waves rumbling the ground under their feet and crashing into the geometric columns stacked like giant's blocks.

The glowing happiness on her face as they walked the glittering white sand beaches of Vatersay, racing over the narrow isthmus separating the east of the isle from the west—the water so achingly blue, it felt sky-kissed.

Isolde plucking wind-blown strands of copper hair from her lips as they climbed over boulders, hiking to reach Loch Coruisk at the bottom of Skye, the Black Cuillin mountains looming overhead. The landscape was so varied, Tristan could scarcely believe he was still within the country of Great Britain.

Isolde's smoldering look at him from across the dining room table of Dunvegan Castle, promising all sorts of wickedness once they were alone, completely distracting Tristan's thoughts as he attempted to converse with their host—the Laird of Clan MacLeod.

Swimming beside Isolde in the glassy-still depths of Loch Shieldaig in the shadow of Ben Alligin, quietly recalling the terror of their own shipwreck and allowing the frigid waters to soothe the edge of the memory of how close they had both come to not being here at all.

Isolde still hadn't said she loved him, but Tristan cataloged her attachment in places outside words.

Surely there was devotion in the urgency of her kisses in the dark of night, tucked into their bed aboard the ship, the shushing of waves swallowing their moans.

Surely it was friendship that took his hand and ran through the *machair* dunes on the west coast of the Isle of Uist.

And surely it was fondness that stroked his hair in the dawn hours and held him close, listening attentively as he told of his plans for his estates.

Every day, his own affections for her deepened, morphing from the obsessive, desperate feeling he had labeled as *love* at the beginning of their marriage into an intense ocean of adoration swelling beneath his sternum.

That wherever Isolde was, there he would belong for as long as she would have him.

The only dark cloud came when they docked in Ullapool, the northernmost village of any size along the west coast of Scotland, and the only town with a direct, well-maintained road to Inverness.

There, Tristan discovered correspondence waiting for him—missives from estate stewards, a long list of questions from his man-of-business, and most significantly, a stack of letters from Ledger.

Lords was still arguing over when to hold Hadley's trial—at the end of July right before Parliament recessed for the year, or wait until the next parliamentary session in February.

But one bit of information sent Tristan's stomach plummeting in his abdominal cavity.

Despite my best efforts, Your Grace, several newspapers have uncovered that you provided information implicating Hadley after your marriage to his daughter. Naturally, the public have seized on the drama of the story. It feels like no matter where I go, I hear people discussing the matter. I fear I have failed you in my . . .

Tristan tossed the rest of the letter aside, anxiety churning in his chest.

Damnation.

He paced his small study aboard ship.

What was he to do?

Sooner or later, Isolde would learn of his behavior, and she would rightly see his actions as a betrayal.

They *were* a betrayal. He had promised that he would recuse himself from the impeachment case against Hadley, and Tristan had deliberately broken that promise. A broken promise that would destroy the fragile, barely-grown trust between them.

Isolde would be justifiably wounded and furious. She would see him for the vindictive blackguard that he was.

His heart already ached for the hurt he would cause her.

After everything he had done, how could he expect her to forgive this, too? At a certain point, her goodwill would wear out.

And without love tethering her, why would she remain with him instead of fleeing back to her parents' loyal arms?

As ever, he had needed more time. More time to learn how to kindle her love. More time to grow and change and prove his trustworthiness.

But this . . . he feared it would be the final nail in his coffin.

Tristan paused before the porthole window, trying to breathe through the despair banding his lungs.

"Oh, Tristan!" Isolde's cheerful voice greeted him from the doorway.

He turned to see her clutching a handful of her own correspondence, eagerly scanning the lines of a letter. Sun from the window at his back washed the sprigged muslin of her dress and highlighted the rosy color of her cheeks.

How had he ever convinced such a lovely creature to remain at his side?

"Uncle Rafe has formally invited us tae stay with him at Dunhelm Castle as we make our way down the coast tae Inverness. I know seeing your brother may be difficult for yourself, but I should so enjoy a visit." She lifted her head, eyes lit with excitement. "Please may we—"

She broke off with a frown, obviously reading something of his distress on his face. Her eyes dropped to the stack of letters atop his desk.

"What is it?" she asked.

He needed to tell her.

He should tell her.

And yet, Tristan simply . . . couldn't. Could not make his lips form the words that would injure her and shatter his own heart.

Not yet.

Please, give me one more day.

One more day of happiness.

Then he would tell her.

"Nothing," he replied instead, tongue numb. "Well, not nothing, obviously. Just the weight of hundreds of questions that I would prefer not to have to spend the time answering."

"Would you like some assistance?"

"No, my love. I shall manage." He crossed and captured her mouth in a heated kiss. "If you are beside me, I will be far too distracted to focus on anything else."

"Tristan." She shook her head on a laugh, looping her arms around his neck.

He managed a smile. "And, yes. Of course, we should visit my brother."

Though he did not relish the thought of spending days in Rafe's company, he could not deny Isolde time with a man who was like an uncle to her.

"Thank you! I shall pen a reply immediately." She kissed him again and then walked back into their bedchamber. Tristan's gaze devoured her.

His decision had been made.

Damn, but he was a lily-livered coward.

Isolde had not told him that she loved him. And once she learned of his actions—and she *would* learn of them—she likely never would. In the glaring light of his perfidy, Tristan could scarcely blame her.

But between now and her discovery, he would cling to these precious days of happiness with both hands.

OVER THE WEEKS of their honeymoon, Isolde discovered she enjoyed hearing her husband talk about himself. His past. His hopes for the future.

She made an unconscious habit of drawing out his thoughts. Every morning, she would choose a new topic she wished to explore.

"Tell me about your estates," she asked as they anchored off the jagged cliffs of Ardnamurchan.

"Eager to claim your role as duchess?" he replied, teasing in his tone.

She elbowed his ribs. "Ye ken what I mean. I want tae hear about your plans for them—what your tenants be like and such."

And so . . . Tristan talked.

About his estates, his dreams for Britain as a country, his time at Oxford, his hunt for Allie in Italy and his mistakes with his sister.

He even spoke of his father in the dead of night, voice hoarse in her ear, his arms trembling around her.

She was coming to love him in truth.

The adoration and joy she felt whenever she heard his voice or noticed his handsome gray head after even the shortest absence spoke volumes.

The flutterings inside the chrysalis of her affections became stronger day after day.

How could her heart have changed so quickly? It had been mere weeks since their wedding.

Perhaps that was why she hesitated to say the words *I love you*. How could love arrive so quickly?

Or perhaps she was waiting for . . . *och*, she wasn't quite sure what precisely. A flash of illumination? The perfect time and place?

Isolde couldn't say.

A potential moment came the night after they left Ullapool.

Seated against the headboard of their bed aboard the *SS Statesman*, she and Tristan talked as the lamplight burned low, his head on her shoulder and an arm thrown over her waist.

Something troubled him still. She could sense it clinging to the edges of his mood, but she had decided to let it be for now. He would tell her when he was ready.

Isolde dragged her fingers through his gray hair.

"I suppose I should finally forgive ye for reading my letters tae Stephen Jarvis," she said, pressing a kiss to his forehead.

Tristan snorted, a quiet huff of sound.

"I shall forever remain unrepentant of that act." He nuzzled her throat.

"Husband! When someone forgives ye, it is considered good form tae extend an apology. Particularly when said someone is your wife."

"Never." He pushed upright, gazing at her. "The moment I opened those letters and realized *you* were their author . . . I was powerless to stop myself. The enchanting loops and curls of your handwriting, the clever bite of your wit. I inhaled every word, enthralled by your spell."

"Now ye be ridiculous!"

"My long-time worship of you is anything but ridiculous, Duchess."

He kissed her to prove his point and then ran his thumb over her tingling lips.

He continued, "When I awoke that night and saw you rummaging through the chest of drawers in my bedchamber . . ." He loosed a long, slow breath. "I was simply undone. You were my every fantasy brought to life."

"I was in my dressing gown," Isolde laughed.

"Indeed, you were." His eyebrows lifted suggestively. "Your bare toes peeking out the bottom, your glorious red hair in a long braid down your back. So enticing I could scarcely breathe."

"And I was desperate to recover my letters!"

"I realized that immediately. I couldn't admit it to myself at the time, but I was insane with jealousy and bursting with rage."

"Over Jarvis?"

"Yes, because that lying, adulterous man had kissed you. He had tasted what I had not. And then, he had thoroughly abused your trust and wounded your affectionate heart. It was not to be borne; he had to be punished. Like the idiot I was, I refused to even consider courting you myself. Instead, I made it my goal to torment Jarvis, to pummel him for his deception and lies."

"And thus, your investigation into his financial dealings began."

"Precisely."

"Implicating my father along the way." She touched his face.

"Yes."

"Are you still convinced of Hadley's guilt?" she asked, voice tentative.

Isolde didn't wish her loyalties to be conflicted between her husband and her father. Perhaps it was better not to know?

Tristan was a long time answering, as if carefully choosing his words.

"Convinced of Hadley's guilt?" he finally repeated slowly. "I cannot say. There are letters between solicitors and your father that appear damning. It is why I wished Lords to further investigate the matter."

"But you didn't have to pursue it. You had prior reason to question my father, to cast doubt on him. I would love to know where your rancor began."

His shoulders sagged as he looked away from her.

"Tell me, Tristan," she urged. "Please."

On a sigh, he nodded.

Isolde listened as he outlined how her father had systematically laid waste to the dukedom's finances. How it had taken years of work on

Tristan's part to restore losses and rectify the trouble. And then, beginning about when Isolde returned from Boston, Hadley began a campaign to embarrass and demean Tristan at every turn. Tristan described his own ill-advised speech in Lords, full of his youthful pride, and Hadley's subsequent public mockery and condemnation.

And all the thousands of stinging cuts since.

"Ye have been at one another's throats for a long while," she said when he had finished. "Perhaps it is time tae bury the hatchet."

"Yes. I suppose it is." He trailed a hand through her hair. "And I have your loving spirit to thank for it."

Isolde smiled at him.

She could have said *I love you* in that moment.

But Tristan kissed her so lushly, so thoroughly, Isolde quite forgot her own name, much less her intended words.

However, in the days that followed, she couldn't shake the sense that something had upset him in the letters he had received in Ullapool.

Was his lovemaking more desperate than amorous? Did he appear anxious to cling to her?

She couldn't say.

Time.

They had both experienced tremendous changes in a matter of weeks.

She simply needed to be patient and help Tristan settle into this new way of being.

And surely, given time, she would seize the perfect moment to tell him *I love you*.

29

The Duke of Kendall has not relinquished his vendetta against Lord Hadley, despite his marriage to the earl's eldest daughter. We learned Wednesday last that Kendall sent more damaging evidence to the impeachment committee. Will anything stem the feud between son and father-in-law?

—ARTICLE IN *THE LONDON TIMES*

The white walls of Dunhelm Castle, Sir Rafe Gordon's Highland residence, gleamed atop a cliff and reflected the golden light of the evening sun.

Tristan studied the structure from the deck of the *SS Statesman*.

The castle appeared a startling jewel, perched dramatically on a wee peninsula, water lapping the base of black basalt cliffs on three sides. The hills of the Caithness coast rose behind, framing the turrets and gables in green heather and gorse.

He had never dreaded a sight more.

Devastation ravaged his chest.

Isolde did not yet know of his betrayal of her trust. The coward in him simply hadn't been able to confess his sins.

Sir Rafe *had* to have heard the tale.

Isolde would likely know the whole of it before morning.

Tell her. Tell her now.

But his tongue stubbornly refused to loosen, to let pass the words stuck in his throat.

And then it was too late, as they were climbing into the tender to be rowed to a rocky beach just north of the castle.

Once inside, Sir Rafe and his wife, Lady Gordon, greeted them at the end of an oak-lined entry hall.

Tristan watched as his wife warmly embraced their hosts, the affectionate familiarity between them obvious.

His own welcome was decidedly more stiff and formal.

Rafe studied Tristan intently as they shook hands, his gaze moving between Tristan and Isolde, most likely assessing the depth of Isolde's blissful ignorance of her husband's deception.

Tristan could feel his *Kendall* self surface. A need to retreat inward, to shield himself from injury. To withdraw like a turtle into its shell, to a place where the weight of his brother's stare and the discomfort of Tristan's own perfidy could not reach.

Clenching his fists, he held the urge at bay. Reverting to his old ways would only make the situation worse and add weight to Isolde's confirmation that he had not changed.

He knew this.

And yet, it was difficult.

Difficult to nod and respond genially to Rafe's questions.

Yes, they had greatly enjoyed exploring the sea stacks at John O'Groats.

No, they had not taken time to examine the ancient steps at Old Wick.

Tristan and Isolde followed their hosts up a flight of stairs to what was once the Great Hall of the medieval castle. Now, the space served as a drawing-room of sorts. To the left, a series of three tall windows provided a dramatic panorama of the ocean.

"Mamma?" Isolde gasped at Tristan's side. "Papa!"

Lord and Lady Hadley stood in front of the fireplace, heads turned expectantly toward the doorway.

Isolde flew from Tristan's side and into the open arms of her parents.

Lady Hadley promptly burst into tears, clutching her daughter close.

Tristan's stomach, already tied in knots, plummeted. A hollow tingling pricked his fingertips.

Why was Hadley here? With Lords still debating a trial date, shouldn't the earl be in London, consulting with solicitors?

Sir Rafe excused himself from Tristan's side.

Lady Gordon crossed to her friends, stopping at Lady Hadley's shoulder.

Leaving Tristan remaining just inside the doorway.

Alone.

Lord and Lady Hadley fussed over their daughter.

"Isolde, my darling! I have been so anxious to see you." Lady Hadley framed her daughter's face between her hands. "I feared for my heart when I heard about your near drowning."

"I am well, Mamma," Isolde laughed, her eyes bright.

Lord Hadley embraced his daughter, but his baleful gaze met Tristan's over her shoulder. Glowering and livid.

Tristan read it all there.

Hadley knew.

Of course, he knew.

And he also, rightly, intuited that Isolde did not.

A series of whoops sounded from the doorway on the opposite side of the room.

"Isolde!"

"Finally!"

Mac and James Langston burst into the room, rushing to sweep their sister into their arms. Lady Mariah Langston followed behind more decorously.

"I cannot believe ye almost died!" Mac laughed, spinning Isolde in a circle as she giggled in delight.

How odd, Tristan thought.

That he could feel such aching tenderness and joy for Isolde and, yet, such wretchedness for himself.

He swallowed and walked over to the windows, studying the view. The sun sank toward the horizon, bathing the ocean in streaks of golden coral.

It felt apropos, the sunset.

An ending. A descent into darkness after a singularly stunning display of light and beauty.

Much like Tristan's marriage.

Granted, the thought was perhaps more than a tad maudlin.

But as he listened to the familial laughter behind him, he also found a thread of solace. If his betrayal drove Isolde away, she would find support and affection within her family's loving embrace.

And he . . .

Well, Tristan would continue on as he always had—isolated and alone, attempting to live out—

"Tristan!" a familiar, ebullient voice cried.

Startled, he turned just in time to catch Allie in his arms. His sister clasped her hands tight around his waist and buried her face in his chest.

And just as Lady Hadley had moments earlier, his twin burst into tears, sobs wracking her frame.

"Allie," he murmured, gathering her close, aghast to feel emotion stinging his eyelids. "You're here."

"Of course, I'm here," she said, the words muffled against his ribcage.

And then she hit his upper arm. Hard.

"Ow!" Tristan yelped. "Whatever is that—"

"A note!" Allie pulled back, gray eyes baleful, cheeks damp. "I was told you had drowned, and yet I felt nothing through our twin bond. Nothing! No sign at all that anything was amiss."

"Allie, we have no twin bond."

"We do!" She pointed a finger in his face. "I thought you gone, and it nearly sent me into an early grave!"

"Aye, that is true," a man's voice agreed.

Tristan lifted his head to see Ethan Penn-Leith walking toward them, Sir Rafe at his side.

"I feared for her health, she was *greiting* so," Ethan continued.

As usual, Tristan's brother-in-law appeared cheerful and ebullient, his green eyes lit with bonhomie. The Scot had no sense of self-preservation, wearing every emotion on his face for all and sundry to see, particularly his devotion to Allie.

In short, Ethan reminded Tristan of an overly-exuberant puppy.

It was not a compliment.

"Exactly!" Allie pointed at her husband before turning back to Tristan. "And then, I received a paltry few sentences in a letter." She placed her hands on her hips and parodied his *Kendall* voice. *"All is well, Sister. The reports of my demise were greatly exaggerated. Have a good life."*

Tristan chuckled. "It was hardly *that* terse."

"I read between the lines."

"I said I loved you."

"Details, Tristan. I needed details!" She smacked the back of one hand against the palm of the other. "How did you survive? Were you injured? How did Isolde fare? Instead, I had to wait for Hadley to arrive and tell me all."

Tristan pulled Allie into his arms again. Over his twin's head, he could see Isolde similarly hugging her younger sister with the rest of her family gathered around.

"I'm sorry, Allie." He pressed a kiss to her hair. "I should have realized."

"Yes, you should have." Her words sounded muffled against his waistcoat. "But thank you for the apology. Marriage appears to have softened your Kendall-ness."

"It has," he confessed readily. "I heeded your advice."

"Finally!" she said on a hiccupping laugh, tears brimming once more.

She stepped out of his embrace, digging for a handkerchief to wipe her eyes.

"I am glad tae see ye be well, Kendall," Ethan said, taking his wife's place in front of Tristan. "The world would have lost a brilliant light had ye perished."

Trust the Highland Poet to have something grandiose to say.

And then, Ethan did the most astonishing thing of all—

He pulled Tristan in for a backslapping hug, a friendly expression of brotherly affection that Tristan had no recollection of ever before receiving.

Something of his amazement must have shown on his expression over Ethan's shoulder, as Sir Rafe nodded in approval.

And Tristan realized.

Sir Rafe had invited Allie and Ethan, as well. And then excused himself from the drawing-room to fetch them. To ensure that—just as Isolde was surrounded by those she loved—Tristan would have his own family to greet him.

The gesture was . . . touching. Astonishing, even. To receive such thoughtful kindness—goodwill that was for his benefit alone. Particularly from a man he had assumed the worst of and always treated with disdain.

"*Uffa!*" Allie stared at her handkerchief in exasperation before tilting her head back in an attempt to staunch her tears. "I detest that I can't stem this weeping!"

Ethan chuckled, tugging her into his arms. "Ye ken why that be, my love."

Tristan's brows lifted in question.

Allie turned in her husband's embrace to look at her twin, gaze suddenly bashful.

Leaning forward, she murmured softly for his ears alone, "I discovered last week that I am in a family way." She added in Italian, "*Sono incinta.*"

Ethan pressed a hand to Allie's middle, his smile wide and radiant.

"Truly? Ah, Allie." Joy flooded Tristan's chest. "That is the best news. Congratulations."

Of course, the words set his sister to weeping in earnest, crying first on Ethan's chest and then Tristan's.

"I'm going to be a t-terrible m-mother," she hiccuped in his ear.

"Nonsense," Tristan laughed. "Your children will adore you."

"No. My children will adore Ethan." She looked to her husband who stood speaking with Sir Rafe. "I mean, he is just impossibly lovable."

As if to emphasize her point, Ethan laughed, a stunningly charismatic smile enveloping his face.

And then Allie began crying once more.

Tristan pressed a kiss to her temple.

"Now." His twin pointed a finger at him, tears still streaming down her face. "Tell me everything that has happened since your marriage! And don't you dare leave out a single detail!"

Allie dragged him to a window seat and forced him to regale her with the entire tale of his shipwreck and time on the island.

Occasionally, Tristan met Isolde's gaze across the room. She sat with her mother, surely recounting the same story.

And the whole scenario felt . . .

Well, it felt like family.

Warm. Accepting. Like the memory of playing blind man's bluff with his mother and Allie in the nursery of Hawthorn as a child.

If only Tristan could find a way to hold on to this feeling . . .

But that hope was quickly dashed.

They had all just stood to retire to dress for dinner when Hadley approached Tristan.

"A word, Kendall, if ye please." It was not a request.

Tristan followed Hadley into an alcove, dread a burning coal in his gut.

The earl got straight to the point.

"I know what ye did. Rafe knows what ye did. Hell, all of London knows what ye did." Hadley's icy stare chilled Tristan's spine. "But it's clear that my Izzy doesn't yet know of your perfidy. I don't care how your new onslaught of information damages myself. But in this, ye have deceived my daughter and hidden your wrongs from her eyes. Ye broke a promise—one of many, I am sure. I should tell her myself right—"

"Hadley," Tristan began.

The earl put up a staying hand. "I *should* tell her right now—and I cannot guarantee that someone else here won't say something—but this is *your* betrayal. Your wrong. And I don't wish my daughter tae be angry with me for being the harbinger of bad news. You will gather what spineless courage ye can muster and tell her. I'll give ye until tomorrow morning tae confess all." Hadley consulted his pocket-watch. "Ye have twelve hours, Duke."

DINNER AND THE ensuing conversation were raucous affairs.

Tristan heard little of either, preferring to remain at the edge of the festivities. It nearly felt like a wake, a celebration of the life he might have had.

His thoughts were still overwrought as he climbed into bed and pulled his wife into his arms.

Tell her.

And yet the words still would not come.

Damnation, he was such a coward.

Once Isolde's breathing evened out, he slipped from underneath the counterpane, pulling on trousers and his silk banyan.

The house was quiet, but he noted light streaming from under the library door.

Pushing it open, Tristan found Sir Rafe and Hadley sitting before the fire, tumblers of whisky in their hands.

"Duke." Sir Rafe stood when he saw Tristan in the doorway. "Join us."

Hadley snorted, pushing to his feet. "Have ye told her, Kendall?"

"Andrew." Rafe's tone held reproach.

"Not yet." Tristan took in a slow breath. "Trying to convince myself I'm not a coward."

"*Och*, at least you're being honest for once." Hadley drained the remainder of his whisky, setting the glass down on a sideboard.

"Despite your opinion of me, Hadley," Tristan said, "I am attempting to grow into a better man. One who is worthy of your daughter."

"That remains tae be seen." Hadley turned for the door. "Night, Rafe. Good luck keeping this one company." He jerked his thumb in Tristan's direction before leaving the room and closing the door.

"Have a seat." Rafe motioned toward the chair Hadley had just vacated. "Whisky?"

"Yes."

Tristan sat.

Rafe handed him two fingers of Scotch before retaking his seat.

"Care tae talk, Kendall?" his brother asked.

Tristan winced. "I hate hearing our father's name on your lips." He paused and then added, "Please, call me Tristan."

Rafe blinked, as if the concession surprised him. The tentative peace offering of it.

"Tristan," he murmured. "I should be honored."

The quiet hush of night and the soreness of Tristan's own heart sent his words tumbling like spillikins.

"Honored?" he repeated, shaking his head and sipping his whisky. "Were our father not a blight upon human existence, you would be Kendall right now. And I . . ." He held his glass up to the firelight, the amber liquid recalling the color of Isolde's hair. ". . . I would not exist."

Rafe remained silent for seven seconds.

Tristan counted them.

"I have never once regretted my decision tae invalidate my parent's marriage," his brother finally said. "It liberated my mother from our father's grasp and gave me immediate freedom, as well. I would make the same decision a thousand times over. I never wished to be Kendall."

Tristan met Rafe's gaze, reading the truth there.

"A dukedom is a privilege," Rafe continued, "but I also recognize its weight. By all accounts, ye be a fair and capable manager of it. Ye are a credit tae our heritage."

The unexpected praise nearly stole Tristan's breath.

"Thank you," he whispered.

They both sipped their drinks in silence for a moment, Tristan pondering.

Sitting with his brother . . .

His brother!

Well, it felt . . .

Tristan searched for the word he wanted.

Accepting.

He felt accepted.

And despite his hurt over Rafe's actions in the past, Tristan sensed he could finally look beyond that.

That maybe, with time, he and Rafe could form a bond of some sort.

Rafe certainly appeared open to the prospect.

"How fairs Hawthorn?" Rafe asked. "I understand ye have undertaken some refurbishment in the south wing?"

They happily settled into talking about Tristan's plans for the estate. An experienced landowner himself, Rafe had keen insights, particularly as he had assisted Old Kendall in managing the ducal lands for several years.

It was invigorating, to speak about the dukedom and its people with someone who knew them as intimately as Tristan himself.

"Does that stretch of ancient forest still cut through the home farm?" Rafe asked.

"Of course. Auld Graeme protected that forest with his life on more than one occasion."

"Graeme MacIntosh?" Rafe's eyebrows lifted in delight, the motion tugging at the scar across his cheek. "I cannot imagine he yet lives. He seemed ancient when I was a lad."

"No, he passed about a decade ago. I ensured his widow received his pension."

"*Och*, that is good of ye. Auld Graeme was a gruff character, but I never met a finer woodsman."

Tristan nodded, as that was only too true.

"I pestered Graeme so thoroughly one summer," Tristan confessed, "he made me chop wood to stay out from underfoot."

"Aye, that sounds like Auld Graeme." Rafe smiled, a dimple popping in his cheek.

"I cannot think he liked me much."

"Don't be daft. Knowing Graeme as I do, I'm sure he adored ye. That man had a heart forged of pure gold."

Tristan raised his eyebrows.

Rafe noted his skepticism.

"Graeme was brusque tae be sure," his brother continued, "and as Scottish as they come. He arrived at Hawthorn when my mother married our father. I actually tried tae lure him back tae Scotland after Father was convicted of bigamy, but Graeme had married an English lass and didn't wish tae leave."

"I never knew any of this."

"Aye, well, Graeme kept his thoughts close. However, ye weren't the first lad Auld Graeme helped heal from Kendall's brutality. He had an affinity for wounded things. Always some recuperating animal in his kitchen."

"A wounded thing," Tristan repeated slowly. "That is an accurate description of the boy I was then."

"Aye. Myself, too. Graeme took me in hand. He taught yourself tae swing an axe, but he schooled me in how tae be a Scot. Made me shed the crisp English accent our father insisted upon and showed me how tae track game. Graeme cared when so few people did not. Though I realized years later, many of the servants at Hawthorn did what they could tae lessen the horror of our father's cruelty. As I said, I am sure they adored ye, though they would have been careful not tae show it."

Rafe's words opened a door in Tristan's mind, abruptly permitting him to see his childhood in a new light.

Many of the same servants who raised Tristan and Allie had also raised Rafe and his siblings.

Snippets of memory surfaced.

A nurse rocking him to sleep even after he was old enough to no longer require such tending.

The cook leaving a plate of still-warm biscuits within easy reach of young hands.

The butler flaring his eyes in Tristan's direction when his father arrived home, the faintest warning that Tristan should make himself scarce.

Evidence of caring that he had never truly understood.

That was the problem with love, he was coming to realize.

It had to be noticed. To be seen in order to be appreciated.

He looked at his brother. At this man who had reached out to him more than once over the years. Who continually extended an olive branch, no matter how cruel or cutting Tristan's response.

That . . .

That was an act of love on Rafe's part.

And Tristan consistently rejected it.

All because he refused to forgive Rafe for a mistake nearly twenty years past. A ghastly mistake that, yes, had cost Tristan dearly.

But given his own behavior over the past few weeks, Tristan hardly felt justified in castigating anyone for not fully thinking through consequences before acting.

Sipping his whisky for courage, Tristan cleared his throat.

"I know I have been angry with you for many years," he began.

Rafe shifted in his chair. "Aye, ye have. I could never quite pinpoint what happened."

The old hurt and anguish reared up, attempting to sink claws into Tristan's lungs. He pushed it away.

"It was . . ." Tristan swallowed. "It was Eton."

"Eton?" Rafe frowned.

"Yes. When first we met."

Tristan described his joy in meeting Rafe for the first time. The excitement that perhaps Tristan might have a friend in John. His happiness in living free of his father for the first time. The hope that he might have a loving relationship with Rafe.

And then the horror of Rafe's words to their father. Of the perceived betrayal that altered the course of Tristan's life.

Rafe was pacing before the fire, pale and teary-eyed, by the time Tristan finished.

"I had no idea," Rafe whispered. "I vaguely remember the encounter with our sire, but ye ken how he was. I'm sure he had riled me, and I said something *glaikit* without thinking. I am so very sorry, Tristan."

"You didn't know." Tristan swallowed, eyes staring into the coals. "But from then on, I hated you. Your thoughtless words stoked Kendall's cruelty and ended any hope of a relationship between you and me. I hated the love you lavished on John and your children, on your friends . . . on anyone but myself. It was the final cruel blow, after losing my sister and my mother . . . to lose my brother, too."

Rafe held out a hand for Tristan.

Setting down his tumbler, Tristan placed a palm in his brother's.

Rafe pulled him to his feet and hauled him into a tight hug.

"I would have given anything to save you from our father's cruelty." His voice hoarse in Tristan's ear. "It breaks me tae know I caused ye so much suffering at his hands. Know this now, Tristan Gilbert. Ye shall always have a loving brother in myself."

Tristan returned his brother's tight, healing embrace.

Bloody hell.

This must be what philosophers called *catharsis*.

The relief of shedding a heavy burden carried for far too long.

Tristan stepped back, only to have Rafe stop him with a hand at the back of his neck.

"I know our father would never have said this, but I am proud of the man ye have become." Rafe's brown eyes glittered with tears. "And I'm doubly glad that ye married Isolde, regardless of the grim circumstances surrounding your marriage. No matter Andrew's opinion, ye and Isolde are a perfect match."

Isolde.

Tristan's wife.

He managed a shuddering breath. "I love her, you know."

Rafe nodded and stepped back. "Aye, it shines in your eyes every time ye look at her. 'Tis precisely how I look at my Sophie."

"I've loved Isolde for nearly a decade," Tristan confessed.

"Is that so?" A grin tugged at Rafe's lips.

Tristan relayed the mishap in Montacute's garden, Isolde mistaking him for John. "One look at her—one conversation—and I was lost. There has never been anyone else for me."

"Aye, that is how it went with Sophie." Rafe put his hands into his pockets. "I saw her at a ball, spoke with her for five minutes, and knew she would be my wife."

"Truly?"

"We Gilbert men can be an obsessive lot when it comes to our women. It explains why our father married his first wife, Catherine. Old Kendall fell in love with her—or as close to love as that black-hearted bastard was capable—and pursued her until she capitulated. Of course, he was unable tae retain her affections and, in his arrogance, married my mother at our grandfather's insistence."

Tristan's head tipped back in understanding. "Hence, from obsession, his bigamy was born."

"Precisely." Rafe clapped Tristan on the back. "I'd like to think you and I are more intelligent. We do the work necessary to retain our wives' hearts."

Yes.

But it all reminded Tristan of the purpose behind his foray into the library. Anxiety twisted in his stomach.

"Will Isolde ever forgive me, do you think?" he asked Rafe quietly.

"Aye, take courage, Brother," Rafe smiled. "Isolde has a loving heart, like her father. Merely stay the course and be honest with her. If ye could forgive the painful repercussions of my own wrongs, I imagine she can forgive ye this."

"Granted, it did take me twenty years."

Rafe laughed. "Hopefully, Isolde will forgive ye a wee bit faster. After all, in the case of a wife, ye do have kisses as a means of persuasion. Though ye will likely have tae grovel." He pushed Tristan toward the door. "Go. Speak with her. Trust in her love for ye."

Tristan nodded, biting back a stab of pain.

Trust in her love for ye.

That was the very problem.

Isolde *didn't* love him.

And now, heaven alone only knew if she ever would.

30

My darling Sophie. I have a brother again. My heart overflows with joy.

—A HASTILY-SCRIBBLED NOTE FROM SIR RAFE GORDON
TO LADY GORDON, LEFT ON HER LADYSHIP'S BEDSIDE TABLE

Isolde opened her eyes to moonlight and a sense that something was not quite right.

Blinking, she rolled over, seeking Tristan's warmth, only to realize what had awakened her.

Her husband sat on the opposite edge of the mattress with his back to her. The drapes were pulled wide and the window shutters opened, sending moonlight spilling into the room and casting him in a silvery outline.

Isolde pushed to sitting.

"Tristan?" she murmured.

"Yes." He turned toward her, his face lost in shadow.

She rubbed her eyes and stretched.

"What time is it?"

"Half three."

Isolde paused, frowning. "Why are ye up?"

"I couldn't sleep." A hesitation. "I had a long conversation with Rafe. We mended fences."

"Oh, Tristan!" She extended a hand toward him. "I am so happy tae hear it. But why are ye over there? Come here." She patted the counterpane beside her. "I want tae hold ye."

"Isolde . . ." he began, her name more sigh than sound. Resigned and so weary.

Her heart kicked in her ribcage.

Something was wrong. But then, she had suspected as much.

"What is it, Tristan? I ken something has been eating at ye. Talk with me." She extended a palm toward him once more.

Quietly, he took her hand in his, shifting more fully onto the bed. But he still didn't come any closer.

"Now I be nervous, Husband," she whispered. "Why do ye hesitate tae speak?"

The clock on the mantel ticked the seconds.

Finally, he cleared his throat, words coming haltingly. "It is difficult . . . to force myself to break . . . my own heart."

"Tristan?"

"And . . . even more difficult . . . to knowingly hurt yours."

Isolde's breathing seized. She shuffled across the bed to him, but he flinched when she placed a hand on his chest.

Fear clamped her lungs in a vise.

"Tristan Gilbert, tell me immediately what has happened!"

"I'm trying," he choked. "I just . . . I wanted to wait . . . wait until you loved me, and then maybe you could forgive—"

His voice broke on a gasp.

He was *greiting*, she realized. Weeping silently, a hand pressed to his eyes.

What the devil had happened to make him weep so?

To be so sure she would reject and abandon him?

Trepidation jittered in her limbs.

"Tell me," she repeated, sitting back.

What the hell had he done?

With a deep, hiccupping breath, he began to speak. "In Oban, Ledger mentioned that Commons had requested . . ."

Silently, Isolde listened as the whole stuttering tale came out. How he had permitted more damning evidence to be given about her father. How he had Ledger obfuscate his perfidy, so she wouldn't learn of it. His regret that he hadn't been more loyal to her, that he had been selfishly thinking only of himself, instead of putting her heart and all she loved before anything else.

In the midst of his confession, she felt it—the sting of his betrayal. For the briefest moment, she imagined the scene. Shouting her fury and casting him from their bedchamber, marshaling her wounded spirit to retaliate in kind.

But like April clouds racing off after rain, sunshine warmed her chest.

And in place of fury or betrayal or hurt . . .

A surge of tenderness and adoration rose from the deepest well of her soul.

In its wake, one thought, and one thought alone, swept through her mind.

I love him.

Oh, how I love him.

The truth of it pulsed, a palpable surety thrumming through her veins, fluttery wings at last taking flight.

This was the truest test, she realized.

To love amid joy, when one was content and blissful and swimming in happiness . . .

Such love was simple. Easily bestowed.

But to love in the thick of crisis . . .

When her beloved wept his regret—not expecting forgiveness to be granted but humbly begging for the chance to win her faith once more.

To feel, in her heart, the pain of his sorrow more deeply than the sting of his betrayal.

"I vow to always put you first in my affections going forward."

Tristan's voice was hoarse. "I will work every hour to rebuild the trust I have shattered. I swear this to you. I love—" His voice cracked. "I love you. I love you more than my pride, more than my vanity or ambitions. You may decide that forgiveness is impossible, given my actions, but—"

Isolde stopped him with a finger to his lips before moving her hand to his heart. It beat a desperate prayer under her palm.

"I forgive ye," she said.

She felt more than heard his stuttered gasp.

"What . . . what did you say?"

"I forgive ye."

His spine straightened, his head lifting.

"But . . . why?" The choked bafflement in his voice nearly made her smile. "How? How can you? I have failed to—"

"I forgive ye because that is what love does."

A long pause . . .

He held impossibly still, as if her slightest move would unravel him.

And then, on the most hesitant of whispers . . .

"Love?" he breathed.

"Aye." Isolde licked a tear from her lip, sure he could hear the emotion in her own voice. "I love ye, Tristan Gilbert. I love the goodness that ye try tae cloak in stern duty. I love how fiercely ye watch over those within your care. I love the way your eyes light when ye see me. I love the way ye make me laugh, how ye meet me as an equal. But most of all, I love that we get tae build a life together."

Anything else she might have said was lost in the hunger of his mouth finding hers, his tears mingling with her own.

He lifted his head, his face a moon-rimmed shadow.

"Truly? You love me?" he asked, so astonished, so awestruck.

"Aye. Would ye like tae hear it again?"

"Please, my darling. Never stop saying it."

"I love ye," she whispered.

And then proceeded to show him precisely what that meant.

THE NEXT MORNING, Isolde lazily refused to leave their bed, preferring instead to remain in her husband's arms and take breakfast there.

She and Tristan talked of nearly everything—the weather, her love for him, the prospect of visiting Inverness, the dozens of details that led her to realize she loved him.

When they finally arrived in the drawing-room close to midday, every head turned in their direction.

Isolde surmised that if her expression was even half as lovestruck as her husband's, everyone read their mutual adoration plain as day.

Everyone, that was, except her father.

He took one look at her radiant smile and marched across the room toward them.

Isolde didn't have to wait to know her father's mind.

"*Och*, ye still haven't told her?" He glared at Tristan. "I knew ye tae be a coward, but tae abuse my Izzy's good faith in such a fashion—"

"Papa," Isolde began.

"Izzy, ye must know that—"

"I know, Papa. Tristan told me all."

Hadley frowned. "About his continued assistance and desires to see me stand trial?"

"Aye."

With an apologetic glance at Tristan, she took her father's arm, leading him to one side of the large room so they could speak more privately.

"That's all ye have tae say, Izzy?" Hadley asked. "Just, *Aye, my turncoat of a husband told me* and all is well?"

"Ye ken it wasn't that simple, Papa. But the matter, ultimately, is between myself and Tristan. And I have chosen tae forgive him."

"Izzy, I know I will never consider any man to be worthy of yourself. But in this, I beg ye tae stop seeing good where there is none."

Isolde tugged her father deeper into a window embrasure, giving them even more privacy.

"Papa, I know your words are born of fear for me, and I love ye for loving me so. But I think ye be looking at this situation with Tristan the wrong way around. In my husband, ye see a man who is your enemy—the same way Tristan has seen you for too long. Ye scrutinize one another's actions to a fault."

"I have just reason for such an opinion, Izzy."

"I ken that, Papa. I do." She placed her palm on her father's shoulder. "But I'm asking ye to try to see Tristan through my eyes. In him, I see a man who is wounded and heart-sore. One who is slowly but surely becoming a better man. One who loves as fiercely as ye do and yearns to be adored in return. He is a man I love as boundlessly as ye taught me to love, Papa. And he loves me with an ardor and tenderness even you could not criticize. Ye need tae decide what version of my husband ye are going to see. Can ye trust my own judgment—that I know him, that Uncle Rafe knows him—better than yourself?"

Her father closed his eyes for a brief moment.

"Think upon it, Papa." She kissed his cheek. "I don't want to spend my days choosing between my husband and my father. 'Twould be a wretched existence. I love ye both, and I want ye tae get along."

Hadley glanced around the room—at his wife and children, at Rafe and Allie and Ethan—clearly noting the harmony between their two families.

"Ye truly love him?" her father asked.

"Aye," she nodded, willing her love to shine through her eyes. "I do. So very much. And he is *worthy* of my love. Moreover, I know your giant heart is capable of forgiveness."

Sighing, Hadley wrapped his strong arms around her.

And as she had since her earliest memories, Isolde curled into the security of her father's love.

HOURS LATER, TRISTAN stood at the railing of a flagstone terrace beside the castle, studying the ocean and trying to come to grips with the earth-moving shifts of the past twenty-four hours.

Allie was here. His twin, his other half.

He had made peace with his brother. He now *had* a brother.

And most surprising—most beautiful, most precious of all— his Isolde had forgiven him.

She *loved* him.

The wonder of it glowed in his chest. He wanted to kneel at her feet in devotion and awe.

They had become a family, the two of them. And within that lay the hope of the future family they would make together.

He could laugh in astonishment.

A faint motion to his right had him turning his head.

Hadley came to a stop beside him on the terrace, forehead furrowed and mouth drawn in a taut line. Leaning forward, he braced a hand on the stone balustrade,

Swallowing, Tristan shoved his own hands into his trouser pockets.

Not everyone was happy with the day's turn of events. And not every relationship could be mended.

But for Isolde's sake, Tristan was willing to try.

He and Hadley stood in silence a long while, shoulder-to-shoulder, listening to the call of gulls and the crash of waves against the cliffs below.

Tristan had no idea what his father-in-law was thinking. Or even what the purpose of this conversation would be. More warnings? Another threat of violence?

Finally, Hadley sighed. "Thank ye for telling my Izzy, Duke."

The words came out gruff, but Tristan heard the olive branch in them.

"I took far longer than needed," he admitted. "Your daughter does have the most loving heart in Christendom."

"That she does, Kendall. That she does." Hadley's lips twitched, as if tempted to smile at the mere thought of his daughter.

Tristan cleared his throat.

If apologies were to be the order of the day, well, he had his own to make.

"I . . . I should like to express my regret for my instigating role in the situation with Jarvis. As a gentleman, I should have discussed my concerns with you privately before making them public."

"Aye, ye should have," Hadley said in that same gruff tone. "But I also should have scrutinized Jarvis's dealings more thoroughly. However, Izzy was insistent—ye might know that side of her by now—and I was distracted by everyday affairs. I found it simpler to appease her with a few thousand pounds invested than to do a proper investigation. I should have been more attentive to the letters I sent my solicitor in Manchester. My actions were not intentionally fraudulent. But had I given more consideration tae the matter, I would have understood the state of affairs with Jarvis sooner."

They stood in silence again.

"I do love her, you know," Tristan said. "More than life itself."

"Aye. She told me as much." Hadley spared him a glance. "Hard tae believe."

"Truly? Loving Isolde is the easiest, most natural thing I have ever done."

"Ah, Duke, ye seem tae be developing a way with words," Hadley chuckled in astonishment. "Must be Penn-Leith's influence."

"Hardly. I have loved Isolde for nearly a decade."

That tidbit of information sent Hadley's brow to furrowing. "*Och,* my Izzy didn't tell me this. How so?"

As he had with Rafe the night before, Tristan described his encounter with Isolde, long ago in Montacute's garden. Of his own instantaneous, free-fall into love with her.

"As you can imagine, after loving your daughter for so long, the gift of her returning affection leaves me awestruck. I intend to worship her for the rest of my days."

"I cannot believe she loves ye in return." Hadley's frown deepened.

"'Tis astonishing. I am unworthy of her love."

"At last!" Hadley pushed off the balustrade, hands moving to his hips. "Something we can agree on."

"But know that I shall endeavor all my days to be worthy."

"Won't we all? But I am glad to hear it, Kendall."

Shifting on his feet, Tristan made yet another decision. "I would actually prefer you call me Tristan. A new name for a new beginning, as it were."

Hadley nodded slowly. "I guess ye should call me Andrew then." He sighed, another heavy gust of air. "Damn and blast! I never guessed I would decide to try tae love a Duke of Kendall."

"Pardon?"

"Have ye read the Bible?"

Tristan floundered.

"A little, I suppose," he said, remembering the passages Isolde had sent him in what felt like eons past.

"Aye, well, ye should read more of it. Turns out, it has much tae say about forgiveness. I've forgiven much worse slights than yours against myself." Hadley held out his palm. "Love my daughter as ye say ye will, Tristan, and all will be well between us."

Tristan shook Hadley's hand.

It was a ruse, of course. Hadley pulled on their joined palms, forcing Tristan closer to give him a thumping embrace.

They broke apart at the sound of a nearby laugh.

Tristan stepped back just in time to watch Isolde run into Hadley's arms. "Thank ye, Papa. I knew ye two could begin to reconcile."

After hugging her father, she immediately turned and wrapped her arms around Tristan's waist. "And you, too, Husband."

Smiling, Tristan met Hadley's gaze over Isolde's head, pressing an affectionate kiss to her hair.

Isolde stepped back, but Tristan kept one arm wrapped around her, snugging her to his side.

"I've been meaning to ask," Tristan said, "why are you here at Dunhelm Castle, Hadley? Did Lords decide to hold the trial in the spring then? I'll do what I can to assist you in——"

"*Och*, that's a braw thought, lad." Hadley waved his arm. "But I have hopes that the whole matter will be resolved soon. Before leaving London last week, I provided the committee with evidence of my innocence. Fortunately, I received word earlier today that, in light of the evidence, the committee have recommended dropping the charges against me. Hopefully, the affair is just a matter of bureaucracy from this point onward. I have already recompensed other investors for what was lost. Those that wanted out, at least. The rest stayed with me, as I have taken over Jarvis's business interests. Truthfully, Jarvis had a good idea. He simply mismanaged it. The lot should turn a profit next year."

Isolde looked at her father. "The trial is no more? 'Tis all finished?!"

Hadley shrugged. "'Tisn't done and dusted yet, but I have hopes it will all be sorted soon. I told ye from the start it wasn't anything tae worry upon." The earl clapped his hands. "I think I shall leave ye both here."

Tristan and Isolde watched Hadley walk away, a bounce in his step.

Shaking his head, Tristan looked down at her. "Your father's endless resilience and bonhomie *can* be annoying, Wife."

Isolde elbowed his ribs. "Ye like him. Say nice things."

"I like his daughter even more." Tristan pulled Isolde closer.

"Go on," she said.

"I adore the joy and happiness that bubbles effortlessly from your heart."

"Oh, I very much like that."

"Shall I keep going?"

"Aye. Can ye mention my eyes next?"

"Shall I say they are the color of an August sky on a cloudless day? Or that I adore seeing my love for you reflected there?"

"Like this?" She leaned back in his arms, her summer-blue gaze radiant with adoration.

"Yes, precisely like that."

"I love you, Tristan."

"I love you, too."

And to prove it, he cupped the back of her neck and kissed her.

EPILOGUE

1853
WILTSHIRE, ENGLAND
HAWTHORN, PRIMARY SEAT OF THE DUKE OF KENDALL

FOUR YEARS LATER

Tristan was rather sure his heart would crack from the *terrorworryanticipation* constricting his lungs.

He paced from the fireplace to the window and then back again, long strides across the blue drawing room of Hawthorn. The lush furnishings—the extravagant rococo mirror over the fireplace, the Rembrandt and Gainsborough on the wall, the Venetian crystal of the chandelier—were invisible to his distracted eyes.

A floor above, Isolde writhed in agony in the large ducal bed, laboring to bring their child into the world.

What heartless fiend had decided that a husband could not hold his wife at such a moment?

Tristan pivoted at the fireplace and strode the sixteen paces to the window, counting each step in an attempt to stem his panic.

. . . three, four, five . . .

"I fear he's making me seasick with all this back and forth," Hadley mused conversationally to Rafe.

"Aye," Rafe replied. "I predict one of us will lose his lunch before this is over."

Hadley crossed his arms. "It shan't be myself."

Tristan turned to stare at his brother and father-in-law, seated so casually before the hearth, unsure if their teasing was meant to enrage or quiet his fears.

Isolde's waters had broken over twelve hours past, waking them both in the dead of night. At first light, Tristan had sent a telegram to London, as he knew Lord and Lady Hadley wished to be present for the birth of their grandchild. The Hadleys had taken the first train out of King's Cross, arriving with Rafe in tow not long after lunch.

Lady Hadley was currently at her daughter's side, providing the support and encouragement Tristan felt nearly feverish to supply himself.

Now he fixed the two men with his ducal gaze. "Were either of you this *blasé* about the births of your own children?"

Both men replied in unison.

"Nae."

"Not at all."

"*Och*, birth is always a worry," Hadley said. "But Isolde birthed wee Beatrice without incident. She'll come through this, too."

As if summoned by her name, the door swung open and Lady Beatrice Gilbert walked into the room, rubbing her eyes. Nearly three years old, she appeared to have just woken from a nap, her fiery red hair wreathing her head like a glowing corona.

"Papa," she said in her high, lisping voice, stretching and yawning. "Where Nurthe go?"

As usual, the mere sight of his daughter filled Tristan with an unfathomable love—the sort that constricted his breathing and left him desperate to safeguard her. He thought nothing could equal the force of his affections for Isolde, but the moment the midwife laid Beatrice in his arms, his heart expanded triple-fold.

Their Honey Bea, as Isolde called her, was her mother's duplicate—bright blue eyes, red hair, and an endlessly inquisitive personality. She had ensnared Tristan the moment she wrapped her tiny finger around his. How could he not adore her? Bea radiated summer sunshine on even the darkest day.

"Nurse is likely with Mamma, Honey Bea." Crossing the room, Tristan scooped her into his arms, holding her small body against his. For her part, Beatrice tucked her arms between them and relaxed into his shoulder, the sleepy-child smell of her igniting a joyous ache.

Tristan stroked her back and gently kissed her forehead.

"Ith Mamma no' well?" she lisped, snuggling closer and closing her eyes.

Her absolute trust in his love and protection overwhelmed him at times. His Honey Bea did not doubt that her parents adored her, a fact Tristan vowed she would always know.

"Mamma is well." Tristan silently prayed that she would be. "You shall have a younger brother or sister soon."

"Mmm," was her only reply, her head tucked beneath Tristan's chin.

Beatrice had made her ambivalence for a sibling clear.

Tristan turned back to the room, only to find Hadley and Rafe staring at him with matching looks of . . . what? Amusement? Surprise? Respect?

They both knew Tristan doted on his wife and daughter. He still remembered his astonishment at Isolde's descriptions of Hadley visiting the nursery to read her bedtime stories.

Now, Tristan understood the emotions that had compelled his father-in-law to cherish his daughter and fear for her choice of husband. Tristan could scarcely tolerate half a day apart from Beatrice and loved nothing more than to cradle her against his side and read her a story. She was the perfect embodiment of his love for Isolde—this bright, happy girl. And he would personally disembowel any devil who mistreated her.

Tristan's transformation from stern, politically-minded duke to devoted family man had not gone unnoticed by Polite Society. The first year of his marriage had been dotted with endless mentions in newspapers and gossip rags, every last observer puzzled by the change in his demeanor. Tristan had ignored them all, too busy enjoying his own love and happiness.

Stirring in Tristan's arms, Bea finally noticed her grandfather sitting before the fire.

"Granda!" she shrieked, wiggling insistently to be put down.

Tristan obliged, watching with a bemused smile as Bea raced across the room to Hadley's open arms, scrambling onto his lap and peppering his face with kisses.

"*Och*, there's my favorite Honey Bea," Hadley laughed, tickling her face with his beard until she lost her breath to giggling.

At times, Tristan marveled at the oddity of sharing the people he loved most—Isolde and Beatrice—with a man he once loathed and who had loathed Tristan in return. But over the years, respect and a grudging love had grown between himself and his father-in-law.

Tristan smiled and met Rafe's gaze, reading admiration there.

Rafe, however, had become a brother in truth. The person Tristan turned to for advice and support.

Recently at Hadley's urging (of all people), Tristan had begun to tiptoe again into politics. Though Her Majesty still objected to Isolde's extensive education, she very much approved of the Duke and Duchess of Kendall's example of domestic felicity.

Moreover, he had discovered that kind and generous behavior was a more productive way to build popularity and support. Tristan had gained many friends over the past three years. Now, a trip to White's involved warm greetings and long conversations with like-minded Peers.

Bea settled in to play a game of pat-a-cake with Hadley, sitting back on his knees and laughing when her grandfather deliberately made a mistake.

Tristan paced back over to the window, swallowing back his anxiety.

Please, he silently pleaded. *Please let my Isolde be well.*

Twenty minutes of nervous pacing later, the cry of a newborn babe rang down the stairwell.

Tristan was already at the drawing-room door when the housekeeper burst in, all radiance and excitement.

"Congratulations, Your Grace," she said on a curtsy. "The duchess has birthed ye a strong and healthy babe. Her Grace fares well. I shall leave it to her to tell you if it's a boy or a girl. Give us thirty minutes and then ye may join us."

The following half an hour was rather the longest of Tristan's life. But he dutifully waited.

Thirty minutes to the second later, Tristan walked into his bedchamber with Bea gathered against his breastbone once more.

Isolde sat in the bed, a tiny bundle in her arms, as the midwife and others fussed around her.

Hair tousled, cheeks flushed, his wife had never looked more lovely.

Frowning, Bea pushed out of his hold and scrambled across the bed to her mother.

"Come see." Isolde beckoned.

Bea eagerly cuddled into her mother's side, looking at the baby's tiny face.

Without a word, Tristan leaned over the bed and kissed Isolde soundly.

His wife returned his kiss before pulling back on a grin.

"Ye kiss me before knowing if I've birthed ye a son or daughter?"

"Always," he rasped. "You are well. The child is well. I need know nothing more."

Isolde laughed at that. "Ye be too easy tae please at times, my love. Come." She patted the bed at her side. And then giving him that wide, summer-bright smile he adored, she added, "Here, hold your son."

THREE HOURS LATER, Tristan was still nestled beside Isolde under the counterpane, his new son cradled in the crook of his arm.

Beatrice had long ago fallen asleep at the foot of the bed, her chubby arms flung with abandon over her head. She needed to return to the nursery, but as usual, both Tristan and Isolde were loathe to part from her.

They had accepted well-wishes and congratulations from Rafe and Lord and Lady Hadley, all of them cooing over the new heir—

Andrew Tristan Rafe Gilbert, Lord Hawthorn.

Hadley, in particular, had surreptitiously wiped his eyes when he realized that the new babe had been named in his honor.

But this moment afterward was Tristan's favorite—the quiet comfort of sitting beside Isolde in the hush of their private bedchamber.

"I can't cease looking at him," Tristan murmured, staring at the babe in the crook of his elbow. "I had wondered if it were possible to love a child as much as I love Beatrice."

"Aye," Isolde agreed. "How could we ever adore another as deeply?"

"And yet, here we are." Tristan pressed a kiss to the boy's forehead, running a finger over the dark hair fuzzing his small, wrinkled head.

Hawthorn scrunched his tiny face and yawned, curling his body and exerting all his strength to open his eyes.

Unlike Beatrice, who had been angry and wailing in the hours after her birth, Hawthorn was quiet and serious. Tristan supposed he himself had likely sported a similar expression at birth—an aged sort of knowing that had led his mother to christen him *triste*.

The babe regarded Tristan intently, gaze earnest and fierce. As if Hawthorn already knew the weight of duty that loomed in his future. The dukedom that would one day rest upon his shoulders.

You will not face it alone, Tristan vowed.

Unlike generations past, the next Duke of Kendall would be raised in affection and light.

This, Tristan realized.

This more than anything else would ensure that Old Kendall was forgotten, blotted out in the glowing light of love.

"Thank you," Tristan murmured, looking at his wife.

"For birthing ye a son? That was more chance and biology than any willful choice on my part."

"Perhaps. But you didn't need to love me. You didn't need to forgive me. You didn't—"

Isolde captured his mouth with a kiss. "I regret nothing, Husband.

I will be forever grateful for the forces that brought us together. For the joy ye give me. The joy of our life together."

"As will I, Wife."

And Tristan kissed her again.

1859
Fettermill, Scotland
Thistle Muir, family home of the Penn-Leiths

Six Years Later

ISOLDE STOOD JUST outside the front door of Thistle Muir—the Penn-Leith childhood home—watching a herd of children race across the front lawn, playing a rambunctious game of *tig*.

"It's astonishing how much love and frustration my children can provoke in me," Allie said conversationally at her side.

"Aye. And how did we all have so many?" Isolde mused.

"Well." Allie shot her a wry sort of look. "We all know precisely why, don't we?"

Isolde laughed. "True. It would help if our husbands weren't quite so alluringly handsome."

They both looked to Allie's Ethan. He stood talking with his older brother, Malcolm Penn-Leith, the men casually leaning against the fence separating the garden from a field dotted with fluffy sheep. Allie's youngest child, Felicity, squealed and scrambled up Ethan's leg to dodge being tagged, her dark, curly hair escaping its braids. Ethan scarcely broke stride in speaking with Malcolm, hitching the wee girl in his arms.

They had assembled, the Penn-Leiths and Kendalls, for their annual family holiday. Sometimes they gathered at Hawthorn. Other years at Laverloch Castle up Glen Laver where Ethan's older sister, Leah, lived with her husband, Mr. Fox Carnegie.

But this year, they had decided to congregate at the Penn-Leith family's place of origin—the modest country house that Ethan's father, Mr. John Penn, had built for his new bride, Isobel Leith.

Of course, the house was far too small to host the combined number of their offspring. Isolde and her family, along with Allie and Ethan's brood, were staying at Hadley's nearby Muirford House.

At the moment, they were waiting for Tristan to arrive from London. He had been held up by a vote in Parliament the day before—his political star was on a shining trajectory toward Prime Minister. Tristan had scheduled his private railway coach to leave earlier that morning, hopefully arriving before dinner.

In the meantime, Isolde relished the sounds of laughter and happiness filling the garden.

The game of *tig* was in full force. At nine years of age, Bea was in her element, racing the boys and dancing around Malcolm's enormous dog—the punnily named Geoffrey Pawcer, who was apparently a welp of Beowoof. Malcolm regularly christened his animals with literary names. Pawcer adored the chaos, barking and running alongside the children. Arthur, the elder of Allie and Ethan's twins, was always two steps behind his cousin, shouting for Bea to wait up.

Naturally, not all of them were so energetic. If Isolde stepped back, she could see Clara, Arthur's twin sister, and her own Hawthorn cuddled into the window seat of Thistle Muir's front parlor, their matching dark heads bent over a book. Clara read while Hawthorn asked questions, his serious eyes studying his cousin's face as he listened.

On the other side of the room, Viola, Malcolm's wife, sat talking with Fox, Leah, and their only son, Jack, who at nineteen years old was just up from his studies at St Andrews University in Fife.

Abruptly, a cheering shout went up from the children on the lawn, their heads turning toward the gravel drive before the house.

A horse cantered round the bend, Tristan on its back.

Shrieks of joy immediately followed.

The children tore down the drive en masse, shouts of "Papa!" and "Uncle Tristan!" and dog yips ringing through the air.

A grin on his face, Tristan dismounted just in time to catch Bea in his arms. Her younger brother and sister, Thomas and Agnes, soon followed. And then Allie and Ethan's brood were upon him. Even Geoffry Pawcer leaped into the mix, licking Tristan's face, tail wagging exuberantly.

Tristan winced, laughing ruefully before pushing the dog down.

Isolde smiled and turned to Allie with some remark about the chaos. But the words died on her tongue.

Allie was *greiting*, enormous tears dripping down to her chin.

"Allie?" Isolde asked, alarm rising in her chest.

"Ignore me." Allie retrieved a handkerchief and wiped her nose. "I'm just overwhelmed by the beauty of . . . of everything. This moment." She sniffed and waved her hand, indicating the garden as a whole. "I envisioned it, you know."

"This moment?"

"Well, not this precisely. But I imagined a time when Tristan would arrive at Thistle Muir and all our children would race to greet him and bury him in the force of their happiness." She pointed at her brother. "And look at him now!"

Tristan was indeed buried in joy. Agnes climbed on his back while Bea jabbered on about a hedgehog she and Arthur had trapped in a fishing basket the day before. Malcolm, bless him, had taken the reins of Tristan's horse, leading the animal toward the barns behind the house.

Isolde and Allie stepped onto the gravel drive.

"Husband," Isolde said as Tristan drew her into a tight embrace and kissed her soundly, Agnes giggling maniacally and clinging like a barnacle to his back.

Tristan turned to greet his sister and then paused, seeing her tears.

"Ah, Allie," he said, holding her close. "It's just like your dream all those years ago."

"Yes!" Allie hiccupped. "How did you know?"

"I remember you telling me of your vision." Tristan tapped his temple. "And also . . . twin sense."

A burble of laughter broke through Allie's tears.

"I knew it!" she crowed. "I knew you would admit it eventually!"

In reply, Tristan pressed a kiss to his twin's forehead.

THAT EVENING, THEY were all seated around a huge table in the garden, the dining room inside too small to hold such a crowd.

It was a glorious Scottish evening. Twilight lingered on the horizon, casting long shadows across the lawn. Dirty plates and half-full glasses dotted the tablecloth, a plate of biscuits sitting in the middle. No one seemed interested in calling for a servant to clear the mess.

Isolde rested her head on Tristan's shoulder. He held a sleeping Agnes in his arms, her head tucked under his chin. Across from them, Allie rocked wee Felicity. Malcolm looped an arm around the back of his wife's chair, causing Viola to turn her shoulders and lean into him. Beside them, Fox reached for Leah's hand, lacing their fingers together.

The remainder of the children had stolen off to the barn to play with a litter of kittens and pet a new lamb. Their laughter drifted in on the wind.

This moment, Isolde thought. *This is the moment I want to remember when I am old and gray.* A perfect evening spent in the company of those she loved.

She nearly said as much to Tristan, but Ethan stood and tapped a fork to his wine glass to command their attention.

"I am grateful we are all gathered together here." Ethan smiled, his habitual charismatic smile—the one that routinely made women swoon at poetry readings. "Though Thistle Muir is my childhood home, I ken that it is now Malcolm and Viola's abode. However on this occasion, my brother bid me say a few words about our family and the house ye see there before us."

"Hear, hear!" Fox lifted a glass of water in salute.

Ethan tilted his head in acknowledgment. "As ye all know, my gentleman-farmer father fell in love with our highborn mother. And as a condition of their marriage, our grandfather required our father tae build his bride this lovely home—a house commensurate with her station in life. And so, for us, the house has always stood as a symbol of our parents' love, both for one another and for ourselves."

"Aye," Malcolm agreed gruffly. "That it has."

On a nod, Ethan continued, "We three siblings experienced our first lessons in love here. And as we all know, love begets love. Nothing demonstrates that more distinctly than our togetherness tonight, surrounded by the laughter and harmony of family. So in honor of us all, I have written a poem, if ye will bear with me."

Ethan unfolded a piece of paper from his waistcoat pocket and cleared his throat.

"I found a heartbeat in these walls.
A rhythmic pulse of hope and care,
From childhood's glee to aging's grace,
The footfalls of time ringing there.

I hear a song within these stones . . ."

Ethan continued, his words evoking the love that Thistle Muir had borne witness to over the years—heartache and laughter, tears and triumphs—a sacred sort of music embedded in its walls.

Isolde watched Leah wipe away a tear before Fox handed her a handkerchief.

Viola dabbed at her eyes.

Soon, Isolde's own nose stung with emotion.

Even Malcolm cleared his throat more vigorously than usual.

Reaching the end, Ethan finished—

" . . . and thus,
With hearts well full and memories drawn
Our symphony of love plays on."

His words echoed across the garden, dissipating into purple shadows of shrubs and trees.

Allie sniffled and reached out to grasp her husband's hand.

"Well said, Penn-Leith," Tristan said at Isolde's side. "I think we can all agree that—"

Whatever he intended to say was drowned in the cacophony of children, a dog, several cats, and a bleating lamb clamoring toward them.

"Biscuits!" Bea and Arthur shrieked in unison, reaching for the plate of sweets at the table's center.

Tristan laughed, catching Bea around the middle.

Ethan swept the plate above his head, causing the rest of the children to jump and stretch for his arm.

"One at a time," he chuckled.

Isolde met Allie's gaze across the table, both of them laughing through their tears.

This, Isolde thought.

This bright, rambunctious chaos was the song Ethan had described in his poem.

The sound of happiness and family.

The sound of love.

Of life full to the brim with joy.

AUTHOR'S NOTE

It feels bittersweet to have reached the end of another series. The Penn-Leiths have had my heart for so long, I struggle to imagine moving on to other characters and stories. In particular, Tristan and Isolde have been difficult to let go. A book hangover is terrible. A book-*writing* hangover? The absolute worst.

But as usual, I can't leave a book without offering some commentary on the history of various plot points.

As the UK built out its rail network in the 1840s, fraudulent railway schemes ran rampant. Numerous ventures failed, often due to corruption. George Hudson, in particular, stands out as a notable example of this. Hudson linked London and Edinburgh by merging railway companies, but he also engaged in what we would call a Ponzi scheme—paying past investors with funds from recent investors. Eventually, Hudson's fraud was uncovered, and he was forced to repay investors, and even spent some time in prison for his actions.

I used Hudson's case as the basis for Stephen Jarvis's failed venture in *A Heart Sufficient*. In my imagination, Jarvis created an elaborate Ponzi scheme and dragged Lord Hadley into the middle of it. But unlike the very real George Hudson, compelling a Peer and member of the House of Lords like Hadley to answer for his crimes is a more complicated matter.

Within the UK, impeachment arose as a way to prosecute a Peer for crimes outside of treason or murder. (This is not *impeachment* as we think of it in the United States; the actual process has little in common between the UK and the US.) In the 1840s and earlier, Peers were considered above the law and could not be tried in UK courts for lesser offenses, like debt, fraud, or bigamy. However, over time, this rankled the non-Peer classes. Impeachment became a way for the House of Commons to compel the House of Lords to try one of their own for an offense. In short, the House of Commons would vote to bring charges against a Peer and then order the House of Lords to conduct a trial. The trial would proceed like a regular trial, only in this case, members of the House of Lords would act as judge and jury. In practice, impeachment was used infrequently and has not been employed in well over 150 years. And the few earlier cases were usually settled before the matter reached the stage of a trial, as Lord Hadley shows.

Broadhurst College, the university in the United States that Lady Isolde attended, is fictitious. However, there were schools in the US at the time that accepted female students, most notably Wesleyan College (not to be confused with Wesleyan University) in Georgia and Bradford Academy in Massachusetts.

Also, the books and philosophies the characters mention are very real. A partial list includes:

Letters to Young Ladies (1835) by Lydia Howard Sigourney.

The Book of St. Albans (1486), attributed to Juliana Berners.

The Philosophy of the Inductive Sciences (1840) by Mr. William Whewell.

Kew Gardens, the Palm House, the Sequoias, the old palace, and the ice house are based on actual places within Kew itself. The gardens are lovely, particularly when the bluebells are in full bloom in the spring.

Steam travel was just starting into its heyday in 1849. The *SS Great Western* was the first steamship built specifically for transatlantic travel, with her maiden voyage occurring in 1838. Trains and rail lines also connected every major city of the UK by 1849.

The Isle of Canna is fictitious, though I based it loosely on the Isle of Muck. The islands of the Hebrides were generally owned and leased by the local clans, usually MacLeod or MacLean.

The Rough Bounds are still very wild. There are few roads and most are narrow single tracks. Even today, many areas and villages of the Rough Bounds are accessible only by sea. But if you ever have a chance to explore the area, I highly recommend it. It is absolutely lovely and astonishingly remote.

The town of Oban is very real, utterly charming, and well worth a stop. All other places mentioned in the book are genuine places you can visit. Consider it a highlight reel of all my favorite spots in the Hebrides.

Sir John MacDougall, Dunollie House, and the Brooch of Lorne are very much genuine historical figures, though I know I took license in how I portrayed Sir John personally.

Dunhelm Castle, Sir Rafe's home, is based on Dunbeath Castle which perches dramatically on the edge of the ocean north of Inverness. If you've ever driven south from John O'Groats along the A9, Dunbeath will take your breath away. As of this writing, Dunbeath Castle is for sale, so Google it if you want to see more photos of the castle. Or, you know, buy yourself an incredible estate in Scotland. If you do, please invite me for a visit.

I know I've mentioned this before, but for those reading one of my Scottish books for the first time, allow me to also comment on the Scottish language. I've used modern spellings of Scottish pronunciations and, even then, restricted myself to a few key words to give a Scottish flavor to the text. So at times, the accent as written is not perfectly consistent; this was done to help readability.

I have created an extensive board on Pinterest with images of things I talk about in the book. So if you want a visual of anything—including Kew Gardens, the Rough Bounds, the white sand beaches of the Hebrides, etc.—pop over there and explore. Just search for NicholeVan.

As usual, writing a book is this bizarre mix of working long hours alone while simultaneously rallying a village to help get the novel to publication.

A HUGE thank you to all my ARC and beta-readers who read, give suggestions, and post about my books. The Bookstagram community has pulled me through many a frustrating day of writing. I feel I cannot thank reviewers enough for the time, thought, and effort they put into posting about my books. Thank you for helping to spread the word and ensuring I can continue to write, year after year.

Also, I cannot give enough thanks to my two primary editors—Erin Rodabough and Shannon Castleton—for their tireless efforts and brilliant suggestions. They always help me take what I see as a so-so manuscript and turn it into something far beyond my own meager efforts. I love that we continue on this journey together, helping one another in our writing efforts.

I also have to give a special shout-out to Rebecca Spencer. Thank you for encouraging two key points with this novel: 1) insisting that the central conflict needed to involve Lord Hadley, and 2) challenging me to write a romance without a third act break-up.

And lastly, I lavish all my love and appreciation on my children and husband. Thank you for your endless words of encouragement and for listening to me ramble my way through a thorny plot issue. The past few years have been a bit of a wild ride, but there is no one I would rather have by my side.

READING GROUP QUESTIONS

Yes, there are reading group questions for this book. They exist mostly as a ploy to encourage readers to congregate and discuss the book, preferably with lots of good chocolate and laughter.

Please note that these questions inherently contain some spoilers.

1. At the beginning of the book, Tristan wants to obliterate his father from history. To ensure that the man's legacy is forgotten. How do you feel about this goal? What values should be inherent in the things we wish for? Discuss this question in terms of loyalty to spouse and family.

2. Initially, Tristan fixates quite a bit on time, on clocks and watches. How does the use of time change over the course of the book? How do you see this mirroring changes in Tristan's personality?

3. Each chapter contains a snippet of outside text—a newspaper article or letter, etc. Did you like those inclusions? Why or why not? Notably, however, the chapters when Isolde and Tristan are stranded in the Isle of Canna do not contain any "found text" headers. Why do you think the author omitted them from those chapters?

4. At its heart, this book is a redemption story. Tristan undergoes a significant character arc. Did you find his change believable? Why or why not? Can one traumatic experience change someone so quickly? Have you ever experienced something similar—where you wake up as one person and go to bed as another?

5. Forgiveness has a strong role in the book. Make a list of the wrongs that need to be forgiven in the book. How do you feel these instances of forgiveness were handled? Were they believable? Why or why not?

6. Love of family—or the lack of it—plays a large part in this story. How much can a parent influence a child's future behavior? What about siblings? Can you overcome a parent's influence that is so damaging?

7. Like Tristan, Lord Hadley experiences a character arc, but his arc is off-screen. How did you feel about that? Also, at times Hadley functions as something of a villain, but based on his appearance in past books, we know he is not a villainous man. What are your thoughts on this idea—we are all the villains of someone else's story?

8. What makes a heart sufficient in a man? What qualities do women love in a "noble" man?

9. Is Isolde's hesitation to tell Tristan *I love you* realistic? What do you need to feel before saying *I love you* to someone? And what does that mean to you? Is it flippant, something you say to a friend in parting? Or should it hold more weight?

10. Who are your favorite characters in the series? Who have you loved and why? Pretend you have been selected as the Thistle Muir Bachelorette, who would you give the rose to?

OTHER BOOKS BY NICHOLE VAN

THE PENN-LEITHS OF THISTLE MUIR

Love Practically
Adjacent But Only Just
One Kiss Alone
A Heart Sufficient

THE BROTHERHOOD OF THE BLACK TARTAN

Suffering the Scot
Romancing the Rake
Loving a Lady
Making the Marquess
Remembering Jamie

OTHER REGENCY ROMANCES

Seeing Miss Heartstone
Vingt-et-Un | Twenty-one (a novella included in *Falling for a Duke*)

BROTHERS *MALEDETTI*

Lovers and Madmen
Gladly Beyond
Love's Shadow
Lightning Struck
A Madness Most Discreet

THE HOUSE OF OAK

Intertwine
Divine
Clandestine
Refine
Outshine

If you haven't yet read *Seeing Miss Heartstone*,
please turn the page for a preview of this
Whitney Award Winner for Best Historical Romance 2018.

SEEING MISS HEARTSTONE

. . . My lord, news of your current financial pressures has reached many ears. I know of an interested party who would be honored to discuss a proposed joint venture. They have asked to meet you along the Long Water in Hyde Park tomorrow morning, where they shall endeavor to lay out the particulars of their proposal . . .

—EXCERPT FROM AN UNSIGNED LETTER POSTED TO LORD BLAKE

In retrospect, Miss Arabella Heartstone had three regrets about 'The Incident.'

She should not have worn her green, wool cloak with the fox fur collar, as Hyde Park was warmer than expected that morning.

She should not have instructed her chaperone, Miss Anne Rutger, to remain politely out of earshot.

And she probably should *not* have proposed marriage to the Marquess of Blake.

"P-pardon?" Lord Blake lifted a quizzical eyebrow, standing straight and tall, rimmed in the morning sunlight bouncing off the Long Water behind him. A gentle breeze wound through the surrounding trees, rustling newly-grown, green leaves. "Would . . . would you mind repeating that last phrase? I fear I did not hear you correctly."

Belle straightened her shoulders, clasped her trembling hands together, and sternly ordered her thumping heart to *Cease this racket.*

Swallowing, she restated her request. "After much consideration, my lord, I feel a marriage between you and myself would be prudent."

Lord Blake stared at her, blinking over and over. Belle was unsure if his reaction denoted surprise or was simply the result of the dazzling sunlight off the water behind her.

Silence.

Birds twittered. Branches creaked. Leaves rustled.

Eternities passed. Millennia ended and were reborn.

Belle gritted her teeth, desperate to bolster her flagging confidence. *You are strong and courageous. You can do this.*

In the past, her passivity over the Marriage Matter had nearly ended in disaster. So, Belle had set her sights on a more forthright course— propose marriage herself. Yes, she struggled to talk with people and preferred anonymity to attention, but her current situation was critical.

She needed a husband. Decidedly. Desperately. Immediately. As in . . . yesterday would not have been soon enough.

At the moment, however, her mental encouragement barely managed to convince the swarming butterflies in her stomach to not free her breakfast along with themselves. Casting up her accounts all over his lordship's dusty Hessian boots would hardly nurture his romantic interest.

At last, Lord Blake stirred, pulling a folded letter from his overcoat. He stared at it, eyebrows drawing down, a sharp "V" appearing above his nose.

"You sent me this message, asking to meet me here?" He flapped the letter in her direction.

"Yes." Belle bit down on her lip and darted a glance behind at her companion. Miss Rutger stood a solid thirty yards off, studiously facing the Long Water. "Well . . . uhm . . . in all truthfulness, Miss Rutger wrote the letter."

Lord Blake raised his eyebrows, clearly uncaring of the minutiae involved. "So you are *not* a gentleman interested in my business venture in the East Indies?" He unfolded the letter, reading from it. "'*I know of an interested party who would be honored to discuss a proposed joint venture. They have asked to meet you along the Long Water*,' et cetera. This 'interested party' is yourself?" He returned the letter to his pocket.

"Yes, my lord." Belle commanded her feet to hold still and not bounce up and down—the bouncing being yet another effect of those dratted nervous butterflies.

Lord Blake's brows rose further. "And you are offering . . . marriage?"

"Yes, my lord," Belle repeated, but she had to clarify the point. Apparently, she had no issue with being thought forward and brazen, but heaven forbid Lord Blake imagine her a liar, too. "Though . . . I *am* proposing a joint endeavor."

"Indeed," he paused. "Marriage usually implies as much."

Lord Blake shuffled a Hessian-booted foot and clasped his hands behind his back. A corner of his mouth twitched.

Was the man . . . amused? If so, was that good? Or bad?

And at this point, did it matter?

Belle soldiered on. "There would be significant advantages to both of us with such a match."

More silence. An errant draft of wind tugged at his coat.

"You have me at a disadvantage, Miss . . ." His voice trailed off.

"Heartstone. Miss Arabella Heartstone."

"I see." He removed his hat and slapped it against his thigh. "And why have we not met in more . . . uh . . . typical circumstances? A ball, perhaps? A dinner party where we could be properly introduced and engage in conversation about the weather and the latest bonnet fashions before leaping straight to marriage?"

"Oh." It was Belle's turn to blink, absorbing his words. *Oh dear.* "We *have* met, my lord. We were introduced at Lord Pemberley's musicale last month. We did discuss the weather, but not bonnets or . . . uhm . . . marriage."

She hadn't expected him to recall everything, but to not even *recognize* her? To not remember their brief conversation—

"How do you do, Miss Heartstone? It's a pleasure to make your acquaintance." Lord Blake bowed.

"The pleasure is all mine, my lord." Belle curtsied. *"Lovely weather we're having."*

"Indeed, we are."

It did not bode well.

The butterflies rushed upward, eager for escape.

"Right." Blake let out a gusting breath and shook his head, sending his hair tumbling across his forehead. The morning sun turned it into molten shades of deep amber, curling softly over his ears.

Lean and several inches taller than her own average height, Lord Blake was not classically handsome, she supposed. His straight nose, square jaw, and high forehead were all too exaggerated for classical handsomeness.

And yet, something about him tugged at her. Perhaps it was the breadth of his shoulders filling out his coat. Or maybe it was the ease of his stance, as if he would face the jaws of Hell itself with a sardonic smile and casual *sang-froid*. Or maybe it was the way he ran a gloved hand through his hair, taking it from fashionably tousled to deliciously rumpled.

Mmmmm.

Belle was going to side with the hair. Though sardonic smiles were a close second.

Regardless, her decision to offer marriage to him had not been based on his physical appearance. She was many things, but *flighty* and *shallow* were two words that had never been attached to her.

Replacing his hat, Lord Blake studied her, blue eyes twinkling.

Yes. Definitely amused.

That was . . . encouraging? Having never proposed marriage to a man before, Belle was unsure.

"Enlighten me, if you would be so kind, as to the particular reasons why you think this . . . joint endeavor . . . would be profitable." He gestured toward her.

Oh! Excellent.

That she had come prepared to do.

With a curt nod, she pulled a paper from her reticule.

"A list?" His lips twitched again.

"I am nothing if not thorough in my planning, my lord." She opened the paper with shaking fingers, her hands clammy inside her gloves.

"Of course. I should have expected as much. You arranged this meeting, after all." He tapped the letter in his pocket.

Belle chose to ignore the wry humor in his tone and merely nodded her head in agreement. "Allow me to proceed with my list. Though please forgive me if my reasons appear forward."

"You have just proposed marriage to a peer of the realm, madam. I cannot imagine anything you say from this point onward will trump that."

"True."

A beat.

Lord Blake pinned her with his gaze—calm and guileless. The forthright look of a man who knew himself and would never be less-than-true to his own values.

His gaze upset her breathing, causing something to catch in her throat.

Belle broke eye-contact, swallowing too loudly.

"Allow me to begin." She snapped the paper in her hand. The words swam in her vision, but she knew them by heart. The paper was more for show than anything else. She had done her calculations most carefully.

Taking a fortifying breath, Belle began, "Firstly, you have newly inherited the Marquisate of Blake from a cousin. Your cousin was somewhat imprudent in his spending habits—"

"I would declare the man to be an utter scapegrace and wastrel, but continue."

"Regardless of the cause, your lands and estates are in dire need of resuscitation." Belle glanced at him over the top of her paper. "You are basically without funds, my lord."

"As my solicitor repeatedly reminds me." He shot her an arch look. "It is why I am trying to fund a business venture in connection with the East India Company, as you are also undoubtedly aware."

"Yes, my lord. That is why I am proposing an enterprise of a slightly different sort. Allow me to continue." Belle cleared her throat, looking down to her paper. "My own family is genteel with connections to the upper aristocracy—my great-great grandfather was the Earl of Stratton—though we have no proper title of our own, leaving my father to make his own way in the world. I, as you might already know, am a considerable heiress. My father was a prominent banker and left the entirety of his estate to me upon his death three years past."

Belle clenched her jaw against the familiar sting in her throat.

Blink, blink, blink.

Now was *not* the time to dwell upon her father.

"Are you indeed?" he asked. "Though I do not wish to sound crass, I feel we left polite discussion in the dust several minutes ago, so I must enquire: How much of an heiress are you, precisely?"

Did she hear keen interest in his tone? Or was Lord Blake simply exceedingly polite?

"I believe the current amount stands somewhere in the region of eighty thousand pounds, my lord," she replied.

Lord Blake froze at that staggering number, just as Belle had predicted he would.

"Eighty thousand pounds, you say? That is a dowry of marquess-saving proportions."

"My thoughts precisely, my lord."

Her father had originally left her a healthy sixty thousand pounds, but she was nothing if not her father's daughter. Numbers and statistics flowed through her brain, a constant rushing river. She had used these skills to grow her fortune.

It was what her father would have wanted. Refusing to see her gender as a barrier, her father had taught his only child everything he knew— financial systems, probabilities, market shares—even soliciting her opinions during that last year before his death.

By the age of sixteen, Belle understood more about supply-and-demand and the mathematics of economics than most noblemen. Knowing this, the conditions in her father's will allowed her to continue to oversee her own interests with the help of his solicitor, Mr. Sloan. At only nineteen years of age, she currently managed a thriving financial empire.

She could hear her father's gruff voice, his hand gently lifting her chin. *I would give you choices, my Little Heart Full. A lady should always have options. I would see you happy.*

Belle swallowed back the painful tightness in her throat.

Now, if she could only land a husband and free herself from the guardianship of her uncle and mother.

Family, it turned out, were not quite as simple to manage as corn shares.

Her mother, hungry for a title for her daughter, was becoming increasingly bold in her attempts to get Belle married. She had all but forced Belle to betroth herself to a cold, aloof viscount the previous Season. Fortunately, the viscount—Lord Linwood—had asked to be released from their betrothal.

But the entire situation had left Belle feeling helpless.

She *detested* feeling helpless, she realized. And so she used that unwelcome sensation to suppress her inherent shyness and overcome her retiring personality.

Belle would solve the husband problem herself. She simply needed to reduce the entire situation to a statistical probability and face it as she would any other business transaction.

"Eighty-thousand pounds," Lord Blake repeated. "Are husbands—particularly the marquess variety—generally so costly?" He clasped his hands behind his back, studying her. "I had not thought to price them before this."

"I cannot say. This is my first venture into, uhmm . . ."

"Purchasing a husband?" he supplied, eyes wide.

Heavens. Was that a hint of displeasure creeping into his voice?

"I am not entirely sure I agree with the word *purchase*, my lord—"

"True. It does smack of trade and all polite society knows we cannot have *that*."

A pause.

"Shall we use the word *negotiate* instead?" she asked.

He cocked his head, considering. "I daresay that would be better. So I receive a sultan's ransom and your lovely self, and you receive . . ." His words drifted off.

"A husband. And in the process, I become Lady Blake, a peeress of the realm."

"Are you truly so hungry to be a marchioness? Surely eighty thousand pounds could purchase—forgive me, *negotiate*—the title of duchess." His words so very, very dry.

"I am sure my mother would agree with you, my lord, but I am more interested in finding a balance between title and the proper gentleman." She cleared her throat. "You come highly recommended."

"Do I?" Again, his tone darkly sardonic.

Oh, dear.

But as she was already in for more than a penny, why not aim for the whole pound?

"I did not arrive at the decision to propose marriage lightly. I had my solicitor hire a Runner to investigate you. I have armed myself with information, my lord."

Belle wisely did not add that, after crunching all the statistical probabilities, Lord Blake had been by far and away her preferred candidate. She was quite sure that, like most people, he would not appreciate being reduced to a number.

"Information? About me?" he asked.

"Yes. For example, I know you recently cashed out of the army, selling the officer's commission you inherited from your father. All those who served with you report you to be an honest and worthy commander—"

"As well they should."

"Additionally, you are a kind son to your mother. You send her and your stepfather funds when you are able. You visit regularly. Your four older sisters dote upon you, and you are godfather to at least one of each of their children. You are a tremendous favorite with all of your nieces and nephews. All of this speaks highly to the kind of husband and father you would be."

After her disastrous betrothal to Lord Linwood last year, Belle was determined to not make the same error twice. She learned from her mistakes. Her mother and uncle would not browbeat her into accepting one of their suitors again.

If nothing else, eighty thousand pounds should purchase—*negotiate*—her a *kindhearted* husband of her own choice.

Lord Blake shuffled his feet. "I-I really am at a loss for words, Miss Heartstone. I am trying to decide if I should be flattered or utterly appalled."

Belle sucked in a deep breath, her mouth as dry as the Sahara.

Stay strong. Argue your case.

She pasted a strained smile on her face. "Might I suggest siding with flattery, my lord?"

Visit www.NicholeVan.com to buy your copy of
Seeing Miss Heartstone today and continue the story.

ABOUT THE AUTHOR

THE SHORT VERSION:

NICHOLE VAN IS a writer, photographer, designer and generally disorganized person. Though originally from the Rocky Mountains, she has lived all over the world, including Italy and the UK. She and her family recently returned to the US after spending six years in Scotland. Nichole currently lives in the heart of the Rockies with her husband and and three children.

THE LONG OVERACHIEVER VERSION:

AN INTERNATIONAL BESTSELLING author, Nichole Van is an artist who feels life is too short to only have one obsession. In former lives, she has been a contemporary dancer, pianist, art historian, choreographer, culinary artist and English professor.

Most notably, however, Nichole is an acclaimed photographer, winning over thirty international accolades for her work, including Portrait of the Year from WPPI in 2007. (Think Oscars for wedding and portrait photographers.) Her unique photography style has been featured in many magazines, including Rangefinder and Professional Photographer.

All that said, Nichole has always been a writer at heart. With an MA in English, she taught technical writing at Brigham Young University for ten years and has written more technical manuals than she can quickly count. She decided in late 2013 to start writing fiction and has since become an Amazon #1 bestselling author. Additionally, she has won a RONE award, as well as been a Whitney Award Finalist several years running. Her late 2018 release, *Seeing Miss Heartstone*, won the Whitney Award Winner for Best Historical Romance.

In 2017, Nichole, her husband and three children moved from the Rocky Mountains in the USA to Scotland. They lived there for six years—residing on the coast of eastern Scotland in an eighteenth century country house—before returning to the USA in 2023. Nichole currently lives in the heart of the Rockies, miles up a mountain canyon.

She is known as NicholeVan all over the web: Facebook, Instagram, Pinterest, etc. Visit http://www.NicholeVan.com to sign up for her author newsletter and be notified of new book releases.

If you enjoyed this book, please leave a short review on Amazon.com. Wonderful reviews are the elixir of life for authors. Even better than dark chocolate.